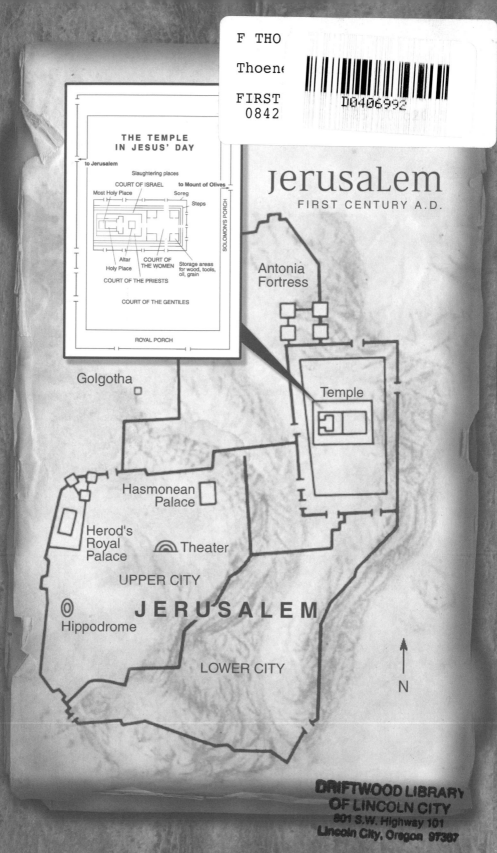

THE TEMPLE
IN JESUS' DAY

to Jerusalem

Slaughtering places

COURT OF ISRAEL   to Mount of Olives

Most Holy Place   Soreg

Most Holy Place   Steps

Altar   COURT OF
Holy Place   THE WOMEN

Storage areas
for wood, tools,
oil, grain

COURT OF THE PRIESTS

COURT OF THE GENTILES

SOLOMON'S PORCH

ROYAL PORCH

JerusaLem
FIRST CENTURY A.D.

Antonia
Fortress

Golgotha

Temple

Hasmonean
Palace

Herod's
Royal
Palace   Theater

UPPER CITY

JERUSALEM

Hippodrome

LOWER CITY

N

FIRST LIGHT

BODIE & BROCK

BOOK ONE

A.D. CHRONICLES

FIRST LIGHT

Tyndale House Publishers, Inc.
Wheaton, Illinois

THOENE

Visit Tyndale's exciting Web site at www.tyndale.com

First Light copyright © 2003 by Bodie and Brock Thoene. All rights reserved.

Cover illustration © 2003 by Chris Hopkins. All rights reserved.

Edited by Ramona Cramer Tucker

Cover designed by RULE 29, www.rule29.com

Interior designed by Dean H. Renninger

Published in association with the literary agency of Alive Communications, Inc., 7680 Goddard Street, Suite 200, Colorado Springs, CO 80920.

Scripture quotations are taken from the *Holy Bible*, New International Version®. NIV® Copyright © 1973, 1978, 1984 by International Bible Society. Used by permission of Zondervan Publishing House. All rights reserved.

Library of Congress Cataloging-in-Publication Data

Thoene, Bodie, date.
  First light / Bodie and Brock Thoene.
     p. cm. — (The A.D. chronicles ; Bk. 1)
  ISBN 0-8423-7506-6 (hc) — ISBN 0-8423-7507-4 (sc)
  1. Jewish families—Fiction. 2. Jerusalem—Fiction. I. Thoene, Brock, - II. Title.
  PS3570.H46 F57 2003
  813′.54—dc21   2003002758

Printed in the United States of America

09   08   07   06   05   04   03
 7   6   5   4   3   2   1

For Anne Rosenfeld, Jean Barrett, Dave Harris,
and Luke Thoene, who gave this story a voice.

Prologue

PASSOVER *seder* had ended. Moshe Sachar kissed his five eldest sons, their wives, and their children good night at the door of his Old City Jerusalem home.

The oldest son, Luke, embraced Moshe. Tears were in his eyes. "Papa. Papa. It just wasn't the same without them tonight."

Moshe patted Luke on the back. "Your mother and sister-in-law could see us all from heaven. Rachel's proud of you boys. And her nineteen grandchildren. Nothing she loved more than being a *bubbe* to all these grandchildren, eh? God blessed us with fifty-three wonderful years. Could I ask for more?"

"It shouldn't have ended the way it did." Luke frowned.

"It didn't end, Son. I see the faces of our grandchildren and it's like your mother isn't gone. I saw Rachel smile when little Leah smiled, nu? I saw Rachel's eyes when Etta looked at me. And I heard Rachel speak when Danielle recited the blessing."

"You sure you'll be all right, Papa?" Luke seemed reluctant to leave.

Moshe gestured toward his youngest son, Shimon, who stood grim-faced with his arms crossed, in the doorway of the study. Moshe whispered, "Pray for your brother. He's having a hard time, eh?"

Shimon, aged thirty-seven, had lost his wife in the same bombing that had killed Rachel. Moshe said in a cheerful voice, "Your brother will be good company."

Alfie, the barrel-chested old gardener, raised his hand and stepped up to embrace Luke. "And me. Don't forget me."

"Sure. Always Alfie." Luke returned the hug of the simpleminded caretaker who had lived with Moshe and the Sachar family for over fifty years.

Alfie assured Luke, "Don't worry none about your papa and brother, eh? Don't worry. I take good care of your papa and Shimon. I been taking care your papa since before you boys was born."

Moshe added, "Me and Alfie and Shimon. Three bachelors. We'll stay up all night with our pipes. Talk about old times. Talk politics and archaeology. What could be better to pass the time on Passover in Jerusalem? We'll be fine. Your mother would approve. Now go on home, Luke. I'll ring you tomorrow."

"Shalom, Papa." Then Luke raised his hand in farewell to his brother. "Shimon. Alfie. Shalom." Luke touched his finger to the *mezuzah* on the doorpost, spoke the blessing of peace, and stepped out to join his family in the lane. It was a short walk home for them.

The door clicked shut. Moshe stood for a moment with his hand on the latch. The clock ticked in the foyer behind him. The house was quiet. Too quiet.

From behind Moshe, Shimon spoke. "You okay, Papa?"

"Sure," Moshe replied. "You?"

"It's been a long night," Shimon said wearily.

"Yes."

"I'll make coffee and bring macaroons before we show him, eh, Moshe?" The old giant lumbered off toward the kitchen.

It was the first Passover Israeli archaeologist Moshe Sachar had spent without Rachel since their marriage in 1948. The vacant chairs of Rachel and thirty-two-year-old daughter-in-law Susan were stark reminders that fifty years had not strengthened the fragile existence of Israel. Nor had time altered the Muslim vow to finish what Hitler had begun with the extermination of Jews in Nazi Germany. Worldwide anti-Semitism was once again escalating to levels unmatched since the days when Hitler began his propaganda campaign against the Jews of

Europe. Through the worldwide media, evil was once again sinking its claws into the minds and cultures of the nations of the world.

Even in the American church many had begun to preach against the nation of Israel in blatant disregard of the eternal promises God gave to the descendants of Abraham, Isaac, and Jacob.

Meanwhile, in Israel, life or death for a Jew was often a matter of missing a bus targeted by a terrorist bomber or simply walking out of a restaurant seconds before a terrorist walked in.

One year had passed since Moshe and Shimon had lost their wives together in the suicide bombing of an Old City café. Moshe's wife, Rachel, had lived through the Holocaust, the Israeli War of Independence in 1948, and each successive war against Israel in the fifty years that followed.

The mother of six strong sons in Israel and one adopted daughter in America, Rachel had often told Moshe that when the Lord called her home she would be ready for a rest after cooking so many holiday meals for such a family!

Rachel had died as she used her body to shield two small children from the blast that ripped through the restaurant.

Shimon's wife, Susan, was an American archaeology student who had met and married Shimon five years earlier. When the *intifada* had begun, her parents had begged her to return to America. Like the biblical heroine in the book of Ruth, Susan had chosen to remain with her new Israeli family. Shimon's people had become her people, she said, and she would not leave. Susan had been six months pregnant when a ball bearing from the bomb exploded through her eye and into her brain, killing her instantly. The baby, a boy, died within minutes inside her. Susan Sachar's life had only begun when a Hamas terrorist murdered her and Rachel and the baby and many others.

On CNN the murderer was called a political activist.

Yasser Arafat declared that the bombing was Israel's fault.

The Muslim mother of the bomber was interviewed with great sympathy, and she told how proud she was of her son. His picture was posted throughout the West Bank and Gaza as a hero and martyr for Islam. His family received a payment of ten thousand dollars from Iraq and five thousand indirectly from Saudi Arabia and Egypt.

No one asked what this loss of their wives and the unborn child meant to Shimon or to Moshe.

Shimon, a professor of antiquities at Hebrew University, was mired in despair and grief. Not a day had passed this last year in which he had not thought of Susan and the baby boy he might have had.

Tonight he sank into the leather wingback chair facing Moshe's desk. Pressing his fingertips together, he stared blankly at the row of ancient pottery above the bookshelf.

Moshe sat down opposite his son. He could hear the *clank* of dishes as Alfie cleaned the kitchen and prepared coffee.

"It's late." Shimon did not look into his father's eyes.

Shimon most resembles me, Moshe noted. Tall, lean, and tanned. Prominent nose, high cheekbones. Dark brown eyes, black curly hair with a touch of gray at the temples. Shimon had the look of his Sephardic ancestors. He had also followed in Moshe's footsteps and had taken up his father's professorship after Moshe retired.

"You are the most like me," Moshe said aloud. "Of all the boys."

Shimon inhaled deeply and turned away. "You and Mama. What, fifty-three years? I wanted it to be like that for me and Susan."

"I won't offer you platitudes, Shimon."

"Good. You know my friends are saying I should begin to date again?" He shifted his weight in the chair in disgust. "You know? Like getting a puppy when the old dog dies or something. Horrible. Horrible."

"Yes," Moshe agreed.

"Papa." Shimon rubbed his brow, as though trying to blot out an image in his brain. "I don't know what to do with myself. You know? I go home to our little flat. Still. You know? I expect Susan'll be there, waiting."

"Yes." Moshe remembered the countless occasions he had forgotten Rachel was gone. He had called out to her, expecting a reply.

"Papa? What can I do?"

"Work. Study."

Shimon shook his head. "I've lost interest in . . . everything. I don't know. I've been granted a sabbatical from the university. I'm not going back after spring break, Papa. I need time away. I . . . everything is dark. I feel blind. Blind without her light."

"You're not alone in your grief."

"Why is that fact no comfort? I keep asking myself, *why?* Why? You and I walked out of the café together. They stayed behind talking. Mama and Susan. I wish . . . you know—Well, you know what I wish."

"That you had lingered long enough to die with her."

"Yes. Yes. That."

"I know, Son. I know. It's not so hard for me. I'm over eighty years old now. I'll see your mother soon. Soon. But you have a long life ahead of you."

"I suppose I'll have to live it in this darkness."

"No. But you'll have to live till you see the light at the end."

Silence. Shimon pressed his lips together.

Alfie entered, carrying a thermos and book bag slung over his shoulder. He stared at Shimon, then addressed Moshe. "You haven't told him about it yet?"

"No," Moshe replied.

"Well, you better tell him," Alfie said slowly. "Your oldest son, Luke, knows. Shimon is the youngest. He should know too. It's not safe only one son knowing the secret. What if something happens? You're old. Me too."

Shimon raised his head and fixed his gaze on Alfie. "What are you going on about, Alf?"

Alfie strode to the bookshelf. He narrowed his eyes and said firmly to Moshe, "He don't know nothing about it, eh? Nothing about his great-grandfather, the rabbi, the way he knew all the paths under the city? Nothing about where you and me disappeared to in 1948 after the Old City fell to the Arabs? Nor what's right under this house? Nothing at all? Shimon don't know? Moshe! We're getting old, you and me. And Rachel said a long time ago that Shimon had to know the secret. Had to know. He's the youngest. Him and Luke need to both of them know. You showed Luke last year. You promised Rachel you'd tell the oldest and the youngest someday before you die."

Shimon reacted with irritation. "What's he talking about, Papa?"

Moshe responded cautiously, "You remind me of myself, Shimon. And so your mother said you were the most likely to succeed me."

"And so I have done. I teach in your same classroom. I would have liked to emulate you in other ways. Your life. But that's out of my hands," Shimon countered.

"Tell him, Moshe," Alfie urged. "I brought coffee. A thermos. We'll take it. It's Passover. Tell him."

Moshe nodded stiffly. "In May 1948 I was commander of the defenders of the Old City. You know that much of the story."

"Yes," Shimon put in. "The Jewish Quarter was surrounded and besieged by five Arab armies. Only two hundred Jewish defenders against thousands. Fifteen hundred Jewish civilians were starving, without water, crammed into the basement of the Hurva Synagogue. And then you ran out of ammunition. You were overrun. Defeated by the Arabs. Taken prisoner of war by the Arabs. The Jewish civilian population was expelled from the Jewish Quarter. Mama was with them when they were driven out of Old City Jerusalem. Uncle Yacov too. Grandfather Shlomo Lebowitz died that same night. The synagogues were burned. For nineteen years Jordan controlled the Jewish Old City, and no Jew was allowed into Old City Jerusalem or allowed to worship at the Western Wall."

Moshe raised his finger in correction. "Mostly true."

"Tell him," Alfie insisted.

"Yes." Shimon leaned forward. "Tell me, Papa."

Moshe cleared his throat. "You know this house is built on the very site where Grandfather Lebowitz's house once stood."

"Yes," Shimon replied. "When Israel recaptured the Old City from Jordan in 1967, this property was returned to you and Mama. You rebuilt the house. You and Alfie rebuilt it with your own hands. Luke and Uncle Yacov helped. I remember."

Moshe smiled enigmatically. "We didn't want anyone else poking around here. Especially in the basement. So we rebuilt this house ourselves. We kept the secret."

"What secret, Papa?"

"Before the Old City fell in 1948, Grandfather showed me a passage in the basement of this house."

"Passage?"

"A tunnel. From ancient times," Moshe continued. "It leads beneath the Old City and then under the Temple Mount itself. Alfie and I . . . as the Arab armies were entering the Jewish Quarter . . . Alfie and I escaped through a second passage from Eliyahu Synagogue into a chamber. A library."

Shimon blinked dumbly at his father. "I heard the legends. Always. Who hasn't? But what, Papa? Are you telling me these are not myths?"

"You're my youngest son, Shimon. You, like me, will know what this treasure means. The secret was shown to me by your great-grandfather. Your uncle Yacov also knew of it. But he died without children. So the ancient guardianship is passed through me to two of my sons. To Luke, who was born the day Alfie and I returned to the surface . . . and now also to you, my youngest."

"Show him," Alfie insisted, bolting the exterior door of the study. "I brought macaroons. Coffee too. Let's show him."

Moshe stood stiffly. "Yes. It's time. I felt it tonight like I have never felt it before. The end of some things. The beginning of others. I'm not young anymore."

Shimon leapt to his feet. "Please! Papa! Yes! Show me!"

"Alfie," Moshe said, deferring to the old caretaker, "open it then."

Alfie shifted the bag of macaroons on his shoulder and reached up to hook a gnarled index finger around the center stem of a seven-branched candlestick. With a slight pressure the menorah tilted forward with a click. One narrow section of the bookshelf slid back, revealing an opening wide enough for only one man to enter.

Shimon gasped. "Is this what you were doing all those times Mama said you were studying and couldn't be disturbed?"

Moshe laughed. "She spoke the truth. You always assumed I worked in this room, eh?"

"Twenty-two steps here," Alfie instructed. "We did it that way because it's the Hebrew alphabet. Twenty-two letters. Moshe taught it to me so I could remember it."

They entered the confined space. Shoulders brushed the walls as the three descended into darkness. Twenty-two steps beginning with *alef.*

Moshe pulled a handle at the bottom. The bookshelf slid closed behind them, bringing absolute blackness.

"Son, give me your hand." Moshe grasped Shimon's fingers. "You'll learn to do this without light." He pulled Shimon's hand forward and brushed his fingertips across the cold stone wall. The raised image of a menorah was carved into the stone. "You feel it?"

"Yes. Yes!" Shimon said in awe.

"Then push each of the seven branches starting from right to left."

Shimon obeyed. The wall groaned as it opened. The space was filled with a sound like a rushing wind and the sweet fragrance of incense.

"How will we move in the dark?" Shimon asked.

"Point your index finger upwards," Moshe explained. "That's right. Reach up to the top of the tunnel. You will feel three separate patterns of grooves in the stone. Fit your finger into the single-finger-width slot. Yes. Yes. Like a trolley car, eh? Now hold on to the back of my jacket. Keep your finger pointing up, fixed into the groove. Alfie will put his hand on your shoulder. Come on then."

The trio entered the low, constricted passageway and inched forward, following the same path by which the ancient high priest of Solomon's day had once entered the Temple.

For the sake of Shimon, Moshe repeated the instructions that old Rabbi Lebowitz had given him over fifty years earlier. "One finger into the groove. This will guide you along the one path you must take to the chamber of scrolls. Take no other path, or you will surely find death."

They did not speak further as they progressed through the darkness. Moshe remembered clearly what the old rabbi had told him about Alfie Halder: *"Alfie is one of the Thirty-Six Righteous. For the sake of such innocent hearts, the Lord is merciful and the judgment of the Almighty against the earth is held back until the day Messiah will come."*

Strange after fifty years how the words of the old man replayed in Moshe's mind as if they had been spoken yesterday. During his time beneath the Temple Mount, Moshe had found the company of Alfie a comfort. Together the two had kept their guardianship a secret. Alfie had accepted the burden of their responsibility with childlike peace, seemingly undaunted by the prospect that they might have spent a lifetime beneath the mountain. Each time the two had made the journey of return into the chamber, Alfie had entered with the joy of praise on his lips.

"Tonight," old Alfie said softly, *"I'd rather be a doorkeeper in the house of the Lord than to dwell in the tents of the wicked."* And then he laughed. "A long time we two been doorkeepers, eh, Moshe? Fifty years and better, eh? Ah, well. Time to pass it on. Almost home. We're almost home, Moshe!"

Sometimes curving, sometimes straight, the stone path beneath their feet was worn smooth from centuries of guardians.

When the guiding groove on the ceiling came to an abrupt end, Moshe, with a practiced hand, found the low stone arch of the entrance. "From here we kneel to pass through," he instructed his son.

"We're pilgrims," Alfie explained as he dropped to his knees.

Moshe prayed the Shema: "Hear, O Israel! The Lord our God is one Lord . . . "[2]

Alfie and Shimon repeated the familiar words. Then Alfie said to Shimon, "They've been waiting for you a long time, Shimon."

"Papa?" Shimon whispered in awe. "Who's been waiting?"

Moshe did not reply. He slid his finger over the cool facade, found an indentation in the stone, and pushed inward. With a *whoosh*, the wall groaned and yielded to his touch. The distant sound of music echoed on the rush of wind that blew past them.

"Come forward, Son," Moshe instructed Shimon. As they entered, the sense of vast space opened up before Shimon. He remained on his knees, shoulder-to-shoulder with Alfie and Moshe. The door slid shut behind them.

"Now," Moshe said. "Look up."

Shimon looked up and gasped. There was light enough to see the face of his father and Alfie clearly. Above them was a perfect replica of the skies above Jerusalem. Luminescent stars, re-created with incredible accuracy, showed the heavens of early summer. There was the North Star, fixed like a diamond in the handle of the Little Dipper.

"There, Shimon," Moshe said. "The polestar by which travelers find their way. So even here, beneath the Temple Mount, you'll always know which direction is north. You can't be lost here. Those who came before us made sure of that. And it's precise in every detail. It's a gift, Shimon."

"A miracle," Alfie said.

"Yes," Shimon agreed. "A miracle, Papa! I remember summer nights when we all slept on the housetop and you taught us the names of the stars."

"And here they are. Old friends, these stars." Moshe was pleased. "The shepherd-king David knew them well by name. Can you name them, Shimon?"

"The summer triangle of Deneb, Altair, and Vega in the east," Shimon replied. "Antares in the south. Regulus there in the paw of Leo in the west. And Arcturus directly overhead."

Woven into the artificial night were the Hebrew letters proclaiming, *In the beginning Elohim created the heavens and the earth.*[3] With a fine golden thread, the names of God were inscribed among the stars: *Adonai. Elohim. El Shaddai. YHWH. King of kings. Lord of lords. Wonderful Counselor. Savior.*

The glory of the heavens provided light enough to read by. "Stand up, my son," Moshe instructed. "Stand and be strong. This is your heritage. The Year of the Lord. *Anno Domini.* Come with us."

Moshe led them through a west-facing entrance to a balcony that overlooked an enormous vaulted library with shelves stacked with row upon row of clay jars. In the center of the hall were three long study tables, additional jars, and a box with flashlights and a supply of batteries.

"Papa?" Shimon questioned. "Tell me."

"The Temple library," Moshe replied. "Seven thousand scrolls remain of the original fifty thousand. Most of these were hidden when Jerusalem was destroyed and the Temple burned. There's one chamber where books penned by eyewitnesses have been added from time to time. And that's where you'll begin your journey. *The A.D. Chronicles*, that section's called. It's where I began when I was a little younger than you are now. There are twelve doors, each leading to another room. Many choices. But after Susan and your mother died, Alfie and I discussed it. There, that center doorway. Carved in the capstone you see the words *The A.D. Chronicles.*" Moshe inclined his head. "I've made a list of the order of reading. Seventy scrolls in all. It'll take you several years. The house will be yours and Luke's, so you can come and go as you like."

Moshe led his son down a spiral staircase to the floor of the library. He swept his hand upward to where the words of three languages—Hebrew, Greek, and Latin—ringed the parapet.

WHAT WAS—WHAT IS—WHAT WILL BE

"It's all here." Moshe took Shimon's hand. "Enough for one man to study for several lifetimes and still not understand the height, the depth, the breadth of God's love for mankind. I've been studying for fifty years and yet haven't made a dent."

"Papa?" Shimon croaked. "I've only been granted a one-year sabbatical!"

Alfie laughed. "Ah, you'll have fun, Shimon! Your mama always said of all the boys you would be the one who would not want to stop reading, eh?"

"Yes. Under the covers with a flashlight," Shimon remarked. "She never could make me quit once I had a good book in my hands."

"That was practice," Alfie said.

Moshe led the way to a study table, where several clay jars were lined up beside a lamp. "I've laid these out for you. Here are the first three Jerusalem scrolls Alfie and I studied. But there, you see this one? I've chosen this fourth scroll for you to begin your studies. I call it *First Light.*" He tapped his fingers affectionately against the pottery. "Here,

Shimon. Inside is light to help guide you through this darkest night of your soul. Yes. Begin here." Moshe pushed the container toward Shimon. "You see what words are pressed into the clay? Read."

Shimon traced the raised Hebrew letters on the rim of the jar with his fingertips. *"My name is Peniel."*

"Yes. His name was Peniel," Moshe whispered affectionately, as if the one who wrote the script was an old friend. "Peniel. 'Face of God.' That's it, Shimon, my boy. *First Light.* Go on. Open it. He's been waiting to speak to you about darkness and light for a very long time. He taught me things I didn't understand until I read his story."

Shimon detached the seal that covered the mouth of the jar. At his father's urging, he removed the scroll. Lambskin. Supple. Almost like new. Shimon sank down to sit on the bench at the study table.

"Now, Shimon," old Alfie instructed, "we'll stay with you tonight, your papa and me. I always liked Peniel. So. We're running out of time, us old men. Almost home. Almost home. Read to us, Shimon."

Shimon unrolled the first sheaf. A flower was pressed on the page. A gardenia? Shimon could not be certain. He scanned the distinct Hebrew letters of the document:

"Those who lived in darkness have seen a great light. . . .

Look at Him. Yes. Look! The ordinariness of it. That's the most extraordinary thing!

He came to us like the great treasure of a king, beyond value, hidden in straw, packed into a common clay jug, shipped to earth among the cargo of a river scow.

Yes, it was something like that when He came. No one really knew. Not really.

Yes, look at Him. Ordinary.

His name? Yeshua. It means 'God is Salvation.'

Thirty-two years old by human reckoning. Just under six feet tall. Sun-bronzed. Slim and strong. Square hands. Calloused hands. Skinned knuckles from pulling up the bucket of a stone well. Brown eyes. Dark brown with gold flecks. Matching brown, curly hair, sun-streaked with hints of copper; tied back and braided at the nape of His neck. Beard thick and dark.

He stroked His beard and smiled often when He considered a question that interested Him or heard a song that pleased

Him. Or when He held a child in His arms and asked, 'What do you want to be when you grow up?' Or more to the point, 'I like you exactly the way you are.'

He was nothing remarkable at first glance. Could blend into a crowd and never be noticed until His eyes locked on you and compassion poured into your soul.

And yet. What is the truth here?

Yeshua.

First Light.

The great red dawning that rises over the mountains of all eternity. The shining bridge of stars that arches up and up and gives us a path from earth into heaven's throne room.

Yeshua: the early cock crow that will wake us from death, after the final night of time has fled.

To our ship, battered by the gale, He is the lighthouse.

To those who wait on shore and search the seas for a sail, He is the ship that safely carries Himself and those, our dear ones, His children, who have left us behind.

He brings the message of eternity to us across the vast gulf of all time.

He is the well of our hope, the bright epitome of all things. The mystery that, even now, is only dimly understood by the human heart.

And yet, listen! Listen! Here is the remarkable thing about it! It seemed so ordinary.

It was a time of sadness, as life has always been. Frightening to those who lived through the darkness of political upheaval, corruption, violence, cruelty, futility, and the manipulation of men's minds. It was a time of striving and longing and smashed hopes . . . and nothing ever, ever, ever turning out the way anyone wished it would!

Like always, eh? So much like every day since the beginning of time that who could notice someone extraordinary had come among us?

The innocent died while evil men thrived. Mothers and fathers stood at the edge of their children's graves and shook their fists at God and cried out, 'Why?'

Why?

At first only a few noticed when He came among us, bringing answers.

Then as His light illuminated the darkness and threatened
to expose evil,

As He challenged self-righteous hypocrisy,

Embraced the lonely, gave hope to the hopeless,

Then they noticed.

Yes.

Only then.

When it looked as though everything might change, they
noticed.

Only then those men of darkness, who liked to keep things
the way they had always been, looked for a way to kill Him.

Yeshua.

This is a story of many ordinary people. Some had met Him
early and were already changed. But there were others, so many,
who still lived in darkness. Waiting. Hoping for something or
someone to come along and heal the wounds of body and soul.

That year at Passover there was a whisper. Maybe. Maybe
now our Deliverer will come! Tens of thousands crowded into
Jerusalem to look for Him. But He did not come.

That year, instead of the Messiah, counterfeit champions
under the command of the rebel bar Abba pulled their swords
and did battle at the Temple against Rome and the forces of the
hated Herod Antipas!

They could not win.

In this brief Passover skirmish the Jewish Zealots, seeking
freedom from bondage, took many innocent pilgrims with them
to the grave.

And anguished cries filled the streets that night. Why?
Why? Where was God in all this? And where was Messiah?
Why did He not intervene? No one knew. No one except three
small boys and an old shepherd named Zadok."

And as Shimon read, the scent of a garden and the hushed whisper
of the wind swirled around them. . . .

PART I

The people walking in darkness
have seen a great light;
On those living in the land of the shadow of death
a light has dawned.
You have enlarged the nation
and increased their joy;
They rejoice before you
as people rejoice at the harvest,
As men rejoice
when dividing the plunder.
For as in the day of Midian's defeat,
You have shattered
the yoke that burdens them,
the bar across their shoulders,
the rod of their oppressor.***

***WE WHO HAVE WALKED IN DARKNESS HAVE
   SEEN A GREAT LIGHT;
    ON ALL WHO LIVED IN A LAND DARK AS DEATH,
    A LIGHT HAS DAWNED.

ISAIAH 9:2-4

1

In a tiny, unpretentious house in the village known as Beth-lehem, "House of Bread," bunches of lavender dried in the rafters of the main room, filling the place with sweet aroma. The seder supper was finished. The stories of Israel's deliverance from bondage in Egypt had all been sung. The clutter of empty dishes remained stacked on the table.

Three boys and a sheepdog shared a bed made of soft fleece. Avel, aged nine, lay between five-year-old Emet and eleven-year-old Ha-or Tov.

Emet and Ha-or Tov were drowsy, nearly asleep. Avel, eyes heavy, listened to the soft voices of two men engaged in conversation. Red Dog blinked at the firelight.

Zadok, Chief Shepherd of the flocks and herds of Israel, was old. A patch covered one eye. Skin was like leather, face split by the scar of an ancient wound. His voice and that of his Passover guest, Yeshua of Nazareth, drifted into the bedchamber.

"But if not now, when?" Zadok inquired of Yeshua.

Avel strained to hear Yeshua's reply.

When?

In the history of the world, had there ever been a more important question? So many things depended on the answer. Redemption. Freedom. Vengeance against Roman oppressors and corrupt religious rulers.

Avel rested his cheek on his hand. Zadok was not asking one question, but many.

When?

When would Yeshua openly declare His right to the throne of David?

When would He take His place at the head of an army to drive the Romans from Jerusalem and Israel?

When would He avenge the blood of those who had fallen victim to Roman swords within the Temple courts only today in Jerusalem?

"If not now, Lord, when?"

And who had more right to know than Zadok? Zadok, who as a young man had been among the first shepherds to see the angels and hear their heavenly proclamation that the Messiah had been born in a lambing barn at Beth-lehem.

Zadok, who had brought first word of the miraculous event to the elders of the Temple as he delivered the young lambs of Beth-lehem and Migdal Eder for the daily sacrifice.

Zadok, who had made room in his own home for the young mother, her husband, and the newborn baby king.

Zadok, who had secretly sent the family on their way to safety as the soldiers of the old butcher king, Herod, had come by night to kill every male child under the age of two in the village.

Zadok, whose face had been ripped open by a Roman gladius in his battle to save his children.

Zadok, who had buried three tiny boys while the keening of his wife, Rachel, echoed across the pastures of Migdal Eder to be heard as far away as Ramah.

Zadok, who had kept his holy vow of silence about the whereabouts of the promised King of Israel for thirty-two years until tonight.

Did a man who suffered so much not deserve to know why? What had it all been for?

When?

Yeshua, His gaze fixed intently on the old man, did not answer at first. Then He grasped Zadok's hand. "You were the first to hear. The first to believe. The first to suffer loss for my sake. Your babies are the first martyrs. Surely you've known, old friend, that it was no accident that the Son of David was born in a stable among the lambs set apart for sacrifice in the Temple of Yerushalayim. That same child born thirty-two years ago in Beth-lehem is *korban,* that which is holy and set apart for the purposes of the heavenly Father."

"But what can it mean?" Zadok's voice was intense.

"Zadok? You're Chief Shepherd of the Temple flock. You tend the lambs for sacrifice. Can it be that you've forgotten the words spoken by the prophet Isaias about the Messiah?"

Zadok waved a hand. Evidently, Avel thought, the old man did not want to be reminded of that part of the Scripture. "So much written about what is *korban.* How can an old man be expected to remember it all?"

Yeshua stroked His beard. Without taking His eyes from the shepherd He said, *"He was oppressed and afflicted, yet he did not open his mouth; he was led as a lamb to slaughter."*[4]

That was all. As if it explained anything!

Ha-or Tov, now wide awake, whispered to Avel, "What does Yeshua mean? What do the sacrificial lambs raised here in the fields of Beth-lehem have to do with Messiah, the Redeemer?"

"I think he's talking about the riots today," Avel replied.

"The penalty for breaking the commands of the Almighty," Yeshua continued, "is death. That curse now rests on every human soul. Redemption costs something, Zadok, my old friend. It is written by Isaias about the Son of Man, *'Surely he took up our infirmities and carried our sorrows. . . . He was pierced for our transgressions, he was crushed for our iniquities. . . . the punishment that brought us peace was upon him, and by his wounds we are healed.'"*[5]

Zadok leaned close. Firelight glowed golden on his face. "Can the cost of our salvation be so high?"

"Tomorrow I'll be teaching in Beth-Anyah."

"So close to Yerushalayim! You'll draw the wolves out along with the sheep. You put yourself at their mercy."

"A day is coming when they will understand God's Mercy."

"But not that way, Lord! Tell me it won't be!"

"God's love for each person is that profound."

"There must be another way! Crush our enemies! Call down fire from heaven! Destroy the wicked! Set up a kingdom in Yerushalayim like our shepherd-king, David! Like you, he was born here in Beth-lehem!"

"Zadok, when the soldiers of Herod came to Beth-lehem to kill every baby boy, you sought to save your three sons." Yeshua touched the scar on Zadok's cheek. Avel fixed his eyes on the scene, remembering his own healing. But this time Yeshua did not make the jagged line smooth again or restore the eye lost in the battle, though Avel knew He could have done so. "This scar is proof of your love for your children."

"I failed. I am alive and my babies are in their graves."

"Not for want of effort. You would have died to save your little ones. I know you. Even now you'd face a lion and lay down your life to save your flocks. Can the Son sent by the Father do any less for the flock given to him? Would you deny the Lord the honor of wounds and scars that will be eternal proof of how much he loves you?"

"I will die for you, Lord."

"He was led like a lamb to slaughter."[6]

"But I am more ready to give up my own life! Gladly!"

"One day it may be so. Anyone who lays down his life for my sake will find it.[7] God so loved the world that whoever believes in his Son will never die but will inherit eternal life.[8] But first, the good shepherd will lay down his life to save his flock. That price must be paid to redeem those the Father has given to me. The prophecy of what will happen is all there, recorded by Moses and the prophets. They longed to see what you see, to hear what you have heard.[9] The battle for mankind will be won."

"Rabbi, will we fight the enemy then? Together?"

"Don't misunderstand, old friend . . . *by his wounds we are healed.*"[10]

The prophecy hung like the scent of lavender on the air. Then, inexplicably, Avel saw a tangible sorrow grip the old man, as if he remembered something. What was the meaning of it? Avel wondered. What had that fragment of verse awakened in the old man's understanding?

Shoulders sagged. With a groan Zadok bowed his head. Ran crooked fingers through his thatch of white hair. What did Zadok hear that Avel did not?

After a long time the aged shepherd pleaded, "Ah! No! And after such a fine beginning. I looked up! Saw the stars shinin' there above us in the field. Such joy we felt. What a beautiful baby boy! Such hope! What's it for? It can't be meant to end so ill!"

Silence descended. Then, finally, Yeshua replied, "It can't be any other way."

"But when?"

"Next year in Yerushalayim. Passover."

"I won't attend." Zadok raised his chin defiantly. But Avel knew the truth of it: Yes, Zadok would be there.

Yeshua stood and smiled. "Never mind, old friend. I'll see you again. Soon." He glanced at Red Dog. "The faithful ones are gone. Wolves lead the flock of Israel. They won't let you rest."

Zadok's lower lip shot out. "Get yourself out of Judea! Y' know what they'll do! The office of high priest is bought and paid for. They fear you. And after today? What happened in the Temple? They'll find some way to blame you for it."

"It isn't yet my time."

"Y' must leave! Thirty years ago I warned your mother and Joseph to leave. Go to Egypt. To Alexandria. There are true Israelites in Alexandria. They have a temple there where some might listen. Them that hold the power in Yerushalayim now will use their might against you as Herod, the great butcher, once tried. Caiaphas as high priest is in league with the Romans. Up to the neck. Herod Antipas depends on Roman soldiers to keep the people from revolution and the Nabatean king from attacking. It's a dangerous time for us all."

"Men's souls have a fiercer enemy than Rome. More terrible than Herod Antipas. Don't be afraid of those who have power to kill the body. Beware of one who will destroy your soul if he can." Yeshua glanced toward Avel, Emet, and Ha-or Tov. "Follow the shepherd," he said to the boys. "Learn from him. Listen to no other voice and you will live!" Then He placed His hand on Zadok's shoulder in farewell. "Teach them Torah as the Lord commands a father to teach his children. Zadok! Take care of my lambs!"

Zadok nodded, unable to speak.

The two clasped hands. "I'll see you soon. Won't I?" A flash of understanding appeared to pass between them.

Avel fought the urge to run to Yeshua, to wrap his arms around Him and beg Him not to leave them unprotected.

Yeshua touched His finger to the mezuzah, the small rectangular case containing a fragment of Scripture. This was the covenant-mark placed on the doorpost of every Jewish house in remembrance of the blood of the Passover lamb.

In a gentle voice Yeshua whispered the blessing: *"The Lord will watch over your coming and going both now and forevermore."*[11]

Yeshua's benediction seemed a promise that the Lord Himself would watch over them, Avel thought. Why then was Avel afraid to see Him go? Even with hope that the Lord would preserve them, death felt very close. Wolves were stalking the flock, nipping at the heels of the Good Shepherd and all who followed Him.

The two men embraced. Without a backward glance, Yeshua strode into the night.

Silhouetted by the fires in the city of Jerusalem, Herod Antipas raised his cup and called for a toast. Two hundred guests, gathered on the rooftop of the old Hasmonean Palace, joined him. Among them were members of the Jewish Sanhedrin, representatives of the High Priest Caiaphas who had taken refuge in the palace when the Passover riot reached a fevered pitch.

"Death to all rebels!" cried the dissipated tetrarch.

"Death!" returned the company.

"Emperor Caesar! Long life!"

"Caesar!" they shouted.

Twenty-year-old Susanna bat Maccabee remained silent. She raised her cup to her lips but did not drink. She would not drink to the death of those who, like her ancestors, the Maccabees, had fallen in an attempt to wrest Jerusalem from the control of a corrupt and oppressive government.

With her flashing eyes, chestnut hair, and uncommonly tall and slender build, it was said that Susanna had the beauty of her ancestral grandmother, wife of the renowned Judas Maccabeus, who had driven the Greeks from the Holy City. As a child of old rebels, conquerors, priests, and kings, Susanna was not merely stubborn. Rebellion was second nature to her. Even a year of official disapproval and exile from Herod Antipas' court had not weakened her resolve to marry the younger brother instead of the older from the family of bar Talmai.

Tonight she was back in Jerusalem to attend the Passover feast. It was expected Susanna would yield to Antipas' wish and consent to marry Demos bar Talmai. But it was Manaen she loved.

That year of banishment in a desert fortress with one personal servant had not changed her determination. She would have told Antipas and all of them plainly what she intended if the riots had not broken out.

Now she stood on the parapet beside Joanna, wife of Herod's steward. The women watched as flames licked the Jerusalem sky. Slaves moved among the guests with wine and trays of food. There was a celebratory mood, laughter and speculation about how many were dead. Bets were made as to the number. What first came as a report of danger dissolved into relief and then excitement, like the anticipation of gladiatorial sport in the arena. The air smelled of death. The rebellion had been brutally crushed. The Messiah had not come after all. Antipas and the Roman governor, Pontius Pilate, were safe. Everyone, for that matter, was safe.

Except Manaen.

Manaen and his old servant, Adam, had not returned. Demos acted unconcerned that his brother might be among the dead. Instead Demos leered drunkenly at Susanna and raised his cup to her.

She turned her back on him.

"Are you all right?" Joanna asked Susanna quietly.

"When Manaen returns. When I see his face again. I've thought of nothing else for months."

Joanna, her ally in years past, was an older confidante who understood the unhappiness of life in the scrutiny of Antipas' court. Though Susanna had not been permitted to communicate with Joanna for a year, tonight they took comfort in one another again.

"What will you do?" Joanna gave a forced smile in the direction of Demos, who appeared triumphant, expectant.

"I know what I *won't* do." Susanna kept her gaze riveted on the fire.

"House arrest in Machaerus hasn't changed your mind?" Joanna queried.

"A hundred years couldn't make me choose Demos over Manaen."

Joanna patted her arm in solidarity. "Well done. Demos has brought his latest eunuch with him tonight. A pretty pair." She shook her head. "I'm taking my son, Bo, and going to stay with his friends in Beth-Anyah. Enough of this. I wouldn't have come if Kuza hadn't insisted. Listen, if you need a place to stay—"

Eglon, commander of Antipas' bodyguard, burst in. He waved a bloody cloak, then dropped to one knee before Antipas. "Lord Antipas! The rebels are utterly crushed, surrounded in a pottery shop. Only a matter of time before the last of them is killed."

Applause and shouts of approval erupted.

Eglon thrust the robe into Demos' hands. "I'm afraid I bring sad news for the house of bar Talmai." He paused.

Demos stared at the cloak and grinned wildly, as if he knew already.

"Lord Demos," Eglon continued, "your brother, Manaen, is dead."

Someone gasped.

Then the world began to spin around Susanna. She took a step toward Demos and Manaen's torn cloak, then drew back as Demos held up the garment in an almost victorious gesture.

"Brave Manaen!" Antipas declared. "Brave lad! No doubt perished fighting our enemies. Well then. We'll have another round in memory of brave Manaen bar Talmai!"

The tetrarch eyed Susanna. "To the god who decides all things, eh? Who shall live and who shall die."

MANAEN BAR TALMAI LAY facedown, bleeding, on the stone floor. When someone kicked him hard in the back, he opened one eye. Nine pairs of filthy, sandaled feet surrounded him. Dancing torchlight seeped in through linen curtains.

He was in a pottery shop. Shattered clay jars lay everywhere. A broom rested against the wall. A dead man sprawled awkwardly in the corner, still clutching a candlestick defensively. His vacant eyes stared at Manaen.

A skinny, teenaged boy clutched his knees, ducked his head, and cowered beside an overturned table. Was he one of the rebels? The ragged creature was not bound and seemed of no more consequence to them than the shards of broken ceramics surrounding him that they trampled underfoot.

The point of a dagger pricked Manaen on his neck. But he could not move. Why? Why was he tied up? How did he get here?

"Wake up! You're not dead yet! Wake up!"

Gagged and trussed like a bull for the slaughter, Manaen at last remembered he was in a rebel hideout near the Sheep Gate in Jerusalem, dragged here after a fight with a score of attackers outside the Temple. He had taken down three before someone smashed him across the face with a leg of roasted mutton. That blow was followed by a wine jar to the back of his skull. He had not seen it coming.

So much for Passover supper. Lamb and wine and plenty of blood were splattered across Jerusalem.

A mix of Roman legionaries and the Samaritan members of Herod Antipas' bodyguard ringed the structure. Flaming torches illuminated the street outside, casting eerie shadows on the walls.

Behind the line of soldiers the angry mob began to chant, *"Burn it down! Burn it down! Burn it down!"*

Manaen's captors, Zealots of the well-known band of bar Abba, huddled over him in the darkness. What hope did they have after a riot that had killed hundreds of innocent pilgrims?

Only one hope. Their hostage.

"The Romans will crucify us if we're taken alive!"

"Burn it down!"

"Did anyone see bar Abba?"

"Burn them alive!"

"He escaped through Damascus Gate just as the Romans attacked."

"Crucify them! Crucify them!"

"Our own people will tear us apart! Listen to them! They blame us for the riot! They think it was us did the slaughter! Not the guards of Herod Antipas! Not the Roman swine, but us!"

"Murderers! Crucify them!"

Another hard kick to Manaen's back.

"He's our passage to freedom! Get him up! Show the hostage to the Roman tribune!"

Rough hands grasped Manaen by hair, arms, and tunic. They lugged him to the door and propped him up on display with three swords pressed to his throat, back, and belly!

For a few seconds the ferocity of the crowd wavered. Screams for vengeance rippled away up a side street and died as whispers asked whose life it was the rebels held balanced on the point of a dagger.

"Tribune Felix!" the rebel commander shouted. "We've got a friend of yours here! Manaen bar Talmai! He's a ward of Herod Antipas and brother of Demos! Hear me, Tribune Felix! We'll kill Manaen bar Talmai for sure if you don't back off! Call off the dogs or Manaen dies first!"

Manaen knew Rome would see to it that these vultures were nailed spread-eagle to their perches by morning.

Manaen could clearly see the young tribune's troubled expression. Of course Felix knew Manaen! They were both twenty-five or so and had things in common. Like the hope of leaving Judea forever, to live in Rome. Surely Felix would not let Manaen die at the hands of rebels!

The blade of a dagger cut away the gag, then prodded Manaen beneath his right ear. The commander hissed, "Speak to Tribune Felix! You're old friends, eh? Come on! Tell Felix how badly you'd like to live, eh? Live to carouse together again?"

Manaen coughed. Tried to find his voice. But his tongue was swollen, his throat parched with thirst. "Tribune . . . ," he croaked.

Tribune Felix looked as if he could use a goblet of wine. He shifted uneasily as his soldiers watched him for direction. There was a slight hesitation, then Felix drew himself erect and addressed the rebels, "Who's this fellow?"

"You know who he is! Manaen bar Talmai! Our hostage. And Herod Antipas won't take kindly to you bringing the guts of his ward home in a jug! Let us pass and we'll set him free."

"He's nothing to me. Nothing to Governor Pilate. Nothing to Rome. Kill him, then."

Could Felix mean this? Manaen's heart pounded harder.

"We'll oblige you, make no mistake," the wild-eyed rebel captain warned. "He's a dead man if you don't let us go. It's scum like him we came to wipe from Yerushalayim!"

The tribune continued coolly. "Kill him. It'll make no difference. You'll be crucified or cooked in a fire of your own kindling."

From the back of the crowd a single voice took up the shout, *"Crucify them! Crucify!"*

Then another and another joined in the chant until a thousand voices shouted for the execution of the Zealots!

The rebels withdrew, shoving Manaen back into the cover of the house. They thrust him roughly onto the stone pavement and, knives drawn, towered over him.

"Listen to them!"

"Crucify! Crucify!"

"They mean to kill us. The Romans and our own people together."

"Murderers! Crucify them!"

"They think it was us who started the panic!"

"Burn it down! Burn it down!"

"We're done for, Dan!"

"Burn it down! Burn it down!"

"Even so," the scar-faced Dan replied, "I'll die fighting Romans. Die with a sword in my hand rather than nailed to a Roman cross!"

"And I."

"Me as well."

"Me too."

They raised their eyes to search one another's solemn faces. Braving certain death, they crossed their swords together above Manaen in a sacred pact.

"Burn it down! Burn it down!"

Manaen knew when the first torch was hurled because it clattered onto the flat roof of the dwelling. Another and then another followed. The mob went wild with pleasure. A blazing brand wheeled through the window and spun across the floor to land in a heap of flax. The wall burst into flame. Smoke swelled in the room. The youth by the table covered his nose and mouth and shrank back from the heat. Manaen struggled to escape, wriggling across the floor.

"What about them two?" A bandit noted Manaen's desperate attempt to scramble away from the fire and the youth who simply sat among the smashed pots as if he welcomed death.

"Leave them to burn."

At that, the nine rebels recited the Shema: "Hear, O Israel! The Lord our God is one Lord; the Lord is One!" They called on the God of Israel to accept the sacrifice of their lives as proof that they loved Him with all their hearts, souls, and minds. Manaen heard them mutter the names of wives or children. Then with a shout they wheeled around almost as one. Flames at their backs, they charged out the door into the swords and armor of their enemy. Screams and cheers erupted outside as a hopeless battle ensued.

Inside, a wave of flame reared up and licked the rafters. Manaen shouted to the cowering youth, "Cut me loose! Come on! Move it!"

The young man, terror on his face, turned his head toward the sound of Manaen's voice. Then, by the light of the searing blaze, Manaen saw the reason he had not moved.

He was blind.

"Where are you?" the teenager cried. "The fire! Where are you?"

"Here! Here, boy!" Manaen struggled to make his voice sound confident, to offer reassurance in place of the panic he felt. "What's your name?"

"Peniel."

"We have a chance, Peniel. But I'm bound! Can't move. Pick up a broken shard. That's it! Yes! By your right hand! Stay low! Crawl forward. Come to my voice and I'll lead you out! I'm here on the floor. That's it. A few paces more!"

The blind boy crept nearer. Manaen extended his hands. "Come on! Cut my wrists loose first!" Too much smoke! A spasm of coughing racked him. "Cut!"

Trembling fingers examined the strands of rope that held Manaen captive. The boy began to cut carefully—too carefully—as the fire consumed the curtains with a roar, then leapt above them. No time remaining! The roof, eagerly grasped by the hungry flames, groaned at the touch. The wood door caught fire. Soon it would be too late.

"Hurry! Hurry, lad!"

At last the blind boy sliced through the cords. Manaen snatched the potsherd from him and attacked the ropes around his ankles, freeing himself with seconds to spare. The roof blazed fiercely now, threatening to collapse. A white sheet of fire roared behind them and above them.

"Come on then!" Squinting his eyes against the furnacelike heat, Manaen grabbed the boy by his arm. He stumbled on numbed feet toward the burning door. "Cover your face!" With a shout Manaen launched himself, ramming his shoulder into the wood. It splintered outward as the two leapt through the charring barrier and tumbled onto the ground.

In an instant the soldiers were upon them, dragging the blind boy away at sword point. "Here's one of their whelps! Kill him!"

"Don't hurt him! Fools!" Manaen cried, scrambling to his feet, his beard scorched and his tunic smoking. "He saved my life! Saved my life! Turn him loose!"

THE CORPSES OF THE NINE REBELS were laid out in a neat row along the street for viewing. If any in the crowd recognized them, they did not speak up or request to take them away for burial. To do so would have implicated them in the rebellion.

"So, my friend, you would've let these fellows kill me?" Manaen asked Felix.

"Only your feathers are singed, Manaen." Felix tugged the charred fringes of Manaen's garment. "I'd wear this when you return to the palace of your benefactor, Herod Antipas. Maybe he and that brother of yours will take pity and buy you something new to wear. Then you can sell it and pay me what you owe me."

"I owe that blind boy over there a sight more than I owe you."

Peniel, under guard, sat on the paving stones near the bodies of the rebels.

"You're in debt to half of Jerusalem."

"Let him go free."

"Who is he? One of them?"

"His name is Peniel. He was in the shop when I woke up. Cowering in the corner. They intended to let him burn. Along with me."

"He'll have to be questioned."

"Who will interrogate him?"

"Captain of Pilate's Praetorian Guard."

"Commander Vara? I won't have it."

"He must be questioned."

"Tortured, you mean."

"Manaen, my friend, you don't have anything to say about it. Nor do I." Felix inclined his head toward where the crowd was roughly parted by a warhorse ridden by a black-clad Praetorian centurion. His armor was caked with blood. Eyes flashed with evident hatred as he urged his mount through the throng. He was preceded by ten tough Samaritan legionaries. "Here comes Vara and his butchers now. Bloodied but unbowed."

"I wonder how many innocent Jews he personally skewered with his sword in the Temple courtyard today. Felix, I can't turn the boy over to the likes of him. You know what Vara will do to him. He'd rack a confession out of his own mother if it advanced him in the eyes of Pilate and Sejanus."

Felix replied sarcastically as Vara approached. "In half an hour Vara will have this blind beggar confessing he saw the faces of every rebel and describing them in detail. Pilate will be pleased."

"Felix, Peniel saved my life."

Felix hesitated, then gave Manaen a nudge. "Stand back. Out of his view, eh?"

Manaen averted his gaze from Vara and blended into the verge of the crowd. But he was near enough to hear every word between Vara and Felix.

Vara reined up his mount and saluted Tribune Felix. With a cursory glance at Manaen, he passed a dispatch to Felix. The red wax seal of Pontius Pilate was on the scroll.

"Orders from the governor," Vara said gruffly. He glowered at the dead men.

Felix broke the seal and skimmed the dispatch with obvious disgust.

"I come to you, Tribune," Vara explained, "by personal order of the governor. Corpses of rebels are to be turned over to me, beheaded, taken outside the city gates, and crucified. Heads will be put on pikes along the wall. Bodies will hang until they rot. A friendly warning against treason for other Jews." Vara scowled at the crowd, which thinned as his soldiers began to decapitate the corpses.

"Take them, Commander Vara. With my blessings. I have no use for nine dead men."

Manaen glanced at the blind boy. Would he, too, become a sacrificial lamb?

Vara dismounted. "The governor commands your soldiers to assist me and my men."

Felix nodded then snapped his fingers, ordering the officer who stood guard over the blind captive to move away and lend a hand in the grisly task.

Vara continued. "And further, Pilate commands that Centurion Marcus Longinus appear before the governor on certain charges."

"What charges?"

"The charge of *maiestas*. Disrespect to the name of Emperor

Tiberius. It was reported to Pilate how unhelpful Marcus Longinus was in quelling the riots today. Interfering with Roman soldiers in their duty. The charge is *maiestas.*"

Manaen was aware that such a crime was punishable by crucifixion. Often a trumped-up accusation of *maiestas* was used by men in power to rid themselves of political enemies.

"Marcus? Accused of treason?" Felix scoffed.

"There are other matters."

"There never was an officer more loyal to Tiberius Caesar than Marcus Longinus," Manaen heard Felix protest. "But Marcus has enemies here. I suppose one may have captured Pilate's ear with such an accusation. It will be sorted out. And whatever envious scum made this false accusation will be held to account."

It was instantly obvious to Manaen that Vara was the one who had indicted Marcus before Pilate.

Vara responded defensively, "Marcus has been known to be friendly with the Jews. To make comments against Sejanus."

"Sejanus isn't Caesar," Felix fired back.

"He's Caesar's right arm."

More like Caesar's iron fist, Manaen thought. With the help of his black-uniformed Praetorian guards, Sejanus kept the puppet rulers throughout the Empire under his control. It was by Sejanus' will that Pilate was governor of Judea. By Sejanus' will that Herod Antipas remained tetrarch in Galilee and Perea.

"Centurion Longinus holds the *corona obsidionalis,*" Felix noted. "The highest award Rome can give an officer for bravery. This he won by saving the Roman army at the battle of Idistaviso."

Vara appeared unimpressed. "I forgot you two are friends. So, Tribune Felix, you outrank me. Perhaps you could bring him in. Tell him if you see him Pilate wishes a word with him. It would be better if he turns himself in. Better for his friends if he turns himself in."

It was clear Felix understood the threat. "If I see Centurion Marcus I will pass along your advice."

The heads were tossed into a basket and bodies loaded onto an oxcart. Vara clapped his hands together. "And now. Where is the Jew who was hostage of these brigands?"

Manaen sensed the blood drain from his face. He retreated deeper into the shadows.

"Gone," Felix lied. "Returned to Herod Antipas, I suppose."

"Well then. Besides him there was a witness, an accomplice, I hear?"

Felix gestured toward the headless body of a rebel being dragged toward the cart. "He's dead."

"No survivors? I heard a young one survived. One left alive for me to question."

"None. All dead."

So Felix had decided not to turn Peniel over to Vara. Inwardly Manaen cheered him. Moving through the crowd, Manaen clapped a hand on the blind boy's shoulder. They dared not linger.

"Come on," he whispered. "Come on, boy. I'll take you home."

BEHIND MANAEN AND the blind youth smoke and flames billowed up from the rebel house, carrying the stench of burning flesh across Jerusalem.

"Where do you live, boy?" Manaen linked arms with him.

"Near Sheep Gate. I can make my way alone."

"It's dark as pitch in that quarter of the city. I'll help you."

"I'm no stranger to darkness, sir. I've been blind since birth. No eyes at all. See? But what's that sound? Wind?"

"Women. On the Temple Mount. Keening."

"How many dead?"

"They're still counting. Laid them out on the causeway from the Temple Mount. Nearly a thousand trampled, last report. More injured will die before sunup."

"So many?"

"Yes. So many." They walked in thoughtful silence toward the Sheep Gate for a while. So the hope of the common folk for deliverance from Rome had come to this. Jews had traveled from Judea, Galilee, and from all over the Roman Empire to celebrate Passover in Jerusalem.

Freedom from bondage in a world ruled by Tiberius Caesar and Sejanus? Never mind. The pilgrims had come to remember that the birth of Israel had been heralded by the wail of grief over the firstborn children of Egypt. Fifteen hundred years had passed since the blood of the first Passover lamb marked the doorposts of Hebrew slaves in Egypt. Once again the descendants of Abraham were enslaved by a harsh master. With the help of Herod Antipas and a corrupt priesthood headed by Caiaphas, Imperial Rome held its boot on the neck of Israel.

Might a new deliverer arrive, like Moses, to liberate them once and for all? they wondered. With the throng had come bar Abba and his band of Zealots. Their plan was first to kill the Jewish ruling council, the high priest, and members of the Sanhedrin, then the Roman overlords. Call the masses to revolt!

But it was not to be.

Tonight the ancient keening of Egyptian mothers for their children echoed in the body-littered streets of Jerusalem.

When? When will Messiah come? When will the Deliverer announce His kingdom and drive out the corrupt high priest and vanquish the oppressors?

Instead of the triumphant entry of the Messiah to reign, Roman soldiers in full battle gear sealed off every entrance to the Temple Mount. Worshippers who had escaped and were brave enough to remain on the streets could only wonder if their missing loved ones were still alive inside.

Waiting at the barricades in the shadows of the city, mothers called out the names of lost children. Husbands called for wives, sons for fathers, children for parents. Somewhere among the fallen, Manaen knew, was Adam, his beloved servant.

Beyond the official blockades? Inside the Temple?

The moon rose, illuminating the carnage.

In their pursuit of victims, the disguised Roman cohort had paid no heed to the Soreg Wall, the low stone barrier that marked the boundary over which no Gentile was allowed to cross.

Adam had been struck down; then Manaen had been hit and swept away in the maelstrom until he was taken captive. How long ago that seemed now.

Manaen broke his inward musing. "Have you got a family, boy?"

"Yes. Parents. Five sisters."

"Are they safe? Do you know?"

"They were at home when I left. Too much work yet to do to go to the Temple. This is the busiest time of year for them. Yes. Safe I think."

"What's your full name, boy?"

"Peniel ben Yahtzar. The potter's son. And I'm seventeen years old. Not a boy. I'm of age. Old enough to pass through Nicanor Gate and enter the Court of the Israelites . . . if I wasn't blind. I'm not a child."

Peniel. It was a curious name for someone blind.

"Yes, sorry," Manaen began. "What I mean is, you acted bravely. Like a warrior. You saved my life. I'm grateful." Manaen wished he had even a few small coins to reward the blind boy.

"I can tell by your accent you're highborn. What's your name, sir?"

"Manaen bar Talmai."

"Manaen means 'Comforter.'"

"I'm no comfort to anyone, I'm afraid. Not in Yerushalayim anyway."

"Bar Talmai? The old treasurer of Herod the Great was called Talmai."

"My father."

"Then you're brother to Demos, who oversees the vineyards of Herod Antipas?" It was plain in the boy's tone that with such family connections he believed Manaen was an important and perhaps wealthy man. "The same Demos who loves Susanna bat Maccabee? But she won't have him for a husband."

"You know a lot. Too much maybe."

"I may be blind but I'm not deaf. I sit with a begging bowl near Nicanor Gate. You'd be surprised what I hear from the lips of the powerful men. To be blind and a beggar makes me invisible. They think I have no tongue to repeat what I hear. So they stand on the steps and their gossip drips into my beggar's bowl. And I keep it to myself. But what happened today . . . well . . . why should I speak to you about it? You're one of them. A juggler of men's lives and conjurer of the fortunes of Israel." There was an edge of anger in the boy's voice. Dangerous.

"If you know all this, then you also know about my brother, Demos, and how he feels about me. But . . . I don't owe you an explanation."

"No sir. You don't owe me anything."

"Nothing except my life. For what it's worth."

"The rabbis teach that one man's life is worth the whole world. The worth of a soul only God can weigh."

"Worth? So far my soul balances on one side of the scales and a sparrow feather rests on the other side. The feather has more weight than me."

"Then come beg with me at the Temple steps! That's enough to make a light heart heavy. They all came looking for Messiah."

"Keep your mouth shut about whatever you've heard, boy. Eglon,

Captain of Herod Antipas' guard, and Vara, that Praetorian butcher, would have you cut to pieces to get at what you know and what you hear."

"Eglon? The one who cut off the head of Yochanan the Baptizer and presented it to Herod's stepdaughter on a platter? That Eglon?"

"Yes. That Eglon. No doubt he's prowling about tonight. Searching for anyone he might trap and torture into confession."

"I'd tell him I saw nothing. No Messiah. He could torture me. Put out my eyes maybe?" Peniel laughed. "I've seen nothing."

"Nor heard anything."

"And here's the truth of it. By the Lord's providence I was collecting payment for my father's clay lamps when the Zealots came. Small, inexpensive lamps for the pilgrims. The men killed old Uri. He put up a fight. The shop was smashed. All my father's lamps."

"They've burned the shop down. And the shopkeeper with it."

Peniel raised his head as if to sniff the wind for direction. "But you and I escaped sword and fire. Why we escaped and others didn't? A complex question. It'll take time to know the answer. Must be a reason. Praised you are, Lord our God, for keeping us alive and helping us reach this moment. Eh? It makes me look forward to the rest of my life. Discovery."

Peniel was an interesting creature, Manaen thought as the boy felt his way along the walls of the street. At last they came to a shabby house tucked in an alleyway near the livestock holding pens. The air reeked of sheep and cattle dung.

Peniel's family lived above a potter's workshop, where ordinary clay pots and utensils of the cheapest variety were manufactured. The sign of a clay lamp hung over the low entryway. An oil lamp burned feebly in the upstairs window.

He called up, "Mother! Father! Shalom!"

A woman glanced out the windowsill. "Peniel's back," she said without enthusiasm. Then without moving, she added, "Who's that with you?"

"Lord Manaen bar Talmai of the court of Herod Antipas."

"Right," she answered, unbelieving. "Why not Elijah? You're late, Peniel. Seder's finished; your sisters in bed hours ago."

"Old Uri's dead. His shop burned, the pilgrim lamps smashed."

The woman muttered, "There. That does it. Two weeks' work. That's what your father gets for sending you to make a collection." At that she blew out the light and vanished, leaving Manaen and Peniel standing awkwardly beneath the sign.

"My mother." Peniel was embarrassed.

"I wanted to tell your kin how you helped."

"Doesn't matter. They're in bed."

"I see." Manaen wondered at the coldness of a mother's reaction at finding her boy alive after such a night. "Will you go up?"

"Up? There? The house is small and crowded. I'm clumsy. That's not good in a potter's house. I'm not permitted. So my *sukkah* is out back. Beside the kiln. There I live with the Ushpizin, the exalted wanderers and exiles of Israel."

Manaen laughed. "Good company to keep."

"I'm never bored. Father Avraham teaches me about sacrifice and promises kept. Yitz'chak discusses his sorrow over two sons who hate one another. Ya'acov often speaks about wrestling with angels, corrupt in-laws, too many wives, and a brood of treacherous sons. Joseph tells me his brothers hate him enough to sell him into slavery."

"I know how he must feel."

"Mosheh has a word or two of advice for me. He tells me life could be worse. As for the Messiah? The Ushpizin speak about him often. They say he's coming. I haven't met him yet. I must one day meet him face-to-face. But like everyone else I'm still hoping . . . hoping he'll come. There are occasional whispers. But he never comes."

Peniel lived in a *sukkah*? A hut beside the kiln? With Ushpizin? He was either mad or had a finely tuned sense of humor about very difficult living arrangements, Manaen thought. He stared up at the window and considered how Peniel, the true light of the potter's family, had been banished to illuminate a *sukkah* beside the kiln. When Manaen turned toward Peniel, the boy had already vanished into an alleyway between two houses.

"Thank you, and Shalom, my friend," Manaen called after him.

"Shalom, Manaen bar Talmai! I'll tell Joseph what you said! Come find me if you ever need a blind guide in the dark world! Shalom tov!"

"Shalom," Peniel whispered as he sat in the eight-foot-square hut where he lived beside his father's pottery kiln. "Anyone here? Besides me?

Mosheh? Ya'acov? Avraham? Elijah? Messiah?" Peniel spoke each name of the Ushpizin, those ancient honored guests whom Jewish tradition invited to be a part of special family gatherings. Exiles and wanderers. Just like Peniel, who had been exiled since his seventh year.

Tonight Peniel was alone. No answer. Empty space. Only the sound of his blood rushing in his ears. Peniel had hoped the Messiah would come for Passover.

"I didn't think so. No matter . . . I waited for you beside the Eastern Gate all day, like I promised I would, but you didn't come. Good thing I left, I suppose. Good thing I didn't bring Gershon's alms bowl. It would have been broken for sure."

Passover, *zeman heiruteinu*, was the season of liberation. And yet in Jerusalem there was only bondage.

The echo of grief descended from the Upper City. Peniel grasped the alms bowl his brother, Gershon, had made for him. He ran his fingers around the rim and read the raised letters. ""'My name is Peniel.' Peniel. Peniel." He traced the pattern of the picture Gershon had etched for him on the side of the bowl.

"I miss Gershon tonight especially," Peniel said to himself. "This time of year I always miss him. It should have been me. Mama always says so. You know, this was not the way I thought it would be tonight. Passover. I always look forward to Passover. Not what I expected. I . . . I was too late. And they didn't wait. The one night a year Mama lets me return from my exile. Enter the house. Sit at table with them. And now I've missed it. And you haven't come either. More important things to do. So many souls to gather up and carry home, I suppose."

The rumble of carts carrying the dead from the city passed by on the cobbled street. Human voices mingled with the high, clear sound of a flute playing a dirge. Peniel covered his ears and tried not to think about what lay outside his cubicle tonight.

"Like Egypt, eh? The night the Angel of Death came? Well, they'll all go home now. No one will want to stay in Yerushalayim. Everyone will leave now. More alms this week than all year. No *ma'ot hittim*, money for bread, this year. Enough alms in seven days to feed me for half a year. Mama will be angry. Bad for business, she'll say. No pilgrims to buy pottery either. Best week of the year, ruined for her and Papa." He shrugged. "Why should I complain? I'm of age. I can feed myself. No use to be a burden."

Peniel placed the precious bowl in the corner. He stretched out on the straw mat and covered himself with a frayed woolen blanket. His stomach rumbled. "But I was looking forward to Passover tonight. Once a year. Lamb and bread. Honey. Eggs. All of it. Only once a year. Maybe next year. Maybe. Maybe you'll come next year. I'll still be here. I'll wait for you like I always wait for you. At the Eastern Gate."

He sighed as weariness swept over him. He lay with his head on his arm. He had no expectation that Ushpizin might still come visit his little *sukkah*. Still, as he drifted toward slumber, he softly sang the invitation as he did on every holy day and Shabbat. It was the polite thing to do.

"U-lu Ush-pi-zin i-la-in ka-di-shin!
Enter, exalted, sacred guests!
Te-vu ush-pi-zin Maher-nu-at, te-vu!
Be seated, faithful guests!"

Outside a breeze rustled the branches of the jacaranda tree. Twigs and leaves tapped together. The aroma of lavender drifted into the *sukkah*.

But no one came. No one came.

3

C H A P T E R

The blackness of the Judean night was nearly impenetrable. Not only were the stars obscured, but a sea of formless clouds swallowed the full moon. A breeze from the north flung itself against the fang of Herodium, moaning softly at the wound inflicted by Herod the Great's watchtower.

Or was the moan human and being carried on the breeze?

Marcus Longinus, onetime Primus Pilus of the First Cohort but now a centurion without a command, paced the battlements. The air was scented with the tang of sage, but in the Roman officer's nostrils there was the aroma of death. Though Jerusalem lay a dozen miles away, all Marcus' attention remained fixed on the Holy City, scene after bloody scene appearing in his mind as if displayed on the hills just below the fortress.

What watch was it? Long past midnight, certainly. Marcus had heard the tramp of the changing sentries, the challenge given and responded to, the decurion's respectful salute, but whether one hour ago or three, he could not have said. He was exhausted, yet would not consider sleep.

Yesterday had been the Day of Preparation for the Jewish Passover. Hundreds of thousands of pilgrims thronged the city; tens of thousands of lambs were readied for the sacrifices and presented at the Temple of the Unnameable God.

Joyful celebrating should have followed the sacrifice and sunset. But instead of feasting, Jerusalem was filled with mourning. Instead of a jubilant memorial of the historical delivery from slavery in Egypt, what the Jews experienced was another brutal lesson in enforced subservience to Rome.

Grief would subside to a dull ache, but it would be replaced with anger. Marcus was certain the aftereffects of the carnage would include even greater Jewish hatred of the Imperial Roman overlords than had already existed in this miserable province.

He tried to piece the sequence together. What was the cycle of blunders that had led to gory disaster?

The Roman governor, Pontius Pilate, trying to curry favor with his obstinate Jewish subjects, had proposed constructing an aqueduct. All well and good so far. Jerusalem was forever short of water for drinking and bathing and the ceremonial sluicing away of the blood of the sacrifices.

Marcus wondered if there was enough water in all the pools and all the cisterns to cleanse the Temple Mount of the human blood spilled there less than twelve hours before.

Pilate's project had run afoul of one of the seemingly incomprehensible religious squabbles for which the Jews were legendary. The money he demanded and received from the Temple treasury had been *korban*, dedicated to the purchase of sacrificial animals and off-limits for any other purpose. So a delegation of Jewish leaders had appeared before Pilate to oppose what they saw as misuse of *korban*. The nervous governor, warned that rebels and assassins were in the city, had placed disguised soldiers amongst the crowd.

The protest had escalated, turned ugly. Then Pilate had unleashed the troopers: Samaritans and Idumeans, happy to break Jewish heads, rampaged through the city. Sturdy Galilean peasants, less likely to flee than easily cowed city dwellers, were especially well represented among the slain and crippled.

Marcus had exerted every effort to stop the conflict, even confronting Vara, the Praetorian officer and leader of the savagery. Parted at last by the arrival of Tribune Felix and a cohort of uniformed legionaries, Vara had promised Marcus death for his interference. That was of little consequence, being only the latest in a long line of scores between the two that would someday have to be settled.

The centurion, battle-hardened for the last sixteen of his thirty-two years, was no stranger to fierce conflict. During the riot there had been no time for the horrors to register, but his mind had not avoided noting them. It had merely stored up tragedy after tragedy; now each was presented for his review.

He saw a Jewish mother and child huddled in a shop's doorway as a legionary raised a club . . .

. . . knew that a pair of Jewish brothers standing back-to-back in mutual defense had both had their skulls crushed.

. . . remembered a Jewish father standing dull-eyed over the trampled body of his son, baring his breast to a dagger and begging to be killed himself.

. . . saw shock become revulsion in the eyes of Nakdimon ben Gurion, member of the Jewish Sanhedrin, who amid the chaos mistook Marcus for one of the ravening wolves.

Yet in all this, Marcus' greatest concern was for Miryam of Magdala. Had she heeded his warning and kept away from Jerusalem? Or had she gone up to the Temple with her brother, El'azar, and sister, Marta? Was she now lying dead in a gutter? Marcus wrenched his thoughts away from that picture.

And what would the sequel be? Open rebellion? Miles of crosses lining the highway from Jerusalem to Caesarea, holding aloft the rotting corpses of Jewish manhood?

It had happened before.

A shaft of moonlight pierced the clouds. Movement on the horizon attracted Marcus' attention. He was too accomplished a soldier not to notice. His senses were not dead, even if his heart was.

A troop of riders emerged from the north. At their head was a horseman good enough to be recognizable in the fitful gleam. Tribune Felix was approaching Herodium.

Marcus left the parapet, descending into the stone heart of the citadel to meet him.

Marcus Longinus encountered Tribune Felix at the bottom of the inverted cone of Herodium, near the marble mausoleum of the butcher king. From Felix's appearance it seemed an apt comparison: The tribune was spattered from helmet to greaves in blood, the leather lacings of his caligae boots crusted and filthy, his face streaked with soot. Although the young tribune was seven years Marcus' junior, by reason of family connections he was already well beyond any rank Marcus could hope for.

Felix looked drained and ready to collapse. "We've been all night cleaning up. Corpses stacked like flour sacks. Some more fighting too. We sealed off the city. A band of rebels tried to cut their way out, got turned back, then holed up in a pottery shop. We ended up burning it down over their heads, and still they came out waving daggers. Killed them all."

"Bar Abba?"

Felix shook his head. "He wasn't among them, but the sicarius, Dan, was." The tribune shuddered, then repeated, "Bodies heaped like ripped-open bags of grain . . . is there any wine?"

"Wine and hot water both," Marcus promised, shouting for servants to come help the tribune out of his armor.

Felix stared at the representation of the Temple carved in high relief on Herod's tomb. "Wine first. And then a bath as hot as you can make it . . . and more wine."

An hour later Felix, scrubbed obsessively clean in a marble tub that had once belonged to Herod's murdered queen, and dressed in a fresh linen tunic, sat beside Marcus in a chair drawn close to a fire. "Did you get the old man and the children safely away?" he asked.

Marcus had escorted Zadok, Chief Shepherd of the Temple flock, and his three young apprentice shepherds, back to Migdal Eder, near Beth-lehem. He nodded.

After taking another long swallow from a brass goblet, Felix sighed. "It's good. Good." He stared at the ceiling for a minute before continuing. "No vultures over the Temple Mount. Did you know that? Smell the blood for a hundred miles but no vultures circle the house of the Jewish god . . . much good he did them today." Felix snorted. His body jerked awkwardly and wine splashed from the goblet onto the floor. "Plenty of human vultures though. On the scene . . . and in the palaces. Some looking to devour others by where they put the blame."

"Felix, what are you talking about?"

Felix was the superior officer. Though the young man and Marcus had been by turns both close and distant in their relationship, clearly something was weighing on the tribune now. He stared at Marcus, raised the wine to his lips, then deliberately set it down and pushed it away from him. "You," he said pointedly. "Praetorian commander Vara is trying to get you blamed for the slaughter. You're to answer a charge of *maiestas.*"

"What?" Marcus exploded. "I did everything I could to stop it! You know I told Pilate to put more men out openly in uniform, but he wouldn't listen. Vara's men were like packs of . . . of wolves. In those cramped streets, against unarmed women and children. I've seen lions in the arena less savage than Vara's cutthroats."

Felix shook his head. "Pilate is in no mood to listen to that. A handful of rebels, and Pilate thinks everything he unleashed was justified. Our mighty governor was scared . . . terrified for his life. Tonight he's exactly like his patron, Praetorian Prefect Sejanus. He'd be happy to rid the world of Jews once and for all. And Vara would have obliged, except you got in the way."

"I should've killed him," Marcus stated bluntly. "Leaned my weight on the sword and . . . "

"And you'd already be hanging from a cross atop Golgotha. Listen," Felix said abruptly, "something has to be done before this province goes up in flames. Pilate marches from one debacle to another. In the last two years he's taken Judea from peaceful and productive to the brink of civil war. I've been talking to Philip."

The shift of topic was just too much. Marcus peered closely at Felix's face.

"I'm not drunk," Felix protested. "Just listen. *Tetrarch* Philip, who rules Trachonitus."

Marcus was familiar with the younger son of Herod the Great, whose small kingdom lay east of the Jordan opposite the Galil. "Tetarch Philip is in Jerusalem for the Passover," Felix said. "I met him first in Rome. He's not like Antipas, not at all."

Herod Antipas, Philip's half brother, ruled the northern and eastern parts of the province—the Galil and Idumea. But he was a plotter and a schemer and a murderer. Antipas had ordered the execution of Yochanan the Baptizer, whom many of the Jews regarded as a prophet.

"Philip has never pushed himself forward, and his tetrarchy has stayed quiet while he sees the danger mounting everywhere else."

Philip's territory lay along the trade route to Damascus, Syria, a much more important province of the Empire than Judea. Syria had a governor of higher rank than Pilate and real Roman legionaries in place of hired mercenary auxiliary troops. All this combined to add to the security of Philip's rule, but Marcus did not mention his observations aloud.

"And what does Tetrarch Philip suggest?" Marcus inquired warily.

Not directly replying, Felix said instead, "Just before I rode from Caesarea to Jerusalem I received a message from Alexandria. There's someone there who wants to see you: You know him as Caligula."

"Caligula? Little Boots?" Not so little anymore, Marcus knew, though Marcus had not seen Caligula since the boy had been around the army camps of Germany and then Syria, where he had gotten his nickname. He was always a strange, secretive child. Manipulative, too. But Caligula must be eighteen or nineteen now.

Felix nodded. "Caligula, great-nephew of Tiberius Caesar and son of your late commander, Germanicus, has expressed a desire to see you. It seems he never forgot your loyalty to his father," Felix added significantly. "And your kindness to him when he was a child . . . it's an opportunity sent by the gods." He raised a speculative eyebrow.

Marcus lifted his hands in protest. "No, Felix. You *will* get me crucified. Centurions don't mix with provincial tetrarchs or Imperial royalty."

Felix drew himself up sternly. "You'd refuse a direct order?"

"No, but . . . "

"Did you know that Sejanus, as head of the Praetorian Guard, has announced that he is *co-emperor* with Tiberius? I believe Sejanus intends to usurp the throne. He'll do to the Empire what his puppets Pilate and Vara are doing here," Felix said frankly. "Philip agrees that they'll have to be brought up short. And you need to be out of Pilate's reach for a time till the Passover massacre fades a bit. In short, you must disappear. Later we can admit Caligula sent for you . . . and a request from a near relative of Tiberius Caesar is also a command."

"But if Caligula asks *my* opinion of this province?"

"You're a soldier of Rome. You'll answer his questions as best you're able."

Marcus conceded, unable to think of any protest that would not be insubordinate and too weary to argue further. "How and when?"

Felix, satisfaction evident on his face, reared back in his chair. "Vara will scour the highways for you, so we must throw him off the scent. The courier ship *Livia* is due at Caesarea day after tomorrow; after that it'll return to Alexandria. I'll instruct the captain to put in at Ashkelon on the return voyage. You'll join it there. I'll have a report and letters for you to carry."

Tetrarch Philip wanted to be the sole king of Judea, as his father had been.

Felix's family, influential in Rome, wanted to see Sejanus brought down. Clearly they pinned their hopes on Caligula.

And Marcus, after ten years of ducking his head and soldiering, was about to be thrust back into Imperial politics. He was not comfortable with the role but saw no escape.

Felix leaned forward, one conspirator to another. "Maybe we can save this province from the fire after all."

oncern for Adam, his aged servant, drove Manaen back to the horror on the Temple Mount. It had been hours since the madness had begun, but still Manaen would not allow himself to rest until he knew Adam's fate.

In his heart he was certain Adam was dead. Manaen's recollections of the riot were confused and fragmentary, but one thing stood out clearly in his memory: seeing Adam struck down by a club. The frail old man's last instinct had been to interpose his thin arms between Manaen and the danger that swirled around them both.

Adam, faithful to the last.

Adam, on whose shoulders Manaen had been carried as a child.

Adam, who had been both teacher and confidant . . . more family to Manaen than his sly, grasping brother would ever be.

Manaen observed as the Jewish sanctuary officers and Herod's bodyguards picked their way through the slaughter by torchlight. In full uniform they searched for hidden weapons . . . some evidence that the mob had intended revolt against the powers of Rome, the high priest, and Tetrarch Herod Antipas.

Who had struck the blow that knocked Manaen unconscious? Had it been a rebel or a disguised soldier?

And the fierce brute who crushed Adam? His face was fully fleshed: Clearly the savage attacker was well fed. Not the picture of one of bar Abba's henchmen, hiding in caves and living off the land.

But then nothing about today made sense.

The scenes of this particular day and night were a vile contrast to the bright, shining metropolis that Manaen always pictured when he considered Jerusalem. A city of a quarter million, crossroads of the Jewish world if not the whole Roman Empire. A city that stretched back to David, to Solomon, humming with business and beauty. Jerusalem was home to grand palaces, imposing towers, reassuring walls, and stirring views.

Arching over all was the Temple: gleaming, awe-inspiring, and grand. An attraction, a point of pride, a boost to the collective ego of a now far-flung people.

By day Jerusalem's streets thronged with austere religious officials and eager pilgrims, with merchants and artisans, importers and the stewards of rich households. White-robed priests mingled with uncouth Galileans—those easily irritated north-country rustics who always suspected they were being made fun of when they came to the capital.

Anyone who walked the confines of Jerusalem's three hundred wall-encompassed acres on any given day would be offered expensive jewelry, imported double-dyed linen, exotic unguents, and silk worth its weight in gold. But a traveler could view all the wonders for free, then feed himself cheaply on figs, grapes, barley bread, wine, dried fish, olives, and pomegranates, or buy a lamb for pennies to roast with friends.

Any needed service could be had for the asking. Tradesmen wore their professional emblems on their lapels. A spray of colored threads denoted a cloth-dyer; an oversized needle called attention to a tailor. Seven specialized markets in cattle, vegetables, wool, bread, and other staples competed with smaller shops of every kind, and they in turn with sidewalk stalls that folded up at night. Hundreds of synagogues catered to every sect, every nationality. A Cyrenian could be hundreds of miles from home and still know exactly where to find others of his speech and dress. Houses of Jewish religious study competed with each other, and also with the pagan entertainment of Greek extraction. Horse racing and theater existed; so did public-bathing establishments and gymnasiums.

But tonight all that was wonderful, urbane, or noteworthy about Jerusalem was hidden, masked by grief and terror. Even the Temple pavilion, normally so aglow with giant lamps that it resembled a full moon resting on the Mount, was tonight darkened and sinister.

Outside the tunnel that connected the city to the Temple Mount, Manaen joined a queue of anxious, tearful citizens waiting their turn to speak to one of the Levites. When it was his opportunity to approach the Temple Guard, Manaen asked for assistance. "My servant . . . can you help me find him? He was wounded . . . or . . ."

The guard appeared to be expecting the question. Not unkindly, but in clipped official tones, he stated, "Only the dead left now, I'm afraid. Wounded taken off already. We're trying to group the dead near where they fell. Do you have any idea where on the mount he was?"

"Yes, I . . . I think so," Manaen returned, struggling to extract that information from the cloud of emotion and fatigue. "I was with him. We were the first group to sacrifice our lambs and so were already headed toward the Hasmonean wall and the double-gate passageway."

"Try the Court of the Gentiles near the Stoa passageway," the guard said dismissively. "Next!"

A neatly ordered row of dead bodies stretched across the plaza. Torchlights bobbed about the pavement. Knots of cloaked and hooded humans seemed to float above the blood-slick stones.

Each cluster of apprehensive seekers huddled briefly over a corpse, debated its marred features in tones of low intensity, reached a conclusion, then drifted off toward another battered relic. A long piercing shriek of bereavement confirmed the discovery of a loved one.

Manaen obtained a torch from the kin of a woman who had already located her murdered son. Dazed and sobbing, she was led away, while Manaen stood at one end of a hundred-foot-long palisade of bodies.

In the end it was Adam's robe, sky blue and trimmed in gold thread, which identified him.

Manaen had scrimped on his pitiful stipend in order to buy the old man the new garment for his seventy-second birthday. It had been Adam's proudest possession for the past five years. Now it was his shroud.

Stopping a passing detail of Levite altar attendants, who tonight were stacking bodies instead of firewood, Manaen arranged for Adam to be taken to the palace.

While he waited for Adam's body to be picked up, he stood for a few seconds. His farewells to his old friend were muddled.

In the midst of these reflections Manaen spotted Eglon, the brutish commander of Herod Antipas' personal defenders, stepping over the dead. All Herod's Samaritan guards were specially chosen for their callous harshness, but Eglon was the worst.

The soldier directed the light of a smoking torch toward an arm that protruded from a stack of corpses. He plucked a gold bracelet and rings from the stiff fingers of a woman's hand. Then, with a furtive glance around, Eglon pocketed the loot.

Manaen coughed, alerting the startled officer to his presence.

Eglon reeked of wine. He seemed relieved to see a familiar face. Manaen was well-known around the court of Herod Antipas. "So it's you, young sir. Thought you were dead. We found your cloak earlier, all ripped and bloody. So you survived, eh? Then what brings you back to this charnel house? Here on tetrarch's business?"

"I came back for Adam," Manaen said, indicating the body of his friend.

"Well, you can tell the tetrarch everyone here is dead but us and those who gather their dead. And there's plenty to gather." Eglon smirked and patted the leather money pouch at his waist. "Plenty for the gathering, you might say."

"Gathering taxes for Herod Antipas?" Manaen queried.

"Baubles. Just payment for treason."

"Whether just or not is God's judgment."

"Here's God's justice for traitors." The officer rubbed the stubble on his chin. "You might do well to line *your* pockets, young sir. Everyone knows your elder brother Demos keeps your inheritance locked up tight. And you are in poverty, as it were. At your brother's mercy, so to speak."

Manaen's temper flared. "You're drunk on blood to speak to a member of the tetrarch's circle this way." Manaen was strong enough to be a threat even to the commander of Herod Antipas' personal attendants.

"It's your elder brother who holds the tetrarch's ear and the estates of your late father, and who hopes to hold the affections of Lady Susanna as well."

"Hold your tongue or I'll hold your ear."

"Whenever you'd like!"

"At the pleasure of Herod!"

The commander, hand on the hilt of his sword, sneered. "We all know about Demos and the money and all. I was just offering a bit of helpful advice. There's so much temptation here for the taking if you'd just humble yourself a bit to pick it up."

"You'll learn the blood of my father flows in my veins equally with my brother's. Though as firstborn son he holds the estates, I humble myself for no man."

"Not even for yourself?"

"Especially not for myself. What would be left of my father in me if I did?"

Eglon shrugged and clinked two gold coins in his hand. "Youth and ignorance," he mocked. "I can teach you a lesson. Suit yourself. I may buy a vineyard in Sychar after this night."

"Then you can drink to your own health whenever you like."

"I'll drink to the health of the dead traitors who paid for my vineyard."

"Adam was no traitor!" Manaen warned. "And how do you know this woman was?"

"She's dead, isn't she?" Eglon observed in a tone that suggested the matter was self-evident.

"You must hope she's dead or else she'll rise up and call you a thief."

Eglon bristled, "Calling me a thief, are you?"

"No. But she would. If she could speak."

"I'm doing my duty. A good soldier."

"Proof of what you are is in your pocket."

The officer touched the fragment of parchment that bore the seal of Antipas. He scowled and said defensively, "I serve my Lord Herod Antipas and Caiaphas, the high priest, and they serve Tiberius Caesar."

"I won't ask what's in *their* pockets," Manaen said.

"It's not thievery to take from a dead traitor," Eglon protested. "Look. For such a task as cleaning up this mess every soldier deserves to take what he finds as payment."

"What's this traitor's name?"

"How should I know?" Eglon fired back, evidently irritated by the question. He glowered at the feminine arm and hand that emerged from beneath a dead boy with a boot print on his bloody face.

"I'm going now," Manaen said curtly. "Adam's body will be carried away soon. He had better arrive in his blue robe, or there'll be one more corpse before the full tally of this day is made!"

MANAEN MADE HIS WAY BACK THROUGH THE narrow streets to the palace.

"Halt! Who goes there?" Herod's Samaritan guard challenged Manaen from the brooding watchtower above the gate.

Manaen recognized the voice as that of a soldier known by all as the Wolf. Jutting lower teeth, hairy body, and beady eyes set beneath a thick brow made his appearance fit the name. In temperament he was unpredictable: either brutal or congenial depending on his mood.

"It's Manaen bar Talmai."

"A ghost then. Or an assassin come to murder Herod Antipas in his bed."

"Neither!" Manaen thumped his fist angrily against the gate.

"But we've heard the report that Manaen bar Talmai is dead by the hand of rebels, and his old servant with him."

So word of Adam's death had already reached the palace. "Adam died fighting. But who he was fighting—rebels or soldiers in disguise— I don't know."

"The old man is dead. And so is his master, Manaen."

"Only half true. I escaped."

"This could yet be an attempt to gain entry into the palace. Slit my throat first."

"Stinking Samaritan mercenary," Manaen muttered under his breath. Then, louder, "I know it's you, Wolf, standing guard up there on the rampart. I recognize your growl. How's that Nabatean mistress of yours? The slave who serves up all the gossip of Herod Antipas' court?"

"Yes, this is Wolf. But you're a ghost if you're Manaen."

"Open up or I'll have you collared and chained!" Frustration boiled over into raging threats.

"Spirit, you may command your fellow demons to chain me, but to-night I fear my master, Herod Antipas, more than the torments of hell."

"I'm as alive as ever, Wolf, and you know it. Let me in. I'm done up." Manaen's weariness and grief overcame the brief flare of his anger.

There was a touch of sadistic enjoyment in the soldier's tone as he kept Manaen waiting in the street. "Eglon, the captain of the guard, brought Manaen's bloody cloak to the banquet tonight as proof Manaen had been taken by rebels and slain. Herod laid the cloak of his ward in a place of honor and drank a toast in his memory."

"I'm touched. Would've liked to have been there. I could use a cup of wine. Now let me in. I'm tired and hungry."

"Lady Susanna ran weeping from the chamber at the sight of Manaen's torn robes."

Manaen considered the image. Having been focused solely on his escape, Adam's death, his confrontation with Eglon, and now his exhaustion, Manaen had not thought about Susanna. He had not imagined that anyone thought him dead . . . much less that she, so beyond his reach, grieved for him.

Manaen felt a surge of concern as well as satisfaction at her anguish.

Wolf continued, "Then Demos, brother of Manaen, said he was certain Manaen would not wish the celebration of victory over the enemies of Herod Antipas and Rome to come to an end just because Manaen was dead. So the feast went forward as if Manaen was still among the living."

Manaen replied caustically, "Ah, my brother, Demos. Always putting affairs of state above personal matters. All right. You've given me the gossip. I'll play your game. Bring down a torch, you Samaritan cretin. See for yourself: I'm alive at the portal. In a mood to tear apart any who hinder me."

"It indeed *seems* to be the sound of Lord Manaen," the guard said slowly.

"There's a flesh-and-blood fist attached to this voice. If I were a ghost I'd fly up and turn you to stone."

After a few seconds the window in the pedestrian gate flew open and a lamp was held up. "Let's have a look," the guard insisted, putting Manaen through the paces. "Step forward."

Manaen moved into the circle of light and scowled into the glare. "All right, Wolf. Done your duty?"

A tone of mock surprise was in the soldier's response. "Lord Manaen! Alive!"

"And kicking."

The clank of bolts and bars rattled as the entrance was opened. Manaen stiffly climbed through the constricted passage. He barely resisted the urge to grab the moronic strongman by the throat.

"By the god! You look half dead anyhow. Do you blame me, sir, for being careful? Listen to that wailing, will you? Makes a man's skin crawl. But all the same there was jubilation in the palace tonight. It's a victory over the common folk. That's what it is. Herod Antipas is preserved against treachery and civil riot. The high priest and the Sanhedrin escaped slaughter. Pilate. All the rest. Not one of the important men killed. Except you. Well . . . you know what I mean. No one with any real power or money killed. Just the Galilean Zealots and those unfortunates who got in the way. Come morning, when the city gates open, thousands of pilgrims will all be running for home. No Jewish Messiah to save them this year. Jubilation among the leaders, that's what."

"There's no victory here," Manaen stated flatly. "Only the living and the dead. And thieves dressed as soldiers collecting bounty from the fallen." The image of Eglon renewed Manaen's anger. He ordered, "Send a cart to fetch back Adam's body from the causeway."

"You've found the old man then."

"Yes. Yes," Manaen admitted wearily, stiffening his resolve not to show his grief. "What about Susanna?" he demanded gruffly. "What's that serving woman of yours say about Susanna?"

"Susanna was commanded by Herod Antipas to return to table. To sit beside your brother, Demos. She wept for you all night and wouldn't eat. She thinks you're dead. You're the lone one of the royal house killed, she thinks. Very unfair of the god to kill you and leave her to Demos, she says to my woman when she gets ready for bed. Susanna'll be glad to see you."

"She may be the only one who is."

MUSIC AND DRUNKEN LAUGHTER ECHOED through the smoky corridors that led from the banqueting hall.

So Herod Antipas and a handful of his guests were still at it, Manaen thought, as though no tragedy had unfolded beyond the high walls of this dark, decrepit place. Manaen recognized the voice of his brother, Demos, calling for another drink. No doubt Demos raised his glass in a toast of the destruction of dreams! A salute to the fable that the God of Jacob had eyes to see, or ears to hear, or heart to care what befell His people!

Hesitating outside the hall, Manaen considered if he should make his entry and ruin the mood of the party, or wait until morning when Demos was too hungover to remember that Manaen was supposed to be dead.

Better wait. Give Demos one night of illusion that he was finally rid of Manaen and that the way to Susanna and the inheritance was clear.

Manaen would find Susanna. Tell her he was alive, still in love with her even after a year of separation. Still living with hope in this hopeless world that someday he would find a way past the objections of Herod and Demos and marry her. And if he was caught breaking the command of Herod that he stay away from her? Well, he would face that when he came to it.

Tonight they were under the same roof again.

Her tears proved she loved him.

He knew the way to her bedchamber. That was enough.

The personal bodyguards of the tetrarch stationed at the entry to her bedchamber eyed Manaen with astonishment. Their curiosity was evident as he passed in the corridor, but they did not speak to him. Though the presence of sentries confirmed she was within, Manaen pretended disinterest.

There was another way in.

Susanna's second-story room opened on an interior courtyard with a fountain at its center. A honeysuckle vine wound round a trellis near her balcony. Manaen knew every handhold.

The splash of water and the scent of newly blooming flowers awakened a thousand memories, urging him on as he climbed.

Her window was open. The candle at her bedside had long since guttered and died, leaving the room in darkness. He listened. Was she asleep?

He clung to the lattice and whispered, "Susanna?"

No reply. Moonlight glared onto the tile rooftop, threatening to reveal him. He slipped over the balustrade and hid in the shadows.

"Susanna?" he called again, at first not daring to enter. "Are you awake?"

A slight cough. A moan. A sleepy voice. "Manaen?"

"Susanna." He crept forward, concealing himself behind the curtain. "It's me!"

"Manaen!" she cried. "Oh! I've gone mad at last! He's dead! He's dead!"

"Susanna! I'm alive!"

Silence. She sat up in bed. "Manaen? Am I dreaming? Is this a dream? A thousand dreams of you." She covered her face with her hands.

"Susanna. Don't be afraid!" He stepped from the shadow. "No dream."

As she raised her face to the moonlight, he saw recognition, relief, and joy in her dark, wide eyes. Chestnut hair cascaded over the shoulders of her white shift.

Longing made him awkward, suddenly clumsy. He stood staring, unable to move or speak.

Wordlessly she reached out to him, clasped his hand. Pulling him down into her arms she touched his face in wonder.

Aching with desire at her touch, he closed his eyes and breathed in the aroma of her skin. "Now *I'm* dreaming."

At last she spoke. "Tonight, when they said you were dead, I knew I couldn't live without you." She raised her face to him.

He kissed her mouth, drinking in her sweetness like a man thirsting for cool water on a hot day. "Susanna!"

"Oh, Manaen!" she said, stroking his dark blond hair. "A year forbidden to see you and now, *now*, how can I live another day without you? What can we do? What *can* we do?"

She leaned against his chest and began to weep quietly. Her thoughts came in choking sobs. "The law of Rome and the guardianship of Herod control my life! My father's will says I may not marry except with Herod's approval. And only then do I gain my inheritance. The will also says I cannot be forced into marriage with a man I don't love. If it wasn't for that clause Herod would have me bound to your brother tomorrow."

Demos.

He would marry Susanna for money, then leave her for the beds of lovers, both male and female. The thought of it was beyond enduring. Yet Manaen, like Susanna, was a prisoner of law and custom. His fortune was controlled by his elder brother.

He was powerless.

After a time she whispered, "I would've died *with* you if you had died tonight. I listened to the women of Israel crying for their children. The keening carried on the wind, and I thought that all of them . . . all of us . . . we're all prisoners."

He had no answer for her. No hope to offer. He held her.

After a while there was a stirring in the corridor outside her room. Voices. Men's voices. Demos. Some of his cronies. Drunk. Demanding the guards stand aside. Bawling her name. Pounding on the door.

"They've come!" She pushed Manaen toward the balcony. "Go now! Please!"

"I'll fight them!"

"You've no sword!"

"I'll fight them!"

"They'll have you killed if you're found here."

"I won't leave you to them."

"The door is bolted. They'll have to break it down. Now go! Go! I won't let them in! Go!"

"Susanna!" Demos' nasal voice crooned. "Open the door! I'm here to console you! News . . . wonderful . . . news. Herod says we are to marry at once! He says you need comforting and I'm just the man!"

Pulling her close yet again, Manaen kissed her hurriedly, then grasped both her arms and peered into her eyes. "I didn't die. We are meant to be together. Believe it."

Then as the hammering on the door redoubled, jostling the bar that secured it, Manaen leapt for the window ledge. Flinging his legs over the edge, he grasped the vine and made a hasty descent.

Halfway to the ground he missed his hold and dropped to the flagstones. At the noise, a guard on the rooftop shouted a challenge.

Manaen ducked into the shadows at the base of the fountain. After a day of rebels and riots no one would ignore a possible assassin in the courtyard. The guard shouted, "Torches. Bring torches!" Manaen heard hobnailed boots clattering up the spiral stairs from the underground barracks.

Picking a dark window below Susanna's room, Manaen threw himself at the drapery that covered the opening. Struggling to free himself from the brocade, rolling onto the floor, he jumped upright, ready to fight his way free.

The chamber, a waiting room for dignitaries calling on the tetrarch, was deserted. A marble bust of Tiberius scowled at Manaen from one wall, while the baleful stare of Herod the Great regarded him from another.

Opening the door a crack, Manaen listened. He heard rushing footsteps, but they seemed to come from the corridor overhead.

Outside the window the voice of the sentry shouted, "He went that way! In the window!"

No time to stop and consider his strategy.

Demos sober was cunningly dangerous; drunk he was viciously so.

Susanna was in danger.

Manaen dashed into the corridor.

As he turned the corner he ran headlong into the arms of a guard. "Let me go!" Manaen blustered. "My brother's calling upstairs. You see to the other disturbance and I'll attend to him. Go!"

The ruse worked.

Taking the stairs three steps at a time, Manaen regained the level of Susanna's chamber as Demos' cronies crashed into her door, bursting the bolt.

"Susanna!" Demos' words were slurred. "No more waiting! Herod says . . . Herod . . . says . . . you'll marry me. Tonight!"

"Demos! You're drunk! Get out! Let go of me!"

Manaen heard Susanna's cry of fear. Rage consumed him. Pushing past the guards, who made no move to interfere, Manaen bellowed at his brother, "Demos! Leave her alone!"

"Manaen! They said you're dead!" Demos slurred. "Dead. But even if you're not, you're too late. Herod says she's mine!"

Demos' companions closed in, one from either side.

Feinting toward the nearer accomplice first, Manaen lunged at the other, kicking the man in the groin, then hammering his face with both fists as he doubled over.

The hands of the second companion pinioned Manaen's arms to his sides. Manaen lashed out with an elbow to the man's ribs, then stomped downward on a slipper-clad foot as he flung a forearm into the man's throat.

Then only he and Demos were still standing. Susanna lay where Demos had flung her across the bed. Her cheek was swollen where he had struck her.

The guards remained outside the chamber, having no wish to interfere on either side of this quarrel between brothers.

Demos drew a dagger from his belt and rushed at Manaen as Susanna screamed a warning.

The blow, aimed at Manaen's heart, came as a downward stroke. Ducking inside it, Manaen battered Demos' arm aside, then launched a blow at his brother's face. The dagger flew end over end, its point igniting a crescent shower of sparks as it struck the wall.

Manaen's right hand closed around his brother's throat. He forced him to his knees. "You went too far this time, Demos," he snarled through gritted teeth. "Too far. You'll never touch her again!"

The tramping steps of an approaching squad of soldiers echoed down the hallway.

"Manaen!" Susanna cried. "Don't kill him! Manaen, stop! Stop! They'll crucify you! Don't!"

Demos struggled feebly, fists without strength striking Manaen's legs. Demos' eyes rolled back in his head as consciousness ebbed.

Susanna's pleading broke through Manaen's fury. "Please, Manaen! They'll kill you! What will become of me? Please!"

With a growl Manaen released his grip and shoved Demos hard against the wall. He stood panting over his brother's prostrate form. "Demos, I'd kill you! Kill you now if it wasn't for the trouble it would bring on her! Hear me, Demos? You lay one hand on her again and I swear I'll—"

At that instant something struck Manaen in the back of the head, hurling him to the floor.

From his knees Manaen heard Eglon's sneering words, "Ah, Manaen. You should've stayed dead!"

Demos gasped for breath and croaked, "He . . . Manaen started it! He tried to kill me, Eglon! You saw him! Tried to . . . kill . . . "

Eglon nudged Manaen with his foot. "Get up, both of you. Herod Antipas wants to see you . . . and the Lady Susanna."

MANAEN'S HEAD THROBBED. A pair of Antipas' guards bound him and dragged him from Susanna's room. He stumbled on the stairs. Eglon shoved him from behind, bouncing him face first into a stone wall.

They pushed Manaen forward through a side passage, past the banqueting hall, and into Antipas' judgment chamber.

Though his eyesight flickered, Manaen knew his whereabouts. The flooring changed from plain buff paving stones to an elaborate mosaic wave pattern in yellows and blues, copied by Antipas from his father's fortress of Machaerus.

Though Antipas was the tetrarch of Galilee and the son of Herod the Great, he had no authority in Jerusalem . . . except where his own subjects were concerned. Manaen and Susanna fell into that category.

At a snarled command from Eglon, the guards hauled Manaen upright and yanked his hair back, forcing him to face Antipas' throne.

The tetrarch's complexion, blotchy with the flush of drink mingled with his normal sallow pastiness, bore an expression of stern regard.

"Manaen," Antipas pronounced with measured disgust, as if regarding a leper. "We were grieved at news of your death. But now we see you are alive again. You are as much trouble as always."

Demos stood beside Manaen. Soldiers flanked him. "My brother has no regard for your commands," Demos asserted quickly. It pleased Manaen that Demos spoke in a strangled rasp. "You ordered him never to see Susanna, yet I found him in her room."

Susanna gasped, "No, my lord! Manaen came to help me!"

"Silence!" Antipas rumbled.

Ignoring the order, Manaen said, "He was going to rape her! Drunk and assaulting her! Should I have stood by—"

"Silence!" Antipas repeated.

Eglon's fist smacked Manaen's ear. "My Lord Antipas," Eglon said, "Master Manaen was seen on the Temple Mount. When I was going about my duties there, he tried to interfere. When I challenged him, he threatened me."

"He was robbing the dead!"

Antipas shouted, "No more accusations, Manaen! It is you who stand to answer charges!"

Eglon cuffed him again, harder this time.

Blood trickled down Manaen's chin to splatter on the mosaic. "I know what I saw," he asserted boldly. "And after what I've seen this day in Yerushalayim, Lord Antipas, you should be worrying about tomorrow! About your tetrarchy! The massacre didn't need to happen. This whole province is on the brink of rebellion! Ever since the death of

Yochanan the Baptizer—" Manaen stopped abruptly. Glaring at Eglon through bruised and swollen eyes, Manaen concluded, "There are too many dead, while too many living people think only of lining their pockets."

Herodias, Antipas' red-haired wife, leaned over her husband's shoulder to whisper to him.

Manaen knew his life hung by a thread. If he could get away from the court of Herod Antipas, however briefly, he would figure out a way to rescue Susanna. Then the two of them would escape from Antipas and Demos forever.

Antipas spoke in a patronizing tone. "Now, Manaen. Our patience wears thin. Very thin with your antics. But justice demands we hear your case. All right, then. What do you have to say for yourself?"

"My lord," Manaen said carefully, "I have no money and no position. I am treated worse by my brother than a . . . than a . . . blind beggar! So I ask you again what I've pleaded for many times: Order my brother to give me my share of the inheritance. Then I'll leave here and never trouble you again. I swear it."

The vixenlike features of Herodias grew sharper than usual as she whispered again to Antipas.

I'm doomed, Manaen thought. *And so is Susanna.*

Adopting an air of pained concern, Antipas said, "A blind beggar, is it? As your guardian I have nothing but your welfare in mind, yet you have always spurned my kindness. My ward, a foster brother upon whom I have lavished my brotherly affection."

"Not you, my Lord Antipas! Demos! Demos withholds my inheritance from me! What my father left to me! I'm a pauper living on the charity of a prince!"

Herodias arched her eyebrow and queried, "You say a blind beggar is treated better than you?"

"What I mean is . . . a blind beggar is better off than I am. At least such a man has reason to hold a bowl and beg, and when he begs he can expect mercy!"

Herodias seemed charmed by his answer. "Well spoken, Manaen. A good example of men you envy." She bent close to Antipas and conferred again. Then she laughed. Antipas joined her mirth.

After wiping his eyes, Antipas regained his stern composure and addressed Demos. "So, Demos. Your own brother would have strangled you. Your dear baby brother. What would you recommend we do with him?"

"Kill him," Demos replied without hesitation. "Execute him!"

"No!" Susanna cried.

"He's a danger!" Demos insisted.

"No!" Susanna shouted again. "He was protecting me! From . . . from . . . that swine!" She tossed her head defiantly at Demos.

Antipas was amused. "Well, yes. Demos stinks of wine and vomit this morning. But underneath it there's a true and loyal heart. One you could love, Susanna, if you put your mind to it."

She shrank back, lowering her eyes and crossing her arms protectively over her chest. "I could not, my Lord Antipas. Not ever."

Antipas bellowed, "You will if I say you will!"

Manaen struggled against the ropes that bound him. "Lord Antipas. I accept the blame for this. The blame—"

"But not the guilt?" Demos challenged.

Antipas held up a jeweled finger. "Susanna. It is clear to us, even after a full year apart from Manaen, that you have not rid yourself of this illusion of affection for him. But you hear him . . . he compares his position with that of a blind beggar. No, no. Worse than a blind beggar, he says. You would still love one so low?"

"I would. I do." She raised her head and held Manaen in her gaze. "I know that now."

"Touching," Herodias interjected. "True love, Antipas. You can't fight that." Another laugh.

Antipas smiled and rubbed his chin thoughtfully. "Manaen, you need time to reflect on your sins . . . and we need time to reflect as well. Stay in Yerushalayim. And stay away from Susanna. We'll hear your case at a more convenient hour."

Manaen and Susanna exchanged a look of relief. Perhaps Antipas was softening toward their plight.

The days ahead would tell.

For a moment at first light, only a moment every dawn, Peniel was happy.

Morning shone on his cheek. It warmed his shoulder and arm. He smelled it in the aroma of baking bread, simmering oats, and eggs frying over the cook fires. He heard it awaken in the cooing of pigeons beneath the eaves of the shop, the stirring in the streets, the voices of mothers calling their children to wash and come to breakfast.

For a moment, only a moment, Peniel imagined he was one of those children. . . .

Gathered in. Fussed over. Ears and face and hands inspected after washing. Embraced. Blessed. Kissed on the forehead. Worried over. Told to eat every crumb.

These were true things, real things, good things in life that Peniel had learned about the summer of his seventh year.

That was the year when, on account of Gershon dying and Peniel being stupid and clumsy, Peniel had been banished from his own house and consigned to live in the hut beside the kiln. He was old enough to beg for his own food, his father told him, as long as he did not beg from the neighbors.

One morning Peniel woke up hungry and followed the aroma of fresh-baked bread into a neighbor's garden. He crept forward and sat quietly outside the window of the shoemaker's house. It was there that Peniel heard morning in a new light.

Children. Lots of them. The mama. The papa. Eating together. Praying together, discussing the day's lesson for Torah school. Spelling. The meaning of verses. A very pleasant time.

Day after day Peniel had risen before daylight and crept into the herb garden beneath the shoemaker's window to listen. Twice the wife of the shoemaker had come into the garden and asked him to join her children inside the house for breakfast.

Knowing how clumsy he was, he had thanked her very much but said it was safer if he stayed outside in the garden. He explained he was not allowed inside his father's house except once a year at Passover and that he would be beaten if he accepted charity from a near neighbor.

She did not ask him to come in again. But from then on, the shoemaker's wife had brought him warm bread slathered in melted butter and honey to eat. She said no one would know.

In all the history of the world there had never been such bread! Such butter! Such sticky, drizzled, sweet honey! There was also a cup of milk after.

Every morning, for an entire summer, Peniel was happy. He often thought how happy a dog must feel to be fed what was left over and allowed to listen to happiness going on around him and above him. In the herb garden of the shoemaker's house, Peniel was as happy as any dog could ever be.

And then one day Peniel was betrayed by his oldest sister, caught in the act of eating his neighbor's bread by his mother. Beaten by his father. He would never forget the scene. . . .

Rasha! Wicked! Baza! Dishonest! Pesha! The transgression of disobeying his parents was unforgivable! He was a reproach to them! He had shamed them before their neighbors! Why had God taken Gershon and not Peniel? By his greed and rebellion he made his own family appear cruel and heartless!

Mama shouted at the shoemaker's wife that the woman was trying to humiliate her before the entire congregation of the synagogue! She sobbed to Papa that others were talking about her behind her back and that it was all the fault of him and Peniel! They said that the potter had created a cracked pot! A marred jug! A broken lamp! They accused Mama of sinning before Peniel was born! They said his blindness was her punishment from God! Imagine! Saying such a thing about her when she had always been moral and upright, and obeyed the commands of Moses!

Even the name of Peniel was meant to mock her!

Had she not been merciful to the sightless infant God had cursed her with? Against her better judgment she had nursed him. It would have been better if she had not, she said. He was greedy even then and demanding even then! She had expected him to die, and that was why she had not named him. Why she had not taken him on the eighth day to be circumcised. It was that nosy rabbi at the synagogue who pushed her to it. The rabbi had chosen this ridiculous name for him!

Peniel! Imagine!

What a joke! To name a blind baby Peniel!

Why had Gershon not let him die?

So Mama's tirade had gone on for several weeks into the fall. Off and on.

Peniel never went back to the shoemaker's garden. Avoided the shoemaker's children. Turned and stumbled away at the approaching voice of the shoemaker's wife. But he remembered her and was grateful. Grateful for more than the bread. Because he remembered how morning was for the shoemaker's children.

Peniel was happy for them. Happy just remembering how it had been for him that summer. Even these long years later the smell of fresh bread at first light made Peniel happy.

But this morning something was different at the home of the shoemaker. Peniel heard the sound of the flute playing a dirge nearby. He rose and made his way out to the street. A crowd had gathered outside the inset doorway of the shop. He recognized the voices of his neighbors whispering together.

"The two little ones, I tell you!"

"The shoemaker's twins?"

"The apple of their mama's eye."

Peniel groaned and gritted his teeth. The babies! Both of them! Sweet girls, five or six years old. They always had a kind word for Peniel when he passed. Could it be that they had fallen too?

"How did it happen?"

"They let go their sister's hand in the panic. In the Court of Women they were separated and . . ."

"Both of them gone? Their mother will never survive such a loss! Her heart will break. Even with seven children, you never get over losing one. But two! Such a sorrow!"

"Crushed in the panic."

"The twins. Never two more beautiful little girls."

"Rabbi's coming. The burial is to be early this morning, to remember that their day on this earth had hardly begun."

The wife of the cantor spotted Peniel, guessed that he was crying, though he could not shed tears. Her voice was shrill, strained, false when she spoke to him. "Oh Shalom, Peniel. Come out from the shadows, boy." He obeyed, turning his body to face her. She asked, "You hear everything. Did you know about this? Did you hear them when they brought the girls home? What time did they bring the bodies back?"

"No. I didn't hear. Didn't know." He held his head and rocked back and forth. "Sweet little girls. The shoemaker's family! Oh! It hurts! It hurts! Poor, dear shoemaker's wife." Peniel squatted down and moaned.

The women turned away from him and talked about him as if he could not hear.

"Look at him. Crouching there in the gutter like an animal. Grieving like they were his own family."

"Peniel. Pathetic."

"Makes you wonder sometimes why. To take a son like Gershon and leave this! Makes you wonder."

"Doesn't it? I mean. For something like him . . . Peniel . . ."

"And who named him anyway? Peniel. Bordering on blasphemy."

"Yes. Well, as I was saying. And now. For him to escape and live when two innocent, perfectly healthy beautiful little girls are killed."

"Makes a person wonder what's going on in the mind of the Almighty."

The rabbi arrived. Peniel heard his voice as the crowd parted and let him through. The door of the shoemaker's house opened. Peniel heard the mother say she could not face the day without her little girls. The flute began to play again, and the women gossiped softly while someone sang the shepherd's psalm.

Some time later Peniel's mother came and found him. She clasped his arm, lifted him from the street, and hissed, "Get up! You have work to do. Look at you. Wringing your hands. Look at your face! Wipe that look off your face! You make people nervous. There's nothing you can do to help. Fuel the kiln."

Peniel did not speak as they followed the procession to the cemetery. Maybe his mama was right. He made people nervous. Maybe she was right. There was nothing he could do. Nothing. Nothing. Death was so final.

IN THE EARLY-MORNING LIGHT MANAEN STOOD, head bowed, beside Adam's grave.

"Hear, O Israel! The Lord our God is one Lord; the Lord is One!"

"Ashes to ashes. Dust to dust."

Fill in the grave and move on to the next.

There was no time for more ceremony. So many killed in the massacre, so many bodies to be buried. Well-off families made hasty farewells; the poor, the unidentified, the unclaimed were all buried in common graves, their friends and families left to wonder forever about their fates.

The loss of Adam would be a long time sinking in, Manaen thought. Being without the aged servant was impossible to contemplate. On first awakening this morning, eyes gummy and burning, hair ragged and singed, smelling of smoke, Manaen's automatic reaction had been to call for his servant, his friend. Even after remembering the events of the previous day and recalling that he had seen Adam dead, Manaen could scarcely believe it.

When Manaen rushed out of the palace and up the Mount of Olives to the cemetery, the rest of the court of Herod Antipas was not in evidence. Almost universally nursing hangovers, none of them would appear before afternoon.

Nor had Manaen seen Susanna this morning. She was probably under lock and key till Antipas relented a little.

Manaen had almost been too late to the grave. In the warmth of the Mediterranean climate Jewish burials always happened rapidly. Today, with hundreds to be interred before the cleansing of the massive defilement of Jerusalem could even begin, the process was swifter and more perfunctory than usual.

Beside Adam's grave, Manaen was the only mourner. Demos had not bothered to come. It was probably better that way.

Knots of family groups milled about uncertainly. Among the mourners Manaen spotted Peniel, standing slightly apart as if someone had placed him there and forgotten to retrieve him. He faced away from the funeral. Had someone in his family died after all? Manaen did not greet him. What was there to say at such a time?

Instead of a return to Jerusalem, the concerted movement Manaen sensed in the crowd was away from the Holy City, along the Bethany Road. Tens and then hundreds of mourners moved off, as if abandoning Jerusalem forever. Peniel and a grim, gray-haired woman headed toward Jerusalem against the flow.

"Tell me, friend," Manaen said, stopping a passerby. "Where is everyone going?"

"To Beth-Anyah, to hear Rabbi Yeshua of Nazareth."

Manaen had heard of the wonder-working teacher but thought of him as a Galilean. "Is he so near? But why are they all going today?"

The man shrugged. "No one has any answers for what's happened here. No one wants to hear some Pharisee tell us that we brought it on ourselves, or some Herodian claim this was all done by rebels." The man stopped abruptly, looking Manaen up and down, as if fearful he had been too indiscreet. But even in his best remaining suit of clothing, Manaen did not look like a courtier. He saw the man relax. "Come along, if you've a mind," the man added. "It'll be days before the stink blows out of Yerushalayim. May as well be somewhere else."

MARCUS RODE AWAY FROM HERODIUM. One sleepy sentry saw him go, and then the morning mists conveniently swallowed him up. Even so, Marcus deliberately set out on the road south toward Hebron. If anyone inquired about the centurion's destination, any conjecture about the sound of hooves would point the opposite way from his real goal.

About a mile from the fortress Marcus reined his black horse, Pavor, in a wide circle. Avoiding the highway altogether, he followed the line of hills back north.

Staying away from the course of the aqueduct, where he might be spotted by a squad of soldiers, Marcus turned Pavor into the hidden mouth of a box canyon. At the back of the ravine was a screen of yellow-flowered mustard plants.

Tying Pavor to a stunted oak tree, Marcus removed the horse's saddle and blanket. Changing out of his uniform, Marcus donned the common garb of a Jewish working man: short, faded tunic and patched, hooded cloak. He had taken the clothing from the locker of a stone-mason close in size to his own 180 pounds.

He added his uniform tunic and short sword to a leather pouch in which his helmet and the corona obsidionalis were already hidden.

Soothing Pavor, who snorted at the unfamiliar appearance and smell of his master, Marcus turned the horse loose. A seep at the base of the cliff provided water and nourished a patch of grass. He assured the animal that he would be back for him as he knotted the lead rope around his own waist as a belt. Pavor would remain in the canyon, grazing near the water source.

After a final nod of approval at the arrangements, Marcus climbed out of the box canyon at its head and hiked cross-country toward Bethany.

CAIAPHAS, HIGH PRIEST OF ISRAEL, WAS fond of quoting Ecclesiastes: *"For everything there is a season . . . a time to kill and a time to heal. A time to plant and a time to uproot."*[12]

The season to uproot any who might oppose his authority in Jerusalem had come. This was the time to kill.

The meeting between Caiaphas, his advisor Annas, and Herod Antipas took place in the tetrarch's audience chamber. The three men had no liking for each other. Caiaphas despised Antipas as an apostate, more Idumean and Samaritan than Jewish. Moreover, the high priest wanted no return to a Herodian dynasty. The last Herod to rule all Judea had summoned and fired high priests at a whim.

Eglon, in full ceremonial uniform, stood behind Antipas—an ominous reminder that the tetrarch had the power of a force at his call.

For his part, Herod Antipas regarded Caiaphas as little more than a stooge for the Roman governor. Like his father-in-law, Annas, before him, Caiaphas held his office at the will and pleasure of the Empire, not by legitimate scriptural authority as a descendant of the priestly line of Levi.

Caiaphas was the son of a wealthy family who, years before, had murdered Onias, the last hereditary high priest, and then had bribed its way into power.

In their affinity for power and their willingness to murder for it, Antipas and Caiaphas were cut from the same cloth.

When the need arose, the two factions were prepared to make common cause. The massacre of the pilgrims represented such a need, but the two men could not refrain from jockeying for position.

The opening volley was launched by Antipas. "Letting Governor Pilate make free with the Temple funds was a bad idea. It's being said the aqueduct project was the main cause of the riot. That makes you and the Sanhedrin partly responsible."

Caiaphas bristled, pursing his lips and squaring his already ramrod-stiff shoulders. "Not at all! The new source of water will aid the Temple sacrifices. Perfectly proper use of the *korban* money! Bar Abba's rebels merely made it an excuse to excite the masses. And even then nothing would have happened if the Pharisees—Gamaliel and his nephew Nakdimon ben Gurion—had not insisted on taking their protest to Pilate."

The sect known as the Pharisees was much more insistent on following the exact letter of religious law than Caiaphas and the majority of the Jewish council. The Pharisees and Pilate made convenient targets on whom to lay blame. Antipas and Caiaphas agreed to put out the word that if Pilate had not been so foolish, so precipitate in unleashing his troopers, the whole ugly scene might have been avoided.

"Most of the dead were your subjects . . . Galileans," Caiaphas noted. "They may blame you for the massacre unless you move decisively. You will, of course, want to lodge a formal complaint with Governor Pilate, as I will about the desecration of the Temple grounds."

"But while we're speaking of your subjects in Galilee," Annas interjected, "there's another matter to bring to your attention. This Yeshua of Nazareth. Was he behind this?"

Antipas squirmed at the mention of the name. "An accomplished conjurer. I would like to meet him, see him perform his tricks in person."

Seated in the third chair gathered within the circuit of the mosaic-tile waves, his hand cupped around his ear, Annas corrected, "The Galil is full of the story how this Yeshua fed an entire crowd by magic.

Bread for five thousand men, plus all their wives and children, out of thin air."

"Fed five thousand—"

"The exact number as an army legion!" Caiaphas confirmed. "Some are comparing him to Elijah or another of the mythical prophets of Israel."

"And that's not the worst of it," Annas hooted impatiently. "Some of the rabble say he's Yochanan the Baptizer back from the dead."

Antipas looked startled. His eyes bulged at all times, but now he resembled a fish brought to the surface from the depths of the Sea of Galilee. "The Baptizer," he repeated, visibly shaken by this news.

Caiaphas glanced knowingly at his father-in-law. "Of course it's foolishness. Yochanan was an insulting fanatic, but at least he followed our customs. Yeshua holds our traditions in contempt. Heals on Shabbat. Makes bread from the air but does not bother to follow the most basic laws of washing before eating. He's no holy man."

Antipas muttered, "Yochanan raised from the dead? Who knows what might happen if someone like that took it into his head to lead an army of peasants seeking revenge! The illiterate mob is still angry at me, blaming me for the execution of the Baptizer. If they believed this Yeshua is the Baptizer raised from the dead and followed him, what happened here over Passover would be a small thing compared to the uprising Yeshua could lead."

"You make the point for us," Caiaphas agreed. "We must suppress him! If he's in your territory, then it's your task."

Caiaphas and Annas left, satisfied they had laid responsibility for the past disasters on Rome and for any future rebellion in Galilee squarely on Antipas' doorstep.

Antipas brooded for a minute, then told Eglon, "I want you to find this Yeshua."

"And?"

"Get rid of him."

"My lord?"

"Track him down! Find out if he was anywhere near Yerush-alayim . . . maybe we can blame him for the riots! But take care of him. I don't dare arrest him, but I don't need any more trouble with any more country preachers. The Baptizer alive!" Antipas stared at Eglon, as if doubting the recollection of Yochanan's head on a platter by his command. "You executed Yochanan . . . unless . . . what if it wasn't Yochanan? A trick. One of his disciples perhaps. Took his place."

"The Baptizer is dead, Lord Antipas," Eglon protested.

"Well, kill him again! Kill whoever this is making bread out of air and raising an army from the rabble of Galil! Kill him, I say! And make it final this time!"

6

CHAPTER

N aomi, at twenty-four, was Susanna bat Maccabee's servant, but she was also a friend and companion. Like the recently rejected first wife of Herod Antipas, Naomi was Nabatean. She was swarthy and stocky like her kinsmen, and often displayed the temper and cunning of her heritage.

She had an intense dislike of Herodias, the new wife of Herod Antipas. Herodias, who had formerly married a half brother of Herod Antipas, was no better than a common prostitute in Naomi's opinion. And Salome, the pampered daughter of Herodias, was the worst kind of she-jackal ever created.

This morning Naomi's muttered tirade against the antics of the royal family was a ray of sunlight in Susanna's otherwise gloomy day.

Naomi brushed Susanna's long, thick hair. "And so you, a royal daughter of the great family of Maccabee, are commanded by this common trash to come to table and sup with them! The nerve! You'd be within your rights to throw a plate of hummus right in the face of that rouged Jezebel and hit Salome on the head with a slab of pork ribs!"

"You've got a dangerous tongue, Naomi," Susanna said, "but your fantasies of violence against Herodias and Salome cheer me up all the same."

"Just between us, Lady Susanna, none of this would've happened if Herod Antipas had not sent his first wife back to Nabatea and married this screeching, preening, finger-biting parrot of a woman. You would have been married to Manaen long ago. The first wife of Antipas? She understood about love, that one! The passion of Nabatean blood! Well, now our Lady the Princess is gone, and good men like Manaen get thrown into irons at the whim of Herodias."

"And other good men are beheaded when Salome dances. A dangerous time, Naomi."

Naomi raised her finger skyward and declared solemnly, "They think the god isn't watching, eh? Well, I heard Yochanan the Baptizer isn't dead at all! He's alive and calling himself by some other name."

"How can that be?"

"The god is paying attention! Yochanan knew what was righteous and wasn't afraid to say it!" She leaned down and said softly, "The Baptizer called Herodias a prostitute and Herod Antipas an adulterer. Wolf told me this. Wolf was in the detail of bodyguards and saw this firsthand. I heard Antipas dressed up like a wool merchant and went out to listen to the Baptizer preach once. Yochanan nearly called down fire and brimstone on the tetrarch's head! Oh yes! The Baptizer knew it was Antipas in disguise, and he let him have it too! A full jug of hummus, so to speak, right in the face! If you get my meaning."

"And look what the Baptizer got for his trouble. I'll be careful in my conversation with Herodias this morning. Careful. She loves flattery but not as much as she loves power. I thought about it last night. There has to be a way around her."

"My father used to keep a long pole in his tent with a noose on the end for catching adders. That's the best way to handle a snake like Herodias." Naomi finished plaiting Susanna's hair.

"Since I have no pole with a noose on the end, I'll have to use my wits to escape her and pray neither Manaen nor I are bitten."

"Go then. Smile sweetly. Be careful what you eat at her table. She's not above using her venom in other ways. If you find yourself in a corner, mention that Yochanan the Baptizer wandered up the corridor last night looking for his head."

THE MEAL WAS A GATHERING OF WIVES of the officials of Herod Antipas' government. Touted as an informal meeting of friends of the court, it was, all the same, a mandatory affair.

Susanna entered the noisy pavilion where the meal was laid out around a fountain. Today Herodias played the role of a regal lioness rather than the adder Naomi had envisioned.

Herodias was the daughter of Mariamne, Herod the Great's murdered Hasmonean queen. As such, the blood of the Maccabees also flowed in her, making her Susanna's distant cousin. Susanna shivered at the thought.

Herodias reclined at the head table on royal blue silk cushions beside her lithe, dark-eyed daughter, Salome. A bevy of fifty chattering, laughing wives of administrators faced the duo in a half circle. Susanna was escorted to a seat next to Joanna, who appeared weary, pale, and drawn.

"You're still here?" Susanna asked.

Joanna replied, "Couldn't miss this. Wanted to. Wished I could. Couldn't. I came for Kuza's sake." Joanna questioned Susanna with a glance. "You all right?" It was clear Joanna had heard about last night.

Susanna lowered her voice and spoke as she raised her cup to drink. "Manaen's the one to worry about."

Joanna took a bunch of grapes. "Kuza told me this morning. Manaen's still free. There's hope in that. Careful," she cautioned. "Herodias is watching you from her perch. Like a cat watches a mouse. Smile, Susanna. Smile. Kuza thinks they'll let you both cool off. Think it over."

"Demos wants him dead."

Joanna threw back her head in a laugh. This seemed to placate Herodias, who turned to stare at other guests. "Dead, is it? They get more and more drunk in their power. If that's the case—smile, she's looking again. You must—if you stay here—play their game. Best to act as if nothing's happened. Divert their attention from Manaen and you. Talk about what interests them. You know the game." Then, "Keep smiling. Whatever you do. Smile when we talk. She's watching. Watching."

"If I had known what lengths Demos would go to, I would have run away with Manaen last year."

"Smile. Don't let her see you're worried. There. That's it."

"I should have gone away with him when he asked me."

"Remember what I told you."

"I wish you'd stay."

"I can't. My world has changed. I'm changed. I don't fit here any more. Can't play the game well."

"What happened?"

"While you were away, I found out there's more to life than this. But to speak of it openly is dangerous," Joanna explained.

"What's happened?"

"If you can get away, come to Beth-Anyah. I got word this morning—"

Just then Herodias raised her goblet. Silence fell. "Welcome! Welcome! We are gathered here together, the best women in Judea, Yerushalayim, and Galilee to honor . . . ourselves, really. And so I offer this toast: to us. Where would our men be without us?"

This was followed by applause, a twittering of laughter, and then the toast.

"Well, that's all I'm going to say," Herodias finished. "Enjoy! Enjoy!" The noise level returned to one similar to a large flock of geese being herded by barking dogs.

Herodias fixed her gaze on Susanna and crooked a finger for her to join her and Salome at the head table.

"Shalom tov," Joanna whispered. "Play the game."

Susanna made her way to Herodias, who patted a cushion indicating that she should sit between Salome and herself.

Smiling, smiling, Susanna sank down beside her.

"And how are we this morning?" Herodias probed.

"Well, though I didn't sleep well."

"True love. Yes, dear. I know about it. I divorced my first husband after all because I loved Antipas. Swept away by love. It was difficult. Difficult. After all, they are brothers. I understand sleepless nights."

"Oh. You thought I meant Manaen? No. No. Dreams. Terrible dreams. A headless spirit walking through the corridors . . . searching for something."

Salome grew ashen. Her eyes widened in terror. "I've seen him too."

Herodias sat up and glared furiously at Susanna. "Is this some sort of joke?"

"Not at all. I called out to my servant. She'll tell you. She didn't see it. But it was so real I almost—"

"Mother?" Salome whined. "You see? It's not a dream! I want to go back to the Galil! Someone else has seen him too!"

"No, Salome." Herodias flicked her fingers in demand for silence. "No more. You're a foolish, silly girl and it was just a dream."

"Yes," Susanna reassured Salome, "I'm sure it was nothing more."

"But, Mother! I've seen it! His body. Wandering through the—"

"Salome!" Herodias interrupted. "You may be excused. Go. Now. Go to your room at once! I told you not to speak of it!"

Susanna pretended apology. "I'm sorry. I didn't mean to."

Salome ran sobbing from the meal. Susanna attempted to engage the lioness in small talk. The weather. The games. The latest fashion from Rome. Conversation fell flat.

"Just a dream," Herodias muttered. "And yet you say . . . you saw it too?"

"Just a dream. Horrible. Surely brought on by all that happened in Yerushalayim."

"Yes. Well. Unpleasant place, this city. Full of blood and gore and . . . sacrifice. I think I'll talk to Antipas. Go home. The Galil is pleasant this time of year." Herodias' hands shook. She spilled her wine and cursed loudly. All eyes were upon her as she stood. "I have a splitting headache. Stay. No, stay. All of you. Stay, enjoy. It's just that . . . my head—" She left abruptly.

Later Susanna took Joanna's arm as they exited together.

"What did you say?" Joanna asked in astonishment.

"I played the game."

GOVERNOR PONTIUS PILATE PACED ALONG the battlements on the eastern flank of the Phasael Tower. His soft, patrician hands were clasped at his back as he stalked the flagstones, dictating aloud in the pleasant air.

Behind Pilate's left shoulder was his private secretary. The harried-looking man moved with a halting lunge. He attempted to take legible notes while juggling a stack of wax tablets and still keep up with the governor's longer stride.

The governor's voice was calmly deliberate, his words carefully measured. But his fingers twitched. Frequently Pilate paused for thought. And at each temporary halt in his narration, he turned his face toward the Temple Mount and scowled.

In the western portion of Jerusalem, above his palace, Herod the Great had built three large towers. He had named one for a wife, another for a friend, and the third, Phasael, for his brother. The top of this structure was the highest point in Jerusalem, so the view over the city was magnificent. But Pilate paid no attention to the scenery.

The commanding fortification included both a miniature palace and its own water supply. It was the last redoubt in case of attack: the easiest to defend and the most secure.

Behind Pilate's right shoulder was the Praetorian officer Vara, his brutish features fixed in what he probably intended as sympathetic commiseration for the difficulties of high rank.

"There were a thousand killed, you say," Pilate demanded of Vara. He motioned for the secretary to cease taking notes and turned to face the Praetorian.

"That is correct, Excellency."

"And of those, how many with known rebel connections?"

Vara cleared his throat. "We're still interrogating, Excellency. More and more conspirators are coming to light as we proceed. It's certain that bar Abba intended to carry out assassinations on a large scale. He would not attempt such a thing if he didn't have a significant force here in the city. Possibly half of the dead were rebels." As Pilate frowned, Vara rapidly amended his statement. "But probably even more. Certainly the rebels were joined by many who also had treason in their hearts. Who knows what's in the thoughts of a Jew? Not to be trusted, any of them."

Nodding at this widely accepted perception, Pilate peered over the edge of the parapet to stare down into the courtyard of the palace that was his Jerusalem home. A phalanx of slaves still scrubbed at the bloodstained cobbles where the riot had begun the day before. "Then the rest have themselves to blame," he noted. "Why didn't they denounce the assassins in the mob before any violence broke out? On their own heads it lies. And many sicarii crowded right into my own courtyard? Dagger-men?"

"We must thank the gods for your Excellency's safety," Vara concurred. "No doubt you were the greatest target of their plot."

"And they came in with those who pretended to offer a peaceful petition," Pilate mused. "Could part of the Sanhedrin be in on the conspiracy?"

"We must follow the trail of the rebels wherever it leads," Vara pronounced forcefully. "No matter who it points to. Well . . . " He paused, as if reluctant to speak. "Centurion Longinus prevented me from carrying out my duties. Because of his interference, more of the rebels escaped . . . perhaps even bar Abba himself."

Pilate's scowl deepened. "The centurion has much to answer for. Has he arrived from Herodium yet?"

"Not yet, Excellency," Vara answered. "But he's expected soon. I sent a rider with an urgent summons."

Another thought appeared to strike the governor. "What about that so-called Messiah? The Galilean?"

"Not reported seen," Vara observed. "But if he's involved, I'll find out."

Pilate returned to pacing and dictating. He worked and reworked the official reports that would go out to the governor of Syria, Pilate's immediate superior, and to the emperor himself. There would be no serious repercussions for Pilate's authority if this was handled properly. Putting down rebellion as forcefully and quickly as possible was acceptable behavior. No blame could attach to Pilate himself for what had happened. His precautions had been fully justified, as any impartial judge would recognize.

And there were plenty of targets available if any blame needed to be shunted aside, especially when Vara produced high-ranking conspirators.

"What do you need to pursue these rebels to their utter destruction?" Pilate inquired.

"The authority to act in your name, without interference," Vara said a shade too fast. Then he added, "Exactly as my commander, Prefect Sejanus, acts for the emperor. That will clarify the lines of authority here in the province."

Pilate nodded. "Take this down," he said to the secretary. "'The bearer of this document has done what he has done for the welfare of the state, and with the approval of Rome.' Will that do?"

Vara smiled. It was an unpleasantly malicious expression, like what a jackal or hyena might display when coming upon a crippled sheep.

"Prepare the document at once," Pilate ordered his secretary, "and bring it to me for my seal."

Steps clattered upwards and an out-of-breath courier arrived at the top of the tower, passing the departing secretary.

The messenger bowed to the governor and saluted Vara.

"This is the man I sent to bring Marcus," Vara said. "Well, where is he?"

With his eyes carefully downward the dispatch rider answered, "I don't know, sir. He was not at Herodium."

"Then where is he?" Vara demanded, not waiting for the governor to speak.

"Tribune Felix said the centurion had been summoned to Alexandria and had already left."

"By whose orders?" Pilate challenged.

"The tribune says the message was from Caligula," the courier returned. "He said you would understand why the centurion had to go immediately."

"Leave us!" Pilate ordered the messenger. Then, after the courier's departure, he said tersely to Vara, "There's more going on here than simply a Jewish rabble upset about their precious sacred treasury! Find the centurion! Now! *Before* he gets to Alexandria. And round up the conspirators."

Miryam.

Marcus held the memory of her love gently, like a tiny bird in his hand. He cherished the image of tenderness he felt toward her.

But honestly? On second thought he had to admit Miryam was more like a knife wound across his palm, which made picking up his life impossible.

She had changed. So had he.

They were better, truer, stronger for having met the Rabbi from Galilee. But they were strong like two tall trees standing on opposite sides of a wide river. They shared the same water; the same wind touched them, moved them. But they were forever planted across from one another. She a Jew. He a Roman. No crossing over.

She knew it.

So did he.

He longed to grow beside her. But it could never be. He asked himself, What were the two of them when the whole earth trembled? In the scope of such turmoil, what were their personal desires?

Noble thoughts. But nobility was little comfort on the long, cold nights when he longed to feel her warmth next to him.

And so he was going to see her in Bethany before he left. To warn her. Tell her that she must carry his warning to Yeshua when she next saw Him. He and His followers must leave the territory of Judea. They must not go into the provinces of Galilee or Perea where Herod Antipas ruled. Marcus was certain, as certain as he had ever been about anything, that the hammer of persecution was raised and poised to strike. Every day Herod Antipas slipped further into paranoia, as his father, the butcher king, had done. His bloodshot eyes turned toward Yeshua now.

Miryam resided in the village of Bethany, nestled against the Mount of Olives east of Jerusalem. After noon the mountain cast its shadow over the great house where Miryam lived with her brother, El'azar, and older sister, Marta.

Marcus could see the humped back of the mountain long before he smelled the cook fires of the village. He cut across a field and met a farmer plowing there as though nothing had happened in Jerusalem. Marcus, who with his beard and stonecutter's tunic looked like a Jew, greeted him.

"Shalom tov."

"Where you headed?" the farmer asked.

"The village of Bethany," Marcus answered.

"No village to speak of. A few scattered farms and orchards. A synagogue. A market square. That mountain there takes up too much room for a proper village to grow." He pointed his ox goad toward the Mount of Olives and the granite terraces and silver-green leaves of the olive trees. "Are you going to Beth-Anyah to hear himself then?"

"Yeshua's there?"

"He is. And the thousands who've fled Yerushalayim have gone after hearing him."

"Where's he staying? Do you know?"

"They say the great house of El'azar and his sisters. Never been there myself. Great friends with them three, I hear. Though madness runs in that family."

"Why don't you come?" Marcus asked.

"Got a field to plant. No time. You see what following after every voice gets you? Told the wife I'm glad we didn't go up to Yerushalayim. Look what it gets you!"

"That's a path." Marcus pointed to a trail beyond the field that wound toward the Mount.

"There's naught but graves that way. No, go round the orchard there by the olive press. Take the proper road. Five miles is all. And there's all the people on the road, going to hear him. I'd show you the way, but I've got this field to plow."

Marcus thanked the farmer and headed on toward Bethany. He would deliver the warning to Yeshua face-to-face, if he was not too late.

MANAEN WAS SWEPT ALONG AS THE THRONG surged the handful of miles separating Jerusalem and the sleepy village of Bethany, known in Hebrew as Beth-Anyah, "House of Misery."

A row of date palms paralleled a stone wall, which in turn enclosed a fig orchard. Manaen made his way through an opening in the barrier and into an already packed field. There, below the brow of a hill where the fig trees stopped, a group of wary-looking Galileans kept open a space. Manaen guessed they were Yeshua's *talmidim*, His disciples, holding off the multitudes from their master.

"Sit down, sit down." The instruction was passed back from the grassy slope to the newer arrivals, and still more came, jamming the space throughout the grove. Then the repeated command was replaced by a low exclamation of recognition. Manaen raised his eyes as a man dressed in rough homespun and a robe of colored stripes came around the side of the hill.

Excited murmuring rippled through the throng.

So this was Yeshua, Manaen thought, disappointed.

The Rabbi was not physically impressive. Of slim build, with brown hair and a thick beard, Yeshua was not noteworthy in appearance. With wide-set dark brown eyes and a ready smile, He was by no means as formidable as His cousin Yochanan the Baptizer, even though there was a strong family resemblance.

It was clear that anger and sorrow simmered just below the surface of the mob. The first words that greeted Yeshua were a challenge issued by Alexander, a relative of the high priest. "Rabbi! Do you agree with the high priest and the Temple authority that those Galileans who perished at the Temple received correct judgment from God for their rebellion against the rulers of Israel?"

A red-faced commoner, evidently a northerner by his accent, angrily rebutted, "They've killed hundreds. Innocent Galileans died just for protesting the use of Temple tithes to build the Roman aqueduct! Pilate's men cut 'em down where they stood. Their blood ran into the gutters with the blood of the lambs!"

Manaen looked for a way to escape in case this argument developed into a violent confrontation. He knew this gathering could easily escalate into another riot. One inflammatory word from Yeshua and yesterday's mayhem would begin all over again.

He glanced around nervously. Certainly Roman legionaries or agents of Herod Antipas and the high priest were in this crowd, just as there had been yesterday. Yes. There. Manaen recognized a trio from Pilate's court—Greeks and Romans dressed as merchants. And Centurion Marcus Longinus, red-bearded, sun-bronzed, stocky, dressed in a commoner's traveling clothes.

There were spies sent from the Sanhedrin. Barak bar Halfi, gruff and defiant in his demeanor. And there, the bull-like figure of Nakdimon ben Gurion, nephew of the revered Rabbi Gamaliel. Had he come on behalf of the Jewish rulers?

How could Yeshua respond without offending one side or challenging the other? If He defended the authorities, the crowds would abandon Him or stone Him where He stood. If He defended the Galileans who died in protest of the aqueduct, He could be taken up for treason, for incitement, or any number of other crimes leading to crucifixion.

Why had Manaen come? This spot was more dangerous than Herod's palace.

Yeshua's reply rang out across the hillside. "Do you think these Galileans were worse sinners than all the other Galileans because they suffered in this way? No, I tell you! *Teshuvah!* Repent! Unless you turn your hearts to God, return to his way of truth and mercy, then you too will perish."

Yeshua turned the accusation on its head. Only Rome and her allies among the Jewish leadership in Jerusalem really believed the Galileans deserved death. The religious leaders had already made a public declaration of the guilt of those who died. It was said that those who were slaughtered while making their sacrifices to the Almighty had been deeply evil. For their rebellion against the high priest, the Almighty had slain them while they sacrificed. The riot that followed, they said, was proof of God's judgment.

And now another challenge rang out: a question meant to trap Yeshua into offending both Rome and the Sanhedrin.

"What about the eighteen Jewish stoneworkers working for Rome to build the Tower of Siloam? Rome paid their wages with sacred money taken from the Temple treasury! They died when the tower collapsed! Surely this was a judgment of God against them because they helped Rome and received wages from forbidden sacred Temple funds!"[13]

Manaen turned to see the identity of the speaker. It was Eglon. And beside him stood Demos. How would Yeshua answer this one?

Yeshua acknowledged Eglon, then examined the opponents He surely knew had come here to trap Him. After a long moment He replied, "Those eighteen who died when the Tower of Siloam fell on them . . . do you think they were more guilty than all the others living in Yerushalayim?[14] *I tell you, no!*" Yeshua's voice boomed out. "All have sinned and fall short of the glory of God!"[14] What has the Lord spoken through the prophet Isaias? All our works of righteousness are no better than filthy rags![15] There is none among mankind who has not sinned! No man stands guiltless before the Almighty, El'Elyon! From Adam until today the wages of sin for every human is death, but the free gift of God is eternal life through the one whom he has sent![16] But unless you repent, you too will perish."

Suddenly Yeshua had turned the issue from politics to repentance!

Had those who died so unexpectedly been prepared? Were they ready for the end of their lives and whatever eternal judgment came next?

With a few words Yeshua had stopped the mouths of those who had come to entrap Him! He forced the crowd from anger and sorrow into introspection. Here were two horrifying examples of sudden death. If it happened to these people, Yeshua appeared to be saying, it could happen to you. Will you be ready to stand before the only Righteous Judge?

Manaen smiled at the smoldering resentment that passed over the faces of Eglon, Demos, and the other hostile witnesses. This Yeshua was carrying on with the same message as His cousin Yochanan, but He was more subtle, more clever.

Manaen would stay and listen. Perhaps Yeshua could help Manaen with the case of his inheritance.

Yeshua pointed at the fig tree, where a group of Pharisees stood. Then He told the crowd a story: "A man had a fig tree, planted in his vineyard. And he went to look for fruit on it but didn't find any. So he said to the gardener who took care of the vineyard, 'For three years now I've been coming to look for fruit on this fig tree and haven't found any. Cut it down! Why should it use up the soil?' 'Sir,' the gardener replied, 'leave it for one more year, and I'll dig around it and fertilize it. If it bears fruit next year, fine! If not, then cut it down.'"[17]

Many of the listeners eyed each other and conversed in low, worried tones. Who was meant by the fig tree? That image had always been a symbol of the nation of Israel. Was Yeshua saying that the nation had failed in something and was about to be destroyed? Was His message a prophecy of doom?

Raising His hand toward Jerusalem, where the Temple edifice glinted in the sun, Yeshua said, "When you see a cloud rising in the west, immediately you say, 'It's going to rain,' and it does."

Manaen looked. Indeed a cloud hung over the Holy City, but perhaps it was the smoke of the still-smoldering fires.

Yeshua continued, "And when the south wind blows, you say, 'It's going to be hot' and it is. Hypocrites! You know how to interpret the appearance of the earth and the sky. How is it that you don't know how to interpret this present time?"[18]

What did He mean? Was some disaster looming for this nation? Or did He mean simply that every man born of woman would someday die? That the tragedies that came to others were simply an indication that one day every life would end?

Manaen considered his own life. He was not ready to die. No. But neither did he want to think about it today.

Still more people came into the field, pressing forward, pushing those already seated into a tighter and tighter mass, trampling on coats and fingers and toes of the unwary.

Manaen glanced toward Demos and Eglon. They inched nearer to where Yeshua stood. Perhaps this was Manaen's chance to receive a judgment in the matter of his inheritance.

"Teacher," Manaen called out suddenly, "tell my brother to divide my inheritance with me."[19]

The question startled Demos, who stopped in his tracks and glared with hatred and surprise at Manaen. Manaen stood and gave his brother a friendly salute.

Yeshua, observing the hostile interaction between brothers, smiled and shook His head. "Man, who appointed me a judge or arbiter between you?" The crowd laughed, recognizing that Yeshua wisely did not wish to stand between two warring siblings.

Then Yeshua fixed His gaze on Demos, speaking directly to him. "Watch out! Be on your guard against all kinds of greed. A man's life doesn't consist in the abundance of what he owns."

The spectators murmured their agreement. Embarrassed at being singled out, Demos sat down quickly.

"I'll tell you a story about a rich man." Yeshua raised His chin and addressed the multitude. "The ground of this certain man produced a very good crop. He thought to himself, *What shall I do? I have no place to store my crops.* Then he said, 'This is what I'll do. I'll tear down my barns and build bigger ones, and there I will store all my grain and my goods. And I'll say to myself, *You have plenty of good things laid up for many years. Take life easy; eat, drink, and be merry.*'

"But God said to him, 'You fool! This very night your life will be demanded from you. Then who will get what you have prepared for yourself?' This is how it will be with anyone who stores up things for himself but is not rich toward God."[20]

And so once again, Yeshua had brought the focus back to issues of the heart. Fixing truth only on foundations laid down by God's Word. Being right before the Lord. Yes! The signs of the times pointed toward something . . . something of great significance. Prophecies were being fulfilled daily! Who in this multitude was ready? What was true for the nation of Israel was true for each individual. If God declared that on this night their lives would be required, who could stand before the Righteous Judge?

Yeshua had escaped the trick questions of His opponents with admirable mental agility.

Wisdom. Until now, it had been only a concept discussed by philosophers. Until now, Manaen had never before been in the presence of a man who truly embodied wisdom.

So this was Yeshua of Nazareth! Manaen was impressed.

It was obvious Demos was humiliated. His face purpled with rage.

Leaning close to Eglon, Demos hissed in his ear. Then the two stood again and slowly began to make their way across the field toward Manaen.

Trouble!

Manaen was pleased at Demos' resentment. Yeshua, while not judging between the two brothers, had revealed the inner motivation of Demos before thousands.

Greed!

Word of this personal insult would surely get back to Herod Antipas. Manaen wanted to be there when it did.

Still poor, but somehow comforted by the words of Yeshua, Manaen slipped away from Bethany and headed back to Jerusalem.

Praetorian Commander Vara presented himself in Herod Antipas' audience chamber. "Sorry to disturb you, Lord Antipas," Vara said. "So many of your Galilean subjects killed."

Antipas waved a ring-encrusted hand dismissively. "Let them all beware the power of Rome! It is a good lesson and will prevent future unrest."

"Just so," Vara said, bobbing his head. "And it's about preventing future unrest that I've come. I've heard one of your subjects . . . indeed, part of your inner circle . . . was in the house occupied by the sicarii."

"No!" Antipas protested. "The same killers you so heroically destroyed in battle? One of my associates?"

Vara nodded. "Manaen bar Talmai. I wish to examine him about what he may have seen or heard . . . names of other rebels, their plans, and so forth. I stress to your Majesty that Manaen is not suspected of actually being a rebel sympathizer . . . yet."

Antipas waited for further explanation, his face set in a sagging mass of suspicion.

Vara continued, "Lord Manaen was present with the rebels, but after we disposed of them, he didn't remain to be questioned or to render aid in exposing their schemes. Doubtless he will be willing to cooperate now."

"Doubtless," Antipas agreed.

Vara added, "It was reported that he was observed leaving the scene with someone who may have been one of the rebels . . . but you know how confused everything was last night. Doubtless he has an adequate explanation."

"Doubtless," Antipas growled. Then to an attendant he barked, "Fetch Manaen here at once."

Several minutes later Antipas and Vara still waited.

At last the servant returned. "Lord Manaen isn't in his chamber," the man reported. "I inquired among the other servants. He hasn't been seen since leaving the palace earlier in the day."

"Ah, well," Vara said. "You'll let him know that I need to question him as soon as possible?"

"Of course," Antipas agreed. "We will be extremely interested in his explanations also."

ALTHOUGH MARCUS SAW MIRYAM AT A DISTANCE, he did not follow after her when she rose to leave with Yeshua and the others.

Among the crowds Marcus had read the signs that a fierce gale was brewing in Judea for Yeshua and His followers. Faces of proud, ambitious men glowered like storm clouds on the horizon. Marcus had spotted the hired assassins sent by Antipas, Caiaphas, and Pilate.

As for the Jewish leadership in attendance, their open hostility to and subsequent humiliation by Yeshua meant only that they would set in motion the wheels that would eventually crush the Teacher and any who dared support Him.

There was Miryam and her brother El'azar, sitting near Yeshua as He taught. And there, the old shepherd Zadok and his three boys among Yeshua's inner circle of friends. Nakdimon ben Gurion, one of perhaps a dozen honest men on the Sanhedrin, stood with arms crossed beside the big fisherman named Shimon.

Did they not realize how closely they were being watched? That names were being recorded by the Temple scribes as Yeshua tied His accusers in knots?

. . . Nakdimon ben Gurion, nephew of Gamaliel, displayed satisfaction in his expression when Yeshua refuted the question about the Galileans . . .

Zadok, Chief Shepherd of the flocks of Israel, was in attendance and by his favorable demeanor appears to be a supporter of the charlatan Yeshua . . .

Yeshua and His talmidim sent the crowds away and then entered the gates of El'azar of Bethany and his sisters . . .

It occurred to Marcus that he too had surely been noted in the lists. He lingered behind the broad trunk of the fig tree as the gates of the villa closed and the crowds dispersed. From this cover he watched as pools of the offended coalesced to compare notes, to embellish and enlarge the transgressions of the Teacher. Their analysis of Yeshua's words poured out was like a gathering of vultures squabbling over a carcass.

"Did you hear what he said . . ."

"Did you see who was beside him!"

"And he seemed to agree with Yeshua!"

"Caiaphas warned Gamaliel about this nephew."

"Doubtful loyalty."

"And Manaen bar Talmai! A member of Herod Antipas' house! Humiliating his brother in front of everyone!"

"Can't be trusted . . ."

"But old Zadok! For the Chief Shepherd to come to this meeting and sit like a Torah schoolboy with such a look of pride on his face!"

"That old man always was one to watch. An insult to the high priest's family!"

"And her! Did you see the way she stared at him? We all know what she is . . . consort to that Roman centurion. Marcus Longinus!"

"He was here too. Dressed like a common Jew."

"Pilate should keep his soldiers on a shorter leash."

"And there was Yeshua talking to her like she had never . . ."

"His followers are scum . . . filth!"

"And Yeshua has the nerve to lump us in with them. As if we're as tainted as they are."

"Caiaphas will have something to say about it!"

"He's dangerous!"

"I agree. For a minute I thought the crowd was on the verge of storming Yerushalayim again with Yeshua as leader!"

And so the fields of Bethany were drenched in the venom of those who viewed Yeshua as a threat to their power. That afternoon, in Marcus' hearing, factions that had never before acknowledged one another joined forces in their opposition to a common enemy.

As they walked, united, back toward Jerusalem, Marcus considered what this meant to Yeshua. His enemies feared that with His personal charisma Yeshua could easily raise an army. Enter Jerusalem as King of the Jews. Strike hard. Storm the citadels of power. Conquer Jerusalem, Judea, and Galilee. Who could oppose a man who could, with one word, heal the wounded among His troops? And feed them bread created out of thin air?

Jewish Zealots like bar Abba certainly hoped this would be the course Yeshua chose. Yet Yeshua had refused a crown, telling His followers that the time to establish His kingdom had not yet come.

As for Rome, sixty years earlier Caesar Augustus had made Herod the great king of the Jews. And Herod the Great was not even a Jew! Could not Yeshua as easily ascend the throne and rule in peace with Rome's approval? This possibility sent currents of terror through the men who now ruled.

Caiaphas and his family held the priesthood in their grasp. They received a cut from all Temple concessions, merchandise, and the sale of goods in the Court of the Gentiles. To lose control of the high priesthood meant not merely loss of power, but loss of wealth, income.

As for Herod Antipas, the tetrarch was so depraved and without morals that even Pilate was disgusted by him. Antipas was also dependent, supporting his life of pleasure from taxes raked in from the common folk. To lose his power meant giving up his lifestyle.

Yeshua, like His cousin, Yochanan the Baptizer, was a voice crying in the wilderness against corruption. And from the wilderness of Judea, Galilee, and the surrounding countryside, the common folk flocked to hear Yeshua's preaching.

There was, to Marcus' way of thinking, *one* hope for Yeshua to survive the coming storm. He would have to leave the territory. Lie low for a while. Bide His time in obscurity until the political tides of Rome turned against Herod Antipas, Caiaphas, and the rest.

The sun was low on the horizon. Shabbat evening was approaching. The field where thousands had gathered was now deserted, except for trash and a few personal effects left behind.

A bird called from the branch above Marcus, who sat alone with his back against the trunk of the tree.

ama was angry. Peniel expected it. Everyone in the city was upset. Mama was just upset for a different reason.

When Peniel considered the loss of so much revenue, he did not blame her entirely, but it was as if she had not noticed people had died. As if it did not really matter about the twins of the shoemaker's family or that the good old man in the pottery shop was dead. The shop burned. How could Mama think about money under such circumstances?

"If you'd only done as you were told! Collected our money and come home!" she shouted at Peniel.

"The old man told me to go away and come back later for the payment. So I did." Peniel stoked the kiln fire with fuel made from dried sheep dung.

"You should have waited! Collected what he owed us and then come straight home. Now he's dead. The lamps are broken. We'll never see the money!"

Peniel knew better than to argue. He did not slow shoveling fuel into the mouth of the furnace.

Mama smacked him hard across the back of the head. "Are you listening to me?"

"Yes."

Another smack. "Put down that shovel! Pay attention when I'm talking to you."

"Yes, Mama." Peniel was grateful for the momentary reprieve from work.

"Where did you go after you left the shop the first time?"

"Back to the Temple."

"Did you collect any alms?"

Peniel dug in his pocket and retrieved a handful of coins.

Mama took it all from him. "That is it?"

"I didn't stay long. So many pilgrims were streaming through the Eastern Gate. Poor folk. Lots of children."

"Eastern Gate? Your station's at Nicanor! That's where the best almsgiving happens, when the rich men are coming and going from the Court of the Israelites. When they're feeling guilty and want to make a big show of giving charity. What were you doing at the Eastern Gate?"

"Just like everyone. There were rumors, you know. I went to see if he would come."

"He?" Another hard slap. "This Messiah again? Hoping for the Messiah? You left our money at the pottery shop! Went to the Temple! Gave up your place beside Nicanor to go wait at the Eastern Gate for a Messiah who'll never come?"

"Yes. I mean . . . no," Peniel admitted. "I mean . . . the rabbis say the years of Daniel's prophecy are complete. Rabbi Gamaliel has the exact years figured out."

Mama slapped him again. "Do you think I care about this nonsense? God has taken from me a son with brains and left me with an idiot! We're trying to make a living here, and you're pretending to be one of Gamaliel's *talmidim!* Is that why you went back to the Temple? You're a blind beggar, not a Torah scholar! You're not Gershon! Learn your place in life and you'll be much happier!"

"I left before the riots. Went back to the old man's shop to pick up the payment. But—"

"Shut up! Shut! Up! Always some excuse! Some reason! Your carelessness cost us weeks of income. You're a disgrace! I'll talk to your father. You can pay back every penny we lost! Every penny from your alms! And I don't care if it takes the rest of your life to work it off! This is your fault, and you're the one to pay for it!"

It was evening. Manaen returned to Jerusalem with newfound resolve. Yeshua of Nazareth had reduced the handpicked conspirators of the Pharisees, the high priest, and Herod Antipas to silence . . . and shamed Demos in the bargain!

The combination restored Manaen's self-confidence. He vowed he would confront Demos again about his inheritance, spelling out his demands to Herod Antipas as being only just and right.

Manaen had spoken to Yeshua on a whim, but perhaps he should threaten to lay the whole affair in front of a magistrate. Surely Tetrarch Antipas had enough to deal with already with all the unrest. Perhaps he would concede, and see that Manaen received what was rightfully his, rather than prolong the debate.

Not that Manaen would ever again ask the Preacher from Galilee to render a decision. Despite Yeshua's quick wit and insight into human nature, the Rabbi had too many enemies to survive for long. Manaen could not think of anyone else who could be on the wrong side of Herod Antipas, the Temple authorities, and Rome—all at the same time. Normally, the Sadducees and Pharisees despised each other, yet in their opposition to Yeshua, they managed to agree.

Manaen decided he would not like to be in Yeshua's sandals. Cleverness and popularity with the crowds were not adequate defenses against an assassin's dagger or a poisoned cup of wine.

Glancing up from his mug of wine, Manaen saw Demos leaning on the door frame. His brother was neither smiling nor scowling, merely staring at Manaen contemplatively.

Manaen could not help gloating. "What an excellent judge of character that Preacher is," he said. "Pegged you right away, didn't he?"

"You were ordered not to leave Yerushalayim, weren't you?" Demos reminded him.

"Don't hand me that!" Manaen returned, laughing. "Everybody is going to see him. Half the city was probably in Beth-Anyah today."

Demos lowered his chin and shook his head in mock despair. "Dear brother, you've really gone and done it this time."

"Nice try, Demos," Manaen scoffed. "It's been a long time since you could frighten me . . . though you always did have a cruel streak that way."

The tramp of hobnailed sandals echoed in the corridor, and Demos stepped aside, a malevolent smile spreading across his face.

The panels of Manaen's door rang hollowly, pounded with the iron-shod butt of a spear.

"Eglon," Manaen said dully, facing the hostile menace of the captain.

"Manaen bar Talmai," Eglon intoned, "you are summoned to Tetrarch Herod Antipas to answer certain charges."

"What nonsense is this?"

"Treason is not nonsense," Eglon said. "Come along."

IN A REPEAT OF THE PREVIOUS NIGHT, Manaen was again hauled up before Antipas. Aside from Susanna's absence, everything was the same as before, except the tetrarch's eyes were bloodshot and he seemed in an even fouler mood.

From behind Antipas' shoulder Herodias watched the proceedings. Her eyes never left Manaen's face, like a cobra's fixed on a futilely jumping rat.

"Manaen bar Talmai, we are severely disappointed in you," Antipas said. "We knew you were an ungrateful, obstinate wretch, but we never suspected you of being a traitor."

"I'm no traitor," Manaen protested.

Herod Antipas raised an authoritative hand. "Not only did you break our express command by leaving Yerushalayim, but you did so in order to consort with a known enemy."

"Yeshua of Nazareth is clever, but not dangerous," Manaen argued. "He tied everyone up in knots. He . . . "

"Silence!" Antipas demanded. "He is a suspected rebel, an inciter of rebellion, near kin to that agitator Yochanan the Baptizer."

Herodias' eyes glittered.

At a slight gesture of Antipas' forefinger, two burly guards and Eglon forced Manaen to his knees, tied his hands behind his back, and stuffed a gag in his mouth. Eglon was taking no chances that Manaen might fight his way clear and escape.

In words freighted with doom, Eglon pronounced the charges

against Manaen. "You stand accused of disobedience to your lord and master, in that you did willfully break his command not to leave Yerushalayim. You are charged with consorting with suspected rebels in the person of Yeshua of Nazareth. You are guilty of slander against Tetrarch Antipas, publicly shaming him with your calumny, as well as slander against your brother. Inasmuch as these things occurred in the presence of two witnesses here present, anything you might say in your own defense is valueless. You are hereby found guilty as charged and are sent to prison to reflect on your crimes."

That was it. No defense, no appeal, no chance of escape.

And Demos' sneer of triumph was the last thing Manaen saw as he was led away.

MARCUS WAITED UNTIL AFTER DARK TO APPROACH the gate of Miryam's villa. He scrutinized the sky for stars setting in the west, but they were blocked by the black arch of the Mount of Olives. Here and there the underbelly of a stray cloud was illuminated by the giant menorahs of the Temple. Even at this distance, Marcus could see the light blazing to welcome the arrival of Shabbat. Tonight began the fifty days of Omer until the celebration of the Jewish feast of Pentecost, which commemorated the giving of the Ten Commandments to Moses.

Marcus had learned much about the Jews in his years of service in the province. The law had been expanded from ten commandments to *611*. Jews who practiced this expanded version of the law were a fierce and stubborn people, weighed down by complex religious obligations.

Only lately had Marcus begun to comprehend the subtle meaning of the writings the Jews called Torah. Yeshua's interpretation of God's commands seemed clear and easy to understand: *Love God and man. Forgive those who hurt you. Show mercy to all. Practice compassion by actions, not just words.*

Was this indeed the Law and the Prophets boiled down, as Yeshua said? Not as difficult to understand but extremely difficult to practice. Perhaps it was easier to be righteous by following 611 rules that covered every aspect of life from which cook pot could be used to how far a man could walk on Shabbat!

If the religion Yeshua preached was as simple as He claimed, could not someone like Marcus take it to heart even though he was not a Jew?

So many things Marcus longed to know appeared out of his grasp. At the core of the wisdom in Torah and Tanakh, he sensed, was Yeshua. Yet Marcus, as a Roman, knew he could never get near enough to be a part of whatever miracle transpired behind the locked gates of Jewish religion. As the low wall of Soreg in the Temple courtyard marked a boundary over which no Gentile could ever cross on pain of death, so Marcus would never be fully allowed to enter into the joy of Miryam's new life.

Marcus' quest for knowledge was like a wind whistling around the corner of a house that contained scholars studying beside a warm fire.

The miracle of simplicity Yeshua brought to the world was meant only for Jews, Marcus had been told. The God Yeshua proclaimed was a Hebrew God. And so Marcus stood back in his place, watching with longing like a hungry man, standing at a distance as others feasted. He decided he would be content merely to glean the scraps that fell from Yeshua's table.

So tonight he waited.

Inside Miryam's house the guests would be finished with Shabbat supper by now. Marcus' arrival, unannounced, would not interrupt their meal.

He knocked on the thick wood panels. No reply. He knocked again. And again.

After ten minutes an aged servant put one rheumy eye to the tiny barred window.

"What do y' want? They've got important visitors."

"I have a message for Lady Miryam."

"Tell it to me then. I'll see she gets it."

"I must speak with her personally."

"You're a foreigner. By your accent. A foreigner."

"We're old friends."

The old man peered out and examined Marcus' clothing. He noted the tradesman's patch sewn onto the tunic. "You're a stonecutter. What's Lady Miryam got to do with a common stonecutter?"

"The clothes are borrowed."

"I'll not go interrupting her when she's in there listening to the Teacher!"

"Tell her Marcus Longinus is at the gate with a message for the Teacher."

"Everybody's got some message for him . . . "

Marcus held up a shiny silver coin. "How's this for your trouble?"

"Why didn't you say so?" The man took the coin and slammed the window shut.

Ten minutes passed before Miryam appeared at the opening. One glance and she laughed. "Marcus! Oh, Marcus!" She unlatched the bolt and threw the door wide for him. "Come in! Come in! Hurry! The most wonderful thing, Marcus!" She took his hands and pulled him into the courtyard. "Yeshua's here!"

"I know," he said quietly. "That's why I've come."

"Well then. Come on! He's teaching! Right here in our house. Oh, Marcus! I'm so glad you've come!" She kissed his cheek and embraced him.

She could not know how her touch coursed through him. Stepping back, he averted his eyes from her. But the image of her smiling face burned on his retina like a lighted candle.

"No. Miryam."

"You've missed supper. He's taken a break, but he's been teaching. All about Avraham! Oh, Marcus!"

"Listen. I can't stay. I . . . I was here this afternoon. I heard him."

"What? Here? Where?"

"So many people."

"But why didn't you come to me?"

"I thought it better not to. I'm out of favor with Pilate. I didn't want to risk . . . for your sake. For Yeshua's sake."

She said cautiously. "We're being watched."

"You know?"

"Everywhere he goes. It's hard to miss."

"Then you know why I'm here. Look." Marcus put a hand on her arm and held her in his direct gaze. "I wasn't expecting to find him here today. Not so close to Jerusalem. Not expecting the crowds. I . . . I'm on my way to Alexandria. But I saw twenty men in the crowd today who I know would kill a man for half a denarius. There's surely a higher bounty than that on the head of Yeshua. Those men weren't all here to-day just to learn."

"But they heard him all the same."

"If they were listening."

She hesitated, as if his destination had just struck her. "Alexandria? You're leaving?" There was disappointment in her voice. "For long?"

"No. I hope not."

She took his hand. "Marcus . . . dangerous times. Don't you feel it? I do. Every day. I'm frightened sometimes. Even though he tells us not to be. Still I feel it closing in. I'm afraid for him. Afraid for us, too . . . if something happened to him. Where would we go?"

"That's why I came here. To warn you . . . to warn Yeshua. He's not safe here in Judea. What happened to the Baptizer could happen to him. It *will* happen if he stays here."

"He knows that. We all know it. Today? Well, you heard them. They're hoping he'll fade away."

"He won't fade away. Not ever, Miryam. But I've seen rivalry before. In Rome. When I was in Syria, General Germanicus was poisoned by someone in his own household. Germanicus was a good man. A young man, too. Grandson of Augustus. Should have been emperor. Instead we got Tiberius. And Tiberius gave us Sejanus, who puts men like Pilate in place to rule Judea.

"Good men—men like Yeshua—don't usually come out the winner. Mostly they don't, from what I've seen. Men like Yeshua play by different rules than men like Caiaphas or Herod Antipas."

"Fifty days from today will be Pentecost," Miryam said. "He intends to go up to Yerushalayim for the feast."

"Talk to his *talmidim*. See if they can convince him otherwise. Keep him out of sight," Marcus insisted.

"Wait here, Marcus." She kissed his cheek and nudged him to sit on the rim of the fountain. Leaving him there, she vanished into the house, emerging moments later with Yeshua at her side.

Marcus stood at attention and clapped his fist against his chest in a Roman salute of authority.

In return Yeshua embraced him, kissing him on each cheek in greeting. "Shalom, friend."

"Shalom, Rabbi." Marcus was unable to raise his eyes to meet Yeshua's searching gaze. The Teacher somehow spoke without words, illuminating Marcus' soul. Such knowledge left Marcus speechless and awkward.

"You've risked much to come here, Centurion," Yeshua said kindly. "What is it you wish to tell me?"

"You . . . already know . . . don't you?" Marcus fixed his eyes on Yeshua's hands. Square, calloused hands. The hands of a laborer.

"Yes. But it was good of you to come, Marcus. To warn me."

"The opposition grows more dangerous every day. I saw assassins in the crowd today."

"Yes." Yeshua smiled and clapped Marcus on the shoulder. "But it's Shabbat. And the first day of the fifty days of Omer. Miryam, Marcus Longinus is a stranger in our midst. He is in need of shelter and mercy."

It was clear Miryam understood Yeshua's intention. "Come in, Marcus . . . Ushpizin. Join us and welcome."

And so the wind of longing was invited to come among the scholars. "Thank you, Rabbi." Marcus saluted again. He was aware that he was the lone non-Jew in the villa tonight.

Yeshua left them standing alone and walked toward the light. Miryam's sister, Marta, intercepted Him at the doorway. With an angry glance toward Miryam she protested, "All day my sister's been sitting at your feet while you teach. And I'm left to do everything! Rabbi! Don't you care that my sister's left me to do all the work by myself? Tell her to help me!"

"Marta, Marta." Yeshua put His finger on the woman's cheek as though speaking to a young child. His voice was calm, quiet. As if He had not just been told there was a price on His head or that murderers were plotting to take His life. It was as though nothing was more important than answering the anxiety and frustration of the woman who stood before Him. "You're worried and upset about many things. Many things. But only one thing is needed. Miryam has chosen what's better, and it won't be taken away from her."[21]

Marta covered her face with her hands at His gentle rebuke.

"This way." Yeshua spun Marta around and nudged her into the room, leaving Miryam and Marcus alone beside the fountain.

Miryam blushed. "Marta." She shrugged. "She's still Marta. But it's getting easier."

"Are you happy, Miryam?" He wanted to ask her if she thought of him, ever missed him, ever remembered. But he held his tongue.

"I *am* . . . happy, I mean." She did not ask how Marcus felt. Perhaps she knew he had not stopped loving her. That he loved her more now than ever.

She touched his cheek. "They're calling us. He's about to begin."

There was so much he wished he could say to her. An awkward silence followed as they simply searched one another's eyes. What would she do if he took her in his arms, kissed her as he used to kiss her?

She broke his reverie. "Come on then. When he teaches sometimes he goes all night. And no one wants the sun to come up."

Marcus followed her into the crowded room. At the curious stares of Yeshua's close circle of disciples, Marcus lagged behind, taking a place at the back, near the door. Miryam moved to the front and resumed her seat.

Marcus recognized each of Yeshua's disciples. Only Judas was missing from them. In a seat of honor was Zadok, Chief Shepherd of the flocks, nearest Yeshua. His three small boys were asleep: one on either side and the youngest in his arms. There was Nakdimon ben Gurion near El'azar, Miryam's brother.

Nakdimon glared at Marcus. It was clear Nakdimon, who had seen Marcus wielding a Roman sword in the previous day's slaughter, assumed Marcus was an enemy of Yeshua. But Zadok, seeing Marcus from across the room, hailed him broadly. Surprise registered on Nakdimon's face.

And then Yeshua began to teach them. "My friends." He addressed Zadok directly. "What you've said in the dark will be heard in the daylight, and what you have whispered in the ear in the inner rooms will be proclaimed from the rooftops."[22]

Zadok's face clouded with emotion at these words. As if he and Yeshua shared a mystery about to be publicly revealed.

Yeshua continued with His gaze fixed on Marcus. "I tell you, my friends, don't be afraid of those who can kill the body and after that can do no more. I'll show you whom you should fear. Fear him who, after killing the body, has the authority to cast you into hell. Yes, I tell you, fear him." Now He inclined his head toward Zadok's three boys. "Aren't five sparrows sold for two pennies? Yet not one of them is forgotten by God. Indeed, the very hairs of your head are numbered. Don't be afraid. You're worth more than many sparrows."[23]

Marta, dirty dishes forsaken, inched nearer and seated herself beside Miryam to listen at Yeshua's feet.

"I tell you, whoever acknowledges me before men, the Son of Man will also acknowledge him before the angels of God. And anyone who speaks a word against the Son of Man will be forgiven. But anyone who blasphemes the Ruach HaKodesh, the Holy Spirit, will not be forgiven." To Zadok again, "When you are brought before synagogues, rulers, and authorities, don't worry about how you will define yourselves or what you will say, for the Holy Spirit will teach you in that moment what you should say."[24]

THE LESSONS CONTINUED for three hours. Tonight Yeshua taught about Abraham and the miraculous birth of the promised son, Isaac. Meaning upon meaning was revealed in the story. Marcus listened in wonder as the Rabbi answered questions, peeling away layer after layer until at last the heart of the lesson was revealed.

"Mercy," said Yeshua. "*Chesed.* God's Mercy toward mankind. And man's mercy toward others. This is the first commandment of Torah."

And then the session ended with a benediction and a song. Marcus, who did not know the words, simply bowed his head and waited until they were dismissed.

That night Marcus slept in the stable. Twice he rose and stood in the darkness outside the house. Crickets fiddled in the grass. A night bird sang beneath the eaves.

He watched the window of Miryam's room until the candle burned out.

hat watch was it? Somewhere between the deepest darkness and first light. Peniel sensed that someone was near. Standing at the entrance. Waiting.

Was he asleep?

A chill of excitement coursed through him. He tried to move Gershon's bowl so the visitor would have a place to sit. But he could not move. He shivered and murmured, *"U-lu Ush-pi-zin!"*

The leather curtain that covered the entrance rustled as a hand drew it back. The aroma of flowers scented the tiny cubicle. Who had entered his hut tonight? What exile of Israel had come to comfort Peniel the blind beggar, Peniel the exile?

The Torah reading for Omer had been about Father Abraham. Details of the passage sprang first to Peniel's mind. He was filled with questions! How he longed to hear the story of Israel's redemption from the beginning!

A strong, mellow voice sighed his name. *Peniel.*

Peniel could not move. He felt warmth. Peace all around him. A dream? "I have a little bread. Take it. It's for you."

Peniel, Adonai has heard your prayer.

"I want to know the why!"

The prophecies are recorded in Torah and Tanakh. His plan of redemption. His love and mercy for mankind. The thoughts of El'Elyon, written down for all to read.

"I can't read. My eyes are blind. But my heart longs to see."

As did mine. Very long ago in a distant land.

"Avraham?"

I was Avram in those days before Adonai changed my name to Avraham. A shepherd over my father's flocks. In a land where a hundred idols were worshipped and sacrificed to. Each night I looked into the heavens and knew that all things were created by only One. That there was no other god but Adonai.

One night Adonai said to me, "Leave your country, your people, and your father's household and go to the land I will show you. I will make you into a great nation and I will bless you. I will make your name great, and you will be a blessing. I will bless those who bless you, and whoever curses you I will curse. And all peoples on earth will be blessed through you."[25]

I was seventy-five years old when Adonai sent me out from my country and father's house. And I gladly went to seek Adonai Elohim's face . . . Peniel."

"That's my name."

Be true to your name. Seek Adonai Elohim's face alone.

"I will."

Then your heart will see Him.

"Like you saw him? Tell me! Tell me!"

Peniel heard a wind in the trees. He sensed the hot sun on his face. Peniel was someplace. Someplace else. Not Jerusalem. The sheep were restless in their pens.

Abraham spoke: *It was near the great trees of Mamre, while I was sitting at the entrance to my tent in the heat of the day. I was one hundred years old. Still without a son. Without hope. I looked up and saw three men standing nearby. And I knew Adonai had come and where He had been sent from. I ran to meet them and bowed myself low to the ground.*

I said, "If I have found favor in Your eyes, my Lord, do not pass Your servant by. You may wash Your feet and rest yourselves beneath this tree. Let me get You something to eat so You can be refreshed and then go on Your way."

"Very well," they answered, "do as you say."

So I hurried to the tent to tell Sarai. Bread, curds and milk, a fine calf—all these things were prepared and set before them. While they ate, I stood near them under a tree.

"Where is your wife, Sarai?" they asked me.

"There in the tent."

Then Adonai said, "I will surely return to you about this time next year and Sarai, your wife, will have a son."

Now Sarai was listening at the entrance of the tent which was behind me. Sarai laughed since she was far past the age of childbearing. "After I am worn out and my master is old, will I now have this pleasure?"

Then Adonai said to me, "Why did Sarai laugh? Is anything too hard for Adonai? I will return to you at the appointed time next year, and Sarai will have a son. And you will call him Yitz'chak. I will establish my covenant with him as an everlasting covenant for his descendants after him."

And so it came to pass exactly as Adonai declared. Sarai bore the promised son of Adonai Elohim's blessing within the year. And so the nation of Israel began. We named the baby Yitz'chak, which means "he will laugh."[26]

Peniel frowned. "Why such a name?"

Because Adonai Most High, El'Elyon, laughs at all who do not believe His promise! Nothing is too hard for Him. He will bless the nations through Yitz'chak's descendants. There is only one plan. Only one promise. Only one Israel. Only one Adonai Elohim, Adonai, Adonai! Only one Son of the Most High, our Messiah!

"When will Messiah come?"

Redemption is near. He stands at the very gates. Freedom is the crown He wears. By His wounds we will be healed. There is healing, mercy, and forgiveness for all who call on His name!

"What is his name?"

Immanu'el! God is with us! Yeshua! Adonai Elohim is Savior!

"But Father Avraham! How will he save us?"

Is anything too hard for Adonai Elohim?

"A Roman governor rules us! Herod Antipas is not a Jew! We're slaves in our own land!"

Is anything too hard for Adonai Elohim?

"Our high priests are corrupt! The religious rulers have been appointed by the Romans for the last hundred years! Yerushalayim is controlled by evil men!"

Is anything too hard . . . for Adonai Elohim?

"Listen to the mourners in the streets! Doesn't Adonai hear his people?"

Peniel had gone too far. Pushed too hard. The night became still.

"Avraham! Sir! Tell me! Tell me when. When?"

There was no reply. The curtain stirred. The Ushpizin had gone. Peniel slipped into a dreamless slumber.

IN DAYLIGHT, IN PUBLIC, MARCUS WOULD NOT acknowledge Miryam, lest her reputation be called into question. He knew that the woman who used to be a harlot had been changed forever by Yeshua. But he did not know if the rest of Bethany was certain of it yet. So they had said their farewells last night. Marcus contented himself now with standing near her in the synagogue.

The synagogue in Bethany was small, nowhere near big enough to hold all those who wanted to hear Yeshua of Nazareth speak. Those who got seats had arrived well before daybreak. By the time the *hazzan* blew his trumpet to announce the time for services, the benches and aisles were full to bursting.

The rest of the crowd flowed out the doors onto the steps, hung around the windows, or waited outside while those in front repeated what had been said.

Marcus, pressed against a wall, could clearly see Miryam and the three boys who belonged to Zadok.

The trio of boys was lucky. Since El'azar was one of the elders of the Bethany congregation, his sisters, Miryam and Marta, had reserved seats in the women's section. Avel, as Miryam's guest, was beside her with Ha-or Tov and Emet.

Two men dressed in rich garments flanked the reading lectern at the front of the chamber. One, a Pharisee named Ezra, was young and thin-faced; the other, gray-haired and fleshy. Marcus had seen the older man before. He was Alexander, brother-in-law of the high priest. The two men, though from opposing sects, looked equally uncomfortable in the cramped surroundings and equally scornful of the mob of commoners assembled to hear Yeshua.

And where was the Rabbi from Nazareth? Instead of being seated in a place of honor facing the congregation, Yeshua sat on a side bench about a third of the way back. Around Him gathered farmers and fishermen, carters and herdsmen, stonecutters and carpenters.

Marcus saw Miryam pat Avel's arm. She squeezed between two other women, calling, "I'll be right back." He spotted Miryam leading someone by the hand, parting the crowd with a soft word. Then Miryam returned to her place with a woman dressed in black, who most closely resembled the stump of a grapevine's trunk.

What her name was scarcely anybody remembered any more. Everyone in the village of Bethany called her Taltal, meaning "curl."

Taltal was not as old as everyone thought. Sometime in her eighteenth year she had awakened with a severe cramp in her neck and the inability to lift her chin off her chest. Each year since then, for the past eighteen, her debility had grown progressively worse, until now her spine was so bent that her nose approached her knees. She ate her meals standing up because when she sat, her head was below the table. She was in constant pain of body and heart because the ruder children of the village called her a witch, pretending to be frightened of her when she approached.

Apparently Taltal was continuing an earlier protest. "No, no, my dear," she remarked to Miryam. "Give my place to someone else. It doesn't matter where I stand, for I can't see the speakers anyway."

"But you need to be where you can hear properly," Miryam replied firmly. "You stay right here next to me."

After a pair of benedictions were intoned, the Shema was recited by the whole congregation.

"Hear, O Israel! The Lord our God is one Lord; the Lord is One. You shall love the Lord your God with all your heart and with all your soul and with all your strength."

Since this was the first Sabbath after the beginning of Passover, it marked the beginning of the Omer: the counting of the seven weeks and one day until Shavuot . . . Pentecost . . . and its commemoration of the giving of the Law on Sinai.

"Praised are you, O Lord, our God, Ruler of the Universe, who has sanctified us with his commandments, commanding us to count the Omer."

Alexander was called to read from the scroll of the prophet Isaiah.

"See, a king will reign in righteousness
and rulers will rule with justice.
Each man will be like a shelter from the wind
and a refuge from the storm.

like streams of water in the desert
and the shadow of a great rock in a thirsty land."[27]

Then came the moment for which the multitude was assembled: Yeshua was asked to come forward and offer a commentary on what had been read.

"A king will rule in righteousness," Yeshua repeated. "What is the Kingdom of God like?" He asked His audience. "What shall I compare it to? It is like a mustard seed, which a man took and planted in his garden. It grew and became a tree, and the birds of the air perched in its branches."[28]

Marcus liked that image. He knew that mustard seeds were tiny, yet when they sprouted they could grow to enormous size.

Continuing the word picture of seeds, Yeshua said, "The Kingdom of God is like a man who sowed good seeds in his fields. But while everyone was sleeping, his enemy came and sowed weeds among the wheat, and went away. When the wheat sprouted and formed heads, then the weeds also appeared. The owner's servants came to him and said, 'Sir, didn't you sow good seed in your field? Where then did the weeds come from?'

"'An enemy did this,' he replied.

"The servants asked him, 'Do you want us to go and pull them up?'

"'No,' he answered, 'because while you are pulling the weeds, you may root up the wheat with them. Let both grow together until harvest. At that time I will tell the harvesters: First collect the weeds and tie them in bundles to be burned; then gather the wheat and bring it into my barn.'"[29]

Marcus imagined Yeshua's parable was meant to be a warning: Do not think that because someone appears upright and pious that he or she really is godly. Of course it was also a warning to the "weeds": Look out! Your deception will not succeed forever!

The religious leaders stirred uneasily in their seats. Scowls deepened as Yeshua continued.

"Another farmer went out to sow his seed. As he was scattering the seed, some fell along the path, and the birds came and ate it up. Some fell on rocky places, where it did not have much soil. It sprang up quickly, because the soil was shallow. But when the sun came up, the plants were scorched, and they withered because they had no root.

Other seed fell among thorns, which grew up and choked the plants. Still other seed fell on good soil, where it produced a crop—a hundred, sixty, or thirty times what was sown. He who has ears, let him hear."[30]

Marcus nodded his comprehension. Yeshua's parables showed how closely connected to the *am ha aretz*, the people of the land, He was. And they responded to His familiar portrayals as well.

"Don't just count each day of the Omer like spilling seeds through your fingers," Yeshua warned them. "It is said that every day of the Omer is meant to be a day of preparation for receiving the Law at Shavuot. Our forefathers, even after being freed from slavery, had to travel in the desert, learning many things, before they were prepared to receive the Law.

"And every seven-day cycle of the Omer," He added, "reminds us of seven important things. Every Sabbath speaks to us of the most important part of the Law. Love, or the way it is expressed to others: *Chesed*, mercy. And the Sabbath rest is all about mercy . . . the mercy of God when we are instructed to rest from our labors and remember that the Sabbath is holy to the Lord.

"It is said that every Sabbath of the Omer is represented by one of the patriarchs, the first of whom is Avraham. This is altogether fitting because the story of Avraham and the Son of Promise is entirely about Mercy . . . mercy to give Avraham and Sarai the son of their old age, and . . . mercy because although Avraham was obedient to God, even to the sacrifice of Yitz'chak, God's Mercy intervened, and a substitute was found and will be found."

Everyone nodded and smiled. This was comfortable and familiar territory. Well-reasoned, too: The first remembrance called to mind by the counting of the Omer was Abraham, and thinking about Abraham reminded a listener of the Mercy of God.

"And mercy," Yeshua instructed them, "is required in your hearts before you can learn any other lessons of the Kingdom. Without mercy, your hearts will be like the stony ground, on which the seed of the Kingdom withered and died. The Law and the Prophets continued until the time of Yochanan the Baptizer. But now the Kingdom of God is at hand."[31]

Now? Did He say now? A buzz ran through the assembly. The Kingdom of God was to be ushered in by the coming of Messiah. Till then it was a concept, a vision of Paradise awaiting a future fulfillment. But

Yeshua seemed to say that the moment was near, perhaps already on the doorstep. The crowd grew restless; some looked shocked.

Then Yeshua did something else completely unexpected. Leaving the platform where He had been speaking, He made His way through the crowd, all the way to the back, where the women's section was located.

There He turned in at Miryam's row. Smiling at the boys, He reached past them to grasp Taltal's hand. As the onlookers moved aside to give Him room, Yeshua crouched even lower than the crippled woman until He could gaze up into her face.

"Come with me," He said. And He led Taltal up to the bema. Once both were on the platform, a hush of expectancy fell over the room. What was He going to do?

"Woman," Yeshua said in a loud voice, "you are set free from your infirmity." Then He put His hands on her. Immediately she straightened up![32]

There was no hesitancy, no testing to see if muscles long tightly coiled would spring back. Taltal stood erect at once . . . face-to-face with Yeshua.

"Praise God!" she shouted, laughing. "Praise and glory to his name!"

The woman was truly beautiful, Marcus thought, with marvelous, sparkling eyes and wide smile. Her countenance radiated joy every way she turned. Though no one had looked her in the face for eighteen years, Taltal returned blessing for abuse, showering them with a picture of the Mercy of God.

Then, amid the flurry of wonder and praise, a harsh, grating bellow broke through. Alexander, jowls quivering, stood at the edge of the platform and shook his fist. "Aren't there six days for work? Come and be healed on those days, not on the Sabbath!"

Behind Alexander, the Pharisee nodded his agreement.

If Alexander expected that his reputation, his connections, or the superiority of his piety would cow Yeshua, he was sadly mistaken. Marcus saw the man take rapid steps backwards when Yeshua advanced on him.

"You hypocrites!" Yeshua shouted in Alexander's face and past the man toward the younger Pharisee. "Doesn't each of you on the Sabbath untie his *ox* . . . or his *donkey* . . . from the stall and lead it out to give it water? Then should not this woman . . . a daughter of Avraham, a daughter of God's Mercy . . . whom Satan has kept bound for eighteen long years, be set free on the Sabbath day from what bound *her?*"[33]

Loud cheering broke out in the synagogue!

What a terribly ironic comparison, Marcus thought. Some people who pretend to be godly have more concern for their animals than they do for people. And they hide their cruelty behind laws that God never meant to be used to abuse. They bury mercy beneath a mountain of pointless rules and empty commands.

Was this what Yeshua had meant when He told Marta that Miryam had chosen the most important thing to focus on? After all, that was the lesson of the Omer: No one could progress in understanding the Kingdom of God unless he first understood and practiced mercy!

Alexander, face mottled with rage and indignation, bustled out of the synagogue, even though the final benediction had not been given. Right behind him in his hasty exit were twenty religious leaders.

El'azar, Miryam's brother, stood to lead the recital of the hymn of the Omer, Psalm 67:

"May God be gracious to us and bless us
and make his face shine upon us,
that your ways may be known on earth,
your salvation among all nations.
May the peoples praise you, O God;
may all the peoples praise you.
May the nations be glad and sing for joy,
for you rule the peoples justly
and guide the nations of the earth.
May the peoples praise you, O God;
may all the peoples praise you.
Then the land will yield its harvest,
and God, our God, will bless us.
God will bless us,
and all the ends of the earth will fear him."[34]

MARCUS' THOUGHTS WERE a confused tangle. His mission to Alexandria and his personal safety seemed utterly insignificant next to the teaching and power wrapped up in Yeshua of Nazareth.

Yeshua was love and mercy in action: not just in good intentions, but in the Teacher's undeniable ability to carry out His plans. Yet He was much more than a miracle-working rabbi.

If Marcus could simply understand what it all meant.

But did anyone fully comprehend who Yeshua was? Marcus wondered. While Yeshua's *talmidim* did not act surprised when their master performed wonders, Marcus had seen them crowd around the Teacher, asking Him to clarify His words, explain His meanings.

This from those who lived with Him every day.

Nor could the disciples' lack of comprehension be assigned to a failure of their education. Even the learned Nakdimon ben Gurion seemed incapable of taking it in.

And many of the most educated, like Alexander and Ezra the Pharisee, rejected Yeshua altogether. They chose, in their pride, to refuse Him and His message because He did not match their image of Messiah. Yet Yeshua did not acknowledge the superiority of their piety. He did not prefer their company to that of the *am ha aretz*.

Yeshua enjoyed people. He enjoyed life. Nor did He reject those labeled "sinners" by the religious establishment.

Marcus had never seen such vehement mercy! Yeshua reserved His scorn and outright condemnation for those who put self-importance above showing kindness.

Yeshua was like a library of creation: every word a meaningful book. His every gesture spoke volumes; His every action was a new revelation.

Marcus suspected a lifetime of study would not be enough for him to comprehend it. All the scrolls of Alexandria could not provide enough paper and ink to record everything Yeshua said and did.

While Marcus stood at the back of the synagogue musing on these things, Zadok approached him.

"Centurion," Zadok said, drawing Marcus into a Torah-school classroom, "it isn't safe for y' to stand here openly. By your dress I recognize that you're hiding, and since it cannot be from us, it must be from your own people. And I reckon y' may be in trouble for helping me and the boys. For breaking the head of Vara on our behalf." The Chief Shepherd paused, then said, "Miryam of Magdala tells me you're bound for Alexandria."

Marcus replied, "I'm better served if no one knows my destination."

Zadok added, "Don't blame Miryam. I told her how y' saved my life and that of the boys. She said she fears you're in danger and asked if I could help . . . blurting out that you'd mentioned Alexandria."

"You do me a kindness if you forget you know where I am. It might be risky for you if anyone thinks you know my whereabouts."

Zadok shook his head. "Then let me say it this way: If y' find yourself going to Alexandria, would y' carry a message for me?"

"If I find myself in Alexandria, of course . . . "

"My brother," Zadok explained. "His name is Rabbi Onias. You'll find him in the quarter called the Delta, near the Canobus Canal. He lives behind a carpenter's shop. Now I won't be a moment."

From a bin of parchment scraps Zadok removed a bit of discarded schoolwork and a scrap of blue twine. The smooth side of the skins was covered with Torah lessons, copied from Scripture. The other face was rough, but free of marks. From a cupboard Zadok produced pen and ink and sat down at a long table to write.

When Zadok's pen finished moving, he laid it aside and reread his letter. Turning it over, he studied the childish scribbles recorded there, then grunted and said to Marcus, "Fitting. The lesson copied here is from the prophet Hosea." The Chief Shepherd quoted, *"Out of Egypt I called my son.'"*[35]

Marcus knew that what he had just heard was somehow connected with Yeshua. But how? "So much I don't understand, old man. So much about Yeshua. So much more I want to know. I offered him my sword. My life in his defense."

Zadok laid a finger on his scar and eyepatch. "There's no defendin' him. Y' cannot defend him. Keep your sword sheathed, Centurion. What's written'll come to pass. His teaching and miracles testify to the power of God. Other events, not yet accomplished, will forever speak of the price of God's love for us. Mercy is not without cost." Tightly rolling the bit of parchment, Zadok secured it with the blue twine and handed it to Marcus. "Here, then. For my brother. Tell him. Tell him what you've seen." The shepherd gestured toward the knot of friends gathered around Taltal. "Yes. Tell him. Onias'll know what it means."

PART II

For to us a child is born,
to us a son is given,
and the government will be on his shoulders.
And he will be called
Wonderful Counselor, Mighty God,
Everlasting Father, Prince of Peace.***

***WE WHO HAVE WALKED IN DARKNESS HAVE
    SEEN A GREAT LIGHT;
   ON ALL WHO LIVED IN A LAND DARK AS DEATH,
   A LIGHT HAS DAWNED.

ISAIAH 9:6

10

anaen's head rocketed to the side from the impact of Vara's knuckles. "Who're you shielding?" Vara demanded for the twentieth time. "What's the connection to bar Abba? To Yeshua of Nazareth? Speak! Who's your contact?"

Spitting blood from his battered lips, Manaen coughed. "Don't know what . . . you're talking about. Almost killed by . . . rebels."

Vara's fist cracked against Manaen's rib cage. "You were seen leaving the rebel house with someone. Who? If you're innocent, then tell me."

Peniel would never survive such a beating, Manaen thought. The blind boy's safety lay in his anonymity. Nor would revealing Peniel's identity secure Manaen's release. This accusation was encouraged by Demos; admitting that Manaen had hidden any information would make things worse.

"You're wrong. Nobody."

"But you know the Galilean preacher?" Vara insisted, striking Manaen in the back of the neck. "Why did you go to Beth-Anyah? To warn him?"

"Everyone . . . went to . . . "

Another blow, this time to Manaen's kidney. Writhing in pain, he sagged on the chains.

"No excuses!" Vara warned. "I have what I need to convict you of treason and have you crucified."

"Still . . . couldn't tell you . . . what I don't know . . . ," Manaen panted.

Vara muttered, "All right. I'll leave you to think it over. I won't have any trouble finding you again, will I?"

THE DAY AFTER SHABBAT MARCUS REACHED THE end of the road connecting Jerusalem with the Valley of Sorek and the port city of Ashkelon, birth-place of Herod the Great. After the recent spring rains, even the canyoned interior of Judea was verdant, but the seashore plain burst with lush greens and the first hints of orange poppies. Rolling hills covered with oaks and olive groves reluctantly displayed occasional outcroppings of the whitest limestone. Vertical pillars of rock, gleaming like marble, made the emerald quality of the landscape all that much more pro-nounced. Stands of ripening barley stood next to already harvested flax fields, like a barber's customers waiting their turns to be shorn.

Nearer the shore, stands of date palms pointed the way toward the harbor.

It was no wonder that the now-vanished Philistines had chosen to establish the Pentapolis, the five cities of their confederation, in this corner of the Mediterranean coast. Known as the Sea People, the Philistines had been the subject of stories Miryam had told him. Their evenings together seemed so long ago, and yet he could remember everything about them.

Many of the narratives recounted as Marcus had lounged in Miryam's villa concerned a Jewish hero named Samson, who always seemed to be fighting Philistines, including taking his revenge in the Valley of Sorek by tying torches to the tails of foxes and setting them loose in the Philistines' barley. Marcus had laughed and laughed at that one.

And Samson, legendary strongman that he was, reportedly carried away the city of Gaza: doors, posts, and bar. Later, it was also in Gaza that the blinded Samson pulled down the pagan temple on the heads of the Philistines . . . and himself.

And of Ashkelon Miryam related that Samson had beaten and robbed thirty of their men in a fit of irritation because they had coerced the answer to a riddle out of Samson's Philistine betrothed.

Miryam had also acted out the part of Samson's temptress, Delilah. She had shown Marcus what Delilah had done to tease Samson into such a frenzy of desire that he unwisely revealed the secret of his strength.[36]

Remembering Miryam then, in the flickering light of the oil lamps—her skin glowing and the scent of her perfume wafting over him—Marcus could easily imagine how Samson had succumbed. . . .

Marcus shook his head to wake up from the vision. That relationship with Miryam was over and done. It was no use tormenting himself with something he could never have.

Marcus returned to his contemplation of the countryside, compelling himself to evaluate the setting with a view toward its military qualities. He took refuge from his personal longings in the enforced discipline of an old campaigner.

Marcus knew that Ashkelon had always been the key to the conquest of the southwestern seaboard of Judea. The pharaohs of Egypt, the Assyrians, the Babylonians, the Chaldeans, the Scythians, the Ptolemies, the Seleucids, and the Jewish Maccabees had each in turn conquered and then exercised authority over Ashkelon until, wisely perhaps, the inhabitants had not waited to be subjugated yet again. They had deliberately asked for the protection of Rome over a hundred years earlier.

It might represent the longest period of peace Ashkelon has ever enjoyed, Marcus thought. *Not everything about Imperial policy is bad.*

It was a curious thought for a centurion of a provincial legion to have. Until recently his reflection would not have admitted that the Empire was *ever* wrong in its treatment of subject peoples.

Perhaps it was a belated influence bequeathed by his captured Briton princess mother.

Perhaps it was the yearning for freedom in the tales recounted by Miryam.

And perhaps Yeshua of Nazareth had something to do with it as well.

Resolutely Marcus set the idea aside and resumed his study of the surroundings. He could see at a glance why Ashkelon had been so easily taken: Open to attack from both land and sea, it had no natural defenses, no rocky ridges or rivers that could be secured. A walled city was an impressive sight but could be starved into submission.

Apparently the Ashkelonites thought more of their bellies than their liberty. They had even torn down the wall.

With the same lavish hand that marked all the elder Herod's building projects, Ashkelon was parklike in the extreme. Herod spared no expense, honoring himself by honoring his birthplace. Steam rose from the marble precincts of a public bathhouse built over natural hot springs. Cool water cascaded over interlocking circlets of stone basins, surmounted by a life-sized statue of Herod.

A grassy knoll that rose from a palisade of palms turned out to be the embankment of an amphitheater, ringed by marble statuary. A statue of the Egyptian goddess Isis kept easy company with a seated figure of Olympian Zeus, and next to him a rendering of winged Victory. A low block, used as a bench, depicted Hadad-rimmon, the thunder god worshipped by some of Marcus' Syrian troopers.

And the Philistines, according to Miryam, had worshipped Beelzebub, the Lord of the Flies.

Ashkelon's every subduer had left behind tokens of their religion. No wonder the place was avoided by pious Jews like Nakdimon ben Gurion and Yeshua of Nazareth.

Past the amphitheater the highway spilled into a central plaza, which in turn opened onto a view of the harbor. Just coming into sight across an expanse of dark blue water was a Roman galley with a double bank of oars.

Marcus had timed his journey to match that of the warship that would carry him to Alexandria. He watched and listened with approval as the sailing master bellowed, "Out oars!" and seventy-two pairs of oars lifted from the sea at precisely the same instant. The galley, being of the lightest class of Roman warship and with a shallow draft, was able to slide directly up onto the shelf of Ashkelon's sandy beach. A gangplank was thrust forward from the decking on the starboard side of the prow.

The *Livia* had arrived.

THE BUSINESS OF HEROD ANTIPAS' COURT CONTINUED even in Jerusalem. Suppliants came to the Hasmonean Palace to beg favors, settle disputes, and seek posts as tax collectors or civil servants within the tetrarch's provinces.

After Manaen's arrest, Susanna had come to wait in the crowded antechamber of the judgment hall. Antipas and Herodias knew she was there, knew what she wanted. But they refused to hear her petition on Manaen's behalf.

Still Susanna came. Still she waited among rich and poor to present her petition.

Today the sun was low in the west. All the other cases had been heard. Susanna sat alone on a hard bench across from a peasant woman from the Galil who had come to see Antipas over settlement of her husband's will.

A strange irony, Susanna thought, *that anyone would come to Herod Antipas with an expectation of receiving justice.* The best anyone could hope for would be that tears and pleading might somehow move him to make a public show of his benevolence and mercy, though she knew Antipas did not comprehend either virtue.

Yet Susanna, for Manaen's sake, would humble herself before the ruler and his consort. As for showing Antipas her tears, that would not be difficult. She had fought to maintain control since word of Manaen's imprisonment had first reached her. Tears would come easily if common sense failed to turn the tetrarch's hard heart.

Reason would be Susanna's first line of defense.

Surely Antipas knew that Manaen's presence at the gathering to hear the Nazarene was simply a matter of curiosity. Had not everyone gone out to hear Yeshua? to measure the Teacher's response to the tragedy in Jerusalem? to seek solace in the loss of loved ones?

Why should Manaen be prosecuted as a criminal when he merely stood among thousands of other onlookers that day? When Manaen had just buried his cherished servant, why would he not go to Bethany to hear if the words of Yeshua contained any comfort? Manaen had not meant disrespect toward the majesty of Herod Antipas! Disloyalty had not been in his heart or mind! He was a loyal subject, a true brother to the tetrarch and to Herodias.

These facts Susanna would lay at the tetrarch's judgment seat on Manaen's behalf. She had rehearsed her speech a hundred times, trying out phrases, turning the words over and over in her mind.

At last the widow was called into Antipas' presence. Susanna smiled and gave her a nod of encouragement.

Once again Susanna was left alone. Sunlight faded. The anteroom grew dim.

At last the widow returned, grinning, trembling, proclaiming loudly what a just and righteous ruler Herod Antipas was: "A Daniel! A Solomon! Truly a great and mighty prince among princes!"

Susanna stood and expectantly approached the guards at the door of the judgment hall.

A lance blocked her entry. "Does he know I'm still here?" she asked.

"He knows, Lady." The Samaritan guard did not look at her.

"Does he know I'm the only one left?"

"He knows, Lady."

"And that I've been waiting for two days?"

"He knows all that, Lady."

"Will he see me then? Will he hear my plea?"

"The session has ended, Lady. The tetrarch and his wife have left the courtroom. They'll be having supper privately tonight."

CHAPTER 11

I t was a whisper; a rumor. Peniel heard it as he sat on the steps of Nicanor.

"He is arrested . . ."

"Manaen bar Talmai. He was in the pottery shop with the rebels. Seen leaving the place with one other. Escaped. Now Manaen is in prison."

"Herod Antipas himself gave the order."

"But the one he was with . . . a scrawny youth, they say . . . he's still at large!"

"No doubt Manaen is guilty of aiding the rebels. Helping the one escape."

"No doubt. Guilty. In prison, isn't he? Arrested. That proves his guilt. Would Antipas throw one of his own in jail if he wasn't guilty? Yes. Everyone knows how he resents the tetrarch."

"Manaen attacked his own brother. Tried to kill Demos!"

"Manaen was seen in the company of Yeshua after Lord Antipas gave him orders not to leave Yerushalayim!"

"He's done for then."

"Praetorian Vara is interrogating witnesses at the Antonia Fortress."

"Has Vara found his accomplice?"

"Not yet. But he will."

Peniel was silent and solemn at this news. He did not ask for alms all day. Instead he listened, sorted through the rumors, and came to the conclusion that the accomplice Praetorian Vara sought was probably him.

Peniel decided he must set the Roman authorities straight. Manaen was no more a conspirator than Peniel was!

Arrested? For what? It was crazy! Manaen had been beaten. Bound. He would have burned to death if Peniel had not cut the ropes on his wrists!

Peniel considered how he could best help Manaen. The Antonia Fortress was at the far side of the Temple. Occupied by Roman soldiers, who could look down onto the sacred mountain, Antonia was both hated and feared by Jews. Within its walls were barracks, a dungeon, and a room where the vestments of the Jewish high priest were kept. The possession of the holy garments was proof that Caiaphas was under the control of Rome, some said.

No matter. Peniel would carry the truth to those who had misunderstood about Manaen. He would explain to them the way it had happened.

Peniel made his way toward the stronghold. He would speak to Praetorian Vara. Tell him everything about that night. Manaen had truly been a captive of the insurgents, not one of their number! Surely Vara would listen to reason and Manaen would be released.

When he asked for help finding the Antonia, everyone shunned him. At last a small boy took his hand and guided him to the entrance. Peniel heard Roman voices talking to one another from within the building.

He called in to them, "Hey, there! Shalom! Hey! Can you help me? I've come to speak to the officer in charge of everything! I've got information about the rebels who died in the pottery shop!"

A Samaritan accent attached to an acrid body odor demanded, "An informant, are you?"

"I've got information."

"You're a beggar."

"Yes, sir," Peniel replied respectfully, though the guard seemed extraordinarily stupid.

"Blind."

"Yes, sir."

The guard laughed. "Just the sort of witness Rome finds useful."

"Yes. I can help."

"What good are you?"

"Ask . . . ask . . . Tribune Felix," Peniel said, remembering the conversation between Manaen and his Roman friend.

"How'd you know that name then?"

"Tribune Felix was at the pottery shop. He'll remember me."

"Wait."

Minutes passed. Peniel recognized the voice of Felix as he emerged from the Antonia.

"That'll be all," Felix said, dismissing the guard. Then to Peniel he said, "You! What are you, crazy? Coming here?"

Felix's strong, rough fingers dug into Peniel's arm. He dragged the youth to one side, beneath an echoing colonnade. He shoved him against a pillar and whispered urgently, "You, boy! What do you want?"

"I came to speak with the Praetorian. Vara."

A shake. "You want to die?"

"No, sir. No, Tribune Felix. I heard that your friend Manaen is arrested."

"What's that to you?"

"He's not a sicarius. That's the truth."

"What's truth got to do with it?"

"Somebody ought to know."

"Vara has the authority of Governor Pilate behind him now. He does what he wants and calls it justice for the good of Rome. He's on a hunt. I can't stop him. Truth won't stop him. Listen, you. You want to live? Forget you were ever there that night. Good thing Vara's gone, or you'd already be hanging from chains in a cell."

"But your friend . . . Manaen . . . he's innocent."

"Manaen's guilty of other things. Stupidity for one."

"But not what they say he's guilty of."

"Boy! Vara will break your arms! Pluck your fingernails out. Burn your eyes out if you had eyes! He'll turn you into a eunuch with his own knife . . . until you confess that Manaen is best friends with bar Abba and planned the whole riot. Truth is not the issue here. Finding a scapegoat is what matters. Scapegoat. A Jewish concept, right? Do you understand me?"

"No, sir."

"Then listen to this. If Vara gets his bloody hands on you, you'll die slowly on a cross. And you won't help Manaen. You can't help him.

He's where he is because he was foolish. Went someplace he wasn't supposed to go. Loved a girl he was forbidden to love. He's the second son of a man who died and left a great fortune. He has a brother who's a snake. It's not your business. So go. Back to wherever you came from. You show up on this side of the platform again and I'll personally see to it you're arrested." Felix spun Peniel around and booted him on the backside as if he were a dog to be driven away. "Go on! Get!"

Peniel got up and stood for a moment to get his bearings. The sounds of the Temple were ahead of him. He reached out and touched the cold stone of a pillar, then hurried away.

OF HEROD THE GREAT'S ADDITIONS TO JERUSALEM, the most Greek in architecture and Roman in spirit was the Hippodrome, where horse and chariot races were held. Located in the southwest quarter of the city, just to the south of Herod's own palace, the Hippodrome was a gigantic, double-decked oval. The ground floor was formed of narrow arched passageways to support the weight of the structure, while the upper story's arcade was more airy: wider arches interspersed with pillars. At intervals decorative towers, capped with red tile roofs, marked the wall.

Governor Pilate, guarded by a decurion and ten legionaries, stalked the uppermost tier of seats in the vacant stadium.

Praetorian Vara arrived, halting several paces away until summoned closer for a private conference.

"For the anniversary of Tiberius' coronation," Pilate mused aloud, "I'll stage the grandest four-day chariot races in the Empire. I'll import teams from Messina and Crete. No province anywhere will do more honor to the emperor than here in Judea." Drawing his attention back to the present, Pilate demanded, "What about Marcus Longinus? Has he been located?"

"Not yet, Excellency," Vara admitted. "I'm certain Tribune Felix knows more than he's telling. If you'd permit me to interrogate him—"

"Absolutely not," Pilate interrupted. "He may be a junior officer, but his uncle's a senator and the family has Imperial connections. You are not to bother the tribune unless you find him guilty of treason." Pilate resumed thinking aloud. "So we must assume that the centurion has escaped to Alexandria and conferred with Caligula."

"Not necessarily, Excellency," Vara corrected. "My source inside Herodium tells me that he saw Tribune Felix preparing a letter. He thinks it's intended for Marcus, and that can only be true if the centurion is still here in the province."

"Do you have the letter?"

"No, Excellency."

"Bah," Pilate scoffed.

"My search has been productive in other ways," Vara suggested. "More information about Marcus has come to light. He pardoned those shepherds who attacked the aqueduct builders . . . on his own authority he let them go free." The governor's face clouded, growing even more full of anger when Vara continued. "Clearly the lack of reprisal encouraged the rebels and the other protestors. And I have interrogated Manaen bar Talmai, Antipas' ward. He's shielding someone . . . perhaps it's Marcus. I'll get to the bottom of it yet."

"Antipas' ward?" Pilate mused. "Perhaps the tetrarch was behind the uprising. He started the Purim bread riots. Be just like that old fox to throw one of his own to the wolves to put us off the scent. No, Commander, Manaen bar Talmai is unimportant. Find our missing centurion; he's the one we want. And if he resists, kill him. Use every means possible."

Vara saluted and turned to leave, then added, "There's another piece of news: Herod Antipas is sending an assassin after that Galilean preacher, Yeshua."

Pilate frowned. Antipas not content with killing only one? This could mean more headaches for me."

"Not if it happens in the tetrarch's domain and away from Judea," Vara prompted. "Yeshua's a troublemaker, that's certain, gathering thousands of men in the wilderness. Better to chop off the head before the body is fully developed. Besides, any violence that results will be directed at Antipas."

"Thank you for your service, Praetorian," Pilate acknowledged. "I'll see that Prefect Sejanus is informed of your assistance."

THAT SAME EVENING DEMOS JOINED Antipas, Herodias, and Eglon in the judgment hall.

"Execute him," Demos insisted. "He's a threat to me. As long as he lives . . . a threat! His malice knows no limits, not even in obedience to you, Lord Antipas. You, his gracious benefactor."

Antipas inclined his head. His sagging jowls rested on a perfumed and manicured hand. "What do you say, Captain?" Antipas asked Eglon.

"Manaen's more than a danger to Demos, my lord. He's disloyal. Disloyal to the point of betraying you. You heard him. Rebellion. People lining their pockets. Does he mean you? Governor Pilate would make a meal fit for the emperor out of such an accusation. Pilate's looking for someone to blame for the riots. Certainly he'll name the rebels, but let a traitor like Manaen suggest that your troops acted wrongly and—"

"Manaen's family is well regarded by the emperor," Herodias hissed. "His lies might carry weight in Rome."

The oil lamps resting on wall sconces had not been trimmed before being hastily relit for this after-hours conference. As a result they sputtered and fumed, streaking the plaster with soot. The flickering light reaching the dais deepened Antipas' eye sockets and sharpened Herodias' nose and chin.

Rubbing his stubbled cheeks, Antipas declared, "There is something in what you say. I've had word that my half brother, Philip, is currying favor with certain factions in Rome. He would love to parade Manaen in front of the emperor if it would spite me. And we do not need the matter of the Baptizer brought up again. Somehow . . . connect this rebellion to the death of the Baptizer. Eh, Eglon?"

"So we're agreed then?" Demos asked eagerly. "Manaen will die?"

Antipas opened his mouth to speak, but Herodias commented scathingly, "Men! You listen, but you don't hear! Manaen's condemned by his own mouth. Let his punishment come from his own words as well." She paused as if her comments needed no explanation.

Eglon and Demos exchanged a glance but did not intrude on the silence. Herodias would clarify the meaning in her own time. Interrupting her dramatic moments was known to make her angry.

"Don't you understand?" she persisted. "He talked at length about what he saw. Well, he's seen too much! And Manaen suggested that a blind beggar is better treated than he is. . . . So be it! Put out his eyes."

Involuntarily Demos blinked and took a step backwards from the dais and away from Herodias.

Even Antipas leaned away from his bedmate.

She expanded her thoughts. "What use will a blind witness be to Pilate? to Philip? to Rome?"

Demos nodded his approval. "Susanna will have her blind beggar. We'll see how long her adoration lasts."

With the wind dead astern and the sail drawing full, the rowers slept on their oars. The muscle that drove the courier ship were all handpicked volunteers. They were not chained to their benches; nevertheless they were grateful for the respite.

A bright orange star that appeared on the southern horizon at midnight outshone all the other lights in the heavens. Marcus, a restless sailor at best, was pacing the gangway forward of the *Livia*'s lone mast when it blazed into view. He pointed it out to the sailing master and asked its name.

"Bless you, sir," the mariner replied. He was a Cypriot by birth and his Aramaic had a pronounced country twang, almost like a Galilean, Marcus thought. "That's not a star. That's Pharos, the lighthouse at Alexandria."

"Are we so close already then?" Marcus asked.

"Not a bit of it," was the chuckling reply. By the light of the lantern hanging nearby, Marcus saw his companion squint at the angle between the light and the horizon and gauge the distance before adding, "Still three hundred stadia off, I should judge. If this wind holds, we'll reach Alexandria by the middle of the morning watch. Not any too soon, neither," the sailing master said with an eye to the east. "There's a storm gathering over the desert."

Long before their arrival the ruddy gleam rose above the horizon and resolved itself into a mammoth tower surmounted by a blazing torch.

Their arrival worked out exactly as the sailor prophesied. Though the wind died away at dawn, then came round to blow out of the opposite quarter, the refreshed oarsmen propelled the slim craft through the calm seas with a speed even greater than they had been making with the breeze.

"Built by King Ptolemy, him that succeeded Alexander the Great. Put there over three hundred years ago," the sailing master supplied in answer to Marcus' query about the tower. "They say it's as tall as seventy men standing one atop the other. I've never climbed it myself, but you can do so if you've a mind."

By the time they gained the entrance to the harbor, Marcus had learned all about what was touted as one of the wonders of the world. The polished bronze panels behind the fire chamber reflected the blaze of several oxcarts of wood at a time, identifying the port to ships far out in the Great Sea. Some said the giant mirrors had been employed to send messages; others that a focused beam of its light could ignite the sails of enemy ships. It was claimed that the secrets of its use had been lost centuries before. The gleaming white marble with which the tower was surfaced identified the harbor by day.

The city of Alexandria had been founded by the great Alexander himself where there had been only an insignificant fishing village before. With Alexandria's growing importance as the capital of Greek rule over Egypt and the southern Mediterranean, the lighthouse constructed on the tiny island of Pharos was a worthy addition to the city.

As the Roman vessel approached nearer, gusts of wind strengthened.

The tower reared up and up, dwarfing the ship's forty-foot-tall mast by more than ten times. Glistening in the sun at the pinnacle of the tower was a bronze statue.

"Zeus," the sailor confided. "Twenty feet tall. It's magic, it is. It moves. His outstretched hand follows the sun across the sky."

Marcus doubted that magic was required to turn the figure on its pedestal, but he had no problem admiring the engineering.

The *Livia* overtook the bulbous form of a grain ship, going home in ballast and riding high in the water. It was also making for the port.

Three galleys emerged from the harbor as the *Livia* rounded the lighthouse. Two were merchant vessels, bound westward along the coast toward Cyrene. The other was a great warship, a *deceres*, half again as long as the *Livia*, twice as wide, with fighting towers fore and aft, triple-banked oars, and a crew of six hundred.

The *Livia* respectfully dipped her Imperial ensign as the two ships passed and the *deceres* returned the gesture.

Marcus' galley entered the port through a channel between Pharos and a breakwater that reached out from the shore. Once inside the harbor the sailing master continued his description of the marvels of the city. "See that big building there? On the hill?"

Marcus observed that it looked like a temple.

"Not a'tall," his companion scoffed. "Unless you're one as thinks Alexander's a god . . . some do, of course. That's his tomb, that is. And straight ahead? That grand building to the left of the wharf? That's the great library. Scholars travel from all over the earth to see that."

"Is that where I'll find Lord Caligula?" Marcus inquired.

The mariner shrugged. "Not from what I hear," he said hesitantly. "But I'll say no more. Port captain'll have messages for you, no doubt."

THE ENORMOUS ARTIFICIAL BAY AT ALEXANDRIA was actually five complete harbors, separated from each other by causeways and breakwaters. Docks for merchant shipping stretched both east and west of Pharos, but the *Livia* was directed toward the centermost wharf.

The stone pier at which the *Livia* docked ended in the blocky building of the customs authority. The quay was lined on both sides by galleys and courier ships from ports all around the Great Sea. *Livia* pulled in next to a truly massive three-decked warship above which floated the banner of the Fourth Legion, which was stationed in Illyricum.

Alexandria, the city named for the Greek general who conquered the world, was second only to Rome in size and importance, and even greater than Rome as a crossroads of the Empire. Its area covered more than Rome, and Alexandria rivaled the Imperial capital in population. If Judea was a backwater posting, Egypt was a plum. If Galilee was full of rustics and bandits and religious Zealots, Alexandria was a cosmopolitan city of wealth and power.

A double file of legionaries was drawn up on the stretch of wharf nearest the Customs House. Forty troopers of the Twenty-second Legion were resplendent in bright blue tunics. The hammered links of their armor glinted silver in the morning sun, and the brass trim on shoulders and sword belts gleamed like gold.

Marcus stared down at the faded red and scratched facings of his own uniform. He knew that the feathers of his plume were bedraggled, despite the fact that he was dressed in the best he had.

These were *real* legionaries, not hired auxiliary soldiers as in Marcus' former Judean command. They were part of the forces of Rome that had taken over from Alexander in ruling the world. Every member was a Roman citizen, superior to any of Marcus' troopers by that fact alone. Each was physically fit, ramrod-straight, and over five feet, ten inches in height. At the end of each file were two men taller and more regal in demeanor than the others. One of these standard bearers was the Signifier, carrying the medallions of Emperor Tiberius and of Sejanus. The other, the Aquilifer, was charged with bearing the legion's prized bronze eagle.

Marcus, proud of his own status as a citizen and secure in his soldiering ability, was humbled nevertheless. He wondered what famous general or client-king was being met by this guard of honor.

To his surprise and chagrin the centurion commanding the ceremonial detail advanced to meet him. The transverse plume on the officer's helmet was as brilliant sapphire as the Egyptian sky, and it matched the enameled dress scabbard of his short sword.

He greeted Marcus with a formal salute of his swagger stick across his chest and apologized for the absence of the tribune and the governor from the welcoming committee. "Both men have gone to Luxor to meet with the commander of the Third Legion," he said. "We'll escort you to your quarters. Caligula will summon you when he's ready."

Marcus' thoughts were spinning. There could not have been any advance word that he was aboard the courier ship, and yet he was expected. For an instant he wondered if the signal mirror of Pharos was a reality. Then his thoughts cleared as he made the appropriate formal responses and fell in with the column of soldiers.

This reception meant that before the vessel had reached Judea the scheme to send him to Alexandria had been in motion. The presence of the honor guard was also explained: The governor would certainly do every honor to Caligula, the son of Germanicus and great-grandson of the deified Augustus, and to anyone Caligula summoned.

But Egypt's governor, a Sejanus appointee like Pilate, had hedged his bets. He would be obliging to the descendant of Augustus, but he would not be present if any anti-Sejanus scheming was underway. Potential heirs to Tiberius had been removed when they threatened Sejanus.

The list might easily expand to include Caligula . . . and Marcus.

A pair of legionaries were detailed to carry Marcus' baggage to the officers' barracks, and then the procession marched away.

13

It was afternoon, the fourth day after Shabbat, the first week of Omer. Peniel reclined against the wall on the north side of Nicanor Gate, cradling his precious begging bowl on his lap. It was his usual spot, and his favorite place in all his sightless world. With his fingers he traced the letters on the rim of the bowl and then the picture Gershon had etched into the clay. "My name is Peniel," he said. Then, "Thanks for the picture, Gershon. Beautiful. Beautiful."

Holding up the bowl he cried, "O tenderhearted, show mercy and by me gain merit before heaven for your own benefit!"

The clink of a coin was the reply.

"May heaven bless you as you bless me!" Peniel thanked the donor.

Mama often dispatched Peniel here when she grew disgusted with his clumsiness, sending him away with the comment that he was good for nothing but begging. Though he never got over being wounded by the cutting remark, Peniel consoled himself with the glory, the grandeur, the wonder of his adopted location.

Even if Peniel had never seen the Temple surroundings, he had heard a decade of awestruck pilgrims gushing words of praise at this exact setting. By now he knew it well: from the columns and chambers surrounding him to the immense structure that was much more than a gate looming behind him. Here, on the semicircular steps that climbed from the Court of Women to the Court of the Israelites, all the adoration of El'Elyon, God Most High, seemed concentrated.

If a pilgrim reaching this platform faced east, he could see over Solomon's Portico to the Mount of Olives. This was the picture Gershon had carved into the clay of Peniel's alms bowl. Beautiful. Beautiful.

Peniel knew if a pilgrim turned round, he gazed through the archway formed by the bronze and marble wonder of Nicanor to the entry of the sanctuary, the earthly dwelling of El'Elyon Himself.

Spread out below Peniel's perch, the Temple commerce was transacted. The courtyard bustled with those bringing offerings to the Temple treasury, or making deliveries to the storehouses of wood, oil, and wine, or presenting themselves to the priests to fulfill a vow.

Amid the clamor and the flurry, Peniel had gained enough knowledge about the magnificence of the Temple that he could tell lost and bewildered Galileans where to get the best view of the Royal Stoa, or instruct Jews from Cyprus or Rome how to reach the Mikveh House for ceremonial cleansing. Those were the times when he felt the most connected to his nation. To sit beside Nicanor, where the heart of Jewish worship throbbed, was to be part of the chosen people . . . and near to the center of creation.

Nor was it merely the noise and commotion that Peniel enjoyed. He also keenly appreciated the times each day when the tumult stopped, when the Levite choir emerged to fill the platform with their white-robed forms and the air of the Temple courts with song. From one side of the bulk of Nicanor half the choir proposed the first part of the verse; then from the opposite, inner court, the second half replied.

Today it was Psalm 94—

"O Lord, the God who avenges,
O God who avenges, shine forth.
Rise up, O judge of the earth;
Pay back to the proud what they deserve.
How long will the wicked, O Lord,
how long will the wicked be jubilant?"[37]

From a door in the structure of the gate behind Peniel, voices emerged. Peniel recognized Caiaphas, the high priest, who shouted to be heard over the antiphon of the choir.

"I tell you, Gamaliel," the high priest boomed, "You and Nakdimon are suspect. Oh, I know you had nothing to do with the riots or the rebels, but the fact remains that it was during your appearance before Pilate that everything came unraveled. Isn't that so?"

Peniel listened to hear the replies of the two men addressed by Caiaphas. Both were prominent, high-ranking Pharisees. Gamaliel was perhaps the most respected scholar in Jerusalem, and Nakdimon the son of Gamaliel's brother.

Nakdimon replied, "The people resent it that you were appointed high priest by a Roman governor. It's more likely you'll be blamed for this than those who by heritage are Israel's judges."

"Who are the common people to determine what's right?" Caiaphas blurted out in an offended tone. "Who are they to discern what's best for Israel?"

"They pour out arrogant words;
all the evildoers are full of boasting.
They crush your people, O Lord."[38]

Then Peniel heard the high priest resume. "Well, you had better get on board with the rest of us! Come now, what possible connection to the rabble of the streets or with the peasants of the Galil can men of study like yourselves possibly have? We have much more in common with Pilate and the Romans than we do with bar Abba or that charlatan Yeshua, wouldn't you say?"

"They slay the widow and the alien;
they murder the fatherless.
They say, 'The Lord does not see;
the God of Jacob pays no heed.'"[39]

Nakdimon replied, "Bar Abba and his rebels have brought death to Yerushalayim. Yeshua brings life! I've seen his works. Heard his teaching. He's no ordinary man. Neither Rome nor the Sanhedrin should interfere if Yeshua is truly the One sent by the Lord."

"Why?" Caiaphas demanded. "Would you be one of his disciples too, Nakdimon? I tell you, these are perilous times. You shouldn't make a remark in favor of an enemy of Rome, even in jest. You know what I always say: 'Better that one man die than that the whole nation perish.' Unless *you* are volunteering to be a martyr, better it be bar Abba or Yeshua, eh? True, Gamaliel? Nakdimon? You better have a talk with your nephew, Gamaliel. He's entirely too stubborn for his own good."

The door slammed again, and Peniel heard two sets of footsteps descend from Nicanor Gate. As they passed him one of them remarked, "Just a moment, Uncle. Here you are, friend Peniel. Shalom tov."

A handful of coins rattled into Peniel's bowl, and he called out, "Bless you, Rabbi Nakdimon. And you, Rabbi Gamaliel."

Behind Peniel the Levites sang:

"You fools, when will you become wise?
Does he who implanted the ear not hear?
Does he who formed the eye not see?"[40]

THAT EVENING DEMOS, DRUNK, WAS AT Susanna's door again. Grinning stupidly, he leaned against the post, blocking her escape. Naomi—arms crossed, expression defiant—stood behind Susanna.

"Get out," Demos ordered the servant. "I'll have some time alone with your mistress."

Naomi did not budge. She seemed not to hear his command.

Demos took a menacing step forward. "Did you hear me, girl? I said, leave us!"

Still Naomi did not move. Susanna linked arms with her. "She's Nabatean. She doesn't understand your language."

"Doesn't understand? She understands well enough when she wants to." Demos scowled. "Tell her to go."

"She's my servant." Susanna lifted her chin. "I want her nearby."

"You mean you don't want to be alone with me."

"You're clever when you're drunk."

"You didn't mind being alone with my brother."

"Truth! Spilling out of you, Demos! You're drunker than I thought."

"Then she can stay. She can watch what I do to you, eh? How would this little Nabatean wench like that? I've been dreaming of you, Susanna." He leered. "If you loved Manaen, you can love me."

"You smell like a wine vat. Get out! You've no right to come to me like this!" Susanna blustered.

"I'll show you how drunk I am." Demos untied his belt, lurched forward, and reached out to tear at Susanna's clothes.

Naomi kicked a footstool in front of his stumbling feet. With a roar, he tripped and lunged facedown on the floor. Naomi snapped up a vase of flowers, held it over his head, and dropped it hard. It cracked into pieces against his skull. Demos groaned, raised his head, and fell back, unconscious.

The servant glared down at him. "In the Nabatean language this means *no!* You think he understands now, Lady Susanna?"

How much time had passed?

Manaen's hands remained shackled behind his back. A chain from his wrists connected to a hook mounted on the wall. Sitting pulled his shoulders awkwardly upward so he knelt on the stone bed to ease the ache. When the throbbing in his knees grew unbearable, he moved. The shackles allowed barely enough freedom for him to exchange one dull pain for another.

The straw on the floor was moldy, stinking of urine and rats.

But the worst torment was the darkness. Not even a stray gleam outlined the crack around the door frame. Day and night had no meaning.

At first Manaen strained his eyes to see around him, as if by force of will he could pierce the blackness. Eventually he gave up. He thought of the blind beggar, Peniel, who lived like this always.

Now Manaen listened to the sound of his own breathing.

Why had he mentioned the execution of Yochanan the Baptizer? Of all the stupid things to bring up. The Jewish prophet had angered Herodias by attacking her immoral life; he had lost his head over it.

Demos would be glad of Manaen's death, and Herodias was

without pity. Antipas never won a contest of wills with his queen. That meant there was no one left to speak up for him, to plead for his life.

Except Susanna. Would she offer herself to Demos in exchange for Manaen's life? He hoped she would not give in.

No one brought food; no guard offered him water. Did they plan to starve him to death? abandon him until the rats gnawed the flesh from his bones?

Manaen had heard of other prisoners left in just such a way. They went mad before they died, gibbering and pleading.

Somehow he slept. Dreamed of Susanna. Of daylight. Of the lakeshore in the Galil where he and Susanna had last been together in freedom and happiness. He reached out for her, trying to caress her face.

Then it was not Susanna anymore, but Herodias. The queen's mouth was parted in a smile; her teeth showed like fangs.

He started up and fell sideways. The yank on the chain brought a scream from his lips as dulled nerves were freshly tortured.

"Water!" he croaked. "For pity's sake, water!"

No one replied.

A light appeared; the glow persisted and grew, seeping around the door like water flooding across the stones.

Manaen heard the tramp of feet. Someone was coming toward his cell. He drew himself erect, grimacing with pain.

Eglon entered. Praetorian Vara was with him. "Look at the brave Manaen now," Eglon commented derisively. "A short while in darkness and he'll be crazy."

Control! Manaen knew he could not look pathetic in front of someone like Antipas' captain.

"Did you know what an honor it is for you to be here, in this very cell?" Eglon queried. "No? Well, this is the very spot where that crazy desert preacher was kept. It was right here that I chopped off his head! What a privilege to die where a prophet of Israel died. I'll say this for him: *He* never asked for mercy. But you, you're not a prophet, are you? Think maybe he'll appear and save you?"

So this was it. Manaen drew his breath and hoped the end would come quickly.

A snap of Vara's fingers brought another guard into the cell. This one carried a charcoal brazier on which coals glowed. And in the center of the coals, glowing a dull red like the head of a viper, was a dagger.

The pot of fire was placed in the cell, directly in front of the prisoner.

Manaen shrank back against the wall. His hands scrabbled uselessly on the shackles, trying to claw the iron bands from his wrists.

"Now pay attention, Eglon," Vara said. "It isn't necessary to gouge out the eye. A heated blade laid just so will sear it. That way he won't frighten the ladies when he begs."

Manaen groaned and steeled himself to fight them.

"'Out of your own mouth,' the queen said," Eglon observed. "She's a rare wit, that one. Sooner sleep with a snake, but by the god, what a warrior she would've made."

"Hold him," Vara ordered. "Eglon, pry his eyelid open . . . unless, of course, he'd like to cooperate by naming his coconspirators?"

Manaen struggled harder, thrashing. He squeezed his eyes shut. It was no use. Nothing would save him from what they planned to do.

The guard put a knee in his midsection, yanked his chin up, pried open one eye. Manaen, unable to look away, watched as Vara fiddled with the dagger's handle, turning the weapon over in the coals.

The Praetorian blew on the embers. Sparks flew up. The tip of the blade blazed from dark crimson to cherry red, the point outlined in yellow.

"Hold him!" Vara directed again. "What a warning he'll be to others! When word of this gets out, informants'll come flooding in, begging to name their friends! And here's another honor for him." Vara laughed harshly. "I'm the last thing he'll ever see in this life!"

JUST AFTER DAYBREAK JOANNA, DRESSED IN traveling clothes, came to Susanna's bedchamber. Her four-year-old son, Boaz, was at her side. "I asked to take you with me. They wouldn't have it. I'm leaving the city before the sun heats up the bodies they've crucified outside the gates."

"How did you get in to see me?"

"It's useful to have the steward of Antipas as a husband. Kuza unlocks all sorts of doors. He bribed the guards."

"Can he help Manaen?"

Joanna did not reply. She called her son back from the open window. Then she took Susanna by the hand. "If you can leave here, you must."

"But I won't. I won't leave Manaen."

"Susanna, you must leave Yerushalayim. This place. Get away from Demos and Antipas and that demon, Herodias. She's worse than Antipas. There's a cruelty in them that knows no limits. I was here the night Eglon executed the Baptizer at the command of Antipas . . . to satisfy Salome and her mother, Herodias. You're in danger if you stay here."

Susanna raised her chin defiantly. "You've known me too long and too well to think I'd ever leave Manaen if there's hope." She retrieved two sealed letters from beneath her pillow. "But you're still an answer to my prayers. Here. Take them. Please take them. A letter to the emperor Tiberius. Another to my mother's sister in Rome. Telling them everything. Everything. Not just about the way I am kept prisoner, but everything that's happened here in Yerushalayim."

Joanna stared at the correspondence as if it were a snake coiled and ready to strike. "I . . . I can't."

"You're my only hope."

"I've got Bo to think about. Kuza too."

"If you love them, take the letters! It's more than Manaen. More than me! It's . . . the way everything is here!"

Joanna put a hand to her head in consternation. After a moment of consideration, she took the letters and slipped them into her pocket.

"Thank you! Oh, Joanna!" Susanna embraced her.

Joanna took her by the arms and gave her a shake. Her voice was a hoarse whisper. "Listen. Listen to me! They've hurt Manaen. Badly."

"No! Hurt him?"

"Eglon. Eglon and Vara . . . at the suggestion of Herodias. Manaen's blind."

"Blind!" Susanna cried out. "Why! But why?"

There was no answer. Joanna's words came in a rush, "If you can escape, you must! Manaen would want you to go, Susanna! Listen to me! You must listen! I have a friend in Beth-Anyah. A few miles from here. Miryam. Her brother is Lord El'azar of Beth-Anyah! If you can get away, go to her. Tell her I said she'd help you get to Capernaum."

DARKNESS—INDESCRIBABLE, COMPLETE—PRESSED down on Manaen. Surmounting the physical agony of his wounds, this tangible darkness pinned him to the dank floor of his cell. *Heavy. A weight pressing, pressing down!*

The smell of charred flesh was his own.

Susanna!

The voice groaning, choking, calling for water was his own.

Susanna!

The nothingness in which he groped was his world. Blackness embraced him. Held him tightly. *Strong! Fierce!* An adversary, darkness would not release him.

Susanna!

No returning to light. No use waiting for dawn. Now eternal night was his. Night without moon or stars. Night without firelight. Night without the flicker of one candle.

Susanna!

Cold stone walls. Rough-hewn stone in a solid square six feet by six feet. He laid his cheek against the stone. *Cool. Cool to soothe the burning.*

What have they done to her?

Thirst. *Terrible.* Thirst. Water. Where was the bucket? Somewhere in the cell there was water. A bucket in the corner. On hands and knees he crept forward, passing his hand before him in an arc.

Susanna!

No water to quench his need.

They meant for him to die then. Some sort of sport. Did they even now stand at the tiny window of the cell and gawk at him? Did they place bets on how long? How long it would take him to go mad and then die?

Trembling, he raised his head. Sat back on his haunches. Propped himself in the corner. Resisted the urge, the need, to touch the useless wounds that had been his eyes.

Resisted the desire to call her name aloud.

Susanna!

He dug his fingers into the stone floor, willing himself to die placidly. No begging. No groping for water. For bread. For light that wasn't there.

THE TOMB OF THE GREAT ALEXANDER WAS located on an artificial mount not far from the harbor. The space around it was clear of other buildings and planted with palm groves. The way its site dominated the city reminded Marcus of Herod's Temple of Augustus in Caesarea, but this was far grander.

As Marcus and his attendant squad of legionaries arrived, the wind increased further, turning palm fronds into pennants, whipping the cloaks of passersby. Anvil-shaped clouds billowed up directly above the city. The sky over Alexandria was forbiddingly blackened by the contrast with the brilliant sunlight that still streamed in underneath the clouds from the west.

Within the ring of palms, at the foot of the steps leading to the tomb's platform, was an encircling array of Roman legionaries acting as guards for Caligula.

While the officers exchanged salutes, Marcus studied the famous sepulchre. Square in shape, the mausoleum's double colonnade enclosed a central hall, surmounted by a dome. The walls were adorned with both Greek friezes—Alexander depicted as Hercules, Alexander as Apollo—and Egyptian wall paintings. One of them showed Alexander being welcomed into the heavenlies by Amun-Ra, whom the Egyptians gladly recognized as Zeus by another name. Another painting portrayed the Greek warrior-king as being enthroned in a chair of state, evidently referring to his status as a deity himself.

At the entry to the rotunda the legionaries halted, leaving Marcus and the escorting centurion to advance alone.

Pale pink marble pillars veined with black supported a golden cupola that mimicked the outer dome. Oil lamps illuminated the space beneath it. Sheltered by this bell-shaped canopy and supported on a golden catafalque was a chamber of translucent crystal containing the mortal remains of the deified Alexander.

Beside the vault, apparently lost in thought and contemplation, was the boy—now a young man—Marcus had known as Little Boots.

As Caligula concentrated on the dead Greek general, Marcus studied the prince he had last seen ten to eleven years earlier. Certainly it had been at least that long. The boy's father had still been alive then, and Germanicus was dead for that many years now, poisoned in Syria by order of Sejanus.

Caligula's pose displayed a three-quarter profile to Marcus' view. Though aged eighteen now, the prince was still as thin as a much younger boy. His nose was too prominent for his narrow face, his chin too weak to balance his broad brow, and his scrawny neck struggled to support a head too large for his sloping shoulders.

"I come here every day," Caligula said without turning. "To pray to Alexander for his guidance. How have you been, Marcus Longinus?"

"I'm well, my lord."

Caligula whipped around. "Leave us," he said to the accompanying officer.

"I am strictly ordered to—"

"Leave us!" Caligula demanded again. "Centurion Longinus is adequate protection for me, unless perhaps you think *he* is a threat?"

The centurion of the Twenty-second Legion bowed deeply and backed away from the scene.

Beckoning Marcus to approach his side, Caligula turned toward the crystalline vault. Reflected by the golden dome, the flames of the lamps so illuminated the crypt that it appeared to glow from within.

Dimly seen, the body of Alexander, apparently a man about the same age as Marcus, floated in an amber fluid.

"Honey," Caligula said absently. "He had a horror of the way Egyptians embalm their dead, taking out their guts and leaving them to dry like fish in the marketplace, so he gave orders to be buried this way. You know that Great-Grandmama died?"

"Yes, my lord," Marcus replied. "I'm sorry for your loss." Marcus recalled that Caligula had been living with his great-grandmother, Livia, who was also Tiberius' mother and had been married to Caesar Augustus. Sejanus' authority was great, but even he scarcely dared challenge the mother of one emperor and the widow of another. Livia had remained a commanding figure well into her eighties, but now she was gone.

"I'm traveling because of my grief," Caligula remarked.

"I understand."

"Oh, not for *her!*" Caligula sniffed. "I'm glad *she's* dead. Horrid old witch! You know she wanted my father dead so Tiberius would be emperor! No, no! My grief is for my mother and brother. Sejanus starved them to death!"

And Caligula's traveling to get away from Rome before Sejanus implicates him in some plot, Marcus thought. *Now that Livia's hand of protection is no more, who knows what will happen?*

"I'm just a simple, private citizen," Caligula stated unconvincingly. "He—" he indicated Alexander's corpse—"he reproaches me with how useless my life has been. When he was eighteen he had already studied with Aristotle! He won the battle of Chaeronea. By twenty he was king of Macedonia . . . by twenty-four wearing the double crown of the pharaohs . . . by twenty-five defeated the Persians! I've done nothing! Nothing!" Caligula's voice managed to sound anguished and petty at the same time.

"His life was a comet," Marcus acknowledged. "And he died at thirty-three."

"He exchanged his body for immortality!" Caligula corrected sharply. "His divinity was too great to be imprisoned any longer in mere flesh! And what was left to accomplish? He had conquered the world! And he was merely a Greek! The blood of the divine Augustus flows in my veins! Besides, I'm smarter than he and better looking too, don't you think?"

Marcus merely bowed.

The interior of the tomb grew darker as the clouds overhead increased. The wind sighed around the pillars.

"Marcus," Caligula said softly, in a much calmer tone, "I can rely on you, can't I? You held the flank at Idistaviso, saving the army. My father gave you the corona obsidionalis on that same day. I saw it. You let me hold it! Later you spurned Sejanus to go with my father to Syria. You remain loyal to my father's memory, don't you?"

"I swore an oath to support him," Marcus replied, "provided I do not break my oath to the emperor."

How awkward that former oath seemed since he'd met Yeshua, Marcus thought. The Nazarene was the one person actually worthy to be emperor of all; it was to Him that Marcus had pledged ultimate loyalty. He knew that now, with no reservation.

Caligula's smile was cunning, his words tinged with sarcasm. "So you've learned politics," he commented. "The charming reply that keeps to the safe side of every hearer."

"I am a soldier," Marcus argued stiffly. "I meant exactly what I said."

There had been a time when to Marcus one god was as good as another. Power existed in legions and men to command them; the rest was superstition and vanity.

But now that he'd met someone with a real claim to miraculous, divine authority, the counterfeits felt worse than mere superstition. They were evil incarnate, condensed into the malicious, spoiled, conceited brat standing in front of him.

As Caligula waved dismissively, Marcus backed away. Apparently the interview was at an end. Was this why he had been summoned all the way to Alexandria? and why he had waited two days to talk with Caligula?

"I am not the son of Germanicus for nothing!" Caligula said, as if addressing Alexander's body. He raised both hands to the crystalline enclosure in supplication. "I am a true descendant of the divine Augustus. I feel the spark of immortality within me! I'm still only eighteen. The mantle of Alexander can yet fall on me! It *will* come to me!"

Outside, the storm that had been gathering finally broke. A crash of thunder split the air, followed by a pulsing rumble that reverberated within the dome. Caligula started, his body jerking awkwardly. "Don't forsake me!" he implored. "I'm surrounded by spies and traitors. I need someone I can trust. Marcus, help me! Come to me again when I summon you, and bring me the news from Judea that will save me from Sejanus."

14

It was Shabbat evening. The second week of Omer. The week of Isaac.

Peniel bought his Shabbat bread at the corner and returned to his hut. Good bread. The first after Passover. Yeasty and still warm. He would eat it with butter tonight. His own Shabbat meal. A thick crust to last Peniel three days. And when it got stale, he would soak it in goat's milk.

Peniel loved Shabbat. He could not beg on Shabbat, but tomorrow he would spend the whole day on the steps listening to the teachers. Listening. No alms bowl. As if he were a true man of Israel: unmarred, seeing, strong. Listening to them teach from Torah. Eating the spiritual bread that satisfied his soul.

These good thoughts ran through his mind as he made his way toward home. Rounding the corner, he heard the voices of his father and mother arguing in the workshop.

"Everybody owes you money!" Mama said. "So we owe everybody money! Show some backbone! Collect what they owe us!"

"You've got enough backbone for both of us!"

"If you'd listen to me—"

"If I had any backbone, I'd have divorced you years ago!"

"You're not worth anything since Gershon died!"

"Leave Gershon out of it!"

"Everything wrong between us started that day!"

"We have another son. You treat him like—"

"I had one son! Gershon! Only one! I'll never believe Peniel didn't—"

"Ridiculous! He was seven! How could a seven-year-old—"

"I had one son I loved—Gershon! He's gone! Gone! He was proof I was blessed. Now I'm left with a sneaking, devious—"

"Bitter! That's what you are! You hang on to everything with your teeth!"

Peniel covered his ears with his hands and hurried past the open window. He did not want to hear it again. Somehow it always came back to Gershon. To Peniel.

Peniel slipped into his shack and sat down cross-legged. He rocked back and forth, humming to try to shut out the noise.

A pot crashed to the floor. The shouting became louder, less understandable. It dissolved into accusations. About everything. About nothing.

"You!"

"No! It's you! You always favor him over me . . . "

"If you wouldn't have . . . "

"Your fault!"

There came one final resounding crash. The banging of a door. Papa was outside. Pacing.

Mama remained inside. Slamming. Breaking. Weeping.

Then, silence.

Peniel heard his father clear his throat. He was outside the shelter.

A tentative knock. "Peniel? You in there?"

"Yes, Papa."

The leather curtain drew back, letting in fresh air. The iron smell of wet clay and smoke from the kiln fire clung to Papa. It was a pleasant aroma for Peniel. He loved his father. Pitied him. Kept his distance because Mama accused Papa of sympathy for Peniel even though Peniel was responsible for what happened. So they seldom spoke.

Papa stopped and peered in. "Your mother is upset."

"You want to come in?"

"No. No, thanks. I just . . . she's touchy, that's all. Things are hard. I mean, the business. I wanted to warn you."

"Sure." Both knew that when things got hard, Mama took it out on Peniel first, Papa second.

"I just thought you should know. Lay low. Don't argue. You know?"

"Thanks."

"Yes. Well . . . you doing well? Sorry you missed the seder."

"It was a bad night for everyone."

"All right then. Just so it's clear. I guess that's all."

"Thanks, Papa."

The curtain fell back into place.

Peniel waited until his father returned to the house before he blessed the bread. "Blessed are you, O Lord Adonai! You have given me bread to eat . . . and I am glad . . . glad. But . . . I would like someone to share it with. You know?"

How could he eat? How could he celebrate Shabbat when Mama and Papa were so unhappy with him?

"If I could give my life for Gershon! If only I could give my life!"

Tonight he did not invite the Ushpizin to the shelter. They never really came. Mama was right about that. He dreamed and dreamed; it kept him going to imagine. But no one ever really came. The Shabbat bread remained untouched.

Peniel wept.

In the hours when Manaen hovered over death's abyss, his thoughts drifted to the blind youth, Peniel, who had saved his life from the fire.

Saved Manaen from the flames! For what reason?

The fire would not be denied. It had sought out Manaen long after he imagined he was safe. Its heat had devoured Manaen's light.

Peniel had parted from Manaen praising God for their preservation for some unknown purpose, some plan, some adventure he believed life held for him.

In the madness of his long night Manaen remembered that Peniel would joyfully sit and talk with the Ushpizin, the ancient wanderers of Israel. And they would speak back to him. Tell him of the world and the world to come: of prophets, priests, and kings.

How lucky Peniel was never to have seen light! Never to know what was lost!

Manaen—alone, without comfort, slipping from sanity—dreamed of seeing. *An orange on a peddler's cart. A coin gleaming in the palm of his hand. Sunlight on the broad leaf of a fig tree.* Nothing was so insignificant but that his memory painted it bright and beautiful on a golden back-drop.

Susanna's eyes: deep brown, warm, knowing him. Her finger twirling a lock of hair. The strap of her gown slipping from her shoulder.

And then, always, *Demos! Herodias, Antipas. Eglon. The brazier of fire. The glowing knife blade . . .*

Words had died in his throat with his final scream. *No light. No color. No food. No water. No hope.*

IT WAS LATE. THE CITY WAS ASLEEP. Peniel's bread remained untouched where he had left it.

There was something moving outside the shelter. Probably one of the million stray cats that haunted Jerusalem.

Peniel sat up. He retrieved the bread. More than once he had awak-ened to find some uninvited furry pest had devoured half his meal.

A step. A scratching.

"Get! Go on!" Peniel defended. "Cats!"

Then a soft knocking on the door. A stranger, a young man, called cheerfully, *Shabbat shalom!*

"Who's there?" Peniel inquired.

Are you Peniel? The blind beggar who sits every day at Nicanor Gate?

Peniel was alarmed but interested. "I haven't got any money out here, if that's what you're after."

No. No. I was sent. He laughed. *We saw you there today. You seem a pleasant sort. They told me you live here. Behind the workshop of your family.*

"Yes. Well. It's too crowded for me to live in the house."

It's crowded here too. He laughed again.

"Not for me. I prefer it."

Yes. Well then, if you say so. I see you haven't eaten your Shabbat challah.

"I wasn't hungry."

I haven't eaten either.

Peniel shook the sleep from his brain. A stranger. At his door. In the middle of the night. In need of bread. Shabbat.

"Come in then, and welcome."

Shabbat shalom, the stranger said again as he ducked low and entered the shelter.

"Shabbat shalom, *u-lu Ush-pi-zin.* Be seated, faithful guest." Peniel indicated the empty spot he always made available to the imaginary Ushpizin. "There's water for washing in the jug in the corner. I have no Shabbat candles, but I have bread. Do you have a name?"

Yitz'chak.

"Well then, I'm Peniel. But you know that. Where are you from, Yitz'chak?"

I first came here to the Holy Mountain from Beersheba. With my old father, one donkey, and two servants. My father left the others near Beth-lehem. You know Beth-lehem? Where the lambs for Temple sacrifice are born and raised? Father and I came on alone. It took us three days for the journey. But that's been quite some time ago. He washed his hands, blessed the bread, and tore off two chunks. One for himself and one for Peniel.

Peniel accepted it and took a bite. He was hungry and grateful for the company. "I've never been anywhere except Yerushalayim. Hardly outside the city gates. I know it well, even though I'm blind."

Mount Moriah is a beautiful place. You can see all the way to Edom and practically to the western sea on a clear day. You're lucky.

"Except that I can't see."

Take my word for it. You're blessed. "I would rather be a doorkeeper in the house of Adonai than dwell in the tents of the wicked," Yitz'chak quoted.[41]

"Well spoken. Point taken. I am lucky; that's true. I like my place at the gate. I hear well enough for ten men. That practically makes me a *minyan* all on my own. And I have a good memory for Torah, for details about the Temple history I overhear. Though I don't get much chance to discuss it."

The Temple. It looks like a snowcap on the mountain when you're coming up the pass. The sun hits it and . . . really. Astounding. It has changed. Always beautiful, even before. But now! Do you know the history? Why they chose this place to build the Temple for the Name of El'Elyon on Mount Moriah?

"It's where Avraham brought his only son, Yitz'chak, to offer him up to Adonai. The exact stone. Still there. Right where it happened. I think about that a lot. Think a lot about Yitz'chak. Avraham scares me a bit sometimes. But Yitz'chak? Brave. Brave."

The story of Yitz'chak isn't the only foreshadowing of the coming Messiah found in Torah, but it may be the clearest and the best, said Yitz'chak. *What do you think?*

Peniel paused midbite. "What do I think? I don't know. Yitz'chak is Yitz'chak. Messiah is Messiah."

Well, you're wrong there. Every word in Torah and Tanakh points to some truth about the Messiah. Foreshadowing. Prophecy. The story of Mount Moriah is one of the best, if I do say so myself.

"What is this? Did you come here to discuss Torah with me? At this hour?"

That's what you wanted. What you asked for. Isn't it? Someone to share your bread this Shabbat? To talk Torah with you?

Peniel did not reply. How did this fellow know what he had whispered in the loneliness of his shelter? Had he mentioned it on the Temple Mount? Had he dozed off at Nicanor Gate and mumbled something out loud?

"Who are you?" Hair stood up on the back of Peniel's neck.

I told you, the stranger replied with a laugh.

"You said . . . Yitz'chak. Yitz'chak. A common enough name. Every other brother, uncle, father, cousin is named Yitz'chak in this land."

That's right.

"How do you know what I said? What I prayed for?"

You were heard.

"Who . . . heard me?"

You were talking to the Almighty. You think He doesn't pay attention? You think the One who made ears doesn't hear?

"I'm dreaming, right?"

Of course.

"Yes. That's it. You're a dream. You're Yitz'chak. Who's your father?"

Avraham.

"A common name. But . . . who . . . sent you?"

Yitz'chak ignored the question. *You listen. You already know in your heart what I'm going to tell you. But they thought it would be good if you heard it from me.*

"Heard what?"

The story about my old father. About me and Mount Moriah. Because it means much more than you think.

"You're Avraham's son. Yitz'chak."

Yes.

"Avraham is your father? *The* Avraham?"

That's it.

"Tell me everything then. And don't let me wake up before you finish. Please!"

Yitz'chak settled in and began to speak what he had seen and heard as a young man. *My father loved me very much. And I loved him. He was a very old man when I was born. I played around him like a lion cub plays with an old lion. Tugging, wrestling, sitting in his lap while he told me stories. Yes, I learned a lot sitting with him. I learned that nothing is too hard for Adonai Elohim. He told me. Told me what Adonai had said about my birth. That I had a future and a hope.*[42] *I believed him.*

One night when I was a little younger than you, I awoke to a distant rumble of thunder over the hills. I heard my father whisper, "Here I am." And I knew Adonai was speaking to Father again. Adonai said to my father, "Take your son, your only son, Yitz'chak, whom you love, and go to the region of Moriah. Sacrifice him there as a burnt offering on one of the mountains I will tell you about."[43]

At first light, Father saddled the donkey. He called me and two of his servants. Father cut the wood himself and loaded it on the donkey. He did not consult my mother. She would have tried to stop us, I believe. So off we went.

Father spoke little except to pray. He fasted and spent the long nights awake, watching over me. I woke up with him sitting beside me. Stroking my hair. "Yitz'chak, Yitz'chak. My son, my only son. You know how much I love you."

"Yes, Father."

On the third day, near what is now Beth-lehem, Father looked up and saw Mount Moriah in the distance. He said to his servants, "Stay here with the donkey while I and the boy go over there. We will worship and then come back to you."[44]

So Father took the wood and placed it on my shoulders to carry. He himself carried the fire and the knife. But I carried the wood alone.

After a while I noticed there was no lamb to sacrifice so I asked him, "Father?"

"Yes, my son?"

"*The fire and the wood are here, but where is the lamb for the burnt offering?*"[45]

Here is a mystery revealed by El Olam, the Eternal God . . . Father answered my question in these exact words and in this precise order as recorded in the Torah, "Elohim He will provide Himself . . . Elohim He will provide Himself . . . the lamb . . . for the burnt offering . . . son of me."

And so we went on together.

As we walked and the wood grew heavy on my shoulders, I thought about what my father said. The words he chose to explain sounded to me as though he meant that Adonai Elohim would provide Himself as the sacrifice! And the lamb for the offering would be His Son! Father knew something about the future which I didn't yet understand. Is anything too hard for God? Avraham was my father, and I trusted him.

When we reached Mount Moriah, where the Temple now stands, I knew this was the place Adonai had told him about. Father built an altar there and arranged the wood on it. He put his hands on my face and looked into my eyes. And then I knew. Suddenly I knew. I was his only son. I knew how much he loved me. How dear I was to him. His future was in me. I was the son of Adonai Elohim's promise to him. And yet I was not afraid. Even if I died there on that altar, I trusted that nothing was too hard for Adonai. He would raise me up again!

"My only son. I love you, my son," Father said to me.

"I love you, my father."

And I laid myself down willingly to be bound: a trusting, obedient son. My father tied me hand and foot, lest instinct make me flinch or jerk away when the knife went into my heart and the sacrifice be ruined. And he laid me on the wood.

Just as my father's hand raised above my chest, prepared to plunge in the knife, in that instant I saw! I saw a bright light! Brighter than the sun! I saw the sacrifice yet to come! I saw the face of Him who had first shown Himself to my father!

And then I heard the voice! Above us. Louder than a thunderclap. "Avraham! Avraham!" It was the voice of the Angel of Adonai!

"Here I am!"

"Do not lay a hand on the boy! Do not do anything to him! Now I know you fear God because you have not withheld from Me your son, your only son!"

Then my eyes were opened, and I saw a ram caught by his horns in a thicket! My father went over, took the ram, and sacrificed it as an offering in-

stead of me. So my father called that place Adonai Yir'eh—"Adonai Will Provide." And to this day it is said, "On the mountain of Adonai it will be provided."

When the sun glinted on the blade of the knife and it flashed toward me, I was dead . . . you know? But my father received me back alive again.

Then the Angel of Adonai called to my father from heaven a second time: "I swear by Myself, declared Adonai, that because you have done this and not withheld your son, your only son, I will surely bless you and make your descendants as numerous as the stars in the sky and as the sand on the seashore. Your descendants will take possession of the cities of their enemies and through your offspring all nations on earth will be blessed because you have obeyed Me."[46]

And so this tells also of a future event. The offering of a son will be played out on the holy mountain once more. Very soon, here, in Yerushalayim. This time it will be Adonai Elohim's only Son who carries the wood on His back and provides Himself as our sacrifice. He will let Himself be bound and will lie down willingly as the Lamb to die for all of us.

Peniel could not speak. But in his mind he asked the question, When?

Soon. Remember, Peniel! This is not only the story of Avraham and Yitz'chak, but the truth of how it will be for the Messiah, Adonai Elohim's beloved Son, His only Son!

For Elohim so loves the world that He gave His only Son, the Messiah, that whoever believes in Him will never die but have eternal life.[47] On the mountain of Adonai our salvation will be provided. He is the lamb of Elohim who takes away the sins of men and blesses the nations. The Messiah will carry the burden of the wood upon which He will die. He will yield to this and lay down His life willingly, knowing that He will be raised again to life after three days' journey into death. And all who call upon His name will be saved! This is the promise of El'Elyon, the One, the Almighty God has sworn this by His name. It is all there, recorded in the Scripture, for all to read and know.

"But how can this be?" Peniel cried out. "It's not what we expected! The teachers who are supposed to know are searching for something entirely different!"

They are blind guides, Yitz'chak replied.

"But how will the people find the way if those who lead them are blind?"

The voice of Yitz'chak was only a whisper in reply: Nothing is too hard . . . for God. . . . Awake, awake, you who dream!

Peniel awoke. He sat up. "Dreaming. Just a dream." He wiped his brow and listened to see if anyone was there. No one. No one. Alone after all.

His stomach rumbled. He remembered he had not had his supper. "I'm hungry." He reached for the Shabbat bread. It was still there. "No cats." He sighed with relief and made the blessing over the bread. Then, picking it up, he touched the broken crust.

Half of the loaf was gone.

15

D ressed in civilian clothes, Marcus hired a donkey to carry him across town to the Jewish Quarter of Alexandria.

Eight million people lived in the province of Egypt. Nearly one million of these were Jews.

Marcus knew a smattering of the history. In the days of Judah Maccabee, when Antiochus Epiphanes set up an idol of himself in the Temple of Jerusalem and sacrificed a pig on the high altar, thousands of Jews fled persecution, escaping to the tolerance of Egypt. Since that time, Alexandria represented the largest Jewish gathering place in the world outside Jerusalem. The last true hereditary high priest had been murdered. Then his son had been given a disused pagan temple in Leontopolis, which he converted into a place of worship for Adonai Elohim. Yet the Sanhedrin in Jerusalem did not recognize its legitimacy. Now there were nearly as many Torah schools and synagogues in Alexandria as in Jerusalem.

Asking directions proved important as Marcus started for the Jewish Quarter near the Canobus Canal. Alexandria was much bigger in area than Jerusalem, even bigger than Rome. Turning aside from the main route, Marcus found a commercial district lively with linen goods, perfumeries, and eating establishments.

Beyond this, to the east, lay the Delta. It was a pleasant area of tree-lined streets and two-story buildings that appeared much more orderly than Jerusalem. Once in the Quarter he discovered a sign announcing Lulav Synagogue, together with the image of a palm branch to illustrate its name.

When Marcus inquired of the synagogue attendant for the residence of Rabbi Onias, he was directed to a carpenter's shop around the corner.

Tying off the donkey to the iron ring set in the wall, Marcus hailed a young man with a load of planks on his shoulder. "I'm looking for Onias, the rabbi."

"Round back. Door's open." The youth jerked his thumb and continued with his task.

The air was fragrant with wood chips. The tiny, one-room structure of the rabbi was half concealed by long planks drying in the sun.

The door was open. Marcus rapped on the doorjamb. An old man, hunched from years of study, sat perusing a scroll. His fingers were clawlike, his feet turned in and useless for walking. A cripple. So unlike his robust brother that Marcus would not have guessed they could be from the same family.

"Shalom. Shalom." The old man raised his eyes only briefly. "You're from the library, are you? Have you brought it then? The scroll of Archimedes?"

"I've come from Jerusalem."

"What's that? Someone else has it?" The old rabbi peered curiously at Marcus. "What's this? You're not from the library."

"Sir, I come with a message from your brother Zadok, Chief Shepherd of the flocks of Israel."

It took a moment for this news to sink in. "Is my brother dead?"

"No, sir. He's sent you a message by my hand."

"You've come a long way to deliver a message from Zadok. I'm pleased." Rabbi Onias held up his hands. Palms displayed scars clearly made by a crucifixion. "Can't stand to greet you properly. Come in. Be seated, honored guest."

Marcus noted the mezuzah on the door of the rabbi. He saluted and bowed slightly as he entered.

"I see you're not a Jew." Onias displayed a toothless grin. "A Roman perhaps? Plainly. Yes. Soldier, yes. An officer at one time by your manner. Your mother . . . a Briton perhaps?"

"Right on all counts," Marcus replied in amazement. "Worthy of a seer in the marketplace."

"You're half a fool for making such an insulting remark to a rabbi."

"Forgive a fool, sir. I meant no offense. The customs of you Jews are beyond me."

"You're forgiven. Sit. Sit. Sit. What's your name?"

"Marcus Longinus." Marcus sank down on a wool sack near the rabbi's table. This gave him clear view of the rabbi's bare feet. These showed the brutal scars of spikes as well.

Marcus took Zadok's scroll from his leather pouch. He placed it before the old man. The rabbi twirled it slowly around, studying the childish scrawl on the exterior of the parchment. He smiled enigmatically yet seemed in no hurry to open it.

"Tell me. What news of my brother? And how is it in Yerushalayim?"

"Your brother is strong. He's well. As for Jerusalem, it balances on the brink of disaster."

"As always. We heard the news of the Passover massacre some days ago. There were pilgrims from Alexandria killed there. It's a pity the Lord did not instruct Solomon to build his Temple in Alexandria. The climate is better. And seldom are the Jews of Alexandria slaughtered." He tapped the scroll lightly against the tabletop and then untied the string. His eyes brimmed with emotion as he scanned the message, turned the parchment over, read the Scripture from Hosea, and then put it to his lips briefly and closed his eyes in murmured prayer. "Blessed are you, O Adonai, Lord of the universe, who in your mercy has let me live to see this day!"

Marcus stirred uneasily, sensing that he had intruded on a profoundly personal moment.

At last Onias spoke with a cracking voice. "You must be a trustworthy man, else my brother Zadok would not have entrusted you with this message."

"Sir, I am a friend of your brother and of your people."

"Then you are extraordinary, for everyone knows how much Zadok hates the Romans."

"And you, sir, do you share his sentiment?"

Onias displayed his right hand, palm up. "I would have reason, as you see by my old wounds."

Marcus nodded and glanced away. The tone, though polite, was clearly confrontational. What was the old man after? Was he testing Marcus?

"A Roman cross?" Marcus asked.

"Herod the Great always did prefer Roman entertainment. I was nailed to the side of my house in Yerushalayim in the days when Herod could not decide if he was builder or butcher. Butcher won."

Marcus nodded once. "Such entertainments have not changed since then. Neither in Rome. Nor in Jerusalem."

The rabbi sighed. "Is there no light for us in this dark and weary world? A beacon to shine out across the void like the lighthouse of Pharos, eh? Bright. Brighter than a star on the horizon. A light to call the hearts of men into safe harbor?"

Marcus leaned forward and answered quietly. "Yes. Yes, sir. I think there is such a light. I've seen him. He's alive. As alive as you and me! His name is Yeshua."

Now the caution and reserve of the rabbi immediately dissolved. Had he simply been waiting for Marcus to speak first? To tell him the good news? There was so little good news these days. Only Yeshua. Only Him. And yet Marcus did not know how to explain what he felt when he heard Yeshua speak. Or saw Him touch the crooked woman and make her straight. How could he explain to someone so far away that Yeshua was not a fable! Not some Greek legend about gods and goddesses! He was real!

Onias asked, "You, son, do you know what my brother has written to me here?"

"No. I didn't read it. He didn't tell me."

"Then I'll read it to you." Onias unrolled the parchment and began:

"My dearest Onias, honored elder brother. Speak his name, Immanu'el, and know that all that was written in the Prophets is true. Our suffering was not in vain. I have seen the Light of the World with my own eyes. Touched him with my hand. Heard his voice. Seen his mighty wonders. God is with us. What we whispered in dark rooms can now be shouted from the housetops! He is Immanu'el."

Onias paused in his reading and eyed Marcus. "My brother would not have sent you to me with such a message if he did not have confidence in you. And so I'll tell you its meaning. First, light the candles for me, my son." Onias directed Marcus to the shelf where beeswax candles were stored. "And we'll break bread together. Break the bread of Torah and nourish our souls on its mysteries."

"Are these mysteries for me? I'm not a Jew."

"Truth is for every soul with ears to hear. You're a child of God. The Lord promised Avraham to bless the world through the seed of his son Yitz'chak."

So much Marcus wanted to know! Had the God of Israel heard his heart and brought him here for a purpose? "How can I learn truth unless someone teaches me?"

"It's right for you to ask every question that comes to your mind. The Lord doesn't resent our questions or turn aside our doubts. Truth transcends doubt like a candle illuminates darkness."

"Where do I begin?"

The old man broke the bread with his crippled hands. "Wherever you like."

"All right then. You. Your hands. Your feet. Who did this to you?"

A shrug. "Thirty years ago and a little more, I was a Torah scholar in Yerushalayim. I dared to teach my talmidim in the court of the Temple that the Messiah, the true King of Israel, would soon come to Yerushalayim just as Mosheh came to the slaves of Egypt to set them free. These ancient prophecies terrified Herod the Great. Knowing the Messiah would be descended from David, Herod destroyed the genealogical records stored in the Temple. Fourteen generations from Avraham to Mosheh. Fourteen generations from Mosheh to David. Fourteen generations from David until our time. Herod silenced any who taught that the year of the Lord was upon us."

Marcus, experienced with the violence and fear of Roman rulers, was not surprised by this. Herod the Great had been a comrade of Roman rulers. "So, as a warning to others who knew the truth of the prophecies, Herod had you arrested and crucified?"

"I was just one of many."

"Yet you survived."

"In a dream the Lord told Simon that he would live to see the Messiah face-to-face. Simon believed the dream, so he didn't fear dying. He took me down from the cross. At great personal risk, Simon and my brother Zadok helped me escape to Alexandria. Here. To this house where I've lived ever since."

"But how could you know the Messiah was coming?" Marcus probed, remembering the prophecies of Roman oracles that also predicted a great king would be born and rule the whole earth.

"The Lord has set forth every detail of Messiah's life in the writings of Mosheh and in the Psalms and the Prophets. Dani'el gives the exact number of years until the Anointed One would come to Yerushalayim and be cut off. The first years of that prophecy are nearly complete. And the signs of the times are clear. Only a man who chooses to disregard the evidence of history and current events can deny that the year of the Lord is near."

Signs. Was this not what Yeshua had said to the multitudes in Bethany? That they refused to acknowledge the plain signs of the times? "What signs?" Marcus asked.

"It is written in Amos that the Lord never does a great thing without telling his prophets.[47] Signs have appeared in our lifetime, like those that appeared to the Hebrew slaves in Egypt. This was before Mosheh, our deliverer, came to us. You call him Moses." The old rabbi opened the scroll of Exodus and skimmed the passage for a long time.

Marcus did not interrupt, though his mind reeled with questions.

At last Onias raised his eyes. "Oh, but you must ask. If you don't ask, how will you find the truth?"

How to boil his quest for truth down to one coherent question? Marcus wondered. He, who knew nothing of Jewish history, did not know what questions to ask. "All right, then. What are the prophecies?"

The rabbi called for another candle. "You are a clean papyrus, Marcus Longinus. Listen then and learn a little." Onias took his time, scrutinizing the Scriptures before he began. "Our people were slaves here in Egypt. Four generations had passed since the Lord told the patriarch Joseph that a deliverer would come and set his people free. The Hebrew slaves looked for a deliverer daily. Our tradition says that two years before Mosheh's birth a bright star appeared in the sky. A conjunction of this magnitude . . . three planets . . . happens rarely. About every eight hundred years. Pharaoh saw it blazing brilliantly within the constellation The Fish, which represents the nation of Israel. Pharaoh asked his astrologers what it could mean. They told him! A deliverer would come out of the Hebrew slaves who lived in Goshen. Pharaoh feared the prophecy, feared the Jews. So he issued a decree, and every Jewish boy under the age of two was slaughtered. Only baby Mosheh survived. Mosheh, whose name spelled backwards is HaShem! 'The Name'! He would reveal The Name of their savior to the slaves of Israel! And Mosheh grew and heard the voice of God and saw him face-to-face. He learned The Name of the Lord. And God gave him the Torah, the Holy Word, on Mount Sinai. He led us to the Promised Land, and yet Mosheh was forbidden to cross over . . . another led us into Eretz-Israel, the land."

"And what was the name of the one who led your nation into their land?"

"His name was Yeshua. The Greeks call him Jesus or Joshua. The name means 'God is Salvation.'"

"This is the same name as the One from Galilee! The Wonder-worker. The Teacher!"

"Yes. The same name as the One who took up where Mosheh left off. That Yeshua is a picture of the Messiah. He who parted the waters and crossed the Jordan River, leading Israel home. Eh? Yeshua, the One who went before and who did not fear the enemies of the nation. Yeshua, who believed the promises. Yeshua, who by the Name and in the power of the Almighty conquered the land. See, everything means something. Everything. But we get ahead of ourselves."

"Then tell me this: Is today like those ancient days? And how is the Messiah like your Mosheh?"

Onias raised his finger and touched his forehead. "Now this is a good question! This is the question of a man who seeks wisdom! How do past events in Scripture reflect our present time? The year of the Lord? I'll tell you. The same bright star that shone before the birth of Mosheh has appeared again! Thirty-two years ago it lit up the eastern sky! It moved until it shone over Beth-lehem! I am one of many witnesses to its appearance. Three times that year the stars you Romans call Jupiter and Saturn came together to form a brilliant spectacle in the sky. And then, one year later, Mars conjoined with them in a sight so bright and beautiful that none of us could take our eyes from it. In the midst of their union the gathered light seemed to form another star, a brand-new star, more brilliant than any other. We gathered on the rooftops to watch each night as the star grew brighter. More luminous than the lighthouse of Pharos it was! We scholars remembered the star that announced the birth of Mosheh, and we spoke of the prophecies. As in the days of Mosheh, this star appeared within the constellation The Fish, which signifies Israel. It seemed to hover over Beth-lehem."

"Why Beth-lehem? An insignificant place."

"Look to the scroll of Micah. Little Beth-lehem, home of David, must be the birthplace of the Messiah." Onias searched the Scriptures and began to read: *'But you, Beth-lehem Ephrathah, though you are small among the clans of Judah, out of you will come for me one who will be ruler over Israel, whose origins are from of old, from ancient times!'*[48]

The old rabbi closed the scroll. "Zadok, my brother, was a shepherd over the sacrificial lambs. He came roaring into the Temple with his comrades! They told old Simon that a great wonder had occurred in Beth-lehem the night before! A baby boy had been born in the lambing cave! Angels appeared above the flocks, declaring to the shepherds of the sacred herds the birth of their King! Immanu'el! 'God-with-us.' Simon, knowing the danger, warned Zadok and the others to keep it to themselves.

"But Herod was told. He trembled with fear because he knew it was true. Beth-lehem was the place to which the kings of the East were directed by Herod's scholars when they came to Yerushalayim in search of the great King of Israel. You see, even while a baby, his light drew men to him. Just as the lighthouse of Pharos serves Alexandria today, so does his light guide all who seek his shelter."

"There's still the memory of what happened next." Marcus recalled the dark rumors about the troops who had lived in the fortress of Herodium.

"Yes." The rabbi shook his head sadly. "Herod, like Pharaoh, sent his troops to murder all the baby boys two and under in Beth-lehem. Zadok's boys were slaughtered. Many others. This is fulfillment of the prophecy of Jeremiah: *'A voice of mourning will be heard in Ramah. Rachel crying for her children because they are no more.'*[49] Zadok, poor Zadok, stayed to fight them. He helped the baby boy and his family escape. Gave them his donkey. They came here to Alexandria. To Egypt. And they lived on the gifts given to the child by the Eastern kings. They lived in safety with me in this house until we got word that Herod died." Onias held out his hands to show Marcus. "The little boy would come to me. See? Little steps. Little steps into my arms. He'd take my hands and lay his cheek against my wounds. Kiss them and say he was sorry I was hurt." The old face clouded with the memory. "He knew even then, I think."

"Knew what?"

Onias sighed. "What is yet to be. What must be. But we're going too fast. Bring your thoughts back to the prophecy of Egypt. To Mosheh, The Name, and to Messiah."

Marcus harnessed his curiosity and focused on details from the sacred writings. "Then show me, sir, if Egypt is also in the prophecy about the Messiah."

"Good. Well done, boy. Ask. Ask the Lord of Heaven who breathed these Scriptures into existence! Ask his Spirit to show you! Is any detail past or present left out? Friend, search the Scriptures and see for yourself!"

"Tell me plainly!"

"The word of the Lord concerning Messiah was recorded by Hosea: '*When Israel, the Prince of God, was a child, I loved him. Out of Egypt I have called my son.*'[50] Every Jew knows this Scripture refers to the Messiah."

"And so the child and his parents returned from Egypt."

"And I had no word about him until you brought this letter from my brother. Yet you've seen the lad grown up! About your age he'd be now. And since I've told you my part of the story, will you tell me? Tell me about him? Tell me what he teaches and what wonders he does. Tell me, son, for I'm as hungry to know the rest of the story as you are to understand the beginning of it."

And so Marcus stayed far into the night. He told what little he knew, beginning with the first time he saw Yeshua heal a child at the Jordan near where Joshua led his people into the land. There was more than enough to spend the hours. The old rabbi knew what questions to ask. Marcus could not fully comprehend the meaning of it, but every detail delighted the old man.

After a time, Onias wrote a long letter to Zadok and sealed it. He cupped Marcus' face in his gnarled hands, kissed his cheek, and said, "This for your kindness, Marcus Longinus, for you've brought water to a thirsty soul. Give this kiss to my brother Zadok." He kissed the other cheek. "And another for Yeshua. Tell him, when you see him, that old Onias of Alexandria remembers him. Tell him I remember the way he held my wounds and looked at me as if they were his wounds. The sorrow on his sweet face. Tell him I pray for him, will you? Tell him Onias is glad to have lived to hear this report. Now go on, friend, and may the peace of the Lord go with you."

It was still dark when Marcus left the house and set out for his quarters. Far from being satisfied with the fragments of knowledge he gleaned from sharing bread with the old rabbi, Marcus longed to know more.

16

CHAPTER

T he prisoner Manaen bar Talmai says nothing, Lord Antipas," the jailor reported. "Doesn't speak a word. Nor reach for food nor water neither."

"The food is brought to my brother? He's aware?" Demos asked.

"Yes, sir. I put it close at hand. Within reach. Beside him. Tell him it's there. All he has to do is reach for it. But he doesn't."

"Does he show signs of pain?" Antipas seemed concerned. Their sport was being ruined by Manaen's obstinate refusal to suffer.

"No, sir. Not when he's awake. Though it's hard to tell sleep or waking, being as he's got no eyes."

Demos, disappointed, remarked, "He's set in his mind he'll not give us satisfaction. He'll never let us know he suffers."

"Strong-willed. Stubborn to the last," Antipas agreed.

The jailor tugged his ragged beard. "He's decided to die, by the look of him. I've seen such signs before. Won't take long without water. If it was only food he was refusing, it could take weeks to waste away. A buck as big and strong as himself. Weeks. But water? You know they're serious when they won't let a drop pass their lips. Days."

Demos sipped his wine and muttered into the cup, "Means to spite us. Proud. Always was too proud for his own good."

"You have heard no word uttered by him?" Antipas probed the jailor further.

"Once I thought I heard him call the name of the Lady Susanna. But that was just after. Delirious. Not right in the head."

"Then she is the food that will break him." Herod sniffed and sat back with satisfaction in his gilded chair. "What do you think, Demos? Is a reunion in order?"

THE FRAGRANT SCENT OF SUSANNA. The swish of her robes. A soft, cool touch on his burning brow. The sweet taste of pressed apple juice held to his lips, dripping from her finger onto his parched tongue. Her voice. *"Manaen! Manaen! Don't leave me! Stay, Manaen! Live!"*

Was it a dream?

"You?" he whispered.

"They told me you won't eat."

"Don't look at me," he moaned. "Don't . . . "

"You can't give up." She began to wash away the dried blood from his face and dripped oil on his crusted eyelids. Her hands trembled as she wrapped a soft, clean bandage around his head. Her breath was shallow, rapid, as if she fought to control her emotions.

"Don't . . . look at me . . . "

"Antipas let me come. To feed you. To care for you."

"Are you . . . all right?"

"Here. I've brought soup."

"Has Demos . . . hurt you?"

"No. No. I'm kept in my chambers. There's a guard. Hush. Softly. They'll hear us."

He lowered his voice. "Why did they let you come?"

"You must . . . here. Good chicken soup for you. A jug of apple cider. Bring you back. Back."

"Back to what?"

"To live. To me, Manaen. To me."

"But my eyes!"

"I'll be forever beautiful to you. Even when we're very old. Very old . . . together. Living together. Somewhere. Somewhere. Not here." Louder then, "Now open your mouth. Good broth for you."

He accepted a spoonful of broth. It hung on his tongue, then slid down his throat. "Good." He sighed. "Yes. Thirsty. Didn't want to . . ."

"Another. There. All right." She leaned close to his ear. "I'll bribe someone. Find a way. We'll run away. Away from this madness."

"They don't mean to let me live. Demos will . . . "

"I've sent a letter to Tiberius. My father never meant for me to be forced into a marriage I didn't want."

"Blind. A blind man. What life can you have?"

"Here. Bread." She soothed him. "You must hang on. Can't give in. *Live, Manaen! God is not blind!*"

The ring of the jailor's keys approached. Susanna laid her head against his chest. "Oh, Manaen!"

"You must go!"

"I can't."

"The trellis. Remember. A way of escape."

"I won't leave you!"

"You must. They won't let you come to me again."

The jailor pounded on the solid oak door. "Time's up!"

"No! No!"

Gruffly he called, "Orders, miss! Come on!"

Manaen touched her face. Smooth skin. High cheekbones. Full lips parted. Aquiline nose. Tears. "They put out my eyes, but I see you still."

She cried, "If they tear out my ears, I'll hear your voice! Cut out my tongue, I'll speak your name! Break off my arms, I'll hold you still! Without feet my soul will run to you! I won't leave you!"

The jailor was in the cell. "Come on, Lady Susanna. Orders from above."

Still she sobbed and clung to Manaen.

"You have my heart. Now go, Susanna," he urged. "Go now. You must!" He hoped she understood his meaning. She must somehow get away from Antipas. Hide herself somewhere. She had friends in Galilee. She could get word to Rome of her abuse and his fate. "Susanna, do you understand me?" He gently pushed her away. "Tell me . . . you understand."

She kissed him one last time. "Yes, yes. But promise . . . if I go . . . you'll try. Try to stay alive."

"Yes. I promise." The panic of knowing he might never be with her again made him desperate inside. Desperate to hold on to her. But he could not show it. This was hard enough without his breaking. "Yes." He groped for the basket she had placed at his right hand. No tears came from his eyes. That was a mercy anyway. Lifting a jug of cider to his lips he tried to swallow. "Good. Very. Good. Yes, I'll be all right now. Go on. Do what I've told you. Go on!"

She struck out at the jailor as he put a hand on her to lead her away. "Keep your muddy paws off!" Then, "Leave him the candle! Don't take the candle from him!"

"What difference to a blind man?"

"Leave the candle!"

Manaen could hear the edge of hysteria growing in her voice. "Susanna? Never mind the candle. There's my girl. Susanna? I'll . . . see you. . . . Remember. Remember what we promised. Go now. Quickly."

The cell door slammed shut and she was led away.

"No light," Susanna said that night as she blew out the candle Naomi placed beside her on the table. "Not tonight."

Somehow sitting in darkness made Susanna feel closer to Manaen. She tasted a bit of bread, a sip of juice. The same food she had taken to his cell.

After a time Naomi remarked, "You can't sit in the dark forever, Lady."

"Manaen will. Darkness. Forever."

"Lady, Wolf says they can make you do whatever they wish. There are ways, Lady Susanna. They'll be patient for a little while and then . . ."

"I can't leave him."

"You mustn't stay. You said so yourself. He told you to leave. Told you to escape. Please, Lady. You can hide awhile. Until the right people receive your letters."

"What if they hurt him? Hurt him because I've gone? Don't you think if I'm here at least they'll be careful what they do to him?"

"They've put out his eyes while you are near," Naomi reminded her. "They've done it to torment you. To bend you to their will. Don't stay."

Susanna felt as though she could not catch her breath. As if she was living through a horrible dream. In the morning she would wake up and none of it would be real.

And yet, she knew Naomi was right. They would torture Manaen in order to break Susanna.

"How? How can I get away?" she asked at last.

"I've thought it through." Naomi drew closer. "Beg Antipas to let you go to the Temple and sacrifice. He can't refuse you that. Think of some excuse. Go in the morning hours, when the sun shines from the east and glints on the gold of the Temple buildings. No one looks at anything else with such a sight! Then you can slip away. Leave through the Eastern Gate. Where was it Joanna was going with her son?"

"Beth-Anyah. The home of a friend."

"Then that's where you must go! A short walk. No distance at all! Bethany! Find Joanna! She'll know what to do!"

17

he second summons from Caligula came early in the morning, when Marcus had neither breakfasted nor finished dressing. Since Caligula had a reputation for loving luxury and sloth, this just-past-dawn communication was unusual. Marcus knew he had to obey at once. The instruction directed him to a Jewish banking establishment known as Alexander of Leontopolis.

Marcus arrived and was escorted into a counting room. Caligula, an enraptured look on his pale face, watched stacks of silver coins being counted and loaded into chests.

"The letters from Tribune Felix and Tetrarch Philip?" Caligula demanded. "You have them?"

Marcus presented a leather courier's pouch.

Stepping to a table set in an alcove, Caligula unrolled the scrolls and studied them, then clucked his tongue. "What a fine mess Sejanus and his pretty puppets have made of Judea," he noted.

Marcus asked, "What message should I bring back to Tribune Felix, my Lord?"

"Sejanus put Pilate in Jerusalem. Vara is one of Sejanus' officers. Tell Felix they're on the way out. Be patient. Corruption. Bungling.

Incompetence. Great-Uncle Tiberius needs to hear this at once. . . . Tell Felix I'm leaving for Rome. Today. Before noon. Wind and tide are favorable. More news has come. Great-Uncle Tiberius has forbidden Sejanus to marry my sister, Livilla. Well, well. A shock to Sejanus, eh? But sister and Sejanus are meeting secretly. A shock to Tiberius when he finds out." Caligula tugged a lock of his hair thoughtfully. "They say my sister poisoned her husband so she could be with Sejanus. Think Tiberius will be interested? Isn't that a choice bit of news?"

Choice was not the descriptive word Marcus would have selected. Marcus did not miss the intrigues of Rome. However, this time more than just gossip would be involved if Caligula's story was true: The murdered husband was the son of Emperor Tiberius.

"You see why I have to go at once? News like this will even distract Great-Uncle Tiberius from his little playthings. After all, who will he turn to in his hour of need? Me, of course. He's killed everyone else." Caligula drew his skinny body up proudly. "Sejanus has much to answer for. Sejanus encouraged Tiberius to exile my mother to an island where she died . . . starved to death. . . . Did you know that? Starved my brother too, not that he would ever have amounted to anything. But now . . . now. The legions of Syria and Germany are tired of Sejanus and his strutting. Much above his station. Ambitious, that's what he is. But the troops worshiped my father; they'll worship me soon enough."

Marcus reflected on what Caligula meant. General Germanicus had been a fine man, a superior soldier. Marcus admired and respected Germanicus and had followed him unquestioningly. But Marcus would no longer worship any man.

Caligula left no doubt what *he* meant by *worship* when he added, "Perhaps you've already heard about the oracle of the Cumaean Sibyl? It's the strangest thing. The oracle predicts that soon all temples of Rome will be dedicated to just one god. Can you imagine that? The oracle says that the god of gods is coming. Why, even the Jews have such a tale, don't they? A god to rule the whole world. Coming soon, they say."

Marcus was sure Caligula saw himself as the embodiment of those prophecies.

Madness.

The two men reentered the counting room. Ten chests of money were strapped shut, awaiting transport, while a further five were still being filled. "My family has used this bank since the days of my great-grandfather Mark Antony and that harlot Cleopatra," he said. "Great-Grandfather left this firm in charge of my grandmother's fortune, and I must say, they've done—"

Just then a pair of slaves, lifting the eleventh chest, stumbled against a table. A handful of coins scattered across the marble floor.

"Idiots!" Caligula shrieked. "Now it'll have to be recounted. Do you think I want to be cheated?" To the overseer of the tally he ordered, "Take them out and have them flogged. . . . Flog them to death!" Then in a calmer tone, "But don't start till I come. I want to watch. Will you join me, Marcus?"

Marcus bowed. "Duty calls me back to Judea." He struggled to keep the disgust he felt out of his reply. "There's a galley sailing today, and I have to prepare to join it."

Caligula grasped Marcus by the wrist and stared into his eyes. "But I can count on you, can't I? When Tiberius dies . . . as he will . . . I'll always be able to count on you, just as my father could? I'll raise you up, Marcus! I've always liked you. And when Tiberius is dead? When my light shines brighter than any in the heavens? I'll make you shine too."

Marcus bowed again, this time lower. "There is no light but the One True Light." He could not bring himself to say more. He raised his eyes and watched as the pathetic creature scurried away to enjoy another's torments. Marcus knew that within Caligula and the rulers of Rome reigned the dark counterfeit that would surely attempt to destroy the One True Light of the World.

The Caesars who commanded the Empire could and would break men at a whim.

Only Yeshua of Nazareth could make broken people whole again.

HEROD ANTIPAS HAD JUST FINISHED DINING IN THE garden with Herodias when Susanna entered the room. She knelt before the couple.

"I've come with a request," she began. "Thank you for receiving me."

Antipas replied coolly, "Request, is it? Susanna has a request, Herodias. What do you think it might be?"

"Well, well, Susanna." Herodias dabbed her thin lips with a napkin.

"Come to report any more ghosts, have you? Yochanan the Baptizer wandering through the corridors?"

"No, Herodias."

"You had quite the effect on Salome. She's left Yerushalayim. Gone to Caesarea to visit her cousin Demetrius. Says she doesn't care if she ever comes back to this place. Can't say I blame her much. Or you for trying to get even. But really, Susanna. Ghosts?"

Eyes lowered, Susanna did not dare gaze directly at her tormentors. They would read her anger and revulsion in an instant. "I want to go to the Temple in the morning."

"Suddenly religious?" Herodias sneered.

"I wish to make a sacrifice."

"Sinned, have we?"

"It's the anniversary of my father's death. Surely you can't refuse me that."

Herod shifted on his couch. "Refuse you? What have we refused you except that which is hurtful to you?"

Susanna would not engage in an argument about Manaen. About her love for him. "I have an obligation to my father's memory."

"Touching," Antipas said. Then, to Herodias, "You think when I die, Salome will go to the Temple and make a sacrifice for me?"

Herodias laughed. "Not Salome. Not here. I'm afraid Salome has become enthralled with the goddess Artemis of Ephesus. She'll travel to see that temple and make a sacrifice for you there if you like."

Susanna felt ill. Color drained from her cheeks. Evil was pervasive in the room. The souls of Antipas and Herodias were dark beyond the blindness of physical eyes. One could live without sight. But how could a soul live without light, without mercy?

Susanna fought to control her voice. She must not let them hear her fear. "My father was a Jew. Honored as an upright man. Would you bring shame on me by refusing this simple request to duty?"

Antipas held up a jeweled hand. "No one said *refuse*. Simply an inquiry as to your motives. I have not thought of my old dear father, the butcher king, in thirty years. Would not pay a penny for a sparrow to sacrifice in the memory of that old bag of guts. So I ask you about this out of curiosity. I am still fascinated by the adherence of my subjects to these religious laws. I lean more to the Sadducee sect, myself. When you die you are dead. No heaven. No hell. It removes so many moral obstacles in life. Does that not make sense?"

"Whatever your belief or unbelief, you do what's right in your own eyes. I must do what's right in *my* conscience. This is my obligation as a daughter to her father."

Antipas sighed. He had wearied of her. "Well then. If it must be done." He snapped his fingers and issued a command to his secretary to arrange for Susanna to go to the Temple in the morning.

18

Most shops in Jerusalem were not yet open. Peniel liked the city at this hour, when he could still hear the birds . . . before the clamor and bustle of buying and selling drowned out the peacefulness of creation. Fingering the raised letters on the rim of his begging bowl, Peniel trudged slowly up the lane toward the Temple Mount.

He sang softly, "Peniel! Peniel! My name is Peniel!"

Maybe today would be the day!

Peniel thought about the gardenia bush. Growing in the shadow outside the wall of Nakdimon ben Gurion's house, the stray shrub had been there as long as anyone could remember. An aged bush, tucked into a north-facing angle of a high wall, it belonged to no one; yet it survived to bloom year after year. And each year the arrival of the first bud to blossom was a cause of celebration and rivalry.

After much discussion, criticism, and deliberation, Torah schools and groups of link boys each chose a bud to represent their faction. Each tightly wound, dark green boll was identified by colored thread and monitored at successive sunrises as the time for opening drew near.

Whoever's bud was the first to bloom won the contest. In the event of a tie, the larger flower won.

The Jerusalem Sparrows—the link boys who lived in the quarry and carried the torches by night—believed that if an orphan like them captured the first blossom, they would have good fortune all year.

The Torah schoolboys competed, one class against another, to carry the first gardenia into their classroom. Such a thing brought luck for exams, they said, and marked divine approval of their rabbi.

But the gardenia bush was more than just luck.

Peniel had heard from the Ushpizin in a dream that the bush was planted by the angel who had stopped Abraham from plunging the knife into the heart of his son Isaac. Drops of blood from the heart of the ram that God provided for sacrifice fell on the ground and nourished the pure white flowers growing there. The fragrance of the bloom was actually the breath of the angel, whispering the name of the one who carried away the flower.

Peniel! Peniel! My name is Peniel!

It made a fine legend.

Abraham's Bush, the Ushpizin called it. It was a wonderful dream. When he awoke, Peniel had prayed that one day the Lord would allow him the honor of picking the first flower from Abraham's gardenia bush at first light.

That had been several years ago.

Peniel was never allowed to participate, of course, not officially. Each year he felt for the threads and bits of colored cloth, then pinned his hopes on some unremarkable and unchosen bud.

His blossom had never won—not surprising since he could not see and was not part of any school group. But all the same, it was a pleasant thing to imagine.

This morning Peniel wondered if Abraham's Bush had managed to survive the violent rampage of the sons of Abraham. The riots had roiled over the streets and alleyways exactly where the gardenia grew.

Stretching out his fingers, Peniel followed the line of the rough stone wall. The wall of Nakdimon was a strong wall, the wall of a rich man. No doubt Nakdimon had vast gardens within. But even so, Peniel would not trade the gardens of Nakdimon for a chance to have the one flower from Abraham's gardenia bush.

Peniel came to the corner of the wall where the bush grew. He put out his hand to feel the waxy leaves. Yes. Yes. It was still there, still growing next to the wall. Safe in the shadow. In some distant past a caring person had erected an awning for the gardenia, and in the shade it had grown to the size of an apple tree.

Peniel drew his breath in deeply. No scent. No flower yet. He reached to feel for the tight buds. Perhaps there were many, but Peniel found only one with a tag on it.

Behind him came the voices of Torah schoolboys. Peniel did not recognize them personally but knew what they were because they discussed the way an old rabbi dabbed his chin with his beard when he dissected the Torah.

They spotted Peniel. "What's this! What's he doing by our lucky bush?"

Peniel straightened but did not turn to face them.

"Hey, you! What're you doing there?"

"Just looking at it," Peniel said. They could not see that he was blind because his back was to them. "I'm just having a good look at it!"

"Well, you're not supposed to touch it! It's ours," declared one with the tone of a plump, arrogant, shopkeeper's child. Proprietary. Like he owned the bush. The street. The wind. The sun. "That's the rule! You can't touch it until the bud opens as wide as three fingers across."

It was a good rule. It meant that little boys with small hands had a better chance to win.

"There's nothing here today." Peniel clucked his tongue. "Maybe somebody got it already."

"No!" argued the second boy. "Look. That one. Right there. That's ours. I asked my father, and he said it would open any day now. All the boys in our class are going to sleep outside the night before it's ready to pick. We'll sleep out and pick it when it's just right. We'll break it in pieces so we each get a petal and a bit of luck."

"Hey!" the shopkeeper's son called. "You're a beggar. And blind! Look at his eyes! What're those letters on your bowl? Peniel? Peniel! What's that supposed to mean?"

"My name. My brother, Gershon, made it for me when I was very young." Peniel clutched the bowl tightly against his heart. His brother had formed the letters. Gershon said Peniel was bright, told Mama Peniel could learn to read with his fingers. But Gershon had died that year, and no one ever again said Peniel was bright. But Peniel carried the bowl his brother made and remembered his kindness. All these things Peniel thought about but did not tell the boys.

"This lucky bush is for Torah schoolboys. Not beggars."

Peniel felt them leering at him, scrutinizing him.

"Hey! Look! Look! I know him! He's the one who sits at Nicanor Gate and begs!"

"Sure! It's the potter's son! The cracked pot himself."

Just then one of the boys snatched Peniel's begging bowl from his hand and sent it spinning. Peniel lunged to retrieve it, but seconds later, it shattered against the pavement.

"My brother . . . Gershon . . . he made that special for me," Peniel whispered. "The letters of my name were raised so I could feel them. Gershon made it for me so I could learn to read with my fingers." Peniel grimaced and moaned. "My name . . . is Peniel. . . ."

The schoolboys danced around Peniel. They tossed bits of broken pottery in his face and chanted, "Broken pot . . . marred pot, the potter's son is a flawed pot!"

Nakdimon ben Gurion—Peniel recognized his voice—emerged from his garden. The man known as The Bull shouted at the Torah students, "Hey! What are you doing there? Get away from there!"

The boys scampered away, laughing.

Peniel heard Nakdimon advance toward him. "You know the rule! No touching the . . . but you're not a Torah student."

"No, sir," Peniel agreed. "I'm a beggar."

"Yes, of course," Nakdimon said. "And I know you. You're Peniel, who sits by Nicanor Gate. But what's happened here?"

"I . . . I came to visit Avraham's Bush. I like the fragrance, you see. But the others . . . they've broken my bowl, the one my brother . . . "

"Well," Nakdimon observed. When there was a faint clicking, Peniel knew Nakdimon was gathering the fragments of clay. "The bowl with your name on it," he said. "I'm sorry. Nothing left." Then, "Wait here a moment."

Nakdimon's footsteps hurried off toward his garden gate, then reemerged seconds later. "Here," he said, thrusting something into Peniel's hands. "It's not so fine as yours, but it will serve. They won't break this."

Peniel ran his hands over the smooth, polished metal surface of the wide, flat bowl. He did not want it. How could Nakdimon know what Gershon's bowl meant to him? "This feels expensive," he said. "I can't take it. Someone will say I stole it."

Peniel could almost feel Nakdimon swell up with indignation, so forceful was his next remark. "You tell them it's a gift from Nakdimon ben Gurion," he said. "In exchange for your prayers. If anyone doubts it, send them to me and I'll set them straight!"

Peniel thanked him. Promised to pray for him. It was a kind gesture. Well meaning. Though it would never replace what had been lost.

THE ALMS BOWL GERSHON HAD MADE FOR Peniel was shattered in a million pieces. Not one fragment was left. Not even one letter of Peniel's name remained intact.

Without the letters on the bowl, who would speak the name of Peniel when they gave their gift to the Lord?

Peniel did not go to his place at Nicanor Gate to collect alms, nor did he eat. His heart was not in it.

He was sorry he had gone to Abraham's gardenia bush, that he had wished for a flower that could never be his. Now he had lost forever Gershon's last gift, the one possession that had meant anything.

And in losing the bowl Gershon had made for him, he felt for the first time that his brother was gone too.

"Who will know my name now?"

Peniel made his way to the Pool of Siloam and sank down in despair against a pillar in the shaded portico.

This was the first time he had come to the great reservoir since Gershon died. If Peniel decided never to go home again, no one would think to look for him here. Who would imagine that, after all these years, Peniel would come back to Siloam?

He had to reason it out. Consider what it meant. What lesson he should learn from this loss.

How different, how ordinary, this day at the pool from the day he lost his brother. And who remembered now what happened, other than Peniel? Even his mother and father refused to speak of it, except in those moments when Mama said it should have been Peniel, not Gershon.

Today women came and went, fetching water for their households. Little children played tag around the pool. Here at least, Peniel thought, no one would bother him. He could sit and grieve without having to explain anything to anyone.

The bowl was a thing, he told himself. Clay and glaze hardened by fire into a useful object. A thing. Yet his hands felt empty without it. He remembered how Gershon had sat at the potter's wheel for days before Peniel's seventh birthday. How he had labored to make it smooth and pleasant to touch. He had shaped each letter from the soft clay and set PENIEL PENIEL PENIEL round the rim among the moon and stars. Carefully Gershon had etched a rainbow over the Mount of Olives on one side and Nicanor Gate on the other. This, he explained, was the picture Peniel would see from Nicanor if he had eyes. Then Gershon had glazed his creation with color and explained to Peniel that color was to the eyes what music was to the ears. A happy, bright thing that touched the soul and made a person thank God for all He created.

Even after Gershon died, Peniel held the Mount of Olives and the color of a rainbow in his hands and sensed his brother near. Even then Peniel remembered to thank Adonai for His beautiful creation! His heart overflowed with joy for what God had made and the gift Gershon had given him by letting him imagine it.

Now Gershon's rainbow was shattered. The mountain vanished. Imagined colors all gone.

How many years had Peniel sat at Nicanor Gate and fingered the raised lettering and in his mind heard Gershon's voice calling, "Peniel! Peniel! Peniel!"

It had kept him company when children mocked him. *Peniel the potter's son! Peniel the cracked pot! Clumsy! Ugly! Useless! Evidence of God's displeasure! Peniel the flawed creation!*

Peniel leaned his head back against the marble pillar and listened to the sounds of Siloam Pool. Mothers. Children. Angry, impatient voices. Blind hearts who did not see anything.

"Come here! You! Listen to me! Did you hear what I said?"

"Stop that right now or I'll have a word with your father and I mean it."

"Mama, Tobias pulled my hair."

"Tabitha splashed water on me."

"He started it."

"I'm hungry."

"Can we go now?"

"Stop it! I've had enough! You drive me crazy! Your father will hear about this!"

Did they ever look at one another? Peniel wondered. Did they ever stop long enough to *really* see one another's hearts?

Did these mothers raise their heads and see the rainbow over the mountains? Though Peniel had no eyes, still he knew the rainbow and the mountain were there! Proof was on Gershon's gift.

They had eyes to see. Why didn't they show their little ones the real rainbow and the real mountains beyond the city walls, where Messiah would come someday? Gershon had made the picture in clay so Peniel could see it plainly with his fingertips every day. Every day. Peniel's view never changed. And yet he never grew tired of it. He would hold the rainbow in his hands and hear his brother's voice echo in the raised letters on the begging bowl. *"Peniel! Peniel! Peniel! Look to the east from where you sit. There is the Mount of Olives, where one day Messiah will descend from heaven! There will be a rainbow around his throne! Yes! Shaped like this! Can your heart see it now? Believe it! One day, like your name says, you will see him face-to-face! His face will be the first thing you see! Believe it, Peniel! This is what faith is!"*

Faith. It was hope for something Peniel could not yet see. It was proof that he was loved by the Lord.

Gershon's gift had made Peniel happy. He had always believed the picture Gershon made for him of a world he could not see with his physical eyes. So now the bowl was broken, but not the gift, Peniel reasoned. He would hold the gift tightly in his heart. He would not let go! No one could smash it. No cruel hand could steal it away from him.

Faith.

Peniel believed color existed beyond the darkness. Yes! The mount where Messiah would stand! The rainbow around his throne! They were real, more wonderful than he could imagine!

As Peniel stood to leave this place of his sorrow, he was certain he would never return to it again.

19 | C H A P T E R

I t was still early that morning when Susanna embraced Naomi and
bid her farewell.

"I'll pray for your safety, Lady. Remember, lose your escort in the
crowd. Join some family. Some band of pilgrims. Leave by way of the
Eastern Gate. And then you're on your way to Bethany."

"I wish you would come with me."

"I have Wolf. They must think you've thought of this on your own.
Now go. Bless you."

"Shalom, dear friend."

Susanna took nothing but what she wore on her back. Hidden beneath her clothing was a pouch of golden coins. Enough for her to survive for a couple months. Perhaps enough to buy passage to Rome. She
would take her petition in person to her mother's sister.

Susanna slipped out the door. The residents of the palace were sleeping after a night of carousing. Only servants and slaves moved about.

Susanna heard voices in the foyer. She hurried down the stairway.

Waiting for her were fifteen of Antipas' personal bodyguards and a
phalanx of Levite priests.

Linen-clad, dressed for Temple service, a priest who was the head of a delegation of six bowed deeply to her. "Lady Susanna bat Maccabee?"

"Yes." Her heart sank. Too many here for her to get free of them.

"The tetrarch is anxious that you be accompanied to the Temple in a manner honoring your father. We have come to escort your litter. We will stay near to you. Anything you need, we are at your command."

She attempted to put them off. "This is a private occasion."

The priest was solicitous. "The tetrarch sent a message personally to High Priest Caiaphas, regarding you and your father. The tetrarch asks that you not be left alone, that we stay nearby at all times. Treachery is yet loose in the streets. Who can say what assassins may still be here in the city? Herod Antipas will not have you out of our sight. You are a prominent woman, of a righteous and honored family. You could be kidnapped and held for ransom."

Susanna did not reply. She was already being held for ransom by Herod Antipas and Demos.

There would be no chance of escape today.

"O TENDERHEARTED, BY YOUR MERCY GAIN MERIT with heaven by me!" Peniel called to the pilgrims as he sat beside the great gate.

The new metal alms dish made a satisfying *clink* whenever a penny was dropped into it. It was a fine, unbreakable dish, cast with flowers around the rim. They were shaped something like the gardenias on Abraham's Bush, Peniel consoled himself. He decided he would be grateful for Nakdimon's gift, that he would thank the Lord of hosts for giving him such a present from the hand of a righteous man like Nakdimon!

As Peniel shook his coins against the dish like a tambourine, a shadow blocked the heat of the sun. A lady. Peniel smelled her perfume. She paused before him.

"Blind man," she said, dropping a weighty coin into the bowl, "please, will you sing a prayer for a friend of mine? He's blind too. And a song for me as well."

"I will, Lady."

"I need your prayers. They say these days heaven hears the prayers of a poor man before the prayers of the priests."

He heard fear and sorrow in her voice. A young voice. Gently pleading.

"Well, I qualify as a poor man. You have my prayers. What should I sing?"

"A psalm to give us courage."

"What's your name, Lady, and I'll mention you often to the Almighty at His gate."

"Does my name matter?"

"No. The Lord knows your name. I'll remember your request. A song for courage." Peniel put his mind to it. Psalm 91 was his favorite. He often sang it when he was alone in his shelter and afraid. "All right then." His clear sweet tenor began to draw a crowd to the steps to listen.

"He who dwells in the shelter of the Most High
will rest in the shadow of the Almighty.
I will say of the Lord, 'He is my refuge
and my fortress,
my God, in whom I trust.'
Surely he will save you from the fowler's snare
and from the deadly pestilence.
He will cover you with his feathers,
and under his wings you will find refuge;
his faithfulness will be your shield and rampart.
You will not fear the terror of night,
nor the arrow that flies by day,
nor the pestilence that stalks in the darkness,
nor the plague that destroys at midday.
A thousand may fall at your side,
ten thousand at your right hand,
but it will not come near you.
You will only observe with your eyes
And see the punishment of the wicked."[51]

Peniel especially liked the part about his eyes seeing. He sang on, finishing the prayer as he shook the bowl with a flourish. Others stooped to drop a penny in as they passed by.

She, the nameless woman, remained transfixed above him. "Why did you choose that song? My great-great-grandfather sang it night and morning. In war and in peace. These were the Scriptures he wore in his phylacteries."

"The promise is yours then. The rabbis say that we're blessed by the old prayers of our grandfathers and by the future prayers of sons yet to be born. Because there is only an eternal present with the Lord. No past. No future. Only now."

"You're young, blind man. How do you know these things?"

"I have sat at this gate and listened since I was seven."

She sighed. "I wish I could sit with you. Listen and believe God hears and sees."

"Believe it. Remember the words of Psalm 94. He who formed the eyes isn't blind. He who implanted the ear isn't deaf.[52] God knows your name," Peniel promised. "Heaven bless you, as you have blessed a blind beggar today. I won't forget to pray for you."

She melted away among the throng gathering for the noon sacrifice, but her perfume lingered. From behind him a man said, "Do you know who that was? The ward of Herod Antipas, Susanna bat Maccabee. Her great-great grandfather won back Yerushalayim from the Greeks. Purified the Temple. Much good it did. Like us, she's at the mercy of Herod Antipas and the Romans."

"They let her come here alone?"

"She's not alone. Look there. Her litter's at the gate. Fifteen of Antipas' bodyguards waiting for her to make her sacrifice. Then they'll cart her back to the palace. She's not going anywhere without Antipas' spies following along."

Peniel began to pray the psalm again for her. For Susanna.

> *"For he will command his angels concerning you,*
> *to guard you in all your ways;*
> *they will lift you up in their hands,*
> *so that you will not strike your foot against a stone."*[53]

Madness was the key to unlock Manaen's cell.

Madness had served David when he hid among the Philistines. Madness gave Samson, the blind giant, victory over his enemies.

Yes. Madness. Useful. Puts them off the scent. Part of the plan. Must let the warden hear.

Manaen's teeth ached. He soaked the crust of bread in water and tore off a chunk.

O Lord, how many are my foes!

It became a game. He placed a morsel in his mouth.

How many rise up against me?

Holding it on his tongue, he tried to see how long he could make each bite last.

Many are saying of me, "God will not deliver him."

How long? An hour until the morsel dissolved?

But You are a shield around me, O Lord! You bestow glory on me and lift up my head.

In this way half a loaf of bread would be made to last until the next meal.

The warden came with his bread. Manaen shrieked, lunged, and rattled his chains.

To the Lord I cry aloud, and He answers me from His holy hill.

He had to have a plan. How could he draw in Demos? Bring Demos' throat within his grasp?

I lie down and sleep.

He savored each crumb, yet allowed himself only half his ration.

I wake again, because the Lord sustains me.

Loud enough for the warden to hear, he called out, inviting Yochanan the Baptizer to join him in the cell!

I will not fear the tens of thousands drawn up against me on every side.

"Come in! Enter, exalted guest! Be seated, faithful guests! Here! A feast of pheasant! Dates and walnuts! Bread and honey. Eggs. Chicken. Lamb *shashlik!*"

Arise, O Lord! Deliver me, O my God!

"Yes. I know. I know. The crust is stale. But if you take your time, it lasts longer than fresh bread. Something to be thankful for. Here. Have another shank of lamb!" The peephole in the door slid open. The warden examined the cell to see if Yochanan the Baptizer had joined Manaen. If there were pheasant and dates to eat.

"Daft!"

Strike all my enemies on the jaw! Break the teeth of the wicked!

"Sure. Yes. Yes. Sure. Tomorrow I'll be on my way. I'm going across the Jordan to the wilderness with you. Honey and wild locusts. Wash in the river. But for now, have another beef rib."

Peephole. Open again. "Look . . . fed him hours ago. Still half a loaf left. He sits in there and talks to spirits. Daft, I tell you. Somebody should report it to Lord Demos. . . . "

From the Lord comes deliverance.[54]

20

The caravansary in Ashkelon where Marcus left Pavor during his Alexandria trip was north of the city, on the road to Ashdod. The stablehands had taken good care of the animal. He was sleek, well fed, and rested . . . none of which applied to Marcus.

Meeting with Caligula had been unnerving to say the least. That the young man was mad was undeniable. Even worse than his delusion was his heartlessness. Worst of all was the suggestion that he might in fact become emperor. Tiberius was ailing in mind and body. Who knew how long he would live?

Rome had been racked before by civil wars. The most recent was when Augustus and Mark Antony battled for supremacy after the death of Julius Caesar.

Civil war had almost come again in Marcus' lifetime. The troops loyal to Germanicus, including Marcus, had lobbied for their commander to succeed Augustus instead of Tiberius.

No one wanted to see the Empire torn apart by such strife again, and yet . . . and yet . . .

What would the Empire be like under the hand of Caligula? Could it possibly be worse than with Sejanus?

And what place in such a world did one as gentle as Yeshua of Nazareth have? How long, in such a world, would it be before men bent on preserving their power moved to eliminate Him as a threat to their control?

Marcus was certain of only one thing: Yeshua was the reality of a king worthy to rule the whole world.

And Caligula was the counterfeit.

These thoughts troubled Marcus as he tried to sleep in a galleried room overlooking the courtyard of the inn. For several hours he wrestled with what to tell Felix. If he informed the tribune that Caligula was heading back to Rome to topple Sejanus, should he also mention that Caligula was crazy? or that the heir of the Imperial family was perhaps demon-possessed?

Sleep refused to come until after midnight, and then it was a fitful doze, full of dreams of Idistaviso. Cherusci tribesmen had swarmed out of the woods. No matter how many of them Marcus hewed down with an ax taken from a fallen enemy, ten more always took their places.

From behind him, toward the river, he heard the neighing of horses: Germanicus marshaling his cavalry for the charge that would sweep the German flank.

If only they arrived in time! If only Marcus' dwindling detachment of unwounded legionaries could hold out. How much longer? He heard the bugle of a warhorse again. In his dream he urged them to hurry, hurry!

And then Marcus was awake. The calling of the horse was Pavor! Instantly wide awake, Marcus reached slowly for the sword hanging from the bedpost. As he did so, he listened carefully.

The explanation for the alarm was not long in coming. A whispered conference took place on the landing outside his room.

"It's him, I tell you," muttered a raspy-voiced Idumean. "I recognize that black beast. We should get Commander Vara."

Vara! So Marcus had been located by the Praetorian commander. Marcus had no expectation that he would live out the night if captured; escape was the single option.

"Nothing doing," argued another higher-pitched voice. "Why share the reward with any others? Unless you're scared, Chabar. Think the four of us can't handle one sleeping centurion?"

Two other voices growled their affirmation.

The one entry to the room was by the door opening onto the landing. But there was a window beside this, unshuttered and covered with a leather curtain. The portal was narrow enough for Marcus to hold it against one attacker at a time, but others could get at him by the window. He needed another plan.

Marcus placed himself where the door would conceal him when it opened. Beside him was a low wooden bench.

Not a moment too soon, either.

The door flew open, shouldered by one of the assailants, and two of them burst into the room. Marcus slammed the door shut and threw the bench against it.

For the moment the odds were only two against one. And Marcus believed his eyes were better adapted to the dark than theirs. The first thrust of his gladius proved him correct. The trooper's parry was late, low, and did nothing to protect his midsection. Marcus buried six inches of his blade's length in the man's gut.

The man crumpled to the floor.

One down.

The other foe circled, bellowing for his comrades outside to hurry up!

Lunging toward the man, Marcus entered the battle again. Their blades rang together, spitting sparks. By the brief flicker Marcus saw a leg thrust over the window ledge.

Have to be quick!

Two more hammering blows, and Marcus moved suddenly to the right, exchanging their positions. The attacker's back was now to the door, which was even then being forced open again.

Hurling himself forward with a flurry of thrusts to make his opponent give ground, Marcus yelled, "He's making a run for it!" just as the portal was forced aside.

Light from the fire in the center of the courtyard gleamed along the blade of a gladius hacking downward from the doorway . . . onto the shoulder of Marcus' adversary.

The man struck by one of his companions screamed and spiraled through the doorway, blocking the opening again.

Two down.

But now the odds favored the attackers. The advantage of surprise was lost.

Worse, the man who arrived through the window had a lance in his hand. With it he parried the jabs of Marcus' short sword, not allowing Marcus to close with him.

Any moment the fourth enemy would be in the room. Marcus could be backed into a corner and pinned.

He doubted if the reward promised by Vara required him to be taken alive.

Marcus batted aside a thrust of the lance, then made a desperate move. Dropping his gladius to dangle from its strap around his wrist, he made a hasty grab for the straw-filled mattress and tossed it upward onto the lance point.

Flying straw and Idumean curses erupted as the attacker attempted to clear the encumbrance from his weapon.

Marcus heard the whistle of air from the descending swipe of a sword. He flung himself to the floor just as the blade passed over the back of his head.

From a crouch, Marcus barreled into the knees of the fourth opponent. The two men crashed back through the doorway. Their weight burst the thin railing, and they plunged ten feet to the cobblestone courtyard.

Fortunately, Marcus fell uppermost. The man underneath was unconscious or dead.

Marcus knew more of Vara's men might be within call. The need to get away was urgent.

As he shook off his daze from the fall, a lance caromed off the pavement with a clang, missing him by mere inches.

Then Marcus swung aboard Pavor and pounded away into the night.

From the ridgeline that connected the pastures of Migdal Eder with the nearby town of Beth-lehem, Marcus watched the valley below and the roads within it. He realized his best chance to avoid attracting attention was to remain hidden by day and approach Migdal Eder after dark.

It was wise that he had taken the precaution. Twice during his vigil he spotted Roman cavalry patrols riding along the highway between Jerusalem and Herodium. Marcus had no way to know if his absence was the object of their missions, but the attack in Ashkelon proved he was being pursued. One of the columns was led by a bulky man with a black plume to his helmet: Vara? The man was too far away for Marcus to be certain, but his instincts told him he was right.

Apart from the Roman legionaries, there were very few travelers on the roads heading up to Jerusalem.

Later, a caravan coming from the south lumbered past. Fifty camels, driven by men who appeared to be Nabateans from the desert kingdom east of the Jordan, bore their loads in stoic silence. The procession brought spices and perfume, fabric and exotic jewelry to sell.

The sun passed meridian height and settled toward the west. Its illumination fell fully on the outline of the aqueduct and the Tower of Siloam. As Marcus' eye followed the orderly march of pillars and arches, it came at last to the heap of wreckage that marked the fall of the Tower of Siloam. The cause was sabotage by bar Abba's rebels, certainly. One of the shepherd boys had overheard enough to convince Marcus of that. But the destruction of Pilate's pet project could not be untangled from the protests and the bloodshed that followed.

And somehow Marcus stood accused for not having prevented it. But he did not waste any time or emotion thinking about how unfair it was. Soldiering since age sixteen had taught Marcus that Roman discipline often consisted of offering up horrifying examples as deterrents. The dead bodies crucified outside Jerusalem's gates bore testimony that justice never took better than second place in the race. Fairness never left the starting line.

At last the sun dipped below the edge of the plateau, separating Beth-lehem from the coastal plain of Judea. Shadows lengthened.

Across the valley was Herodium, higher than all the surrounding hills. The fortress remained sunlit long after the canyons and pastures were shaded, as if the last thing anyone in Judea was allowed to see each day was a reflection of light upon Roman rule.

Nearer at hand, surrounded by flocks of sheep, the Tower of the Flock, also known as Migdal Eder, glowed warmly golden from the cook fires within and the watch fire on its summit.

And still Marcus remained rooted in place. He was certain that at least one of the Roman cavalry details would return to Jerusalem before nightfall. Marcus did not want to arrive at Zadok's at the same time some troopers stopped to ask questions.

Finally, dressed again as a Jewish peasant, he made up his mind to risk it.

The home of the Chief Shepherd was between Migdal Eder and little Bethlehem.

Concealing himself behind a row of sycamore figs, Marcus studied the house. It appeared peaceful enough; smoke came from its chimney, and there was a low murmur of conversation from the windows.

The door creaked open a crack.

Marcus drew back into the shelter of the trees.

A red sheepdog emerged, sniffing the air. Its head swiveled instantly toward Marcus' hiding place, and its ears pricked forward. A low growl rumbled in the animal's throat.

There was the tromp of heavy boots within the house and then Zadok, gleaming white hair and beard both braided into thick cords, stepped out.

The dog snarled once. "Get by, dog," Zadok commanded sharply. "I already know he's there." Advancing a half score of paces, Zadok spoke again: "You can come in any time, Centurion. You missed supper, but we saved you bread and an egg or two."

Marcus was stunned. No one knew his plan. How had the old man guessed his identity there in the darkness?

Marcus emerged from the shadows.

"You were right to wait till after sunset," Zadok volunteered. "Soldiers came to Migdal Eder lookin' for y'. I was ordered—me, the Chief Shepherd of Israel, *ordered* by a Samaritan trooper!—to report your whereabouts if y' came round. Come in and eat. Afterwards y' can explain all this to me."

The red dog lay across the doorway, seriously fulfilling his role as guardian of the little flock sheltered by Zadok's two rooms. In the rear chamber, in a tangle of arms, heads, and sheep-fleece bedding, lay Zadok's three adopted boys. Marcus watched with amusement as one by one the three lost the battle with the need to sleep.

"They have reason to be exhausted," Zadok observed. "This is the busiest season of the year for us, what with taking ten thousand lambs to the Temple. But of course you can stay amongst the keepers of Migdal Eder." Zadok glanced again at the letter Marcus had brought from Onias. "There is nothing I won't do for you if it's within my power and does not offend the Almighty."

"It'll be dangerous," Marcus said, disturbed that permission was given so quickly. "I'm not a deserter, but I'll be treated like one if Praetorian Vara has his way. And that puts an extra threat on your own head. Vara hates people enough to kill them, and he especially hates those who manage to escape him once."

Fingering the black eyepatch and laying a calloused finger in the scar that creased his face, Zadok said wryly, "I'm not so easy to kill. He may find it's more trouble than it's worth."

"There are the boys to think of," Marcus urged.

"They are shepherds of Israel," Zadok said proudly. "Proved their mettle, they did. King David got his start right here, rescuing lambs from bears and lions. Is a Praetorian fiercer than a bear or a lion?"

Marcus nodded slowly. "Yes. And more cruel. A lion kills for food, Vara for sport."

Zadok waved away the caution. "My boys'll do well enough. It's yourself we must think on. With your beard, and dressed the way you are, y' look the part. Add a shepherd's crook, and no one'll guess a centurion hides beneath! Now y' must live here with us. The boys know who y' are, of course, but they'll keep silent about it. Never fear. I'll let it be known about that you're a distant relative of mine, come from . . . Alexandria? We of Judea think the Egyptian Jews are strange anyway. Y' speak Greek with the ease of an Alexandrian. That'll explain any awkwardness about your speech. Your name. Marcus is fine for someone from Alexandria. There'll be gossip in Beth-lehem about y', so if we give them a story. . . . Tell me, did you kill anyone in Alexandria, or are y' running from creditors?"

"Neither." Marcus laughed. "My two wives found out about one another."

"That'll do!" Zadok agreed. "Two wives are enough to make any man leave home for a far country! All right, rest tonight. Tomorrow y' start your duties tending the flocks of the Most High."

The lambing barns of Migdal Eder were contained within a series of low-ceilinged caverns. Dry, sheltered from cold and wind, their still air was redolent of fresh straw, fragrant fodder, manure, and the peculiar oily smell of fleece. The arrival of new life in such a familiar place was a pleasant duty for Zadok to supervise.

Eleven-year-old Ha-or Tov, his mop of curly red hair wagging with his concentrated breathing, struggled to bring a baby lamb into the world. Blind before meeting Yeshua, the boy had a keen instinct for the work. His finely tapered hands slid easily into the birth canal of the laboring ewe. He was comfortable using senses other than sight to sort out the puzzle within the ewe. Under Zadok's tutelage, Ha-or Tov had learned when an application of muscle was required and when to let nature do the work.

The presentation with which he was coping was not unusual: a pair of lambs tangled in the womb. Eyes closed, Ha-or Tov sorted forelegs from hind, properly assigning limbs to lambs before proceeding.

Nine-year-old Avel sat atop a fence rail, watching, while Zadok offered instruction. "Find the hock. There. Y' have it? Now trace it back to the shoulder. Is there another leg hooked over it?"

Lev, an older stablehand of perhaps twenty years, appeared beside Zadok. The new arrival shuffled sideways and kept his face downturned, like a submissive herding dog approaching the chief male of the pack. When the three orphan boys had first arrived, Lev had been surly, jealous. But something miraculous had happened, and now he was humbled and deferential. "Sir," he said softly to Zadok, "the men—that is, some of the men—well, they have a question to put to you, a question for me to ask you, if it isn't too much bother."

"Eh?" Zadok said with a frown, not really listening. "What is't?"

"The men . . . Ephraim as their spokesman . . . they wanted me to ask you . . ." Lev's words trailed away.

Zadok never allowed loud noises to disturb the pregnant or newly birthed ewes, so he whispered fiercely, "Speak up! What is this about?"

"The new man, sir. The one as is out with young Emet, tending the goats. Ephraim says, well, he says we could get in trouble if the Romans find out."

"Ephraim says that, does he?" Zadok demanded.

"Well, sir, since we know who he is, for real, like."

"No, y' don't!" Zadok corrected in a bass rumble like thunder over the mountains of Moab. "Here, Ha-or Tov, you keep on there. Lev, you and Avel come outside with me."

Once outside the entry to the caverns Zadok commanded, "Lev, bring Ephraim to me!" Then as Lev hurried away with a worried what-have-I-gotten-into look on his face, Zadok remarked to Avel, "Y' must nip this sort of thing in the bud, Avel. When y' are Chief Shepherd here, remember that."

The two shepherds arrived from the direction of the tower. Both were shamefaced and nervous.

"So y' thought to question me, eh?" Zadok roared. The Chief Shepherd's complexion flushed, the line of his jaw turned to granite, and his eye flashed like fire. "Well, y' must keep your opinions to yerself, see?"

Haltingly, Ephraim queried, "He's no shepherd. Who is he?"

"He brought me a letter from Onias, in Alexandria. Tell yerselves he's one of the Ushpizin . . . an exiled wanderer . . . and treat him honorably . . . if y' must tell yerselves anything a'tall."

"But he's a Gentile."

"Then perhaps he's one of the Thirty-Six Righteous, the *Lamedvov* who wander the earth and hold back the judgment of the Almighty from the earth! Let be, do I make myself clear? Y' do me no good service by prattling. Don't speak of it, not in village, not in sheepfold. I say he *is* my brother. He *is* son to me, eh? That's enough! If I get word that anything further is spoken of this matter, him who does will have me to answer to, see?"

Ephraim and Lev nodded vigorously and bowed away from the blustering Chief Shepherd. "Wait," Zadok said, calling them back. "There's another matter. I'll have no cowards here, Ephraim. If y've got aught to ask me, do it yerself! Don't be sendin' poor lads like Lev to do yer dirty work for y'!"

After the inquisitive shepherds fled under Zadok's baleful eye, the Chief Shepherd turned to Avel and bent near the boy. "And that," Zadok said with a wink, "is part of yer training."

21 | CHAPTER

The dome of the Sanhedrin council chamber was awash in churning waves of opinion. Caiaphas and the other Temple authorities were anxious to maintain their control over the internal life of Judea, but first they had to subdue the Jewish elders.

"There will be serious consequences if there are more disturbances of the sort that led to the late rioting," Caiaphas intoned. "The Roman governors allow us a great deal of latitude." Caiaphas shook his finger at the crowded room. "But if any more petty squabbles over religious opinions get out of hand, then we'll have Roman magistrates deciding purely Jewish questions."

"Petty issues like using money set apart for the Almighty for another purpose altogether?" Nakdimon inquired sarcastically. "Like turning over control of sacred money to a pagan governor?"

"Let's keep to the matter at hand," Caiaphas remarked hastily.

"So we should give in on the big things so as to maintain control of the little ones?" Gamaliel observed wryly.

"This council will not be allowed to govern Jewish affairs if we can't demonstrate that we can control the Jewish rabble," Annas, Caiaphas' father-in-law, whined.

"Exactly my point," Caiaphas resumed. "Now about this Yeshua of Nazareth. He claims to be the Messiah. Not only is that blasphemous, but every false messiah in the past has been a rebel leader. Rome has crucified would-be messiahs before, but even worse, Rome is watching to see if *we* tolerate any such fanatics."

"It seems to me," Gamaliel said, "that there are two questions. The first is, has Yeshua of Nazareth actually made such a claim?"

At that, Caiaphas snapped his fingers. One of the Temple Guard retreated to an anteroom and returned with a fawning, smiling figure in tow. "Barak bar Halfi, a gentleman of Galilee, is a witness. Bar Halfi, speak of what you heard Yeshua of Nazareth say."

"Noble sirs," bar Halfi began, "it was in the home of . . . a notable Pharisee."

Nakdimon leaned over to his uncle Gamaliel and said softly, "Where bar Halfi got in without an invitation."

Regardless of who the unnamed notable Pharisee was, Barak bar Halfi was a notable paid informer, known to accept commissions from both the Temple authorities and the Romans.

"Yeshua claimed that he was the Light of the World."

There was a rumbling in the chamber. It had been reported that Yeshua had made that claim about himself on more than one occasion.

"You see?" demanded Caiaphas. "In the commentary on the Book of Beginnings it is written, 'O Lord of the universe, you commanded us to light lamps for you, yet you are the light of the world.' Clearly Yeshua connects himself with this passage."

"And in the book of the prophet Isaias," added an aged rabbi in a shaky, high-pitched voice, "we read that the Almighty says Messiah will be placed here as a light for the nations, to take the saving power of the Almighty to all the world. What else can Yeshua mean by that phrase?"

"Point taken," Gamaliel said, rising to his feet. "But if you recall, I said there were *two* issues. The first is what Yeshua says of himself. The second is—what if he really is the Messiah?"

The uproar in the chamber increased in pitch until a squad of guards posted outside the room flung open the doors to see if another riot had broken out.

Accusations and counteraccusations volleyed back and forth across the chamber.

"Listen to me," Nakdimon said. "No one ever did the things

Yeshua of Nazareth is doing. No one ever spoke as he speaks. I myself was present when he brought a dead girl back to life."

"Preposterous! The tricks of a charlatan. She was only asleep, or faking!"

"He took a handful of bread and fish, and fed twenty thousand people!" Nakdimon shouted over the tumult.

"More trickery! He sets himself up to be greater than Mosheh?"

When the roaring subsided, Gamaliel continued. "I do not say that he is the Messiah. I merely point out that if Yeshua of Nazareth *is* the Anointed One of the Almighty, I, for one, would not care to be on record as opposing him."

"A Messiah from the Galil?" Caiaphas scoffed. "Will Messiah come from the sticks? No, he must be born in Beth-lehem of Judea. Isn't that so? And you a teacher of renown."

Gamaliel ignored the scorn and addressed another question to bar Halfi. "What else did Yeshua say? Did he offer to validate his claim by proofs?"

Bar Halfi stared at the high priest as if hoping for instruction, but when he received none he said, "No."

"Come, come," Gamaliel insisted. "A moment ago you weren't so terse with your information. Isn't it true that signs were asked of him?"

Bar Halfi only nodded, once.

"And what was his response?"

"He said," bar Halfi answered reluctantly, "that this was an evil generation and that no sign would be given it except the sign of Jonah."

"Did he say what he meant by that?"

Again a curt motion of bar Halfi's head was the negative reply.

"Learned council," Gamaliel said, "I cannot explain what Yeshua meant by the *sign* of Jonah. Can any in this room? No? Yet we all know the *message* of Jonah. It is: Change your evil ways or be destroyed by the Almighty! From what I hear of Yeshua's preaching, it sounds to me like he is joining us Pharisees in calling for greater holiness in the world."

There were only a handful of the Pharisee sect on the council, but another of these rose in rebuttal. "You go too far," he admonished Gamaliel. "Yeshua could never be one of us. He does not even wash his hands before meals."

There was a general groan from the majority of the members,

which Gamaliel concluded with the words, "I stand corrected. Perhaps Yeshua would not wish to be one of us."

There were shouts of rage, laughter, and many shaking fists.

Caiaphas motioned with his finger, and an attendant banged his staff on the flagstones to call the meeting back to order. "I say again: Yeshua of Nazareth is dangerous. Some of the rabble call him Isaias or Elijah . . . some even say he's Yochanan the Baptizer, back from the dead. It is said that Herod Antipas thinks it may be true."

"If I were Herod Antipas," Gamaliel said, "I would be right to be worried about that."

"Enough banter!" Annas declared. "It should be unlawful for anyone to claim that Yeshua is the Messiah."

"That is the proposal before this body," Caiaphas noted. "Anyone asserting that Yeshua of Nazareth is the Messiah of Israel will be put out of the synagogue. Any license such a one holds to transact business will be withdrawn. Anyone who speaks up for Yeshua will be shunned as an enemy of our people."

The sects of Pharisees and Sadducees disagreed about many things, but in regard to this proposal most of the Sanhedrin concurred, regardless of their party. The measure was adopted by an overwhelming majority.

Only Gamaliel, Nakdimon, and a handful of others abstained from the vote.

PENIEL WAS IN HIS USUAL PLACE BESIDE Nicanor Gate when Gamaliel and Nakdimon arrived. He recognized their voices and listened to their discussion.

"Caiaphas is determined to destroy Yeshua," Nakdimon said.

"Caiaphas is protecting himself and his position. He's determined to sacrifice Yeshua to save his power and his family's political influence," Gamaliel corrected. "They are, after all, appointed by Rome."

This was the kind of gossip Peniel often overheard. No one commented on his presence. Most people did not bother lowering their voices.

Nakdimon protested, "Yeshua's a good man . . . no, he's much more than that. At the very least he's a prophet."

"Even if he calls himself The Light of the World? Some arrogance there, Nephew, you must admit. That title is strictly reserved for Messiah."

Peniel had listened to and memorized the earliest teachings about the Book of Beginnings. The phrase "God separated the Light from the Darkness" did not simply mean that God had divided night from day.

Nakdimon confirmed this. "From the Book of Beginnings we learn that Elohim saw the Light of Messiah before the world was created, and reserved The Light of the World under his throne until it would be revealed in the last days. It's said that when Satan wanted to know who the special light was for, God showed him."

Peniel knew the rest of the story before Nakdimon continued. "When he saw Messiah's light, Satan fell on his face in terror. He screamed that unless he could stop the Messiah, The Light of the World would one day cast him and all idol-worshippers into hell. And he and the demons fled."

"So," Gamaliel continued with his interrogation, "is Yeshua of Nazareth capable of subduing Satan? Is he The Light? Does he cast out demons? Can he cast the Prince of Darkness into hell?"

Peniel understood the two learned men were speaking of the Messiah, the same person Peniel awaited every Passover beside the Eastern Gate. Yet Nakdimon and Gamaliel spoke as if Messiah were possibly already living in the person of Yeshua of Nazareth.

Could it be? Peniel desperately wanted to ask but knew it would be wrong of him to overhear a private conversation and then butt in with a question.

The high priest bustled toward Nicanor, surrounded by his entourage. Then he cleared his throat, demanding attention.

"Now that the council has voted to cast out any who say Yeshua is Messiah or any who call him The Light," Caiaphas said, "I trust we'll have no more awkward comments that might be misinterpreted as support for this upstart from the Galil. It would be embarrassing for the two of you to be put out of the synagogue. Besides, it's clear Yeshua is a fraud. No prophet comes from the Galil."

Peniel knew that statement was wrong. The prophet Jonah, the only prophet recorded who ever successfully preached repentance, was from the Galil.

But beggars did not correct high priests.

The high priest and his followers moved off.

"Caiaphas is as ignorant as he is arrogant," Gamaliel observed when Caiaphas had gone.

Nakdimon agreed. "The Romans did not choose Caiaphas as high priest because he's a man whose mind is illuminated by the candle of the Torah."

"What does the prophet Isaias say about the time when Messiah comes: '*In the past God humbled the land of Zebulun and the land of Naphtali, but in the future he will honor Galilee of the Gentiles.*' And how will he honor it? '*The people walking in darkness have seen a great light; on those living in the land of the shadow of death a light has dawned.*'⁵⁵ Yet Caiaphas dismissed Yeshua's claims out of hand because he's from the Galil?" Gamaliel paused. "And Caiaphas threatens those of us who are searching for truth in this matter. Most definitely a threat, Nakdimon; he makes no attempt to hide it."

Nakdimon blustered, "But what will Caiaphas do to *Yeshua?* Have him arrested?"

"Not yet, I shouldn't think. He'll collect more evidence first, to convict Yeshua out of his own mouth. Besides, Caiaphas is afraid of what the common folk might do if he arrested Yeshua openly. Public anger about the death of Yochanan is too fresh. Caiaphas doesn't want to provoke them. No, I'd say Yeshua has more to fear from an assassin than from court. At least for now."

Peniel had heard much talk of Yeshua before. Who in Jerusalem had not? After all, Peniel had been present when Yeshua tipped over the tables of the money changers, accusing them of the corruption everyone agreed was true.

So now he would be stabbed in the back.

"What do *you* think Yeshua means about being the Light of the World?" Nakdimon asked his uncle.

Peniel heard the shrug in Gamaliel's voice. "The psalmist says God's Word is a lamp unto our feet. Our sages say Messiah is *The* Light! Our brother Philo of Alexandria calls the creative force of God *The Logos* . . . *The Word.* Torah, the written Word, is a lamp that illuminates our path. Its truth leads us to the Great Light of God's mercy. To Messiah. Perhaps Yeshua sees himself as that Light, the Living Word of God."

"I'm a witness," Nakdimon said. "I know what I've seen with my own eyes. His deeds may prove that he is *The* Light, Uncle. More than a lamp in the darkness. I think . . . perhaps . . . all God's Light may be contained inside an ordinary jar of Galilean clay."

"If he is the One sent from heaven, we'll know. He won't fade away. Perhaps he'll explain further . . . if he lives that long."

The two men continued their conversation, but their voices moved off toward the Temple treasury and out of earshot.

But what did that discussion mean?

Peniel had no clue. He pondered the mystery. Interesting, but what was light to a blind man? And no one to discuss it with. The air around the courtyard hummed with resentment against Yeshua. The voices of Israel's rulers echoed the hope that Yeshua of Galilee would soon be swallowed by darkness and never be seen again.

FROM SOMEWHERE IN THE DEPTHS OF THE dungeon, a long, agonized wail awakened Manaen from his nightmare.

What tormented prisoner cried for mercy? Who called the name of Susanna and cursed Demos with Manaen's voice?

The jailor heard it too. *"You! Shut up in there, you! Shut up, Manaen bar Talmai! Or I've got orders to shut you up!"*

"Was it me, Mama? My own voice?" Manaen groaned and lay in the straw for a time, trying to sort out the dream from reality. He called for his mother as he had done as a child when visions of demons had haunted his sleep.

Mama would bring the lamp into his room and show him. Show him there was nothing in the shadows that could harm him.

"The light! Mama, please! Bring the light!" he moaned.

And then he remembered where he was. There would be no candle. No friendly hand to soothe away this dream.

He sat up slowly. Leg irons were simply a cruel reminder that once he might have been a threat to Demos. Once he might have been able to fight or walk away. Now blindness was the chain that shackled him forever.

Darkness had ripped the sword from Manaen's hand but not from his heart. Yet he was disarmed, powerless . . . in a prison from which there was no release.

The memory of Yeshua's words haunted him: *"A man's life does not exist in the abundance of what he owns. . . ."*

What had Yeshua meant? Manaen had nothing. Not even hope. Was there some inner vision that gave a hopeless man the will to live?

Manaen cradled his head in his hands. What glimmer of light could he fix his hope on? Susanna? No. She was beyond his reach. He would not live with a love that had turned to pity. It did not matter what she told him. She could not imagine what their lives would be like if she gave up everything for him! The misery of it. Her love for him would slowly turn to pity and then resentment! No use! No use!

He would extinguish the wavering flame of his love for her! She could never be his! She must escape! Must contact Rome! Somehow she must help secure his release! And if she could not? He must survive long enough to take revenge on his brother.

Revenge! The light that burned within him.

Yes! To live long enough to kill Demos!

Surely Demos no longer considered him a threat. Perhaps he would be given an alms bowl. Put out on the streets of Jerusalem as a lesson to others who questioned authority. Left to grope his way to some corner. And there he would wait.

Wait in darkness as the sun rose.

Hope in darkness at high noon!

Listen in darkness as the sun arched across the sky.

And one day, one day, in darkness he would hear the voice of his brother approach! In darkness he would hear the mocking laughter of Demos as he came near!

And then, in darkness, Manaen would reach for Demos. Touch his arm. Grasp his throat. Slam his head against a wall! Pull him down, down onto the pavement and choke him until Demos descended into the pit of judgment and eternity without light!

And if Manaen was confined to live out the rest of his days in this cell? What then?

Someday Demos would come to gloat. And that would be the last thing he ever did.

Revenge! A light for Manaen's dark soul! To kill his brother! Something to live for! Something to keep him breathing. Eating. Hoping. Planning.

22

CHAPTER

The flock of lambs from Migdal Eder slowed their pace as they climbed the incline into Jerusalem.

Legionaries marched up and down the roads, stopping passersby at random, requiring name, origin, destination, purpose. The authorities allowed no chance that the embers of resentment might again be fanned into the flame of rebellion.

There was an enormous need for lambs for Temple sacrifices. Many residents of Jerusalem made Vows of Remembrance for those who died. Others performed Thank-offerings for their family's safety. It amounted to a surge in the delivery of lambs from Migdal Eder to the Holy City.

For this purpose the flock was driven to the Sheep Gate by Ephraim and Lev, accompanied by Avel and Red Dog.

Avel did not like being back at the scene of the riot. He was anxious to see the mission completed and get back to Beth-lehem.

Red Dog apparently shared the anxiety. The normally phlegmatic sheepdog prodded the lagging animals, then raced to the front of the flock to prevent the leaders from turning the wrong way, then hurried back to Avel as if to check on the boy.

Lev and Ephraim looked equally uneasy. "Be glad to get shed of this lot," Lev muttered to Ephraim. "Place still don't feel right, someways."

They reached the spot where their path jogged left, away from the main road and east toward the Temple's holding pens. Lev stopped, scratched his head, stared. Whining, Red Dog paced ahead, turned back, sat down on the cobbles. "Where'd we miss the way?" Lev inquired.

Avel knew what was wrong. At the fork in the road there used to be a pottery shop, a dealer in cheap housewares: lamps, water jugs, and the like.

Now that landmark was gone. In its place was a heap of ashes and bricks. A charred roof beam, jagged at the end, pointed skyward like a last appeal for help. The shepherds, able to wander from nameless watering hole to characterless canyon with only rock, trees, and stars for signs, were unsure of themselves in the city.

"It's this way," Avel said confidently. In the city he could feel his way around, knew instinctively which way to turn. Then a crunching underfoot made him look down. The ground was littered with potsherds. Avel stooped to retrieve one lone oil lamp, no bigger than his fist, unaccountably intact amid the ruins.

Red Dog barked. Lev rocked uncertainly on his heels. Ephraim started ahead, then stopped. The lambs, sensing the confusion, straggled about, bawling.

Red Dog barked again, this time with a note of alarm.

Hooves clattered toward them. A black-uniformed legionary on a flashing gray horse appeared suddenly. Making no attempt to slow or swerve, the rider scattered lambs too slow about getting out of the way.

Red Dog made a dash at the horse's hind legs, throwing him off stride. The horse kicked awkwardly, prancing, jostling the rider.

Avel recognized the horse. It was the same snorting creature that had trampled his friend Hayyim to death at the Purim Bread riots. And the rider was the same too: Praetorian Vara. The man who would have killed Zadok if Centurion Marcus had not stopped him.

"Clear this road!" Vara commanded harshly. "Control that dog or I'll kill it!"

Avel bristled. "Hey!" But Lev grabbed Avel from behind, sweeping him off his feet. Lev's calloused, meaty palm clamped over Avel's mouth.

"Pardon, Officer," Ephraim said, restraining Red Dog with difficulty. "We're on our way to the Temple sheep pens."

"I know you," Vara said contemptuously. "Beth-lehem. Migdal Eder, is it? Keep these stinking sheep out of our way." His hooves lashing out at any lambs that came within range, Vara's horse picked its way forward till it was head to head with Ephraim.

Avel stared from within Lev's arms. He constrained the urge to shout at the cruel Roman officer, to curse him as a killer. One nudge of Vara's heels and the charger would be unleashed, crushing Ephraim like a grape in a winepress. Just as the horse had crushed Hayyim.

"I've not forgotten how stubborn you shepherds are," Vara remarked. "Tell your leader—old Zadok, is it?—tell him I've got my eye on him." Vara nudged the horse into a sidestep, then turned back to stare at Ephraim. "We'll be searching for rebels and deserters in Bethlehem. Tell that old man. I never forget a face. Or an insult! I saw him and that brat there in the company of Marcus Longinus the day of the riot." So he remembered Avel as well. "Tell Zadok that Praetorian Vara never forgets. So. Do yourselves a favor. Tell Zadok to hand over anyone who's talked treason in your camp. Else you'll be held accountable."

"S-so many strangers around this time of year," Ephraim stammered.

"Look to it. And take a good look at the bodies crucified at the gates of this cursed city. That's the fate of any who challenge Rome. And he who harbors an enemy of Rome gets the same justice as a rebel," Vara declared. With that warning he spurred his mount and rode out the gate.

AVEL AND RED DOG RAN AHEAD OF Ephraim and Lev.

When the boy arrived at the Tower of the Flock, he was frustrated to find that neither Zadok nor Marcus was present. The Chief Shepherd and the disguised centurion had left together earlier in the day. Neither had been seen around the sheepfold since.

Had Avel come too late? Was it possible that Vara and a troop of legionaries had already swooped in and arrested both men?

None of the other shepherds knew what to make of Avel's incoherent alarm; no legionaries had come near. What was the boy ranting about?

What if Zadok and Marcus had been intercepted somewhere between Beth-lehem and Migdal Eder? Were they even now on the way to trial and execution?

Avel's mind saw them already dead, hanging suspended from wooden beams while Vara gloated at their feet.

Avel's thoughts raced even faster than his beating heart. With Red Dog dashing up and circling back, boy and dog panted over the limestone ridge, past the lambing caverns, and down the path to Zadok's house.

When he reached the door, Avel burst in. The room was empty, the cook fire only ashes.

Where was Zadok? Had Vara already made good on his threats?

And now Red Dog had disappeared as well.

Avel heard voices coming from the garden behind the house.

Flinging himself outside again, Avel tumbled around the corner, running headlong into Zadok and the dog.

"What's this?" the old shepherd rumbled. "Boy, you are whiter than any newborn lamb. Has Satan himself been after you?"

Nodding furiously and trying to catch his breath, Avel wheezed, "Praetorian . . . who beat you. Said . . . crucify everybody . . . coming back for traitors."

"Easy, boy," Zadok suggested. "Here, have some water." Behind Zadok was Marcus, who handed Avel a drinking gourd.

Several swallows later Avel was able to explain. "Vara's coming here again . . . looking for Marcus. Said if he was found here, then . . . " The boy gulped, hung his head. "I saw the crosses lined on the hill. I don't want that to happen to you." He buried his face in Zadok's midsection, hugging the old man around the waist.

"It's all right," Zadok comforted, his heavy hands thumping Avel between the shoulder blades. "You're right to warn us; you've done well. Here's what we'll do."

Zadok explained that Ha-or Tov would keep watch from the top of Migdal Eder. When any Roman soldiers appeared, Ha-or Tov would signal Avel, who in turn would run to warn Marcus. Then man, boy, and Red Dog could easily elude prying eyes by keeping to remote canyons till the danger had passed.

"Do y' think that'll serve?" Zadok asked.

Swallowing hard, Avel nodded that he understood. But it was a long time before he released his grip on Zadok's waist.

23

C H A P T E R

 few hours later, heat shimmered up from the road, surrounding the lone traveler in a silver cloud that moved with
him.

Marcus and Zadok, hauling bales of newly sheared fleece in the
cart, saw him coming at a distance. Staff in hand and leather rucksack
slung over his shoulder, he was a Jew. Bearded, dressed like a city
dweller, of the sect of Pharisees, in his mid-twenties.

"I know the man." Zadok halted the donkey and waited in the middle of the road. "One of Gamaliel's *talmidim*. Saul of Tarsus, his name
is. A Pharisee of Pharisees. Can argue the holy writ backwards and for-
wards until it makes no sense at all. Strain at a gnat and swallow a camel,
as an old friend would say."

"What's he doing out here?" Marcus queried. "He's not dressed for
traveling far."

"Messenger boy, I reckon. I've been expecting it."

"From the Sanhedrin?"

"Not officially. They would have sent the Temple Guard if they intended to arrest me. No, something informal."

"I'll leave you to it."

Zadok thumped him once on the back and walked out to meet Gamaliel's student halfway.

Marcus took the heavily laden cart toward the barns and unloaded the greasy cargo.

What would a summons mean for Zadok? Was he finally to be interrogated about the part his shepherds had played in the revolt? Or was there more? The official hearings were finally set to begin at the first of the month. No one doubted that Zadok would be called in to testify then. The question was not if, but when.

Zadok joined Marcus in the barn. "He's an arrogant one, that Saul! Rabbi Gamaliel's a good sort. Why he keeps that lout around I'll never know. Easy to see the pride of Lucifer in him. Religion is his god. And God's not in his religion. Loves to hear himself talk. He'd topple Gamaliel if he could and run the academy his own way." Zadok dipped the gourd in the water jug and drank. Then he held up a parchment. "I'm called to Yerushalayim."

"By which faction?"

"Private meeting. Gamaliel and Nakdimon. Secret. They'll not be seen coming here to the flocks. Not my house at Beth-lehem. Nor risk meeting me in their houses. Nor at the Temple in their offices. I'm to speak with them at the watch fire near the Sheep Gate. After dark."

Marcus did not ask what business they could have that would require such secrecy. Nor did the old shepherd volunteer the information.

Zadok mulled the prospects over. "By law my testimony must be confirmed by one other witness. I'll take Avel with me. He's not likely to be shy about what he knows or easily tripped up."

IT WAS ZADOK'S TURN TO KEEP WATCH over the yearlings in the distant western pasture that night. Flocks slept in the open fields beyond the encampment.

Marcus warmed his hands as the three boys, Avel, Emet, and Ha-or Tov, roasted chunks of lamb on sticks over the open fire. Since Marcus had come to Migdal Eder, he had puzzled over Avel and Emet, the littlest of Zadok's three apprentice shepherds. The boys were familiar and yet not exactly like the Jerusalem street urchins Marcus remembered.

Emet picked off a bit of meat from the skewer and tossed it to Red Dog, who caught it effortlessly in his mouth. Emet laughed with delight and removed another morsel for the dog.

Zadok, especially fearsome in the flickering light, reproved him. "Emet! It isn't right to give children's meat to the dog."

Undeterred, Emet grinned. "Yes, sir. But even a dog can eat the crumbs that fall from his master's table. I've seen you drop a bit when you thought I wasn't looking."

"Well then. Well now." Zadok was caught.

Red Dog whined, licked his chops, and sat up on his hind legs to beg. Zadok scowled, then covertly dropped a chunk of meat at his feet. "Well!" declared the old man as Red Dog dashed in to devour the morsel. "So it would seem there's plenty to spare." With a snap of his fingers he called Red Dog to his side. He playfully tugged the animal's ears. "Now lay down, y' poor, underfed, unloved beast!"

Underfed! Unloved! The words jarred Marcus' memory. The first time he had seen Avel and Emet they had been little more than nameless street urchins. Avel had been an underfed torch bearer, a link boy, an orphan Sparrow in Jerusalem. Little Emet, his bedraggled companion, had been deaf and mute. Sick. Near to dying. And yet now? How could this be?

"You boys are from Jerusalem?" Marcus probed.

"I was," Avel replied. "And so was Emet."

"When I met you first . . . "

"It was cold," Emet declared, taking a seat on a log beside Zadok. "You gave us two denarii."

Marcus recalled the incident clearly. "And Avel? You said you would go and find the rebels. Bar Abba. Kill Romans."

"That was before." Avel licked grease from his fingers.

"Before what?"

"Yeshua of Nazareth found us."

"I was deaf," Emet declared.

Ha-or Tov piped, "And I was blind." He gazed up at the star-studded sky and smiled. "No stars before."

Marcus studied them in wonder. "And what about you, Avel? What did Yeshua do for you?"

Avel tapped his chest. "Broken heart. But no more. No more."

Marcus pondered their stories and his own experiences. The

unarguable fact of their healing. The recovery of Carta, Marcus' servant boy, whose body and soul had been battered beyond human repair! And then there was the miracle Marcus witnessed in the healing of Miryam's soul months ago. "I've seen enough of Yeshua's power this past year that I don't doubt what you say."

Zadok stretched and settled back against a stump. "No room for doubt anymore."

"I believe it! I mean, I'm sure of his great power. His kindness. He healed my servant! But I'm a Roman. Not a Jew. Your brother told me Yeshua is the one, but I don't know enough . . . understand enough . . . to know what it is I'm supposed to believe."

"I'm just beginning to grasp it myself." Zadok accepted a morsel of lamb from Ha-or Tov. He blew on it, then popped it into his mouth.

Marcus queried, "You're a Jew. A learned man. I know you Jews believe in one God. Only one. Then who is Yeshua?"

"Where to begin?" Zadok mused.

"At the beginning. In these matters I'm more a child than these three are. I understand nothing. Nothing about this Hebrew God."

"The beginning then," Zadok agreed. "There is only one God. In the beginning, the limitless past, by his word he called the worlds into existence. What he has made is there. Look. Above you."

Marcus shivered as he gazed up into the vast universe. "Yes. I've often felt that a divine being made it. Just studying the stars I know the truth of that. But I don't know his name."

Zadok continued, "He is called Elohim in the story of creation."

Marcus whispered the name.

"The Lord, Elohim, is so vast," Zadok recounted, "so filled with power, that we are told if any man sees him as he truly is, then that man could not survive. Not even the angels have seen the face of the One who dwells in the Cloud of Unknowing." The old shepherd fixed his eye on Ha-or Tov. "Who made those stars you're so fond of looking at, boy?"

"Elohim. The Word. The One True God," Ha-or Tov replied. "The first words he spoke were, *'Let there be light!'*"[56]

"True. True. Well spoken, boy. And if the universe is so vast that earth and mankind are only a speck of dust within God's creation? What sort of power must the Creator have then?"

"Big," Emet declared, spreading his arms wide. "Very big!"

"That's right. Creation is not greater than the One who created it! The clay pot is not better than the potter! The Lord is not a stone image. Not a carved tree. Not a thing man has created! And yet man has made so many false gods to worship! Elohim, the One True God, inhabits the limitless past. The unseen future."

"And now?" Marcus leaned forward, longing for the answer to questions that had plagued him for months.

"Now?" Zadok poked the fire with a stick. "Yes. The Word, the Light, has come to live among us. And yet we prefer blindness to seeing."

"I want to understand," Marcus pleaded.

"The One True Lord, Adonai, Elohim, has always spoken to men and to angels by emerging from the Cloud of Unknowing in a form they can bear to look on. The Angel of the Lord, he is called, but he is much more than an angel! Messiah. He is the Lord of Hosts! No one has ever seen the true face of the Almighty Father except the One who ascends and descends from the Holy Mountain of the Lord, and he who goes in and out *is* the Lord."

"This Messiah, this Angel of the Lord . . . where is he now?"

"He walked in the garden with our first father and mother. He appeared to our ancestor Avraham and made an everlasting covenant with him meant for us now and for the nation of Israel forever. He wrestled with Ya'acov, who called the place where they wrestled *Peniel* because he had met the Lord face-to-face and lived! Torah teaches us that the Lord God spoke to Mosheh face-to-face in the tent of meeting, just as a man speaks to a man. Friend to friend."

Marcus nodded slowly. "But that was so long ago."

Zadok continued, "And so in the past, the One True God, mighty and awesome, appeared to certain men through the ages, in an incarnation men could comprehend without perishing. It's all recorded in the Holy Scriptures. And always the Lord's message was the same. Mosheh and the prophets wrote that one day the Lord himself would descend from the Cloud of Unknowing in heaven! The Messiah! The Holy One of Israel. A man, but the Son of God. Conceived by the Holy Spirit, born of a virgin, born here in Beth-lehem, a descendant of King David! He would live among mankind as Savior and Kinsman-Redeemer! Men would reject him and despise him. And yet one day Messiah will reign in Yerushalayim as King over all the earth."

Marcus sat back in awe as the rudimentary facts fell into place. "Tell me plainly, old man, because after what I've seen I'll believe it if you say it's true. Is this coming King, foretold in your Scriptures, Yeshua of Nazareth?"

Zadok inclined his head solemnly. "Yeshua is Lord."

LATE THAT NIGHT MANAEN HEARD THE prison warden speak the warning to the new guard in hushed tones. "The Baptizer was beheaded in this cell by Eglon. An eerie place it is. Place of dreams and visions. More than one prisoner's gone mad in this one. Herod saves it for them as offended him personally."

"Who's in here now?"

"Manaen bar Talmai."

"That one? Brother of Demos."

"Eglon blinded him."

"He is the taller brother of the two? the younger? I saw him wrestle a Roman officer once at the baths. Pinned him in three minutes. Could have snapped his neck like a twig. That Manaen? Strong as an ox."

"The same. Half mad now. Fierce. Howls revenge against his brother in his sleep. Better watch yourself with him."

Key rattled in the lock. The hinges groaned. Manaen heard the flutter of the torch flame. He smiled, certain his plan was working.

The warden placed a bowl of soup on the floor at the threshold. Carefully he pushed it toward Manaen with a long pole.

Manaen bolted upright and growled at the two guards, who yelped and sprang back, slamming the door.

"See what I mean?" The warden sighed and extracted the key. "They never last long in that cell. Visions and dreams take them. Ghosts, some say. He'll die. They all die in there. He'll die."

Manaen laughed at his entertainment for the day and groped for the thin soup. "I'll outlive you, half-wit," Manaen muttered. "I'll outwit you too. And my brother."

Thoughts of revenge had grown from embers to a raging fire burning in Manaen's heart.

Hatred was something to keep him warm! The death of Demos was something to pray for! And then he would die contented.

*May those who seek my life be put to shame . . . chaff before the wind . . .
their path dark and slippery . . . may ruin overtake them by surprise . . . may
they fall into a pit, to their ruin . . . and then my soul will rejoice.*[57]

24 CHAPTER

ama finally noticed the beautiful alms bowl, and she was not happy. "Liar! What have you done to us?" Mama grabbed the new dish from Peniel and threw it beside the heap of fuel.

"He gave it to me," Peniel defended. "Mama, Nakdimon ben Gurion gave it to me!"

"Liar! You're a liar and a thief!" She slapped him hard across the mouth, sending him to his knees beside the kiln.

"Ask him." He tasted blood. "Ask Nakdimon."

"What happened to the bowl your brother, Gershon, made for you? It's not good enough for you anymore?"

"Broken."

"Broken! Stupid! Clumsy! Do you know how long Gershon worked on that for you? Do you have any idea how your brother labored over it! He did everything for you! Now here's gratitude! He reworked everything until it was perfect. He said you were worth the effort. 'Peniel's a bright little boy,' he said! 'Devious,' I said. He said you'd appreciate it. Now here's the thanks dear Gershon gets from you! First you kill him by your carelessness; then you break his bowl and steal another!"

Peniel did not attempt to rise. It was no use getting up or trying to speak until she was finished. Each accusation entered his heart like a knife. And just when he thought she was finished, it started up again!

"Pride! You pretend to know things! Just because you sit all day and listen to the rabbis! You quote Torah and Tanakh, and talk about Torah in your little hovel when no one is there! Oh, you think I don't hear you in there? Talking, talking to no one . . . about Torah! You wander off and look for a Messiah who doesn't exist! Well, this is what I think of your learning!" She spit on him. "You'll have us thrown out of the synagogue when they find out you've stolen such an expensive bowl! They'll throw us out of the synagogue, and no one will be allowed to buy from us! If they throw us out of the synagogue we'll be ruined! Nakdimon will bring charges! We'll be put out of business because you're clumsy and arrogant and stupid and greedy!"

Peniel resigned himself to the fact that she would never believe him. "I'll take it back to him, Mama."

"Oh yes! You'll take it back to Nakdimon! You tell him you picked it up by mistake! By mistake! You're blind! He'll accept that you made a mistake! If he doesn't, it's off to prison for you, and don't think I'll ransom you either! If they ask me, I'll tell them you're of age! You can answer for yourself! It's none of my business that you break the commandments not to steal and not to lie and not to dishonor your mother and father!"

"Sure, Mama. I'll take it back to him. Tonight."

"Yes! Take it now! I won't have it in my house when they come looking for it! I won't have it here! It'll get us arrested. Me, your sisters, your father. You're on your own. That's it. From this moment on, you're on your own. Don't come back. I won't have a thief and a liar living under my roof!"

Peniel did not remind her that he had not lived under her roof since he was seven. "Sure, Mama."

"You're the poor son of a poor man. A worthless failure of a man! That's your father. But at least he has his honesty! You'll tarnish even that! Do you know the abuse and insults we've endured because of you? Because you were born without eyes? You'll never know how we've suffered because of you! Isn't a plain clay bowl good enough for you? No! You've got to have one with your name in raised letters so you can read it! Poor Gershon! What a fool he was to think you'd appreciate it. I told him you'd break it within a fortnight!"

The bowl had been Peniel's most cherished possession for ten years. "I love Gershon."

"Oh yes! Sure! That's why he's dead and you're alive!"

He held his tongue. What was the use? What?

"If I take it back to Nakdimon, Mama, can I come home again?"

"No! Clear out!"

"Where will I go?"

"How should I know?" She picked up Nakdimon's bowl and thrust it into Peniel's hands. "You'll get us arrested! Get out of my sight! It should have been you lying there! Not Gershon! And now you've broken the last thing he made! I saw it in your hands, and it kept me from saying what I thought about you because I remembered how much Gershon thought of you! So I held my tongue for Gershon's sake. Well, it's gone now. Gershon's gone. Stupid! Clumsy! Why have we let you stay here for so long? Why?"

She turned on her heel and left Peniel kneeling there beside the kiln.

Peniel ran his fingertip around the rim of Nakdimon's gift. He felt the cool metal flowers. Beautiful workmanship. Even a blind man could see that. Kind rabbi, Nakdimon. A good man doing his best to survive in a den of jackals. He had meant well. Maybe Mama was right. It *was* too good for the likes of Peniel. Too good for him. Yes. It should have been Peniel lying there, not Gershon. Never Gershon.

THAT EVENING PENIEL WAITED WITH THE METAL BOWL in the garden outside the gate of Nakdimon's house.

The night was surprisingly cold for spring. Peniel wondered if there would be a late snow. Where would he go now? Where would he shelter?

But first Peniel had a duty to perform.

Voices carried far in the keenly felt air. Peniel heard the approaching Jerusalem Sparrows when they were still up the Herodian Way. Their incessant chatter was birdlike . . . and not pleasant in Peniel's ears after the mindless and cruel destruction of Gershon's bowl.

An elderly servant with the profound resonance of a dignified Ethiopian had informed Peniel that the master was not at home, but he was expected. Peniel was invited to enter the garden and wait there, but he had declined.

A few minutes passed, and then the voices of two men in serious discussion penetrated the prattle of the accompanying torchbearers. Nakdimon was indeed returning, accompanied by his uncle Gamaliel.

"Review the list of qualifications," Gamaliel urged his nephew. "What does Torah require of Messiah?"

"Besides being a descendant of David?" Nakdimon returned.

"Yes, yes," Gamaliel replied impatiently. "There may be a thousand applicants for David's throne by bloodline alone. Come now! You're skirting the issue. Why? What do you hesitate to say to me?"

Nakdimon's answer was quiet and yet Peniel heard it clearly. "When I questioned him myself, he showed that his wisdom exceeds any man's I've ever met."

"And so?"

"And so I'm trying hard to find a way in which he could not be the Messiah . . . and I'm frightened."

"Because?"

"Because he passes every test. And if he is and we reject him . . . the consequences . . . consider what it means." Nakdimon did not finish the thought.

Gamaliel harrumphed. "Here's your house. More of this later. After we return. It's time I see for myself, eh?"

They embraced. "Shalom until then."

Nakdimon addressed the Sparrows. "As cold as it is, I'm very doubtful anything will bloom soon, but I suppose you'll all be back here early tomorrow to check on Avraham's Bush."

"Before dawn," was the assertive reply. "This year we're going to win."

Gamaliel and two of the link boys proceeded onward. Peniel did not speak. By the light of the remaining torches Nakdimon discovered him.

"You. Peniel?" Nakdimon inquired. "Why aren't you home at this hour?"

One of the Sparrows sniggered, "He needs a torch."

Nakdimon rounded on them sharply. "Here's your penny," he said brusquely. "You may go." Then to Peniel he urged, "Come in and warm yourself, boy. I imagine there's a bit of broth as well."

"No, thank you, sir," Peniel refused. "I've come about the bowl . . . to return the alms bowl, you see." He extended the metal dish and waited.

"I don't understand," Nakdimon said. "I gave that to you to keep."

"I know, sir, and I'm grateful. But Mama says it's too fine for me. She made me promise . . . I mean, I promised her I'd return it."

There was a pause, and then Nakdimon said, "But it's yours. Silver. If it doesn't suit your needs, sell it and buy another."

"Please, sir," Peniel asked. "Please take it back. I promised my mother, you see."

"Very well," Nakdimon said. "I won't encourage someone to break the fifth commandment. But wait a moment." There was the sound of coins jingling and then, in place of the bowl, Peniel received a fistful of money. "The bowl was yours," Nakdimon said firmly. "However, I've decided to keep it and redeem it from you. Here is the full price. It was a gift from my mother, and it was wrong of me to sell it . . . thoughtless, eh? Thank you for letting me buy it back." Swiftly changing topics, Nakdimon added, "And you'll be here tomorrow to check for blossoms on Avraham's Bush as well?"

"I have no bud."

"Doesn't matter. There are a hundred unclaimed. Who knows? Now go on home, but be back tomorrow."

"Yes, sir. Before first light." Peniel did not explain that he had no place to go.

"That's good," Nakdimon said, approving. "Mazel tov . . . good luck to you . . . and Shalom."

"Shalom, sir."

The gate opened and closed, and Peniel heard the bolt shoot into the latch. His fingertips brushing the stone, Peniel advanced carefully around the angle of the wall until his outstretched hands brushed the waxy leaves of the gardenia bush.

Avoiding its overhanging limbs, Peniel slumped down beside the wall. He found remaining warmth from the daytime sun stored in the masonry. At least this took the chill off the air. Careful not to touch the bush, Peniel hunched his shoulders against his sense of loss and tried to sleep.

PENIEL! PENIEL!

"Here I am." Peniel snuggled beneath his cloak as the wind entered the canopy of branches where he slept. Who had come to him tonight? The footsteps that approached were those of a man who had a limp. Who among the Ushpizin walked with a limp?

"Te-vu Ushpizin," Peniel murmured.

Peniel. I know the name well. It was I, the wrestler, who named the place beside the river Peniel.

"You wrestled Adonai," Peniel remembered.

And would not let Him go until He blessed me.

"Then Adonai changed your name from Ya'acov to Isra'el, which means 'He Wrestles With God'!"

You know your Torah.

"I'm surrounded by it all day long."

And what have you learned best sitting at the feet of the teachers of the law?

The wrestler sat near. Peniel heard his breath. Smelled wood smoke on his cloak.

Peniel thought it over for a long time before he answered the wrestler's question. "I have learned that those who make religion their god will not have God for their religion."

Well spoken.

"Not original. Someone else said it about the religious leaders. They forget what it all means. They enjoy the great performance of religion. Acting. Loud prayers. Trumpets. They drop their coins into my bowl with a flair, making certain everyone sees them. Applause. Approval. That is their god. Their hearts are dark."

And perhaps you wrestle with the question, "Where is the Light of Adonai Elohim in the midst of this dark world?"

"I wait for Messiah to come. But he hasn't come yet. I think he doesn't want to be an actor in their charade. Caught up and waved about like a prop in their hypocrisy."

You think true thoughts, Peniel.

"I have nothing, see? No reason to be proud. My father is a potter. I am blind. We are poor. I'm an exile. I have no exalted history. I don't want to pretend I'm something I'm not. Everyone could tell by looking at me anyway. I have just one ambition: that Messiah will come, and I will see him face-to-face. Like you. Only I don't want to wrestle with him."

I understand your meaning. I was once among the blind of heart. I concealed my true self behind deception. I enjoyed tricking others so I could have the world the way I wanted it. I accepted the religion of my grandfather, Avraham, and my father, Yitz'chak, but I did not know Adonai Elohim or see Him face-to-face for myself for many years.

I was Ya'acov. A liar. I tricked my elder brother, Esau, out of his birthright and stole my father Yitz'chak's blessing by deceit. I acted as if I was my older brother. Put on a costume. Made the old man think I was his favorite son. I got my father's blessing . . . and earned my brother's hatred.

"You made up for it." Peniel knew these stories about Ya'acov, and yet he did not think it polite to hold old sins against him.

No. Not me. Adonai Elohim's Mercy made up for it. The sin of my deception haunted me all my life. The same things I did to my brother were done to me. I went away to find a wife and was deceived by my father-in-law into taking the other sister as my bride. I got two wives for it, but life was never easy. Many years later my sons sold Joseph, my beloved son, into slavery and deceived me into thinking he was dead. It's a long story. My boys mostly took after me. Jealous. Devious. Brutal. Liars also. No. My life was never easy.

Peniel asked, "When did your name change to Isra'el? And what about your brother, Esau?"

There's the story. I was still Ya'acov, the deceiver, the night I came home after twenty years. Yes. Ya'acov, the deceiver. My heart was full of fear and darkness. My brother, Esau, heard I was coming and was coming to meet me with four hundred men. Esau had never forgiven me. The plain truth of it . . . I knew Esau was coming to slaughter me and my wives and my eleven sons, and take everything I had worked for all those years. I was terrified. Terrified to my core. As I had never been in my life. Because it wasn't just me, remember; it was my wives and my children whom I loved. It was everything. Would they pay for my sin?

I paused long enough to make an offering to the God of my father Yitz'chak and the God of my grandfather Avraham. Their God, not mine. And I prayed and reminded the God of my fathers that He had promised to prosper me if I would return to my country and the country of my relatives.

I divided my goods, thinking Esau might fall upon some and seize them, but I would still have some left. Then I sent my family and my possessions ahead of me across the river at the ford of Jabbok. I remained behind. Trembling. Frightened. Sitting on the riverbank and waiting for death. Thinking perhaps I might save my family and pacify the anger of Esau if he came to kill me.

Had the God of my fathers not made promises about my children? To bless them? Ah, yes. But I was still Ya'acov, the deceiver, trying to work it out on my own.

Moonless night. More stars than I had ever seen. And yet the darkness was so thick I could feel it. I listened to hear if anything happened in the camp across the river. I could hear the cattle and the sheep. But all was peaceful except for inside my heart. I was glad for the quiet but dreaded what morning light would bring.

"Darkness, cover me! Hide me from what I deserve for my sin against my brother!"

I asked the God of my fathers if He had forgotten His promise. I asked Him if everything I had heard about Him from my fathers was true. I asked Him how He would bless me if I was dead. I wrestled with my heart. I was afraid.

Then, around midnight, I sensed a presence near me. Someone had come. Not a man like you or me. I did not hear His footsteps. He was simply there.

I leapt to my feet and whirled to face Him! "Adonai! God of my fathers! Help me!" I cried, thinking at first perhaps Esau had sent a giant to kill me!

He did not answer.

And then I knew! Adonai had sent an angel to slay me. Perhaps Adonai had deceived me into returning home so I would die here, as I deserved!

The angel did not answer. He was tall. I saw His shape outlined against the river. He was strong. He put out His arms toward me, and I charged, trying to knock Him into the river! I would drown Him, I thought. Or He would drown me!

He pushed me down with one hand. Such power! I jumped up and grasped Him again!

"Who are you?" I cried, knowing that He was not a man born of woman, but something more.

What strength! I had once fought a lion and killed it with my bare hands, but this! I was fighting for my life! He wrestled me to the ground, pinning one shoulder. But I broke free.

"Tell me your name!" I shouted.

He did not answer, nor did He let go. And I would not let Him go. We were locked together, struggling. I knew this one could kill me if He wanted. So mighty He was! Never was man so strong as this one! And then it came to me that He had not been sent to destroy my life but to protect me!

And still I would not let Him go! I held Him tightly, so tightly! Here was the One who had all the strength! Here was the power that had revealed itself to my fathers: to Avraham and to Yitz'chak! Now He had come to me!

"I will not let You go!" I cried.

He touched the socket of my hip so that my hip was wrenched as we wrestled.

In my pain I cried out, "Adonai! Adonai! Save me! Remember Your promises! My God! My God! Do not abandon me to what I fear most! Do not let me drown in my despair! Adonai! Have mercy on me! Adonai! Save me!"

For the first time in my life I called upon the Lord, not as my father's God or my grandfather's God, but as my God!

He did not reply. But I did not let go of Him!

First light.

At last He spoke, "Let Me go, for it is dawn."

But I replied, "I will not let You go unless you bless me!"

By this I meant that He had blessed my grandfather, Avraham. He had blessed my father, Yitz'chak. But I had only the stolen blessing on my life! Every blessing that was mine I had won by trickery. How I longed for the God of my fathers to bless me as well!

Then the angel asked me, "What is your name?"

"Ya'acov."

And He answered, "Your name will no longer be Ya'acov, but Isra'el! Because you have struggled with Adonai and with men and have overcome!"

What light flooded my heart! The long night of my soul had ended. Here was the dawning of my vision! I was forgiven by Adonai Elohim. Blessed by Him! Loved by Him as He loved my fathers. Now He was my own!

I still did not let go of the angel. I wept and asked Him, "Please, tell me Your name."

But He smiled and replied, "Why do you ask My name?" Then He put His hand upon my head and blessed me there. A true blessing. The blessing of a son I had longed for all my life.

And then He vanished. But I knew I was not alone. I rose from the ground and named the place Peniel, saying, "It is because I saw Elohim face-to-face, and yet my life was spared!"

And I went from there after that and faced my worst fears. But I was no longer afraid!

I humbled myself as a servant and bowed seven times before the brother I had wronged. And Esau, my brother, saw me and ran to meet me and threw his arms around my neck and kissed me. And I was forgiven.

I traveled safely, and as my journey home to my country and my family ended, I bought land and set up an altar that I called El Elohe Isra'el, which means "God, the God of Isra'el." And this land was not just the land of my fathers but my land . . . the land of Isra'el.[58]

The voice grew faint in Peniel's ears.

Isra'el spoke quietly to Peniel. *The One Who Is Truth was sent to set me free from my own darkness. Face-to-face I wrestled with Him. And He is no longer a story I heard around the watch fires of my fathers. He is the God of me.*

25 | CHAPTER

F irst light.

The link boys and Torah schoolboys gathered early around Abraham's gardenia bush outside the wall of Nakdimon's house.

But no flower had bloomed in the night.

The factions eyed one another with animosity and speculated on which bud would burst forth at sunrise tomorrow into a prize blossom at least three fingers wide.

Nothing doing this morning.

Peniel stood at the back of the crowd as Nakdimon ben Gurion and his uncle Gamaliel searched the bush for a properly numbered bud that had perhaps bloomed at sunrise.

"Nothing. Nothing. Not one flower yet on the bush," said Nakdimon. "Sorry, boys!"

There was an adolescent groaning from the crowd.

Gamaliel called to them, "All right! That's it for today. Try again tomorrow, dawn. Off with you! Off with you!"

The crowd began to disperse.

Peniel heard the two who had broken Gershon's bowl.

"Look there! It's that blind beggar lolling around. Trip him up! Get him!"

Peniel turned toward the whispers. He grimaced and raised his hands like claws. "I'll haunt you in your sleep," he growled.

His tormentors left in a hurry.

Even so, Peniel decided that he would not be in a rush to leave. There was something lingering in the air. Peniel smelled a bloom! One! First of the season. He had been waiting for it. Waiting! Hoping!

Where was it hiding?

Nakdimon called cheerfully, "Tomorrow then, boys! Come back tomorrow!"

Peniel squatted against the wall as the remaining boys trudged away from the scene.

Nakdimon spotted Peniel and greeted him. "You're the last. You'll be late, Peniel. Someone else will take your seat at Nicanor if you don't hurry along."

Peniel stood and raised his arms. "Sun's not up yet."

"In a minute it will be," Gamaliel said.

Peniel insisted, "There's a flower blooming on Avraham's Bush. A big one, too."

"No," Nakdimon argued. "I've looked it over. Nothing today."

Peniel reached out to him. "It's there. I smell it."

"None of the numbered buds. I've checked every one of them."

Peniel clasped Nakdimon's arm and pleaded. "It's another one. Hiding. Waiting."

Nakdimon laughed. "Well, Peniel, if you can smell a gardenia on this bush, then you have better eyes than me."

"The sun isn't up yet. It's there. Let me see."

Gamaliel agreed that as long as none of the myriad of buds identified for schoolboys and link boys were touched, Peniel could indeed have a flower if there was one to be found.

Peniel smiled and dropped to his hands and knees. "God knows my name," he said. "And he gave me two good ears and a nose to see with."

"Then see for yourself. It's too early in the season."

Peniel followed the unmistakable aroma of gardenia to the lowest foliage on the bush. His fingers searched between the leaves and discovered one soft blossom. Four fingers broad. And there was no tag on it.

"Here it is," Peniel called.

Nakdimon bent down and gave a low whistle. Gamaliel patted

Peniel stoutly on the back. "Well now. Well now! First light! The sun is rising, boy. The prize is claimed by you and no one else. Take it. Take it then. It's yours."

Peniel laughed. "Happy. I'm happy!" Plucking the flower, he held it to his nose and drank in the fragrance like cool water. Then he tucked it in his hair, where the aroma would keep him company all day amid the stink and crush of the crowds.

"Congratulations, Peniel!" Nakdimon said.

"Thanks." He blushed. He had never won anything before. "Now if it's the same to you, don't tell anyone. Let the boys have their contest. They didn't want this bud anyway. It was too low for them. Too low on the branch to be noticed. It took a blind man to see it. So I'll take my flower and go."

"Wise decision," Gamaliel congratulated him. "What will you do with it?"

"I'll praise God with it." And Peniel began to pray as he walked on. "I'm happy! Happy! Smell that, Lord? *And it is good!* Here it is. Proof! God knows my name! I'm Peniel and I am loved! Praise you, O Adonai! Praised be your name in all creation, O Lord of heaven and earth! On the third day you spoke the word and created gardenias, knowing that this one would bloom for me today! You provided the ram instead of Avraham's beloved son. You planted the gardenia bush! And praise to you, O Adonai, that I, Peniel, have a nose to see its beauty! I'm a rich man!"

The Temple gates would not be open for another half hour. But it was always wise for him to arrive early. Walking through Jerusalem during business hours was never easy for him. Merchants placed their wares on display outside shops. On every corner itinerant vendors hawked everything from discount wool fabric to vegetables and cups of diluted barley beer. Things to trip him up. Bullies lurking around corners.

This morning he heard the voice of the shoemaker's wife behind him. Two children were with her. Steps with short, quick strides. Steps hurrying to keep up with her steps.

Usually at her approach Peniel would have ducked into a side street to avoid her. The shame he felt at his mother's behavior toward the shoemaker's wife was still fresh and raw after many years.

But today Peniel set aside his embarrassment. He stopped. Turned. Waited for her. The Lord put an idea in his head.

She fell silent as she approached Peniel.

He knew she saw him there. Peniel, whose mother had shouted at her after she had been kind to him. Peniel the beggar. Waiting.

He took the gardenia from his hair and held it out to her. There was hesitation in her footfall and then faster steps, as if she would pass by in silence. As if she thought maybe he didn't know what he was doing. Or who she was. As if she thought he was trying to sell her the flower.

"Please," Peniel blurted. "Take it. For you."

She paused. He felt her shadow on him. She did not speak. Did not accept his gift. He heard her dig in her money pouch for alms.

He tried again, holding the flower in his hand. Shaking it. "No. No money. Just . . . please. I know it's you. No alms. I'm sorry about the little ones. My heart's cracked open for you. I wanted to tell you. Please. The flower. For you."

She made a humming sound that meant, "I cannot speak right now or I will break, but thank you, Peniel old friend. Please pray for us; we are hurting."

And she clasped his hand in both her hands. After a long moment she plucked the flower from his fingers. He heard her inhale the fragrance. Another humming of appreciation.

She said quietly, "Nothing quite so sweet, so pure, as a gardenia. So fragile. They bloom such a short time. But while they're with us, they fill the air we breathe with such joy!"

Peniel knew she was not really talking about flowers. "I wish I had two for you."

"Ah, Peniel, your kindness couldn't mean more to me today if this were twenty. We're leaving Yerushalayim, you see. Going to Galilee to stay with my sister for a time. I'll remember you in my prayers, today and every day."

She patted him gently and pressed on. He let her go ahead of him. He lingered, knowing she was going to the Temple, where she would buy turtledoves and offer them as a sacrifice in memory of the children she had lost.

At the end of the day she would carry the first gardenia from Abraham's Bush home with her. It was good.

The fragrance of gardenia lingered on Peniel's fingers.

Her kind words at his small gift comforted him, stirred him with hope. Who was Peniel, the blind beggar, that he could give comfort to another when he himself was so in need of comfort?

Nakdimon's coins jingled in his pocket.

Mama said he owed her and Papa for the broken pottery, for the lost income. Said he'd be in debt to them for a long time.

But the price of the silver bowl was significant. Nakdimon had given Peniel a month's income for a sturdy laborer, a whole year's living for a poor beggar.

Surely it would satisfy his debt; surely Mama would accept it when he explained. Let him come home again.

It was early yet. There was time to take the money to Mama and Papa. Everything would be forgiven and the day would be perfect.

Jerusalem stirred to life. Doors creaked open. Shutters rattled as they were thrown back. Oxen bawled in chorus with ungreased cart wheels as they levered the commerce of a new day into position. Soldiers grumbled as they tramped toward the city gates.

Peniel stopped to see it all with his ears. In the midst of it he recognized another familiar sound. *Thump . . . scrape. Thump . . . scrape.* Pause. Repeat.

"Shalom, Peniel! What's happened? You look like half a shekel in my alms bowl."

"Shalom, Gideon!" Peniel hailed his friend as the noise neared him. "I'm brighter than that!"

"I'm not talking about your brains. There's a seven-branch menorah blazing on a half-shekel coin, and your face is shining just that bright."

"I wouldn't know, but if light is happy, then I shine."

"Share the news. Come on. Good news is no use unless it's shared."

"I won the first gardenia from Avraham's Bush."

"Let me see it. Let me see. A year of good fortune. Where is it then? I've never known anyone personally who actually won the flower."

Gideon was a cripple near to Peniel's age, whose begging spot was near the Temple Gate called Beautiful. His legs, useless from his birth, were twisted and thin. He made his way around Jerusalem on a pair of short crutches, stabbing the rough pavement and dragging his body up to join them.

Ten minutes' hard labor to travel a city block . . . an hour's toil to climb a flight of stairs.

Thump . . . scrape.

"I gave it to . . . a friend."

"A friend!" Gideon wailed. "A friend, he says! Gave the blossom of first light to a friend! Who? Who's a better friend to you than me? You couldn't give a year's good fortune to me? Well, that's the thanks I get for riding on your back through the *souk* and telling you where to step and which way to turn!"

"She had more need of it than me or you."

"She? She who? You should've let me be the judge of that! Next time come find me first. I take back what I said about the half shekel. You're dull as a widow's mite."

"Avraham's blessing came to me last night. Even before I won the flower."

"You could've shared it. Gave it away? Gave it away, he says!"

Gideon was too poor to pay for lodging, so he lived in the culvert under the viaduct connecting the Upper City with the Temple Mount. Every day Gideon dragged himself across Jerusalem and back, all the way from the depths of the culvert to the farthest east entry to Temple grounds in hopes of receiving alms for bread.

But not today. Today Gideon would not have to travel to the Temple for alms. Peniel wanted the blessings of the bowl and the flower to go on and on.

Peniel would give a tithe to Gideon. Keep the blessing in circulation. Not even Mama could object when it was put like that.

"Gideon, my friend," Peniel said, laying a hand on Gideon's muscle-knotted forearm. "The Almighty has blessed me. And he told me to do the same for you." Reaching into his pocket, Peniel withdrew a single silver coin. A whole shekel. He felt sorry he could not give more, but reckoned that it was a tithe. The rest was not his to give, since it was to repay a debt.

"Here," he said to Gideon. "Go buy food, clothes, whatever you need. Then rest today. You don't need to climb up to the gate and back, not today."

"Did you find it? How?" Gideon asked, astonished. "I watch the gutter all the time for lost pennies and you, blind, find silver! How?"

Peniel smiled. "Not important. Avraham's blessing. First flower of first light. Can't stay to talk. I've got to get home. Mama said I couldn't live with her and Papa anymore, but I think, you know, I think now she'll let me come back."

"Listen," Gideon said, holding on to Peniel's arm in turn, "if she doesn't want you, you can always come and stay with me. Such a blessing! A year of good fortune. You can share my place in the culvert."

"Thanks, Gideon," Peniel said sincerely. It was a handsome offer. "But I've got a place, you know. My *sukkah* beside Papa's kiln."

26

CHAPTER

The business of the great city returned to normal. Jerusalem could not set aside commerce, religion, or the commerce of religion for very long.

Artisans again hammered loudly on bright brass and sturdy ironwork. Carvers turned out olivewood replicas of the Temple. Pilgrims, with money to spend, would doubtless return for the Feast of Pentecost, now not many Sabbaths away.

Phalanxes of Pharisees, broad in phylacteries, garment fringes, girth, and self-importance, swept up the avenues. Like ships laden with weighty matters of piety, they brushed aside lesser, more common vessels.

Learned rabbis scowled at dull pupils left speechless by arcane questions of no consequence, while Torah scholars smirked.

Gawking Galileans pointed out sights to their children, had their pockets picked, cursed soundly, and were scolded by passing Levites. The northern folk congratulated themselves that the bulk of their traveling money was safely tucked inside the sashes of their robes. Then the country cousins spent their remaining pennies on grilled lamb skewers and freshly baked bread drizzled with honey.

Peniel loved it all: the sounds, the smells, the bustle, the confusion. The great city was his, though he had never seen it. Today, of all days, he was at home in Jerusalem, and he was going home besides.

Over the clamor of a sidewalk vendor hawking dates and raisins, Peniel heard the whirring of the potter's wheel before he entered his father's workshop. *Studio*, he reminded himself. He must remember to use the grander word; Mama preferred it.

With the ease of familiarity, Peniel turned precisely at the center of the doorway, not having to feel for the edges of the frame to know exactly where he stood. "Papa," he called out. "Papa, it's me."

There was a squelching sound, like water crowding down a blocked drain, followed by his father's muttered oath. "I've spoiled it," Peniel's father said with irritation. "You made me spoil it, Peniel. A wine jar. I'll have to begin all over again!"

"I'm sorry, Papa," Peniel began. "But wait till you hear—"

"What are you doing back here?" Papa hissed. "You're not supposed to come back. She," he whispered pointedly, "she's upstairs. She'll hear you. Get out of here."

"Papa," Peniel said urgently, holding out a handful of coins. "I have the money to pay for what was lost at Uri's shop. A month's wages. Look, Papa. I can pay you back. Mama said if I paid—"

"Where'd you get it? Have you turned thief? You would bring even *more* reproach on us? Peniel, I've told myself a thousand times if you were clay I could remake you . . . but there's nothing I can do for you! Nothing."

"Papa! Just listen! Nakdimon ben Gurion gave me the silver bowl. I returned it, like Mama said, but he paid me for it. Said he insisted on redeeming it. Honest, Papa. Can't I go back to firing the kiln for you? Live in my *sukkah?* Can't things be like they used to be? Papa?"

"No!" Peniel's father said forcefully. The kicks to set the potter's wheel turning again were more forceful than necessary. It whirred and Peniel's father busied himself in his work. This meant that Peniel must not speak or disturb him.

Papa had turned his back to the door and to his son. Over his shoulder, as if from a distance, he said, "Leave the money and go. Take a shekel. You'll need it. It's all I can do for you. Go, quickly."

"Papa!" Peniel implored.

"Just go!"

Peniel grasped both the uprights of the doorway, and the world spun beneath his feet. Advancing unsteadily, he begged, "Papa! Bless me! I had a dream about Ya'acov! The blessing by the river! Papa, please—"

Staggering brought Peniel's shoulder in contact with a shelf of penny lamps. The ledge tipped sideways, spilling a cascade of lamps onto the floor in a torrent of small explosions.

Lunging to catch the shelf before all the lamps fell, Peniel knocked it loose from its brackets. The entire stock dumped with a resounding crash.

"Now you've done it!"

Vigorous, angry footsteps thumped overhead.

"Now you've done it," Peniel's father repeated, only both knew he no longer referred to the breakage but to the approach of Mama.

"What's this?" she demanded, while Peniel and his father remained transfixed amid the ruins. "What's he doing here, except causing more trouble? Why did you let him in?"

She would not even say Peniel's name.

"Mama," Peniel tried. "I'm sorry! So sorry! But I brought the money to pay for what was lost . . . maybe enough for what I've spoiled here. See, look! Take it!"

Mama took the coins from Peniel's imploring hands.

Now everything would be all right! Now Peniel could come home. Like the silver bowl, he had redeemed himself and could be home again.

"Where'd you get this?" she asked, suspicion in her tone.

Peniel explained.

"All this for that one bowl?"

"Yes," Peniel said. "And it's all there too, except for one coin I gave to Gideon the cripple."

"You gave what you owed us to a crippled beggar?" Each word glistened with ice; each measured syllable was more disdainful than the last.

"I . . . a tithe . . . it seemed—"

"And you come back and destroy more of our livelihood and reputation? You've always destroyed what was important to me!" Her voice was a river brimming over its banks with fury. "You're of age. Did you think we'd go on supporting you forever? Get out! Go on! Get out!"

NIGHT HUNG ON THE AIR. Pots of lentil stew cooked on the fire. Mothers called children in from play. Shops shuttered. The makeshift stands of peddlers were broken down and carted away.

Peniel had lost his way. Lost his joy. Lost the light that this morning had shone like a half-shekel coin in his heart. He grieved for the hope like a child misses a forgotten good night and goes to sleep with his heart aching.

So he still could not go home? How would the Ushpizin know where to find him? It was not surprising he had a visit while he slept beside Abraham's Bush. After all, that was a world-famous spot. But how could the Ushpizin come to visit Peniel's dreams and speak to him of things of God if he was not in his little *sukkah* beside the potter's kiln? Did the Ushpizin keep track of people when they wandered off?

Where to go? Where to, now that Abraham's blessing had lasted less than one day? False hope. A flower. Nothing different. Things much worse since he had no hope.

Gideon's offer—a place in the culvert—came to Peniel's mind and with it a sense of shame. How could he go to his beggar friend and beg to stay with him tonight after he had made such a show out of his good fortune? Even though Peniel would have liked the company, he did not ask the passing stranger in the street, "Which way to the viaduct? Where is the culvert where the beggars sleep at night?"

Instead he groped forward, listening for familiar sounds to tell him where he was. He stumbled, fell. Rose with the help of someone who took his arm and asked him where he was headed. Did he need help? Need a hand?

Peniel muttered thanks and admitted he was turned around. The stranger could not know that Peniel meant his hopes had all gone south.

"I'm looking for . . . " Peniel paused and listened. What was that sound? Sheep? So he was near the sheep pens. The place they were held until they could be washed and made ready for sacrifice.

"Where are you headed?" the stranger asked again. "It's almost dark."

As if it mattered.

"The sheepfold. Near, I think. But I missed a turning."

"I'm headed that way myself, boy. Come on. I'll show you. No, no. No problem. It's a *mitzvah.*"

So Peniel went with the stranger. Never asking his name. Never knowing where he had come from. Better that way. A stranger would not know his heart was broken and that he was lost. Truly lost.

Peniel walked beside the stranger, right arm linked in his and left hand stretched out to prevent crashing into something. His feet shuffled, searching the cobbles for a stumbling stone. Peniel walked like he was blind.

He heard sheep. Loud. Milling in their unfamiliar pens. Strong smells and voices of the shepherds across the way.

The stranger asked, "Anyone in particular you're looking for?"

"Thanks. No. Leave me near the Temple gate. You know the one. Where they bring the lambs in at dawn."

"Sure. I know the place. Where the shepherds of Migdal Eder sleep and keep their watch fire when they've made a delivery."

"Yes. Thanks."

And so the stranger took Peniel to the gate.

There Peniel stood, waiting. As if there would be someone waiting for him. As if he had not simply chosen this location at random because he could not think of any other place in Jerusalem to spend the night.

And then a boy's voice—familiar, cheerful—called out to him. "Peniel! Look! Look! It's my old friend Peniel!"

Peniel's guide, evidently satisfied with this meeting as if it had been arranged beforehand, wished Peniel well and left him standing there.

The boy sounded familiar. Yes. One of the Jerusalem Sparrows. Avel. One of the link boys, was it not?

"Peniel!" the child called again. "It's almost night. What are you doing here?"

"Avel? Avel lo Ahava, is it you?"

"Yes! Shalom! It's Avel! You never forget a voice, eh?"

Of course it was Avel. A good-hearted boy, this. A talkative boy whose mother had abandoned him at the stone quarry when he was very young. Avel, the mourner, who had lost his dear friend Hayyim several months before and then had vanished.

Peniel did not want to tell why he was here, so he turned the question on Avel. "Why are you here?"

"I'm an apprentice shepherd. At Migdal Eder."

"I heard you ran away from Yerushalayim. Or were killed by the blackmailers who rule the link boys."

"No. Not me. I've got a place now. A real home in Beth-lehem with Zadok the shepherd and my friends. I work. See? I've just fed the lambs. Here's our dog. Red Dog is his name. We're going home tomorrow after the delivery."

The dog licked Peniel's hand and nudged against his leg. Peniel patted his head and felt comforted.

"Well then, a blessing. I'm glad you're not dead. I like your dog."

"You hungry? There's a stew cooking if you can stay awhile. Zadok won't mind. Zadok's over there. Waiting for someone. He's been sitting there for two hours. Waiting. See? But they haven't come. Maybe we got the wrong day, see?"

Peniel did not see, but he said, "Sure." He stroked Red Dog's silken ears.

"Will you stay and eat with us?"

"Sure." Red Dog licked his hand.

"Why aren't you home? In your *sukkah* at your father's workshop?"

"I thought someone named Avel might be here," Peniel hedged. "I came to see for myself if it was you. This is a fine dog. I like him."

"We'll eat and then you must stay the night! The straw's fresh. You went to a lot of trouble to see if I was alive." Avel took Peniel's arms and led him to an upturned half barrel and seated him there. The stew smelled wonderful.

"Well, Avel, tell me, where have you been all this time? Since you left Yerushalayim?"

"Stew'll be ready soon. Zadok and his friends will come, and we can eat together. I'll tell you everything while we wait and the stew cooks!"

For an hour Avel told Peniel the details of his wandering. It was, thought Peniel, as entertaining as the stories of the Ushpizin.

Hayyim was killed, and I was expelled from the company of Jerusalem Sparrows. I left Yerushalayim with Emet, who was deaf, and met Ha-or Tov, who was blind. We set off to find bar Abba, the rebel, so we could join his band. We wanted to kill Romans. We found the bandits in their wadi hideout. They were cruel, you see. They killed our pet sparrow after we ran away in Capernaum and hid in a barn. Deborah, the beautiful daughter of the synagogue cantor, took care of us. She got sick

and died, but the Rabbi Yeshua woke her from her sleep! Then He fed
the thousands who followed after Him with just five loaves and two fish!
And I thought if He could do all that, then surely He could heal my
friends. But there were so many people we couldn't get near Him, and
bar Abba meant to make Him king and bring Him here to
Yerushalayim for Passover. But Yeshua didn't want to be king and left
before we could get close enough to touch Him. So we set off alone into
the mountains. Very sad we were too. Then when we had given up hope,
Yeshua found us wandering in the hills. He fed us and fixed Emet's ears
and Ha-or Tov's eyes, and He breathed life into the sparrow, who flew
away. And I'm no longer called The Mourner. Then Yeshua sent us
south to Beth-lehem to carry a message to Zadok, who knew Him from
when He was a baby. On Passover we took the lambs to Yerushalayim
and survived bar Abba's korban riots. But the Holy One didn't come. So
we went home for supper, and a place was set for the Holy One. We in-
vited the Ushpizin to come sup with us, as is the custom. But instead of
Elijah, Yeshua came and ate the seder at our house. He talked all night
to Zadok and then went away. He's coming again. Beth-lehem's a good
place to wait for Him. And here I am, about to eat lamb stew with you.

Peniel applauded at the end Avel's adventure. It was a good one.
Good like Peniel's dreams of the Ushpizin. Full of the twists and turns
of the best campfire story.

"Well spoken, Avel," Peniel said, feeling better. "I like it better
than the one you used to tell about the old man with no legs who used
to drag himself around the stone quarry."

"All true. Every word of it."

Avel had always been known as a teller of tales in the days when he
carried torches through Jerusalem's streets. Stories of cruel old spirits
lurking in the dark alleyways had been his specialty. This tale had a
more cheerful outcome than the others.

"You should write your stories down."

"Someday, maybe."

"Well done." Peniel had almost forgotten his misery as he listened.
He was hungry. "The stew smells good."

The gruff, aged voice of Zadok approached the campfire. "It does
smell good, Avel! We'll eat. Go lay down, dog! My friends haven't

come. But I see the Lord has blessed us with a guest just the same. No use waiting. We'll eat. What's your name, young fellow?"

Peniel replied, "Peniel ben Yahtzar. The potter's son."

"May Adonai bless y', Peniel. Shalom and welcome."

"Shalom and may the blessing be returned to you and your camp." Peniel touched his forehead in the proper greeting.

Avel said, "His father's workshop isn't far from here. Beyond the turning of the Sheep Gate. I knew Peniel when I was a Sparrow living in the quarry."

"I've seen the potter's workshop there," Zadok said. Peniel heard something disquieting in the shepherd's tone. Too cheerful. Trying too hard to convey that all was well. "And is the father of Peniel well?"

"He is, sir. As well as the sons of Avraham in Yerushalayim can be at such a time."

Long silence at that reply. Then Zadok cleared his throat. "Yes. Then he's not as well as we might pray. The days are dark."

"Yes, sir."

Zadok replied, "It's good to break bread with a brother." Water sloshed as the old man intoned the blessing of the washing. He held the waterskin for Peniel, who rubbed his hands in the water and wiped them on his cloak.

"Yes, sir," agreed Peniel. And they ate while Avel regaled them with stories of the rebel camp and the Galilean rebels who had meant to take back Jerusalem but had failed.

Peniel said little in response. He listened, envying Avel's eyes, which had seen so much, which let him find and follow the road away from Jerusalem. Peniel would have liked to go. But he was stuck here.

Never had the darkness seemed so dark before. Never had Peniel felt so hopeless, so alone.

PENIEL LAY SNUGGLED IN THE STRAW BESIDE Red Dog. Avel snored slightly as he slept near the old shepherd. The watch fires burned low. Only Zadok remained alert, watching, waiting.

Peniel recognized the ancient Hebrew hymn of exile as the old man whispered prayers:

O come, thou rod of Jesse, free
Thine own from Satan's tyranny;
From depths of hell thy people save,
And give them victory o'er the grave.

O come, thou Key of David, come
And open wide our heavenly home;
Make safe the way that leads on high,
And close the path to misery.

Then, the groaning of a hinge in the sheep pen. Stirring of the sheep. The voices of two men moving toward the fire.

"Is he there?"

"There."

"That's him."

Peniel recognized the tenor of Gamaliel and the husky bass of Nakdimon ben Gurion.

Zadok did not stand as they approached. "Shalom. Y've missed supper."

"We thought it best to wait."

Zadok said, "The boy's asleep. He could tell you more than I. He was up in the Galil. Saw Yeshua. Firsthand."

Nakdimon replied, "So was I there. Witness to it all. Astounding, what I saw."

Zadok asked, "Then why do y' need me? Why ask an old man? Surely you know. Surely there's proof enough."

Gamaliel replied, "You were there at the beginning. You know what went before. You've refused to speak till now."

Zadok tossed another branch on the fire. "Come sit by the fire, faithful guests. It's turned cold. Warm yourselves." The two sank to the ground beside the old shepherd.

Zadok greeted them as if they were Ushpizin, Peniel thought as he lay completely still, afraid to move, afraid to give away the fact that he was not asleep.

Gamaliel began again. "And if you can't speak in the open? Zadok, if you could tell us privately what it was you saw out there that night. What you heard! You told it to my old father Simeon when you were a young man. He told me before he died that he had seen the Messiah.

Held the son of David in his arms. But he refused to tell me more. For my safety, he said. For the safety of the Coming One."

Zadok sighed. "He was a wise man, old Simeon. Full of the Spirit of Adonai. None of us dared to talk about it, not that we feared for ourselves. No. But for fear they'd kill the child. And now, even now, y' come to question me about what I saw and heard . . . and y' come at night."

"To protect you, old man," Nakdimon explained.

Gamaliel added cryptically, "There are rumors."

"Those who are witnesses are not safe. You see?" queried Nakdimon. "It's best we not involve the boy Avel. Not name him as a witness if they call a hearing on this matter. And we'll try to keep your name out of it."

Zadok hummed an unintelligible tune. "Keep my name out of it? This scar. This cleft made by the sword of Herod's captain. This speaks the truth of what I know. I'm too old to care now if they kill me, too, for speaking the truth aloud. I would've shouted it from the rooftop except I took a vow of silence."

"And now?"

"Now? Himself came to my house in Beth-lehem."

Gamaliel pressed him. "He came to your house? You've spoken with him? When?"

"He released me from my vow of silence. There's no danger to my soul if I speak the truth. He released me. Only danger to my body. And what's this body? A jug of plain clay that holds the Light of my soul."

"Truth is out of favor these days," Nakdimon warned. "Dangerous for those who speak up."

Zadok laughed. "Why abandon truth because it's out of favor? Hold on to truth long enough and, without a doubt, the world will turn and someone will see you've got it and ask if there's enough to share! You'll hand it out with joy, and there will be more and more to go around."

Nakdimon interjected, "Like the bread he gave the people."

"Yes, like bread. Like wheat planted in a field. And it'll grow again in the hearts of those you meet. That's the way of things."

"A terrible darkness has taken hold of the world, old man," Nakdimon said grimly. "Dangerous for anyone who holds fast to The Light."

"Most of the darkness in this world is due to truth being out of favor," Zadok said. "And folks being scared to death to stand up, hold up The Light, and speak the truth about the Lord for fear they'll be out of favor too. So we betray The Light for safety's sake. Hide the fire inside a clay pot. Prefer the darkness. The blindness. Because it's safer. You don't get noticed that way. The Light shines again when someone brave—it only takes one—stands up and says, 'Here it is! Here's the truth!'"

"Nakdimon's right. Dangerous," Gamaliel said. "I have to warn you of that. It's not just your life at stake. Your home. Your position. The flocks. Everything."

"Everything, y' say? I could lose everything? But what's it mean if I gain everything and lose my soul? And if, because I fear to speak out now, some other soul perishes because I did not want to be out of favor? Isn't that lost soul my responsibility? How do I weigh possessions compared to the value of eternal life? Fear? Humiliation? One day I'll stand before my Lord and King, and he will ask me what I did with the light of his love and mercy. Now *that* moment, sirs, makes me tremble to think of it!"

Nakdimon cleared his throat and said simply, "Yes. Yes. Yes, of course you're right."

Gamaliel added, "You had to be warned. It would be unfair of us to ask you . . . to speak openly . . . if we didn't warn you first."

Zadok said quietly, "I've heard the warning before. It was for his sake, when he was growing up like a tender tree in Nazareth, that I held my tongue through these years. They wouldn't have let him live to manhood if I'd broken the vow. But now. Now he's said I can speak of what I saw when I'm asked. I intend to do it."

THE OLD SHEPHERD AND AVEL WERE up before dawn and ready to leave the city when the gates were opened at first light.

"You'll come see me at Nicanor Gate, won't you, Avel? When you come back to Yerushalayim? You'll stop by and say hello? Catch me up on your stories?"

Avel embraced him. "I will. I'll look for you where you always sit."

"I'll be there. I'm always there," Peniel promised. "Where else would I go?"

Peniel clasped the rough, calloused hand of Zadok in farewell. He resisted the urge to beg the old man to take him back to Beth-lehem. What good would a blind shepherd be? Peniel fought back the panic that gripped him when they left him near the entrance of the Temple.

Red Dog licked his fingers; then he too was gone.

It was a good thing, Peniel thought, that he did not have eyes or tears that fell like ordinary men's. No one in the Temple courtyard could see that he was crying as he made his way to Nicanor Gate. As long as no one spoke to him, said his name, or wished him Shalom tov, his grief would not be discovered in his voice!

He remembered the words the Lord spoke through Jeremiah, the weeping prophet: *"Restrain your voice from weeping and your eyes from tears, for your work will be rewarded."*[59]

No tears. *It was a mercy.* No one spoke as he passed the familiar landmarks and took up his station on the steps of Nicanor even before the rabbis began to gather with their *talmidim* to teach in the courts.

No eyes! How Peniel longed for sight! If only he could read the Word of the Lord! Oh! To sit in the gates of the Temple and study like the rabbis and their *talmidim!* To discuss Torah! To seek the truth within the Scriptures and find it! To teach it to others!

And then the words of the Lord to Jeremiah came again to Peniel's mind: *"This is the covenant I will make with the house of Israel after that time. I will put my law in their minds and write it on their hearts. I will be their God, and they will be my people. No longer will a man teach his neighbor, or a man his brother, saying, 'Know the Lord,' because they will all know me, from the least of them to the greatest."*[60]

Peniel, who did not have an alms bowl, held up his empty hands to heaven and begged, "O you of tender mercies! Please! Because you are righteousness! Because you see one who has no eyes and yet longs to see your face! Have mercy on me! Have mercy on the son of a potter! Imperfect clay am I. A man created flawed from my birth! O you of tender mercies, have mercy on one who lives in darkness and longs to see you face-to-face!"

Rabbis, priests, and scholars must have thought the blind man was calling to them as they passed. They tossed spare change onto his cloak and went away pleased by their own righteousness.

But it was not men Peniel cried out to. He knew their hearts too well for that.

AT THE END OF THE DAY, PENIEL FOUND Gideon the lame, begging where he always begged.

"Ho, Peniel!" Gideon shouted. "Shalom tov!"

"Shalom tov!" Peniel replied. "How are things with you?"

"Your good blessing rubbed off on me. My bowl isn't empty today. I'm keeping the coin you gave me. It's good luck."

Peniel remembered Gideon's offer of shelter. An idea came to him. "I've got to buy bread in the *souk*. Will you be my eyes? I'll carry you."

And so the two joined forces. Peniel became legs for Gideon, the lame. Gideon, riding on his back, became his eyes.

It was a convenient arrangement for both. They made their way around the city in one-quarter of the time.

Now, when Gideon offered to share his shelter beneath the viaduct, Peniel accepted.

MANAEN SMELLED SUSANNA'S PERFUME before he heard her voice.

The jailor said, "I'll warn y', Lady, he's not what he was when last you saw him. He's mad. Got a demon. Dangerous. I ought not leave y' alone in there with him."

"I'm promised time alone with him this evening. Herod Antipas himself has given me leave. You'll stand aside or I'll report you."

"Well, it's not to my liking, Lady. And I had to warn you. He's got a demon, that one."

"Open the door."

The lock clicked. Hinges groaned. Manaen lay motionless with his face toward the wall. The smell of oil and sputter of the flame preceded Susanna.

"Leave us," she commanded.

The nervous jailor replied, "As you wish. I'll be locking you in, Lady. Lest he breaks his chains and kills us all like a true Samson."

The jailor bolted the door.

Manaen inhaled, drinking in her fragrance.

She knelt beside him in the filth and touched his head with her fingertips. She stroked his hair. He did not move but let her gentleness course through him. He was certain this would be the last time he would be with her.

"Manaen?"

He turned to face her. Heedless of his appearance, she embraced him. Kissed his forehead. His wounded eyes. His mouth.

She spoke softly, like a mother tending a sick child. "I brought water. Oil to anoint you. Clean clothes."

He did not speak as she washed his body with warm water and soothed his skin with oil.

Longing for her and the memories of their times together filled his mind. But he did not reach out to take her into his arms. He contented himself with visions of her. Her face was as clear before him as if he had sight. Chestnut hair shining in the sun. Warm brown eyes, caressing him with a look, worrying over his wounds. Smooth, delicate hands, scrubbing him like a servant girl washes the child of her master.

She dried him and helped him dress in a fresh tunic and wrapped a warm woolen cloak around his shoulders.

"There now. My Manaen. I'll see if I can bribe the guard and get you clean straw," she said.

At last he spoke. "They've let you come again."

"Yes." There was some hesitation in her voice. Something she needed to say.

"I didn't think I'd see you again. Why?"

She drew back from his question. Rummaged in the basket. "I've brought you food as well."

"Why did they let you come again?"

"I tried to escape. Tried to leave. Hopeless. Hopeless. My letters. Still no word from anyone."

"You must try again. Go, Susanna. Leave this place."

"I can't."

"I've got a plan. And they won't let you see me again." He touched her cheek and remembered.

She rested against his chest. "Oh, Manaen. I can't let you die here."

He warned, "You can't stop it. Can't change it."

What was it she had to tell him? Why had they let her come? "I must! I can help you get free."

"Susanna, I've thought it through. I have a plan. I won't be here long. You have to leave Yerushalayim. Hide."

She protested, "Guards are everywhere. Watching."

"You know the way. I came to you a hundred times. No one saw me. You have to go! They mean to kill me. I've heard the warden talking. I'm a dead man."

"No, Manaen! Don't say it!"

"And I don't mind so much."

"It doesn't have to be!"

"I don't . . . not so much. Not if I can keep you safe from Demos. But you have to listen to me, Susanna!"

"I won't leave you! I love you!"

"You pity me!"

"No! It's not that way!"

"What life would we have together?"

"I can't let them kill you!"

"Listen! Do as I say! If you love me . . ."

"I do!"

"Then promise . . . if you hear I'm dead . . . promise you'll run!"

"They won't kill you!"

"Hide! You can go to Rome. Your mother's sister."

"Demos promises you will live! If only I . . . you can go free if I will . . . "

He shook her before she could finish. "Don't, Susanna. Don't leave me alone today thinking of you in the bed of Demos!"

She collapsed, sobbing, against him. "There's no other way!"

"Don't! Don't give in to it! I've got a plan! Demos won't have you! He'll never hurt anyone again! Promise me! When you hear I'm dead, don't wait!"

The warden banged hard against the door. "A moment more, Lady."

"This can't be the end!" she cried. "How will I live?"

"Be ready." He held her close. "My beauty! My lioness! Be strong for me." He wiped her tears and kissed her farewell.

"I . . . will . . . always . . . always . . ."

"Yes. Yes. Shalom, my love. Shalom tov."

PART III

Of the increase of his government and peace
there will be no end.
He will reign on David's throne
and over his kingdom,
establishing and upholding it
with justice and righteousness
from that time on and forever.
The zeal of the Lord Almighty
will accomplish this.***

***WE WHO HAVE WALKED IN DARKNESS HAVE
    SEEN A GREAT LIGHT
    ON ALL WHO LIVED IN A LAND DARK AS DEATH,
    A LIGHT HAS DAWNED.

ISAIAH 9:7

27

Two days after Susanna visited Manaen, a draft blew in from the crack under the door.

Manaen heard the hoarse commentary of the jailor but not the replies of the other onlooker through the peephole. "Bless you, sir, he's nearly done. Mostly lays there, moanin' like."

The wreath of filthy straw with which Manaen had crowned his head rustled when he moved, so he lay motionless to listen.

"Rational, sir?" The warden was apparently repeating a question. "Not like anyone I know. See, he talks rational sometimes, plain as you or me . . . but only if he's speakin' to *him*! You know, sir, the Baptizer . . . him as was . . . you know. This one speaks right plain, but just when the dead man's with him, as one might say. For the rest, it's just babble."

The bolt snapped back; the hinges creaked open.

Stalks of straw protruded from Manaen's beard like quills. A thin froth daubed the corners of his mouth. "Ah," he groaned. "Too far! Too far! Can't reach it!"

"You see, sir?" queried the jailor. "Gibberish. He won't last long, sir. Surely you see that plain as I do. Raving mad and harmless, if you see what I mean."

"Yes, I do see," replied the other visitor.

Demos!

A jolt of energy surged through Manaen. Demos was in the cell, and by the sounds, there was just one other present. As the guard added his testimony to the believability of Manaen's performance, Manaen held his breath.

If Demos would come closer!

"Ahh," Manaen moaned again. "Look, Father. Look what Demos caught. Can we keep it, Father?"

"Livin' in the past, he is," the jailor noted. "Seen plenty of 'em do that, come the end."

"Demos," Manaen slurred, softer than before. "Must see Demos . . . must tell Demos . . . "

"He's callin' for you, sir."

Footsteps drew nearer.

A thin trickle of spittle escaped Manaen's lips. "Must tell . . . Demos. Must . . . tell." Manaen let his voice trail away.

"This might be it," the warden suggested.

The draft blowing into Manaen's face stopped.

Someone had moved close enough to stand directly between him and the door!

"Deee . . . mohhhs." Manaen let the name whistle through his lips as if it were his last word on earth.

The smell of sour wine flooded his nostrils, and warm breath touched his cheek.

Now!

Lunging, Manaen willed his hands to be relentless claws. With one he grasped a handful of beard; with the other a fistful of hair.

A sharp yelp of pain and a strangled cry for help!

Manaen bolted up from the pallet. Driving across the cell with all the force he possessed, he wrenched sideways on the head he grasped and drove it into the cell door.

The neck snapped; the body went limp.

An exultant yell escaped Manaen's lips! He was doomed, but he had sent Demos to Sheol ahead of him!

"Guards! Guards!" Manaen heard the screech over the top of his shout of revenge.

It was Demos' voice.

The dead man was not his brother but the stupid, meddling, interfering jailor.

There was still a chance. The dead man blocked the exit. Demos was trapped in the cell with Manaen.

Throwing the body aside with a snarl, Manaen dove at the sound of his brother's cry of alarm. He tripped, fell, grabbed a length of robe.

Demos struck at the top of Manaen's head, bellowed for the guards, tried to pull free.

Shouts responded from the corridor.

More guards were coming!

Hurry!

Manaen clawed his way upwards. If he could once get his hands around Demos' neck, they'd have to kill him to break his hold. One hand was on the lapel of the robe, the other on the sash.

So close!

Manaen tripped again over the body of the guard, and the length of sash pulled free. The lapel ripped loose.

The cell door was forced open, pushing aside the dead jailor.

Manaen gave a despairing bellow and lunged a final time, only to be smashed in the face with the cell door as the rescuing squad of guards hurled it open.

Forced against the wall, Manaen was again shackled by wrists and ankles and left alone.

There was a final scraping sound as the lifeless warden was dragged across the floor and out of the cell, and then the stillness of desolation closed in.

TWO MORNINGS LATER RIDERS APPROACHED Beth-lehem in a cloud of dust.

"Temple Guard," Zadok said to Marcus as they moved up the hill.

"What do they want?" Marcus eyed the high ground for a possible escape route.

"Not you. Me."

"They're armed," Marcus warned him. This was not a friendly visit; that was clear.

"I've been expecting them. They'll be after me testifying to the Sanhedrin."

"About Yeshua?" Marcus was alarmed.

"About the child who was born here thirty years ago." He put a hand to his eyepatch in a familiar gesture. "They'll want to hear the details of how I came by this."

"Is there danger in it?"

Zadok grinned. "You tell me when there isn't danger walking into a snake pit. Aye. They'll not be happy with what I've got to say."

"Can I help? Send word to Felix?"

"I'd sooner shout for the devil to help me than ask a Roman for help. No offense, Marcus Longinus. But you're but half a jackal at that. Yer heart's as faithful as a sheepdog's."

Marcus laughed, somehow pleased by the strange compliment. "Well then, is there anything I can do?"

Zadok considered the offer. "Aye. If I don't come back?"

"Yes?"

"See to it my boys are cared for, will y'?"

"On my word."

"I can't ask for more guarantee than that."

THE THREE-STORY STRUCTURE CALLED Nicanor Gate towered above Peniel's porch. Besides framing the division between the Court of Women and the Court of the Israelites, the massive archway also housed offices and conference rooms.

The lesser Sanhedrin usually held its meetings in the Chamber of Hewn Stone, west of the sanctuary proper. Due to ongoing renovations in that hall, today's assembly of twenty-three members plus witnesses and guests convened in a second-floor chamber directly over Peniel's head.

Any speaker addressing the assembly stood at an angle between two windows. An overhanging cornice deflected the sound downward, so Peniel, with his acute hearing, took in every word as if he had been in the room himself.

This afternoon Gamaliel addressed the company. "Given the disturbances throughout the land," the rabbi said, "it is important for us, as elders of Israel, to understand what is taking place. Many times in the past, popular leaders have arisen, and many of them have claimed the title *Messiah*. Some have lost their followers and faded away; others have brought bloody retribution on their heads. But never in our history have so many been spoken of in connection with the Holy One of Israel as has lately been true. The rebel, bar Abba, has been proclaimed by some. So was Yochanan the Baptizer. And so has Yeshua of Nazareth."

Peniel heard the murmuring within the chamber swell in volume and hostility until it bubbled from the window.

"Decrying such claims as mere rabble-rousing and deploring them as politically dangerous doesn't serve any good purpose," Gamaliel chided. "There remain two fundamental questions: Is it possible that the true Messiah is alive? And if so, who is he?"

"How can we know?" a strident voice unknown to Peniel demanded.

"All the signs are in place," Gamaliel responded. "Here is one simple, straightforward indication: Just as it was fourteen generations from Avraham to David and fourteen generations from David to the Exile, so also have passed another fourteen generations from the Exile to our own day."[61]

The sounds of scoffing did not escape Peniel's notice. Then came a sharper rebuke from the high priest. "But Messiah will reveal himself by unmistakable signs, not like any of these imposters!"

"My father, Simeon, of revered memory," Gamaliel replied, "told me that he held the infant Messiah in his arms . . . here, on this sacred mountain."

The level of whispered commentary dropped dramatically.

"My father said it happened about the same time that King Herod, the butcher king, destroyed the genealogy records stored in the Temple archives—an infamous deed that many in this assembly may recall. Some thirty or thirty-two years ago it was, yet my father's words remain with me: These are the words Simeon spoke to Adonai, 'Sovereign Lord, as you have promised, you may dismiss your servant in peace. For my eyes have seen your salvation.'"[62]

"Then where is he?" Caiaphas insisted. "He would be old enough to be known to us all."

Peniel could almost hear Gamaliel's nod. "Though my father is not living to speak on his own behalf," Gamaliel said, "there is one here whom my father called the first witness: Zadok, Chief Shepherd of Israel."

After calls of welcome subsided, Peniel heard Zadok's gruff country twang: "I haven't spoken of these things before because of a vow binding me to silence. I've only lately been freed of that bond, so yer among the first to hear my story. It was on this wise: Thirty-two years ago this lambing season was the census decreed by Caesar Augustus. And everyone went to his own town to register. Now a man named Joseph went up to Beth-lehem, because he belonged to the house and line of David."

Murmurs of remembrance accompanied Zadok's words.

"He went there to register with Mary, who was pledged to be married to him and was expecting a child. While they were there, the time came for the baby to be born, and she gave birth to her firstborn, a son. She wrapped him in cloths and placed him in a manger, because there was no room for them in the inn."

Peniel imagined the scene. It must have been very hard to travel during the wet season of the year. And with the whole country in flux because of the Roman census, it was easy to imagine how a young, poor couple might find themselves in an awful predicament, like having a baby in a stable.

"I was on duty in the fields," Zadok continued. "I was a young shepherd attached to getting the Temple sacrificial lambs ready for Passover. About the middle watch of the night something amazing happened: An angel appeared to us. Not just to me, but to all the shepherds in charge of Temple flocks with me."

There was a lull in both Zadok's testimony and in the response of his audience. Skeptical men of the world were inclined to discount miraculous visions, yet the history of the Jews was full of such tales. Nor was the Chief Shepherd of Israel a voice to be taken lightly.

Zadok resumed, apparently satisfied that no immediate rebuttal was coming. "This angel appeared, surrounded by the glory of the Lord. I don't mind tellin' y', I was frightened! Terrified! Bright as sun at noonday, he was. With shining face and booming voice. And he said, 'Do not be afraid. I bring you good news of great joy that will be for all the people. Today in the town of David a Savior has been born to you; he is Christ the Lord.'"

The hum of comment overflowed the room like water from a too-full basin, so much so that Zadok raised his voice to be heard over the top of it: "'This will be a sign to you,' the angel said. 'You'll find the baby wrapped in cloths and lying in a manger.' Then suddenly a great company of the heavenly host appeared with the angel, praising God and saying, 'Glory to God in the highest, and on earth peace to men on whom his favor rests.'"

"Why have we never heard of this before?" challenged a deep, angry voice.

"I heard it," Peniel heard Gamaliel respond. "From my father. But in courtesy to our guest, let Zadok finish. Save your questions for after."

The muttering simmered down again.

Zadok continued, "Now after the angels left, we shepherds said to each other, 'Let's go to Beth-lehem and see this thing that has happened, which the Lord has told us about.' So we hurried off and found Mary and Joseph and the baby, who was lyin' in the manger. It was just as the angel said.[63]

"The next day we took the lambs here to the Temple. Did we speak of it? What do y' think? We told everyone! When the delivery was made we stayed here in the courts, tellin' the story over and over. Old Simeon, Gamaliel's father, was one who came and listened and listened. He quizzed me special, to see if he could find any prank to my tale, or if we had drunk too much wine and dreamed it. But he could not, because we spoke the truth! Later he told me that he himself met the young couple and held the baby when they brought him here for his circumcision."

"Then who is he?" many voices clamored. "If the learned Rabbi Simeon was there to hear him named, who is he? Is he alive today?"

"A moment more," Zadok insisted. "My story's not yet finished. My wife, Rachel, and I gave the family a place to live. . . ." Zadok's words trailed away, but not before Peniel detected that the shepherd was in the grip of powerful emotion. When Zadok spoke again, Peniel heard the tremor of grief. "Herod likewise heard about the birth. But he wanted no rival king of Israel, not even a future one if not of his own choosin'! So he sent his butchers to slaughter the boy babies two years and younger. Burst in at night they did, and they killed . . . they murdered . . . my babies, my own dear ones!" At the memory a sigh as gaping as a grave escaped the shepherd.

"I fought them . . . to no use," Zadok finished. "Left me with this scar on my face to remember it, every day for the rest of my life."

"But the child?" Caiaphas hissed. "Was he killed? What became of him? Did he escape?"

Controlling his voice with evident struggles, Zadok answered, "The boy's father was warned in a dream to take his family and flee to Egypt. I alone knew their destination; I alone knew their secret. And I have kept it all these years."[64]

Again there was silence in the chamber as the assembly, and Peniel, took it in. Zadok might have saved his children, his own flesh and blood, if he had betrayed the whereabouts of the baby. He had protected a stranger, but at a horrific cost.

Finally the elders could stand the suspense no longer. One after another, several of them shouted, "Who is he? Where is he? Tell us!"

Peniel too was anxious to hear the conclusion.

"He's alive," Zadok declared. "He walks among us and has released me from my vow. He is . . . Yeshua of Nazareth."

The torrent of derision, wonder, disbelief, and exclamation drowned every previous comment. The tumult was so furious that passersby on the steps of Nicanor stopped to stare up at the window. The uproar buried conversations taking place around the courtyard.

Several minutes passed before the racket subsided, and then Peniel heard an oily, placating tone address Zadok. "Clearly the Chief Shepherd can be excused for such an ill-timed joke. Obviously he does not know that comments in support of Yeshua the charlatan are expressly forbidden."

Zadok's voice again quavered in the grasp of intense passion, but Peniel recognized this expression as barely controlled rage. "Do y' think I'm jokin'?" Zadok thundered. "Not a day of my whole life has passed since, that I have not longed to see that baby grown a man and come into his own! Still more: Do y' imagine I'd change my story to suit the likes of you? to change the truth for a lie because of fear of yer disapproval? By the Almighty, if I did not waver then, why would I draw back now?"

Inwardly Peniel applauded the old man. What power in his words, his convictions! How impressed Peniel was with the way Zadok stood up to them.

"Anyone supporting the claims of Yeshua of Nazareth will be put out of the synagogue," the high priest warned. "We make allowance for you, as Chief Shepherd, because of your age, your good service, and your painful family history. But you are strictly enjoined to keep it to yourself. You may not speak of it to anyone else, under pain of severe penalty."

Zadok's words were daggers, lancing a precise, razor-sharp response. "His secret I have kept for two and thirty years, no matter what penalty was applied. I will do as he wills, if it is to speak or no, whenever and wherever he chooses, and no threats will stop me!"

"Master Zadok," the high priest intoned, "you are dismissed. We will consider your case in council, and you shall hear of our deliberations at a later time."

Though Zadok did not speak again, the ensuing clamor, outrage, and argument no longer resembled an outpouring of water. It was much harsher, more brittle, than that. It sounded to Peniel like an entire warehouse of clay pots smashing to pieces on the paving stones of the Temple courts, and it went on and on.

28

The stretch of the city wall of Jerusalem above the Gennath Gate was one of the loneliest places possible in a city of close to a million souls. The ground fell away steeply on both sides. To the north lay a barren potter's field, planted fresh with new graves. A winding dirt road let to the place of execution called Golgotha.

To the south was Antipas' palace, but this lay across a broad avenue.

There was a watchtower above the gate, but the space where Demos and Wolf walked late that afternoon was a hundred yards east of it.

Reaching into the layers of his robe, Demos withdrew a folded scrap of parchment.

Wolf could not read, but he recognized the seal of Herod Antipas.

"The tetrarch has given Manaen to me to dispose of as I see fit," Demos said. "All Antipas requires is that nothing be done to Manaen where Yerushalayim will learn of it."

"Even blind, the Lady Susanna still prefers him?" Wolf ventured shrewdly.

Demos' anger flared. "Well, she can't prefer him when he's dead, can she?"

"My woman, Susanna's maid," Wolf noted, "says she loves him

more than ever. Says she'll redeem him when she comes into her inheritance—poor, blind, and pathetic as he is. Says she'll have his heart, no matter what."

Demos pondered the problem for a time. "Have his heart, eh?" he said at last. "From her lips. Take him out of the city by night. Kill him. Dump the body, but bring me his heart. I'll pay you well. Antipas left matters with me, and I in turn will trust it to you."

"How much?" Wolf demanded.

"A hundred denarii."

"Make it two hundred."

"Done! Paid tomorrow . . . when you lay Manaen's heart in my hand."

HOLLOW ECHOES. FOOTSTEPS. The clank of keys. Laughter. The familiar Samaritan drawl of Wolf and the Syrian accent of the new warden.

"Antipas has lost patience."

"A lion he was when they caged him," the jailor said. "Would've died with dignity. Now look. 'Twas that visit from the Lady killed his heart." The door creaked open. "Not half alive anymore. Eats well enough after she came to him. Peculiar kind of cruelty, that. Them as lives upstairs above us knows how to twist the knife with more skill than most. Still, never a word from his mouth."

"Better off dead," Wolf replied. "See to the cart. I'll do the rest."

Manaen gave no sign that he understood a word.

The one thing requiring the use of an oxcart was the disposal of Manaen's dead body. So Antipas had given permission to finish him off.

Manaen determined to remain silent to the last. He would not give anyone the satisfaction of hearing he had begged for his life. Expecting at any instant to feel a blade slice through his throat, Manaen raised his chin defiantly. He hoped Wolf would make it quick.

"So, Master Manaen," Wolf observed, "you *are* still in there. Despite what Eglon said, I never thought you'd break as easy as that. Here, have a drink of water. Take it!"

A wooden cup thrust into Manaen's hands was so unexpected he almost dropped it.

"May as well drink it. You're to be gagged."

Gagged?

What new torture was planned?

Despite his unwillingness to show weakness in front of his captors, he drank.

Hands were bound, and a gag was thrust into his mouth and tied behind his neck. "You're being moved," Wolf said. "If you struggle or try to attract attention in any way, I'll stick you like a pig."

Manaen stumbled on the steps as they ascended from the dungeon.

Cool night air drew him upwards. He emerged into the open. Insects thrummed. *The sky must be clear*, he thought. Stars sliding across the heavens. Was the moon up? Manaen inhaled the clean aroma of honeysuckle.

Susanna!

He would not ask Wolf for news of her. Would not ask.

The oxcart rumbled over the cobblestones. Buried and half smothered under a heap of sheep fleeces, Manaen stood no chance of being rescued.

The only sound came from the groan of the wheels. There was no conversation, no bustle of the mighty city.

The cart came to a halt at the city gates. Wolf responded to a challenge by a Roman sentry.

Should Manaen cry out? Try to make himself heard through the muffling layers? That Wolf would kill him there was no doubt.

Wolf showed some documentation and explained he was on business for Herod Antipas. The gates were opened and they lurched onward.

Hours passed and still the wagon whined and jolted on its way.

It stopped at last. Wolf removed the layer of fleece.

"Just so you don't get any stupid ideas," Wolf instructed as he lifted his prisoner out of the cart, dragged him some distance, and threw him to the ground, "we're miles from Yerushalayim, see? You try to run you'll break your own fool neck, so sit and listen."

Manaen had little choice in the matter, so he nodded.

"Right, then," Wolf said. "You're not a bad sort. A bit above yourself, but you always treated me fairly. So here it is: My orders are to kill you and bring Demos your heart as proof. Your brother pays well."

Manaen was not surprised to learn his fate. He had long known that Demos envied him Susanna's love enough to eliminate him. Now that time had arrived.

"My woman," Wolf continued, "dearly loves your Lady Susanna. And Naomi put it to me, she did: 'Can't you save him some way?' Well, not at the cost of my own life, says I. But I've been studying on it."

From the darkness came the noise of something thrashing about, breaking branches and making an angry bleating sound.

"And right here it come to me," Wolf said. "There's a ram caught by his horns in that bramble back where I turned off the road. Demos won't know a ram's heart from a man's, will he?"

The point of Wolf's knife poked under Manaen's chin. "Know this," Wolf said sternly. "If I spare your miserable life, you're bound, bound by oath, to tell no one . . . hear me? You tell anyone who you are or where you come from, it'll mean the end of Susanna . . . of me . . . you too, when they find you. You have no name. No past. No brother. You never knew Lord Antipas. Nor saw Rome. Nor loved a woman named Susanna. So you daren't speak of it, 'cause you'll never know for sure who it is you're talkin' to, will you? One wrong word and . . . "

The tip of the dagger thrust upwards. Manaen felt a sharp pain and the ooze of blood before the sting was withdrawn. The blade hissed as it sawed through Manaen's gag. Wolf yanked it clear of the captive's mouth.

"Likely you'll die out here anyway," Wolf added, "but if the god decides to preserve your life, swear on the life of Susanna never to tell who you are and never, never, to seek for her. Her safety is in believing Manaen bar Talmai is dead. Swear it!"

"I swear . . . "

Wolf grabbed Manaen by the hair and pulled his head back, exposing his throat to the razor-edged knife blade. "Ha! I knew you could speak! Swear again."

"I swear!"

"By the life of Susanna bat Maccabee!"

"By Susanna," Manaen croaked.

Satisfied, Wolf flung him aside and strode to retrieve the ram. "Won't take a minute."

The bleating stopped abruptly.

To his left, Manaen heard the sound of ripping flesh as Wolf labored to cut out the heart of the beast.

"There," Wolf said. "I've prepared your Passover lamb for you."

An instant later the cords were sliced from Manaen's limbs, and he was free. He rubbed his wrists. "Water?" he suggested. "Food?"

" 'Bout two hours till sunup," Wolf noted, ignoring the plea. "There's a cliff close by, a sharp drop onto some rocks. If I was you I'd sit still. That's the best I can do for you."

"One . . . favor . . . Wolf . . . "

"Favor, is it? It's not enough I spare you?"

"One word . . . news . . . how is she?"

"She'll marry your brother in a fortnight or be locked away in her quarters till she rots."

The cart rattled away, leaving Manaen utterly alone.

Upon his return Wolf went directly to find Manaen's brother. His clothes were still dusty. In his hands he carried a pouch cut from a scrap of sheep fleece.

Wolf found Demos lounging on a couch in the main courtyard of Antipas' palace, enjoying the morning sun. While one serving girl offered him a tray of figs and dates, another stood by with a jug of wine. Seated near him, laughing at everything Demos uttered, was a eunuch Demos especially favored. Arrayed in silk, his eyes outlined in kohl and his cheeks rouged, Demos' companion was too pretty to be a man but fawned and simpered more than any woman.

The guard felt a surge of revulsion, followed by pity for the Lady Susanna.

Demos glanced up, spotted Wolf, and frowned. The other seated figure pursed his lips, wrinkled his nose, and patted his forehead with a fold of his robe.

"Wolf," Demos said disdainfully. "Go bathe! The air has a delightful scent of honeysuckle . . . or did have, until you polluted it."

Demos' companion snickered and repeated behind his kerchief, "Wolf!"

Wolf said through gritted teeth, "I always report in when I complete an important mission." Advancing two steps, Wolf saluted and tossed the woolen bag into Demos' lap.

An ooze of dark crimson appeared at the opening of the pouch, like the edge of a wound.

Demos jumped upright, as did the eunuch, who also squeaked and danced out of the way.

The bag slid off, dragging a smear of blood down Demos' robe. It plopped heavily onto the pavement.

"Leave!" Demos ordered. "All of you! Get out!"

The attendants and the eunuch scattered like birds taken to flight. Demos waited a minute, then barked at Wolf, "Are you crazy?"

"You said I don't get paid till I prove the job is done," Wolf countered. "You said it. Go on and look . . . the heart of a true ram delivered at the whim and for the pleasure of a jealous bellwether."

"Your insults are noted."

"Come now, you don't hide the fact that eunuchs are to your liking."

"Just give me what I asked for."

"You mean what you've paid for. Should I call your eunuch back? Watch him swoon?"

"Shut up. Or I'll . . . "

"You'll what? Report me? I think not. Not after this. Pay me and we'll be done with it. This is, as I said, the heart."

Stooping over slowly, as if drawn unwillingly but irresistibly toward the blood-spattered sack, Demos' fingers twitched as he plucked it open. He peered in for a second, then stood quickly upright. "Not like this. I don't want it like this. Put it in something . . . a jar or something. Quickly. Take it away!"

"And my pay?" Wolf said calmly.

"Yes! Yes!" Demos concurred. "Do something with that . . . thing. When you bring it back in a jar, I'll pay you then."

THAT AFTERNOON NAOMI SEEMED desperate as she clasped the hands of her mistress. "Leave this place, Lady Susanna! This dark and terrible place!"

"I won't! Not while Manaen is alive."

"I'll help you! You can go north. Hide! Make your way first to Bethany. Then north! Hide in the Galil with Joanna! In Capernaum. Contact friends in Rome."

"They might let me see him again. I can't go, Naomi. Not while there's any hope!"

"I'll bring you a disguise. Down the trellis! As he used to come to you!"

"He may yet come to me. I'll be here when he does!"

"Oh, Lady Susanna!" Naomi sank to the floor in despair and wept into her hands. "Please go. He would have wanted you to escape from them!"

Dread knotted the pit of Susanna's stomach. There was more to Naomi's pleading than she was revealing. What news had the servant heard? Susanna turned away from her and stood at the window. Honeysuckle crept over the sill and into the room.

"What? What is it? What are you trying to tell me?" Susanna asked dully, knowing before the answer could be given.

Three firm knocks sounded on the door.

Naomi continued to weep, unable to rise. "Oh, my lady! Poor my lady!"

Susanna squared her shoulders and steeled herself as she opened the door. A tall, black-skinned servant carried an earthenware jar in his hands. A diminutive papyrus scroll was tied to the handle.

"What's this?" Susanna asked.

He did not reply. With a deep bow he extended the gift. Susanna accepted it, and he backed away without a word.

She kicked the door shut with her foot and carried the jar to the bedside table.

"It's nothing. Nothing, Naomi. Stop crying."

But Naomi did not look up.

Susanna broke the red wax seal and opened the message:

A gift from Manaen bar Talmai,
Enclosed within this jar of clay.
His heart is now yours to keep forever.

29

That evening a collective shudder passed through the band of beggars who lived beneath the viaduct.

Peniel and Gideon shared a loaf of bread and discussed the meaning of the latest edict handed down from the high priest and his political faction in the Sanhedrin.

"They've made it law. You know that, Peniel. We can't talk about him anymore." Gideon, the lame beggar, rapped his stick on the stone for emphasis. "We should not mention his name!"

Peniel disagreed. "They only said no one can call him Et Ha-or, The Light of the World."

"Messiah, they mean," Gideon whispered. "No one is to say he is Messiah. Or else we'll be put out of the synagogue!"

"All right. So he's not Messiah. But what if he's a prophet sent from Adonai?"

"Peniel! Think of it! Put out of the synagogue! It's as good as a death sentence for us beggars."

Peniel considered the edict of the Sanhedrin. "That's true. We wouldn't be allowed to ask for alms. And no one would offer them to us."

"Worse than that! We'd starve," Gideon said as he munched his meager supper.

"But they say in Galilee he makes bread for the people out of the air. Like manna in the wilderness. Maybe if he's Et Ha-or he could send us bread to eat."

"Et Ha-or! The Light! Are you crazy? Shut up! This is just what they mean. Don't mention it."

"But the miracles . . . "

"Rumors. Everybody's crazy. Everybody loves rumors."

"But what if it really happened? What if he heals people? Casts out demons and such?"

"You have a demon if you think this is anything but a pack of lies. Let it go! False hope. What's The Light of the World mean to a blind man?" Gideon muttered. "Should be easy enough for you to stay out of it."

"Rabbi Gamaliel and Nakdimon think he could be the one." Peniel shrugged.

Gideon argued, "Then let *them* talk! They're rich men. If they get into trouble with their own kind and are cast out of fellowship as punishment for a week or even a month, what's that to them? They still have food to eat. They still have money and a roof over their heads. But think what it would mean to the likes of us! Even a month! If you speak openly about Yeshua, we won't be allowed to sit on the steps of the Temple anymore. We'll be marked for all to see. We'll be as if we're lepers. No one will be allowed to speak to us or help us in any way. I'll lose the right to shelter here beneath the viaduct! My home! Listen to the thunder! A storm is coming! I'd die in a week!"

"But what if he is Messiah? I'm saying, what if they're wrong?"

Gideon grasped Peniel's arm hard. He dug his fingers in and gave Peniel a shake. He hissed through clenched teeth, "Are you crazy? Shut up! Shut up! The high priest is never wrong! Don't even mention it, fool! Or, I warn you, once more and I'll have nothing to do with you."

"But if he is?"

"That's it! You're going to get me in trouble! And I can't afford trouble! You've got legs! So go! Walk!" Gideon was angry. "Go on! Go find another shelter! I offered you a place to sleep because I thought you were generous. Now I see the truth! I see plainly why God made you blind! You're stubborn and rebellious. You have a big mouth!

They'll ask me if you said anything about him and I'll tell the truth. You said he might be. Then they'll ask me why I didn't report you! Why I let you go on begging at Nicanor after such remarks! Get out of here! I won't be put out of the synagogue because of your big mouth!"

"Then Shalom, Gideon. I wish you well."

"Get out of my sight! Go!"

Peniel gathered up his mat and stood. Where would he go? Where? Should he sneak back to his little *sukkah* by the kiln? No. His mother would hear him and drive him away.

He thought of the shoemaker's shop. Deserted now. They'd gone away to Galilee. He remembered the entrance to the shop was deep set. Room enough for a stray dog to take shelter. Maybe there would be room enough for him.

PENI-EL. THE NAME WAS PRONOUNCED DELIBERATELY, as if the speaker was trying it out. Considering what it could mean. The name, *Peni-el.*

From the depths of his slumber Peniel explained, "Peniel. Face of El. It is my name, sir. It means 'Face of God.'"

The voice—pleasant, solemn, and resonant—replied, *Peni-el. The Face of Elohim was not always familiar to me. But always, like you, I wanted to see His face. Elohim. El'Elyon. El Shaddai. Adonai. Yahweh. Ehyeh. His face. Even before my long exile I wondered about the place beside the river where my ancestor Ya'acov wrestled with the Lord. Where he called the site of his struggle Peni-el, because Ya'acov had met God face-to-face and lived.*

In his slumber Peniel muttered the greeting of hospitality. *"Te-vu Ush-pi-zin, i-la-in, Ush-piz-in. . . ."*

The voice came near. *What will you offer me since I have been sent from such a far distant place to speak to you, Peniel?*

Peniel thought. "I have no chair. No food. No roof of my own. No eyes to see your face. But I have ears to hear you speak and a willing heart to learn. Here I am."

It is enough, the visitor replied.

"What should I call you?" Peniel inquired of his guest.

Foreigner. Wanderer. Seeker. Exile.

"Exile? Gershon? My brother's name was Gershon too. But you're not Gershon. I would recognize Gershon's voice."

No, I'm not Gershon. But I was an exile long ago. In the land of Midian. I was alone in the dark like you.

"I'm not alone. Not alone. So many suffer. I wish I was the only one who suffers. I wish it was me, alone, beneath the viaduct. Even now I hear them. The poor. Moaning in their sleep. They're hungry. Maybe a hundred there beneath the viaduct. Beggars like me. And lepers out beyond the shelter. Lepers. Can you smell them? Who will help them?"

God knows their names.

"Do they hear your voice when you speak?"

Some are dreamers of dreams, like you. Some have hope.

"Can they see you?"

No. Only you see me.

"But I don't see. I dream my dreams in darkness. I have no eyes. I'm blind from birth. I don't see you."

Your heart has eyes. You see me. That's why I AM sent me to you. Because you want more than anything to have what your name declares: You long to see God's face. Immanu'el, "God-with-us."

"I know I'll see God face-to-face one day. One day when I die. I'll see. Then I'll understand about light."

Understand this, Peniel. Fix your eyes on the Light that is unseen. Not the things that men see. And so your soul will not be blind.

"I suppose. If that's your definition. But Mama thinks I'm blind. Mama didn't like it when I invited Ushpizin into my *sukkah* and talked with them out loud."

She does not see.

"Life has been hard on her. Mostly on account of me. Like what happened to Gershon."

And so you are exiled.

"Pray for her, Ushpizin! I love her. She's my mother. I've thought it through. She was so bitter about what happened she had to blame someone."

You.

"Yes. But I love her. I hope she'll let me come home someday."

We all have wandered.

"You know my name is Peniel. But who are you?"

I AM . . . sent me. Ehyeh. I AM . . . sent me. You have heard His name before. Ehyeh means I AM. Yahweh, the One who was, is, and will be, the One who dwells at once in all of time and all of space and fills the universe with His glory. It is He, the I AM, who sent me.

"Then you are Mosheh? Prince of Egypt. Deliverer. Lawgiver. I know your name. I know that your name spelled backwards means HaShem, The Name. Because the Lord revealed his name first to you on the mountain and sent you to tell Israel he would redeem them."

I'm Mosheh. Child of a Hebrew slave. Rescued from the water like you, Peniel, while others died. Raised in wealth and privilege by a daughter of Pharaoh. In my own arrogance and by my own strength I killed an Egyptian in an attempt to free my people. I failed. Failed to accomplish what I most longed for. I tried to accomplish by my own power what only the power of the Lord can accomplish. Deliverance. I was arrogant. My motives were to glorify myself. To be a leader, beloved by a downtrodden people. But they saw me for what I was. They saw my motives and they rejected me too. My heart was blind, you see. So I became a fugitive and a wanderer. An exile searching for light. Seeking answers. Searching for the face of God.

Peniel settled in. "Will you tell me about the plagues and crossing the Red Sea? Or about going up on the mountain to receive the tablets of commandments?"

For now, just listen. I will tell of the time when I was a stranger in a strange land . . . a wanderer . . . an exile.

Peniel nodded.

Mosheh began, *I wandered alone in the desert. Escaped to the land of Midian, where I found work as a shepherd. I married. Made a life for myself. We had a son. I named him Gershon.*

"My brother's name," Peniel pointed out.

Foreigner. *A lonely name,* Mosheh said. *Full of homesickness and longing.*

One day I was herding the sheep and the goats of Jethro, my father-in-law. I led the flock beyond Horeb, to the mountain of God. There I saw an amazing thing! A bush, the seven-branched sage that looks like a menorah, was on fire . . . flames shooting up to the heavens! And yet, even though it blazed and blazed, it did not crumble to ashes. The bush of seven branches was not consumed. So I said to myself, "I will go see this strange sight—why the bush does not burn up."

As I approached, the Lord spoke to me . . . called me by name. "Mosheh! Mosheh!"

"Here I am."

And He said, "Do not come any closer. Take off your sandals—the ground where you stand is holy. I AM the God of your ancestors. The God of Avraham, the God of Yitz'chak, AND the God of Ya'acov."

At this I hid my face because I was afraid to look at Him.

The Lord said, "Indeed I HAVE SEEN the misery of My people in Egypt! I HAVE HEARD them crying out because of their slave drivers. I AM concerned about their suffering! So I HAVE COME DOWN to rescue them and bring them up out of the land into a good and spacious land. A land flowing with milk and honey! And now the cry of the Israelites has reached Me, and I HAVE SEEN the way the Egyptians are oppressing them. So now, go! I AM SENDING you to Pharaoh to bring My people the Israelites out of Egypt!"[65]

I asked, "Who am I? Who am I that I should go to Pharaoh and bring the Israelites out of Egypt?"

And the Lord replied, "I WILL BE with you. And this will be a sign to you that it is I Who have sent you: When you have brought the people out of Egypt, you will worship God on this mountain."

I said, "I will tell the people of Israel that the God their ancestors worshipped has sent me to them. But when they ask me, 'What is His name?' what shall I tell them?"

He answered me, "Ehyeh Asher Ehyeh . . . I AM WHO I AM."

By this I understood the meaning of the Lord's name: He always was. He is now. And He always will be.

Then the Lord told me, "This is what you are to say to the Israelites: 'Ehyeh, I AM, has sent me to you.'"

He also said to me, "Say to the Israelites, 'Yod-Heh-Vav-Heh.' Yahweh, the God of your fathers—the God of Avraham, the God of Yitz'chak, and the God of Ya'acov—has sent me to you. This is My name forever, the name by which I AM to be remembered from generation to generation."

Peniel was suddenly very tired. Mosheh whispered, *Peniel! Yahweh has seen! Yahweh has heard! Yahweh of light and life and mercy HAS COME DOWN again to bring His people out of bondage!*

Mosheh stood, receded from Peniel.

The man of God's last words came as a whisper, like someone calling Peniel's name from a distance, like a sigh carried on the breeze: *Peniel! Peniel! Yahweh speaks this truth to the heart of every man: "It is not who you are that will save you! It is Who I AM! Ehyeh! Call on My mercy, and you will not be turned away! Call on My name! Yeshua! For this means,*

'God Saves'! I will come to you! Only by seeing the True Light can you be healed and delivered from the blindness in your heart!"

Then Mosheh bent near Peniel's ear. *Peniel! Yahweh knows your name! Yahweh hears your cry! Yahweh loves you! Yahweh has come down to rescue you! Yahweh is your light! Yahweh is your hope! The One who is sent, I AM, Ehyeh, will soon send you to tell others that only God saves! Have courage! You will see the face of Him! Peniel! Is anything too hard for God?*

SEARING HEAT, NO SHADE. Scorching wind, no water. Bone-numbing cold, no shelter. By these signs alone Manaen knew the passage from night to day and then night again of his time alone in the wilderness.

Curled in a fetal position, he shivered uncontrollably. To sleep when his body temperature was so low meant that he would never wake up. Exhaustion muddled his senses as he wrestled to reason out how to survive.

He thought of Peniel: sightless Peniel, the potter's son, who skillfully navigated the crooked alleyways of Jerusalem day and night without need of vision. Peniel would know what to do! A blind beggar would have more chance than Manaen! It was clear that he must somehow think and act as though he had never had eyes, as if his world had always been bathed in darkness.

How would Peniel survive such cold? the debilitating thirst? the hunger?

Manaen catalogued what he knew for certain. He was exposed to the elements on a wilderness hillside several hours' walking distance from Jerusalem. The carcass of a dead ram lay somewhere to his left, judging from the sounds of Wolf's slaughter. Behind him and above was the track upon which Wolf had driven the cart. Wolf had indicated that a precipice dropped away into a canyon. Certain death.

None of these facts provided an answer. Manaen determined to live long enough to have revenge against his brother and Eglon. Then Manaen would yield willingly to death. But not now! Not yet! Not here on a hillside, where he would be devoured by vultures and his bones left to bleach in the sun!

Manaen cried in anguish, "Oh, God! Oh, God of Avraham! You've forgotten me! My inheritance is dust in the wind!"

The wind whistled an eerie reply up from the valley floor. Its howling cowed him. Manaen covered his head with his arms, feeling dread as if someone fierce and terrible had flown in on the gale and towered over him with drawn sword! Panic seized him, paralyzed him. Nothing in his life had prepared him for this!

Within the wind came an urgent whisper: *Get up, Manaen! Get up! Find the sacrifice and live!*

Imagination? Manaen strained to hear the voice again. *Just the wind. Only the wind!*

No! Someone was there! He felt it. "Who's there?" he asked. "Help me!" he pleaded.

And then he was filled with the sense that this thing was more than human, and he shouted in terror, *"Numen inest!* There is a Presence here! Leave me! Leave me!"

Several moments passed before the gust died away and, with it, Manaen's fear. He shuddered, certain this hallucination was a prelude to death, a waking nightmare brought on by intense thirst.

The thought came to him: Had Wolf been lying about the cliff? Pinning Manaen to the ground with fear? If indeed there was a precipice, it would be either to Manaen's right or straight ahead.

What was it Wolf had said? *"I've prepared your Passover lamb."*

Manaen sat up slowly and raised his face to the breeze. His teeth chattered. The smell of spilled entrails was distinct. The butchered ram was meat and moisture. The warmth of a fleece.

Manaen dropped to hands and knees and crawled toward the scent of the carcass. Torturous. Stones cut his palms. Thornbushes tore at flesh and clothing. Blocked by a hedge of sage from moving directly toward the creature, he hesitated, rose up on his haunches, and pawed the air in search of a clear route.

An hour of trial and error passed. Using his sense of smell, Manaen traveled a mere forty feet, at last laying his hand on the bloody carcass of the ram. He thrust his arm into the open chest cavity. Some warmth remained. Desperate to moisten swollen tongue and parched lips, he licked the blood from his fingers.

Too tired to tear at the muscle for a morsel of meat, Manaen hefted the beast and climbed beneath its body. The weight of the ram and the thick fleece covered him, warmed him.

He was asleep before his body stopped shaking.

The clay jar containing the heart sat on the floor beneath the window. Susanna leaned against the sill and inhaled the cool night air.

"Rain coming."

Susanna wondered where among all the heavens Manaen was now. She felt his presence somehow, as though he was still living on this night. Yet here was the proof that they would never meet again in this world. She had no tears left to cry. Cold reason and the understanding of her precarious position had taken over.

She would have to escape or she too would perish.

Naomi returned to Susanna's unlit room.

"I told them everything, Lady Susanna. As you said I must. That you're prostrate with grief that you and Manaen had so displeased Antipas and the Lord Demos in your disobedience. That Manaen had you under his spell. Now that he's dead you're thinking clearly."

"Clearly enough!" Susanna turned from her.

"That you're at the mercy of Antipas. You have a sick heartache.

You're determined that you must have this night to be alone to think upon your own fate."

"Well done, Naomi," Susanna responded flatly. "The guards?"

"Two. They've been given orders you are not to be disturbed until morning."

"You brought the clothes?"

"From the stable boy." The servant tossed a bundle to Susanna.

"By morning I'll be safe."

"Let me go with you, Lady Susanna," Naomi begged her mistress as Susanna shed her gown and dressed in the disguise of an adolescent boy.

"Too dangerous for you, Naomi."

"Don't condemn me to stay without you!"

"It would go badly for you if you were caught with me. I may be captured and dragged back here to marry Demos. But you know what it means if a runaway slave is caught."

"I'm yours! We played together when we were children! The first wife of Antipas made a gift of me to you, before Antipas forced her to return to her father, King Aretas, in Petra. If I'm yours and I go with you, what can they do to me?"

"Antipas will claim you belong to him."

"I can't think of being captured! I can't stay in this place if you're gone from it. No light left here. No staying, even for Wolf. Wolf has murdered your Lord Manaen by his own hand. And that hand that cut out the heart of your love will never touch me again." Naomi pleaded, "Let me go with you!"

"You have nothing to wear."

Naomi produced a second bundle of clothes from beneath her cloak. "I came ready."

"Get dressed then," Susanna reluctantly agreed.

"Thank you! Oh, thank you, Lady Susanna!"

"If you address me as Lady Susanna in public, we'll be arrested before you can turn around."

"What will I call you then? Master?"

"We'll be brothers, equals," Susanna announced resolutely. "Sons of a farmer in the Galil."

Naomi grinned broadly at the idea. "I had six brothers in Nabatea. I can act the part of a brother. You be the elder brother since you're so much taller than I am. Then you can slap me and order me about at your pleasure as true brothers will do."

"When have I ever slapped you?"

"Never. But now that we're brothers, you must cuff me regularly. And tell me often I'm a stupid lout. Wouldn't be natural if you didn't."

"Well then, is that the way of things?"

"It was with my brothers."

"Maybe it is." Susanna considered how much Demos had hated Manaen. "The pretense will not go on for long."

THE CITY STREETS WERE DESERTED. Somewhere a dog barked. Link boys bearing torches guided late travelers to their destinations through Jerusalem.

Escape!

Susanna's heart raced as she looked down toward the pavement in the dark courtyard below. One slip and she would fall and break her skull on the stones. Manaen had made the climb into her room dozens of times. It was easy, he had told her once, when he had begged her to come away with him.

Nothing to it.

Why then was she so frightened?

She slipped the precious jar into a leather pouch and slung the strap over her shoulder. Hesitating at the ledge, she tried to steady her nerves. What if the trellis was weak? the vine treacherous? What if she lost her handhold? It was a long way down.

Susanna's terror was not based on the fact that she might kill herself in a fall. True fear gripped her in the thought that she might simply be injured, be forced to stay here beneath the roof of Herod Antipas.

Naomi took her arm. "I'll go first, brother Suza. If the trellis breaks, I'll fall. And once I'm safely on the ground, if you fall you'll land on me. A brotherly thing to do."

"Brother Naaman, this is one argument you win. No matter that I'm supposed to do battle with you. Argue over the slightest thing. One brother to another, I admit I'm a coward, through and through. Terrified of heights. Of living through a fall. Go then. Call me when you've made it down."

Naomi slipped over the sill. There was a slight hesitation, then the rustle of leaves and the scent of crushed flowers as she clambered down the trellis.

"Psssssst! Come on then!" Naomi croaked, giddy with excitement. "Nothing to it!"

Susanna patted the pouch and followed after. Groping for handholds, she descended cautiously.

One step. Two. Leaves scratched her cheek. A spiderweb clung to her face.

Three. Four. Splinters from the lattice pricked her soft hands. One-quarter of the way down.

Five.

Male voices sounded from beneath the portico on the opposite side of the fountain. Susanna froze, clinging to the vine as Naomi crouched in the shrubbery and hissed a warning.

Susanna recognized the voices of Herod Antipas and Demos as they strolled in the shadows.

"Handled intelligently," Antipas said. "Eglon will be disappointed he could not perform the deed himself. Eglon had a distinct dislike for Manaen."

"Manaen! Never a more stubborn man," Demos responded. "Disobedient. Dangerous."

"Out of the way now. All behind us." Antipas spit. "Nor will it take Susanna long to think her transgressions over. Tonight she will come to it. Survival instinct will take over. Always does. I know the type. She is of the soft aristocracy, you see. Pampered her whole life. Not an ounce of backbone in her, in spite of her illustrious heritage. Manaen stuffed her mushy little brain with romantic notions. There is no real resistance there. You will see. You will have her and the estates within a fortnight."

Demos laughed. "Women don't know their own minds in such matters. One husband is as good as another. I'll dally with her awhile. Give her a child to play with. Something to keep her occupied. When the lamp is out, she'll never know the difference if I'm Demos or Manaen."

Fury nearly choked Susanna. She clung more tightly to the vine. Oh, that she were a man! Demos would find out what courage she possessed!

"Clearly we were compelled to force her to make the decision. According to the will, four months from now, on her twenty-first birth-day, the entire estate is hers, regardless of whether she is married or not. Thus the timely demise of your brother, Manaen, will work in our favor. With him gone, she will marry you."

"Does she know this provision?"

"You must be joking! I never tell my wards more than is useful. Such a clause is far from useful. To either me or you."

At last everything became clear to Susanna! Four months and the control others had over her life would be finished! This explained so much! No wonder Manaen had to be eliminated!

"All behind us now. Things are working in our favor, I think. Any word from Eglon in Galilee?" Demos was cheerful, confident.

"A message yesterday confirmed my suspicions that Yeshua may be the Baptizer alive again. Somehow Eglon has not yet found him at a vul-nerable moment but writes that the two men reportedly look very much alike. Uncanny. A trick to it, no doubt. Salome has nightmares every night that the Baptizer returns, head in hand, for revenge. Herodias says that Yeshua has placed a curse on Salome to make her suffer for her part in the Baptizer's death. I've spoken about it to Caiaphas. The high priest has secretly given his blessing for Yeshua to be discreetly killed. Noth-ing like a dead Messiah to send the peasants back to their fields. Yeshua works his wonders by the power of Satan, Caiaphas believes. He agrees this Galilean troublemaker must be removed."

"Eglon's the one to accomplish it."

"I have sent Wolf out as a backup. In case Eglon fails. Between the two of them, they have been very reliable."

At that, the two reentered the palace. Further conversation was swallowed as the door closed behind them.

Susanna remained stock-still as she clung to the honeysuckle. All fear, every thought of intimidation had vanished! She clambered down to the courtyard and stared in fury in the direction the two men had gone.

Naomi linked arms with hers. "No time for reflection. Come on! You'll have to kill the snake later, as my father used to say. Demos is right about one thing: They'll never know when the lamp is out if you are Susanna or Suza! Come on, brother! Out the back way! Through the cattle pens! The sentry there is always drunk. I know the way."

The hinges of the stable gate groaned as it slammed shut behind Susanna and Naomi.

Where were the Jerusalem Sparrows? That flock of torchbearing orphan boys who, two for a penny, lit the dark streets of the city and led travelers safely to their destinations?

The two women spoke in urgent whispers.

Naomi fretted, "Dark! Dark night! Moon's behind the clouds. Where are the link boys?"

"Tonight of all nights." Susanna could not see her hand in front of her face. She slid her fingers along the rough exterior wall of the Hasmonean palace. "And we're left without a torchbearer! We'll have to find our own way through this maze. Which way to the city gate?"

"Which gate?" Naomi asked, clutching Susanna's sleeve. "There are eleven or twelve. Nobody but a prophet or a Torah schoolboy studying for exams knows the names of all of them."

"The one . . . you know . . . we've got to get to Beth-Anyah."

"Through the Temple! Eastern Gate!"

"No. No," Susanna corrected. "Temple's closed. Barred and bolted at sunset."

"Then the gate near Siloam Pool!"

"Yes, Naaman! Well done! That's the one!"

"Just follow your nose. The Lower City's an open sewer."

"Do you know the way from here? They've never let me walk openly through Yerushalayim. Only traveled by litter."

"With good reason. The chamber pots of Jerusalem drain into the gutters of the Lower City. No proper lady puts the sole of her sandal on those streets," Naomi replied, clutching Susanna's hand. "A slum. Full of poor folk. The haunt of thieves. Murderers. Prostitutes."

Susanna shuddered. "Sounds exactly like the members of Herod Antipas' court. Can't be any worse than the palaces of the Upper City."

"Point well taken," Naomi agreed dryly. "Probably less dangerous."

It was this thought that drove Susanna onward through the pitch-black night. To remain a pampered captive in the care of her guardian meant she was no more than a slave to the whims of Antipas, Herodias, and Demos! Never mind that her father's estate was legally hers. Until the four months passed and the terms of the will were met, she was no better than a slave in the total control of a brutal taskmaster!

Better to brave the dangers of a world she had never experienced than to stay one more hour in this captivity! Better to wade knee-deep through the swill of the Lower City and emerge on a straight road to freedom! She would not remain a captive within clean marble walls, where death and human treachery were honored guests!

"We'll leave what we were behind, Naomi!" Susanna declared. "Something better waits for us! I know it! I know it!"

"Susanna," Demos bellowed outside the locked chamber door, to the unexpressed amusement of the guards. "Susanna, this is madness. Why make things more difficult? Susanna, open this door!"

Herod Antipas, accompanied by Herodias, appeared in the corridor. "Not again," Antipas said scornfully. "If you cannot control this woman now, Demos, how will you ever manage her?"

Demos did not reply.

"I thought you said she was resigned to the marriage," Herodias queried. "That you had eliminated the last obstacle."

"I did," Demos protested.

A distant grumble of thunder prophesied an approaching storm.

"She knows that pining away for Manaen is pointless," Demos continued. "I sent her his heart as proof."

Herodias and Antipas exchanged looks of consternation, and then Herodias spoke. "Charming gift," she said sarcastically. Then to Antipas: "Why are we standing around? Are you going to give the order to break down the door, or shall I?"

With the use of a table from the dining hall, the guards battered loose the panels of the bedroom door.

"She's gone," Demos remarked dully.

"Not without help," Herodias observed. "At the very least her slave helped her with a ladder. Possibly others were bribed as well. I will get to the bottom of it," she said with relish. Then she added, "And what are you going to do to get her back?"

Antipas dispatched the guards with a message to the barracks: "Soldiers to search every room in the palace in case they are still hiding around here. Post sentries at every gate out of the city. Let no woman pass unchallenged. Move!"

THUNDER, RUMBLING FAR OFF IN THE HILLS. A quickening breeze, stirring branches on the trees, carrying the scent of blossoms and new grass.

It was nights like this Peniel hated more than any other time. A storm was coming. He smelled it. Felt the charge of energy building around him.

The restless breezes stirred up loneliness from deep within him as he sat beneath the eaves of the empty shoemaker's shop and wished for sleep, a good dream, and a visit from the Ushpizin.

He heard the tramp of soldiers in the streets. At their approach Peniel got up, groped his way along the wall, and hid to listen to their conversation when they stopped a link boy.

"Two women . . . a noble lady and her slave. Have you seen them?"

"Just prostitutes out this hour, sir," the Sparrow answered. "And not many of them. No customers for them nor us on such a night. There's a big rain coming. We're headed for shelter."

"Keep your eyes open. Tetrarch Herod Antipas is offering a large reward if they're found. He wants them back. The slave has a value of thirty denarii. Antipas will pay a quarter of her value for the pleasure of making an example of her!"

"How much for the lady?"

"Twice that. Pass the word to the other Sparrows in the quarry, will you? If one finds them, there's reward enough for all of you."

"Sure! We'll keep our eyes open."

"Two women won't get far on such a night, don't you know. City gates closed tight at sundown due to the riot. Nobody in. Nobody out."

"You're right about that. No business for us Sparrows. Got two pennies, sir? We ain't had customers since the riots. No bread for two days."

"Keep your eyes and ears open for the women. If you find them and they ask you for a link, lead them back to one of the guard stations. The reward'll give the whole Sparrow population coin enough to eat well for a year."

The link boys departed empty-handed but hopeful. The soldiers pressed on.

Peniel remained where he was, listening. Listening. Thinking what to do. Thinking about the reward. Wondering what two women from the court of Antipas were doing wandering through the streets of Jerusalem at night.

Escaping.

From what?

From whom?

Why?

Peniel had a pretty good idea about the answers. If the gossip he gathered on the steps of Nicanor Gate was even half true, then the lady would most likely be Susanna.

The tramp of hobnailed sandals receded.

These soldiers of Antipas! Stupid, loudmouthed Samaritan recruits! The two women they sought would have to be deaf idiots not to hear them coming. But the women might not know that the link boys had been enlisted by Antipas' troops to find them!

Peniel knew what Antipas and Herodias would do to the slave. Herodias loved the spectacle of bloodletting. Even a male slave rarely survived the thirty-nine lashes when Herodias ordered a beating.

As for the Lady Susanna? Peniel was certain what would happen to her if she was dragged back to face the judgment of Antipas, Herodias, and Demos.

Peniel raised his hands to beg, "O Lord, send the Ushpizin to guide them! And wind!" Peniel whispered. "O tenderhearted Lord! Come! By your mercy gain merit by granting me this prayer! Fill my broken alms bowl with wind! Blow up a wind to put the torches out! The soldiers and link boys can't see without light from torches! They're lost without their eyes! Not like me! Not like me! O Lord! You gave me ears to see in the dark! Even in the dark! Eyes in my soul to hear the breath of those who are hunted. Ears to see them tremble in the shadows. Ears to find the lost ones! I see! I'm ready! Send rain to drown the fires of the evil one!"

The air crackled. Thunder boomed a warning.

A frightened child called for its mother several streets away. A shutter banged. A dog howled. Tree branches rattled and bowed low as the gale increased.

Peniel stood quietly. Patiently. Listening. Listening. Listening.

31 CHAPTER

J udging by the stink, we're in the right quarter," Naomi said encouragingly.

"We're lost," Susanna answered, hoping her fear was not evident in her tone.

The darkness and sense of foreboding that hung over the great city were palpable. A storm was approaching. No wonder all the link boys had put out their torches and scurried for shelter.

The sky vanished behind dense clouds. Thunderheads reared up over the mountains of Moab, blocking every star. The distant rumble of thunder taunted the two women as they stumbled down a flight of stone steps that seemed to lead nowhere.

Then the rain began. A single plump drop splashed a warning on Susanna's cheek. She could hear the crackle of the approaching deluge as it moved across the city in a solid sheet. And then it was upon them. A stream poured over the slick steps of the lane like a waterfall. Susanna consoled herself that at least the torrent washed the sewage from the Lower City and cleaned the torpid air!

A flash of lightning illuminated her for an instant. The boom of thunder followed immediately. The storm was directly above them. Forked fire struck at the giant menorah in the Temple courtyard!

Susanna called out to Naomi, "Dangerous! The lightning! Too close! Too close! Where should we go?"

"Come on!" Naomi grabbed her hand and pulled her up an alley-way. "I just saw the entrance to a shop. That way! We can shelter until the storm passes!"

Naomi tugged Susanna beneath the arch of a deep-set doorway. The sign of a shoemaker hung above it. They huddled together in complete darkness, listening to the rain.

"We'll never get to Beth-Anyah tonight," Susanna said at last.

Then a cough from behind them, in the recess, broke their momentary sense of security. Sitting on the step was a man. The women screamed and clutched one another.

"Who's there?" Susanna demanded.

"You're not the only one caught in the rain," a youthful voice answered. "The city gates are long closed. You won't get out now till morning. The question is—and never mind the storm—what are two women doing out? doing out in this quarter of Yerushalayim after dark?"

"We're not women," Susanna replied.

"I'm no fool. I know the difference between male and female. High-born woman. And her Nabatean servant. I'm guessing about the servant part. Pretty sure about the Nabatean bit. But it seems to fit."

"I tell you we're not!" Susanna would have run if the lightning had not illuminated the stranger for an instant. He was blind. Grinning. His impish face raised up as if to drink in their conversation.

"Suit yourself," remarked the blind youth. "I was caught in the rain. I know this area. But you? You don't belong here. I don't know much, but I can tell you're not one of the prostitutes who work this lane. Why are you trying to get to Beth-Anyah in the middle of the night?"

"You're impudent!"

"So I've been told. Many times before you. But these are questions which should be asked, eh?"

Susanna mustered her courage. Who was he to question her? "It's none of your business who we are!"

Naomi chimed in, "Or where we're from!"

"Nabatean. Yes. I'm sure of it," answered the youth.

"Or why we want to go to Beth-Anyah!" Susanna finished.

"All right," conceded the blind youth. "None of my business. But I can tell you you're altogether going the wrong way. You'll never get there from here. To Beth-Anyah, I mean."

"How would you know?" Susanna blurted.

"I may be blind, but I'm not stupid. This is my neighborhood. Day or night. It's all the same to me. I know my way around."

"Then why aren't you home?"

"Out for a stroll with the Ushpizin."

"Ushpizin. You're crazy." Susanna drew back and instinctively checked for additional humans in the shadows.

"Yes. Crazy. Comes of living in Yerushalayim, I guess. All the same, I was told I'd meet you."

Naomi dug her fingers into Susanna's arm. "Let's go! He's crazy!"

Susanna's heart raced. "What's your name?"

"Peniel."

"Peniel. Can you lead us to the right gate? Help us get on the road to Beth-Anyah?"

"Sure," he agreed, stepping forward as another bolt of lightning illuminated his face. "Lead you? Sure. With my eyes closed."

PENIEL DID NOT NEED TO SEE THEIR TREMBLING; he heard it in their breathing, noted it in their shaky speech. The scent of perfumed soap clung to their hair.

Perfume! How did they expect to pass as men?

Following a lightning flash, thunder boomed. Susanna gasped. "I know you! The blind beggar from Nicanor Gate. You sang for me."

Up ahead somewhere was the sound of a sentry calling out a challenge and a reply from another soldier.

Both women jumped.

"They're nothing. Nothing," Peniel said with deliberate composure. "Do you remember how the psalm goes? Say it in your heart."

He who dwells in the shelter of the Most High
will rest in the shadow of the Almighty.

I will say of the Lord, 'He is my refuge and my fortress,
My God, in whom I trust.'[66]

Peniel added, "Few honest men are out on a night like this, and even fewer honest women. Even if the guards *were* fooled about you being women, they'll still arrest us if we don't get moving. Do you have a scarf? Both of you? The coarser, the better."

"Yes, but—"

"Hurry!" Peniel urged. "Tie them over your eyes."

"But we'll be blind!" Naomi protested.

He snorted. "Good thinking. So you can see anyway on a night like this?"

Susanna said firmly, "Naomi, do what he says!"

"Good," Peniel praised. "Now you, Susanna. Your right hand on my shoulder. There. That's it. Your servant's hand on your shoulder. Don't let go! We're three blind beggars caught out in the storm."

Peniel led them down the lanes of the Lower City. His steps never faltered as they descended past the Valley Gate leading to the Tyropoean Valley. "I'll take you to a caravansary just inside the Water Gate," Peniel said. "It's the nearest exit to the Beth-Anyah road. We'll spend the night there."

You will not fear the terror of night,
Nor the arrow that flies by day,
Nor the pestilence that stalks in the darkness,
Nor the plague that destroys at midday.[67]

Rain lashed their faces, stinging like the gravel thrown by a sandstorm from the desert. Peniel hoped the driving shower would remove the last traces of scent from his companions' hair.

The thunder over the city hid many of the clues Peniel depended on to recognize when others were near. He wouldn't hear a guard standing very still till it was too late to choose another road.

Peniel had no doubt that if they were discovered it would mean his death. A beggar aiding a fugitive from Herod Antipas would be crushed with no more thought than one gave to swatting a fly. But somehow he was not afraid.

"Halt!" challenged a gruff voice. Peniel felt the heat of a torch thrust near his face, then waved past his shoulder toward the women.

"Oh, beggars, is it? Lost in the dark?"

Peniel answered for the three. "We usually sleep in the culvert below the viaduct, but it's running level full of water tonight. Nearly drowned, we were."

The man cuffed Peniel in the back of the head. "What's that to me?" growled the guard. "Go on then."

"Yes, sir. Thank you, sir."

Peniel smelled the caravansary two blocks before the entrance. The aroma of camel dung and donkey urine was powerful, even when masked by rain and the metallic bite left behind by the lightning.

At the entry Peniel called out, "Ho, Hemath. Are you on duty tonight? Or is it you, Jalon?"

"It's Jalon," answered the porter. "Who calls? Peniel? Why so far from home, on such a night, too?"

Peniel explained that he had the care of two brother beggars, come to Jerusalem on a pilgrimage. They were caught in the storm and needed a place to sleep. Was there a dry corner with some straw?

"You know I can't give away space," Jalon protested. "My master'd have my hide."

Fumbling in the pocket of his robe, Peniel produced a handful of pennies. "Is that enough?" he asked. "For three of us?"

THEY WERE FAR FROM FREE, yet Susanna enjoyed a delicious sense of freedom.

Rain fell steadily on the roof and dripped from the eaves of the caravansary. Naomi and Peniel breathed deeply as they slept.

Susanna lay awake in the straw between her companions. She dared not remove the bandage that covered her eyes lest someone looking at her see she was not blind. In comfortable darkness that hid the poverty of those around her, she tuned her senses to the sounds of snoring drovers and the rustling of livestock in the night.

Gold enough to last her half a year was hidden beneath the strip of cloth that bound her breasts. There were some, no doubt, who would have slit her throat for such a treasure if they had known. But no one knew except Naomi, her conspirator, and God.

Susanna and Naomi were as poor and beggarly as Peniel on the surface. She liked it. Anonymity. She, who had never walked unescorted through the filth of the street, smelled like sheep dung and wet wool.

There was freedom in that.

She wished she had run away and married Manaen and been content to live a life of poverty with him. A farmer's wife, perhaps. They would have had children by now. Maybe two. Boys looking just like Manaen. Bright round faces and chirping voices. The children would have crept into the bed to sleep between her and Manaen when it thundered. He would have told them stories. She would have milked goats and served them warm milk for breakfast. They would have made pilgrimage together at the Feast of Tabernacles with the other folk from Galilee and Judea. They would have camped out under the stars and talked about who made the heavens and the earth.

About who made *them*.

I cared too much about things that didn't matter, she realized.

If only she had not clung to her right, her inheritance, her father's money, she and Manaen would have been happy. They would have found a way. Now it was too late.

The jar containing the heart was wrapped in a spare cloak and concealed beneath the bedding. Someday she would take it to Hebron, she decided, and bury it in the cave where Abraham was buried. The heart of her beloved, eternally in the bosom of Father Abraham.

It seemed only right.

She touched the jar and whispered, "Forgive me. Forgive me. I was blind."

32 | CHAPTER

The life of a caravansary began early. Well before first light the drovers and the camels began hacking and coughing, groaning and complaining. Beasts of burden, two-legged and four, bellowed for food, for water, and griped about the quality of both.

In a secluded alcove, buried nearest the rear wall of the stable, Peniel kept vigil. Tucked under a mound of relatively clean straw with a tiled cornice providing shelter from the rain, Peniel's group of travelers had passed an uneventful night. As Susanna awakened, she stretched and moaned, at which point Peniel grabbed her arm and shook her awake.

"What?" she muttered sleepily. "Where?"

"Shhh!" he said harshly. "You make noise like a woman!"

"Sorry," she offered, lowering her voice in volume and pitch.

"Pay attention," Peniel commanded. "Both of you. Last night we had the advantage because of the dark. In the day it's different. There'll be guards at the gate, and I heard they're checking all women, yes? It's not enough for you to dress like a man, even as a blind beggar. You must act like a man too. Swagger. Spit. Scratch yourself. If anyone speaks to you, curse him soundly, then leave any other talking to me. Even if you get kicked or cuffed for it, do what I say. Understand?"

Naomi giggled. "I'll sound like Wolf."

"You laugh?" Peniel replied. "If anyone gets suspicious, your mistress will be taken back, I'll be beheaded, and you'll be stoned for dressing in men's clothing . . . got it?"

There was one more thing needed. Finding a pile of steaming camel dung, Peniel liberally smeared his tunic and theirs with it. "Now."

Within minutes of exiting the stable the trio reached the Water Gate at the extreme south end of Jerusalem. Beyond it was the highway leading toward Bethany. But first they had to pass a gauntlet of Herod Antipas' soldiers checking exiting travelers.

Peniel waited till he heard the clamor at the gate reach its loudest. A Nabatean nobleman, accompanied by his four wives, objected vigorously to the insult of having them scrutinized by guards.

A spice merchant from Arabia protested loudly that such a delay was all well and good for someone wealthy enough to afford four wives, but some people had to work for a living, and since he was alone, could he not bypass the search?

Since the sentries were palace guards and not Roman legionaries, a drover with a string of braying donkeys felt safe in adding vociferous commentary on the guards' parentage, intellect, and manhood.

"Here we go," Peniel announced. "Hands on shoulders. Right!"

Keeping close to the city wall to avoid being trampled underfoot, Peniel guided his charges right past the drover, the spice merchant, and the nobleman. Beside the harried captain of the guard detail, Peniel said, "Sir, may we proceed? Or will you search us now?"

"By the god!" the guard swore. "You stink! Get on with you!"

And just like that they were past the checkpoint and on the road east.

After a hundred paces Peniel muttered to Susanna, "Lift the corner of the scarf enough to peek out. As soon as you spot a place where we can get off the road, tell me."

Within another hundred paces there was a stand of willows growing beside the stream alongside the highway. Susanna directed them to it.

"This is where I leave you," Peniel said. "I know every inch of Yerushalayim, but out here I'm worse than no use. You know what they say: 'If the blind lead the blind, they both fall in the ditch.'"

The two women protested, "Please. Come with us!"

Sensing their discomfort, Peniel said, "Take off the scarves from your eyes. You'll be all right after this. They say this road leads straight to Beth-Anyah. Walk in the dirt off to the side of the lane, give way to anyone who wants more room, and speak to no one."

"Peniel," Susanna begged, "we need you with us. I've never been out on a highway alone. What if someone would speak to us? ask us? Then we'd have to answer and you said yourself we sound like women. It would be a *mitzvah* if you go with us."

Peniel considered the request. No one had ever asked for his protection before. "Torah says never to refuse to do good if it's in your hand to do it."

"And so we are in your hand, Peniel," Susanna insisted. "Will you come with us?"

"I will." Peniel took her hand. "And we three shall be in the hands of the Almighty."

THE JAUNTY RHYTHM FROM THE HARNESS BELLS of a passing caravan reflected Peniel's mood. The morning sun on his face felt good. Peniel basked in a newfound sense of purpose.

He was outside Jerusalem for almost the first time in his life. Even though he was blind, he was not useless. He had already saved Susanna and Naomi from the dangers of the night and from almost certain detection and capture at the gate. With every passing yard gained on the road toward Bethany, Peniel increased in his confidence.

He remembered what he had said to Manaen after they survived the rebels: *"You and I escaped sword and fire. Why we escaped and others didn't? A complex question. It'll take time to know the answer. Must be a reason. Praised you are, Lord our God, for keeping us alive and helping us reach this moment. Eh? It makes me look forward to the rest of my life. Discovery."*

After being shut out of his *sukkah* and sent away, Peniel had forgotten to look for a purpose. His world had crumbled, and he had assumed he was useless and clumsy, just as Mama said.

But today, though blind, he was not useless. The two women were fearful. They were not blind, and yet they were more afraid than he. Peniel imagined that his duty lay in being cheerful and self-assured.

To give other people hope: It was a *mitzvah* fulfilled.

Not an earthshaking accomplishment perhaps, but Peniel felt God's approval . . . and had a renewed belief in his future.

STIFLING HOT. LATE MORNING. How long had Manaen slept? Too long. Too late.

Ache. Breath labored beneath the weight of the stiff and heavy carcass.

The drone of flies. The stink of offal, ripening guts, and dried blood.

The itch of filth and creeping insects.

And above him, the high shriek of a vulture's cry.

One. Then two. Answering screams of discovery from five or six more.

The flapping of wings. Close. How close? Descending. Flurry of gathering! Swooping! Landing! Frenzy!

"Get back! Let go! Oh! O God, save me!"

Bites of vicious beaks, unable to tell the difference between the ram and the man struggling to free himself from beneath it!

"Get! Get away!" Manaen flailed his arms and whooped wildly as the enormous birds dashed in, ripped the sinew of the ram, then fell back. "Get! Back!" Still they came, the vultures, a hungry rabble unintimidated by a puny man. They would have a piece of Manaen's fresh, living meat as well. Or wait and tend to him later. He was no threat.

Manaen battled his way up from the corpse of the ram and fought his way through the flock of carrion. Fingers and arms were bitten multiple times. He managed to stand, to lash out with his feet, to protect his face. Instinctively covering useless eyes as if they mattered.

Plunging through the brush, he ran headlong across the rocky terrain, stumbling! Tumbling down! Scraping knees and elbows! Thorns piercing tender skin. Clawing his way upright! Running! Falling! Crawling!

Away! Must get away!

s the track leading to Bethany wound around the side of the Mount of Olives, it went through a steep, rocky stretch, well up on the side of the hill. No longer the broad highway it had been just outside Jerusalem, the path was here a constricted, rutted lane.

"Peniel?" Susanna queried. "We've missed the main road. Should've taken the left fork."

Peniel could not comment on that. He did not know the road to Bethany. He never imagined that sighted people might not either.

Peniel cautioned Susanna, "There's a herd of cattle coming. Hear them? Beyond the next bend or two."

"Yes, I hear them," Susanna responded.

The bawling of the cows increased in volume. The shouts of the herdsmen mingled with the racket. It sounded to Peniel like a big herd, perhaps a hundred cows or more.

"It's so narrow here," Naomi observed nervously. "On one side there's a rock wall and on the other a ravine. What do we do?"

Peniel visualized the scene. "Can we get up the slope?"

"Too high and too steep."

"Is there a tree near?"

Susanna directed their steps to a lone acacia tree just off the side of the dirt track. It grew on the brink of the canyon.

"Keep the tree between you and the herd," Peniel warned, "and stand still. If you move or flap your arms, the animals might balk or turn back. It makes the drovers angry. They might strike you." Peniel expected no danger from the animals themselves, but the women were used to the ways of a palace.

"Such a skinny tree," Naomi remarked. "Not room for the three of us."

The ground rumbled under Peniel's feet with the approach of the cattle. The combination of sound and vibration stretched in front of him, completely blocking the way ahead. "Is the tree big enough to climb?"

Naomi's voice quaked. "For one!"

"Then Lady Susanna must climb it," he said. "Hurry."

"I'll take the jar, Lady," Naomi said, then reported, "She's up."

The leaders of the herd arrived.

"Now what?" Naomi asked.

"Is there a place I can get out of the way? Over the lip of the cliff?" Peniel asked.

"Yes," Naomi said doubtfully. "A ledge. Down about the height of a man."

The bulk of the herd had arrived, pushing past the three. "I'll go," Peniel volunteered. "You stay behind the tree trunk till they're past."

Bowing himself to the ground, he groped forward and stretched his legs over the edge of the drop-off. His feet scrabbled on the rocky hillside to find purchase.

At the fullest extension of his arms, Peniel's toes touched a flat spot. It was not wide, barely enough room for both feet, but it would do. He let go with his hands and stood on the ledge.

"Don't worry!" he called up. "They'll get by us."

As Peniel listened to the cattle scuffling and the bellows of the herdsmen, he detected another animal sound: a horse's hooves.

Herdsmen did not ride horses. The people who could afford horses were royalty . . . or soldiers.

"Keep still," he cautioned.

The mass of the cattle herd arrived at the narrowest part of the road. One of them, pushed out from the rest, brushed the tree trunk. The women cried in alarm.

A shower of dust and gravel landed on Peniel's head as hooves scrabbled above him.

At the second collision of beast and tree Naomi shouted, "Hold on, Lady! Hang on!"

The noise of the herd diminished toward the west.

Then a man's voice called from the road, "I see you there in the tree. Seems I guessed right. Thought you'd come this way."

The horse approached.

"Peniel," Naomi hissed, "keep out of sight. He won't hurt us, but he'd kill you!" Louder she pleaded, "Wolf! Let us go, Wolf. You don't want to take my Lady back to Demos. Please! Don't do this!"

"Shut up, Naomi," Wolf growled. To Susanna he said apologetically, "Can't let you go free, Lady. There's a price on your head. I like you, but if I don't collect the reward, someone else will. You stick out like a fig on a rosebush. Climb down, or I'll chop the tree down and you with it."

The branches of the acacia rustled.

"More like it," Wolf said.

Naomi pleaded with him once more to let them go, let them escape from Antipas and Demos.

"Woman, shut up! You're a lot of trouble," Wolf said. "But if I take you back, Herodias will have your hide off one stripe at a time. I wouldn't like to think about that. No, Lady Susanna goes back with me. You go where you like. Nabatea for all I care. You've been nothing but trouble to me."

"I won't leave Lady Susanna!"

"Naomi, go," Susanna ordered. "Go on. Please, Naomi." She lowered her voice. "Like we planned. Tell them what's happened." Then she said, more loudly, "Just give me Manaen's heart."

"Come on then, Lady. No dawdling," Wolf scolded. "Get up on this horse and I'll lead you."

"Hold this for me?"

Wolf grunted with disgust. "Manaen's heart, you say? In the jug? Enough of this."

Both women shrieked. Peniel felt a rush of air as something flew past his head and out into the canyon. Seconds later there was a crash of broken pottery in the depths of the ravine.

And the sound of Susanna weeping.

"Right," Wolf said to Naomi. "Naomi, don't let me catch you again, understand? Don't let anyone catch you, or it'll go bad for both of us."

THE SOUND OF THE HORSE'S HOOVES HAD RETREATED. Wolf was gone, and he had taken Susanna with him.

"Peniel, reach up," Naomi instructed. "Take my hand. Here."

Clawing with fingers and toes, Peniel regained the rim of the wadi. Dust-covered, disheveled, and distraught, he sat down against the tree trunk in abject misery.

"I've failed," he said.

"What could you do, I ask you?" Naomi responded. "Poor Lady Susanna. It's fate. It's the decree of the god. Cruel god he can be at times too. What could anyone have done? Wolf heard my voice and recognized it. Fate. Besides, what do you expect? You're blind."

Peniel shook his head but did not explain. His blindness was inescapable, but that alone did not account for his uselessness. Mama was right: He *was* the burden.

Sensing his wretchedness, Naomi offered, "We'd never've made it so far without you. And thanks to Wolf, I'm free. I'll go to Bethany. Susanna has friends there. Friends who may even know how to help. Come with me, Peniel."

"I led you wrong. Couldn't save her. Clumsy. No use outside Yerushalayim; small use in it. I'm going back. I can beg, and no one gets hurt by it."

The jangle of a donkey's harness attracted Peniel's attention. It sounded anything but cheerful. A donkey had more brains than he. A donkey could find its way back to Jerusalem.

"Wait!" he called to the passing traveler. "Earn favor with heaven by me! I need help getting home to Yerushalayim."

He parted from Naomi without a good-bye, clinging to the donkey's tail. The dumb beast of burden was a better guide than he had been.

THE *FRIGIDARIUM*, OR COLD ROOM, of the Scorpio Bathhouse was a spacious square chamber topped by a dome. In each corner of the room was a semicircular pool of cool water. The mosaic floor forming the deck between the plunges was of white and blue squares outlined in gold.

On the far side of the *frigidarium*, through an archway, was a gaming room. Here bets were placed on horse races, cockfights, and other diversions held away from the bathing establishment. Roman officers, government officials, and wealthy traders also played at a board game called Kings and Crowns, but the most popular entertainment was dice.

It was at a dice table with three other players that Demos found Praetorian Vara: the same table where Demos, Vara, and others played every Sabbath when most entertainments in Jerusalem were closed.

As Demos approached, Vara shook the dice in an ivory cup and made his cast.

"Ha!" Vara exclaimed. "Another triple! Pay up."

Demos edged up alongside until Vara noticed him.

"You're late," Vara said coldly. "You have my money?"

"I . . . I will . . . soon," Demos returned. "You know how stingy Antipas is. But I'll have it soon."

"Have to run back to the tetrarch for an advance on your allowance?" Vara suggested.

"I said I'll have it soon."

"Don't think you can take off to Galilee and skip out on paying, do you?" Vara warned, raising his bushy eyebrows to stare at Demos.

"I'm good for it," Demos vowed.

"You better be."

Demos examined the stacks of silver coins on the dicing table and licked his lips thoughtfully. "Why not let me win some of it back?"

"On credit?" Vara inquired. Then he eyed his companions and noted, "Why not? It's not like I don't know where to find you."

Vara's gambling buddies snickered.

Demos pulled up a low bench, calling for a wax tablet and stylus to prepare a promissory note. "Shall we say fifty?" he suggested.

Vara waved his beefy hand nonchalantly. "Say a hundred. You might win enough to cover what you owe me."

Rubbing his hands together nervously, Demos signed the wax tablet then reached for the dice cup. "What's the count?"

Wolf, sweaty and dusty from travel, arrived. "Lord Demos, I was told I'd find you here."

"So?" Demos sniffed, shaking the cup. "You've found me. Now what?"

Stiffly Wolf reported, "The Lady Susanna has been located and returned to the tetrarch's custody."

"There, you see," Demos said. "My luck has changed already."

He made his throw . . . and lost again.

𐤖

SUN BEATING DOWN LIKE A HAMMER. Thirst. Skin burned. Lips blistered.

Manaen gripped his knees and tucked his head, trying to protect himself against the scorching rays. He was afraid to move.

The precipice. Somewhere. How close?

Vultures still worked on the ram. More were coming. The chorus of a Greek tragedy. Screeching at one another where they sat scattered on the hillside. Impatiently waiting their turns.

Waiting for Manaen to die.

The bleating of sheep, close by. How many? A handful maybe? Part of the ram's harem. Wild? Lost? A shepherd close by?

The Lord is my shepherd. . . .

Manaen raised his chin and tried to call, "Help . . . me." But his voice was a strangled whisper.

Hopeless. Hopeless.

Though I walk in the valley of the shadow of death . . . I will fear . . .

"Susanna!" He managed. "Susanna!" Was she well? Had they told her he was dead? given her the ram's heart in a box? Would she be forced into Demos' bed?

No evil . . .

Vengeance! To live and somehow bring Demos to his knees!

In the presence of my enemies . . .[68]

"O God, help me!"

Thirst. Try not to think about water. Try not to think about the vultures.

It would be over soon.

𐤖

EARLY THAT EVENING SUSANNA, iron manacles on her wrists, was shoved to the floor of Herod Antipas' judgment chamber.

"Where is the slave woman, Wolf?" Antipas demanded.

"Dead, my Lord," Wolf lied.

"You were fond of her, were you not?" Herodias inquired of Wolf.

"She was a lot of trouble," Wolf replied.

"I would have liked to have her back. To flog her myself." Clearly Herodias was disappointed.

"She drew a dagger and killed herself. She was a Nabatean, after all."

Antipas smirked, as if he liked the answer. "Yes, well. I know about Nabatean women. My first wife was crazy too. Nothing you can do but stay out of the way. Ship them off as soon as possible."

Wolf nodded. "She was a lot of trouble."

Herodias, imperious and disdainful, shifted in her seat and eyed Susanna. "Well, you see, Antipas, what a woman will do for love. Susanna has dressed herself in the clothing of a man."

Antipas' left eye twitched nervously. "In the days of the old kings would that not be a stoning offense? Here. Ask the priests." He snapped his fingers at Wolf. "Bring me a priest. Let him look in the scrolls and see if I am not right in this point of law."

Wolf, smelling of sweat and barley beer, saluted the tetrarch and Herodias and left the room.

"Well, *Cousin*," Herodias said harshly, "what do you have to say for yourself? A stoning offense."

Susanna did not raise her eyes. Exhausted, beaten, she hoped for death. "You've already killed my heart," she replied quietly.

"No, no!" Antipas argued. "Wolf killed your heart. Yet Demos can raise it from the dead, I think. We will let Demos see you dressed like this. He prefers little boys, after all. Perhaps this will arouse his passion. Make a man of him, eh, Herodias?"

"Yes. We will let Susanna dress as a man for the wedding ceremony. Demos will like that."

Antipas laughed. "We will issue a decree that Susanna is no longer a woman, but a man. Yes. A wedding gift for Demos."

Wolf returned with the court priest.

"Ah!" Antipas announced. "Here is our scholar! Cohen! Look at this thing on the floor before me. What do you see?"

The priest replied, "A beggar boy. A filthy beggar boy."

"Not so!" Antipas laughed. "Strip away those clothes—" he paused. "Shall we? Shall we strip you in front of everyone, beggar boy?"

Susanna felt sick. The room spun around her. "Please. May I go back to my room?"

The priest drew back at the sound of her voice. "It's a woman!"

"Right," Herodias said dryly.

Antipas probed, "Now here is the question. What does the Scripture say about a woman who dresses as a man? pretends to be a man?"

"It's an abomination," the priest answered.

Antipas snapped his fingers. "Ha! See! I was right. Well then, priest, what should we do with her? Stone her?"

"Be merciful, Lord Antipas. Today is the day when the attribute of mercy is discussed among the rabbis. Put her away," the priest replied.

"Good idea," Antipas concluded.

"We'll have to lock her in a room without windows," Herodias taunted. "Or the little bird will fly."

"Or . . . maybe this," Antipas said slowly.

Susanna knew Antipas was toying with her.

"Marry her to Demos today," he finished.

"There can be no marriages until after Pentecost," the priest argued. "Only after the Festival of Weeks has ended is it lawful for anyone to marry."

Antipas scowled. "Where does it say that?"

"It's the way it's always been, Lord Antipas," the priest explained. "There are no weddings during the fifty days between Passover and Pentecost."

The tetrarch blew his nose loudly. "Well, we cannot change it if that is the way it is. But the evening Pentecost ends there will be a wedding between Susanna bat Maccabee and Demos bar Talmai. Or there will be a funeral in the Potter's Field for a woman who transgressed the laws of God and dressed herself in a man's clothing."

A FEW MINUTES LATER WOLF ESCORTED Susanna to a bare room with a tiny window set high in the wall. There was a bed. A basket of fruit. Bread. A jug of water and one of wine.

Men's clean clothing was neatly folded on the pillow.

"I'm to be locked up in here, then?" Susanna asked.

"I'm sorry for you, Lady," Wolf said. "You'll stay here until you agree to the terms of Antipas and Demos. At least you're alive."

"And Naomi."

Wolf put a finger to his thick lips. "You'll want to do as they tell you. Life is better. No matter what you may think. Maybe, you know, the god will someday give you children. That would be something to cheer you up."

"By Demos." She glanced at the male clothing set out for her and knew the implication of it.

"Does it matter? We all know what he is. He'll get tired of you after a while. He'll leave you alone. Don't give up."

Susanna sighed. "You love Naomi, don't you?"

"She's a lot of trouble. And I could get into trouble if I say more to you."

"Then go on. And ask the priest if I may have a scroll of Psalms to read for the days between now and Pentecost."

"I'll do that, my Lady." Wolf bowed curtly and backed from the room.

The door closed and the lock closed securely. This time there would be no escape.

34

This is as far as you go, lad," the merchant told Peniel.

Peniel, who had been lost in gloomy thoughts on the way back to Jerusalem, came to himself with a start.

"I don't mind you hitching a ride, but I'm traveling with ladies' goods, see?" the peddler said. "Can't have you with me when I reach the shop I'm calling on. You smell, see? Can't have them think you work for me, can I? No offense."

"Where are we?" Peniel asked.

"Pool of Siloam. Just there. A washup will do you good, eh?"

Peniel thanked the man, then made his way down the steps and into the courtyard of Siloam.

Exhausted, he groped toward a wall and sat down against it. The cool of evening enveloped him. The last conversations of women floated through the porticos. And then he was alone. The doors were closed. No one had noticed that he remained behind.

This place was an appropriate place to end this awful day, he thought. Here. It was the site of his greatest loss; the first blow of his deepest wound was delivered here. Siloam Pool, where his long and lonely exile had begun.

Here at Siloam Peniel had ruined the lives of others with his clumsiness. He had turned seven that day. His brother, Gershon, was sixteen. Seven was a righteous number, Gershon said. And at breakfast he gave Peniel the bowl with his name on it.

Peniel! Peniel! Peniel! Raised letters all around. What a gift! To read his name with his fingers! Had anyone ever had a brother like Gershon?

It was on Hoshana Rabbah, the last and greatest day of the Feast of Tabernacles, that it had all happened. . . .

Despite Mama's protests, Gershon promised to bring Peniel along to the drawing out of the water by the priests in the sacred gold pitcher. Since Peniel was not allowed inside the inner Court of the Israelites because he was blind, this was the best place for him to be part of the day of forgiveness! He would be there at the beginning, even if he could not be there at the end!

Mama had scoffed. "What difference will being there make to a blind boy?"

Gershon had prevailed. It was Peniel's birthday, after all.

Papa had overridden Mama's protest, allowing the boys to go.

The brothers got there before first light, long before the crowd. In plenty of time to find the best location, Gershon said: on the far side of the pool, exactly opposite where the priests would perform the ceremony!

Peniel! Peniel! Peniel! Had anyone ever had such a brother as Gershon?

The space around the colonnaded reservoir was soon packed with onlookers. They pressed into every imaginable space, pushing and shoving long after the first-comers shouted, "No more! No more room!"

Gershon gripped Peniel's hand. Kept him safe from the depths of the pool. He fought to keep their place in the front rank. To those who protested that Peniel was blind and it was a waste, Gershon retorted angrily that he was there to see for both of them!

Peniel heard the trumpets blow all the way from the pinnacle of the Temple, ringing tones that thrilled him. The murmur of the spectators echoed along Herodian Way, shouting hosanna to the priests! Singing and cheering in a wave of joy rolling ahead of the procession.

And then the Psalms reached his ears: the Great Hosanna. The last day of the redemption cycle began with the Day of Atonement. The last chance for forgiveness, to be entered in the rolls of the blessed, the fa-vored of Adonai!

Peniel! Peniel! Peniel! Had anyone ever had a brother kinder than Gershon?

"See it, Peniel? See it in your heart! Beautiful! Light! Look! The sky is red this morning. Red. How can I tell you what red is? Red is like the scent of cin-namon! Like apples baking! That is what the sky looks like. Yes! Cinnamon banners of color! There'll be rain tomorrow!"

Gershon protected Peniel. He elbowed encroaching onlookers aside. He described to Peniel the white-robed priests, the golden pitcher passed forward with pomp and ceremony. He recounted the blessing over the water, the prayers for rain for the coming year. Re-peated for Peniel the benediction as the pageant moved off toward the Temple again, where the high priest would pour out the pitcher of Siloam's water at the base of the altar as a sign of the outpouring of God's Mercy.

The crowd, anxious to see the completion of the rite, surged around Gershon and Peniel toward the single exit on the far side. For an instant Gershon let go of Peniel's hand. Only an instant. And the two were parted.

Terror! Where was Gershon? Where?

Peniel! Peniel! Peniel! Was there ever a brother who loved like Gershon?

"Gershon! Where are you? Gershon!" Peniel dropped to his knees and called out. The crowd pushed him from behind. Too near. Too near the rim of Siloam!

And Peniel fell. He shouted Gershon's name as the water closed over his head.

His tunic and robe lapped up water, dragging him down in the deepest part of the tank.

He could not swim, could not see which direction to swim.

Heard Gershon yell his name, *"Peniel! Peniel! Peniel!"*

Then there was a mighty splash as his brother leapt in to save him!

Down and down Peniel sank, struggling, tangled in folds of cloth. His lungs filled with water. Choking! Fighting to breathe! Kicking! Struggling to find air!

Then, a miracle! Gershon's arms encircled him, lifted him, pushed him toward the surface not once but three times. Gershon shouted, *"Someone help! Peniel! Take Peniel!"*

Peniel was lifted by his wrists, aided by one final heave upwards by his brother.

Gershon fell back into the pool with a strangled cry. *"Save . . . Peniel!"*

Hauled dripping and choking onto the pavement, Peniel was nearly unconscious.

"Saved his brother, he did. Pity the elder one couldn't swim either. He's done for."

Peniel! Peniel! Peniel! Since that day no earthly voice had ever spoken his name with love. *"Why isn't Peniel in the grave instead of Gershon? Why should the blind brother live and not the boy with talent and brains and a future?"*

These questions were whispered by men and women as they discussed the tragedy. And Peniel heard them. Heard his mother and his father in the night through their tears.

He did not blame them when they banished him to the little hut out back beside the kiln. No. Did not blame them.

And how he missed Gershon! Every day. Every night! Peniel held the bowl that Gershon made and remembered that he had once been loved. That his brother had loved him enough to die for him.

Peniel! Peniel! Peniel!

Tonight the wound was fresh again as he sat beside the Pool of Siloam and remembered. He wished the bowl was not broken. He grieved over his worthless life. Tonight Peniel himself asked the questions. Why had Adonai not let Gershon live and taken Peniel instead?

Who am I, Lord? Who am I to live when my brother didn't?

What right did Peniel, a blind man, have to hold on to life when the life he had was of no value to anyone?

Gershon could have found the way to Bethany. Gershon would have saved Susanna and Naomi the servant. He would not have gotten lost!

Who am I to be here when my brother is gone? he pleaded.

But there was no answer.

35

irst warning came after noon the next day. Marcus was drawing water from the well for a flock of yearlings when Avel and Red Dog ran to fetch him.

"Zadok wants you to come," the boy panted.

"Almost finished."

"No! He says you're to come *now!* Straightaway to the house! He'll send someone back to finish here."

"What is it, boy? What's wrong?" Marcus hefted the stone slab over the open mouth of the well, then instinctively raised his head to the wind.

Avel explained, "Riders coming. Ha-or Tov saw them from the hill. Cavalry. They'll be wanting water for their mounts. Stop here at the well first. Zadok says you're to come now."

Marcus retrieved his staff and shepherd's bag from the corral post and they set off together.

"Are they Roman?"

Avel nodded.

The meaning was clear to Marcus. They were not the soldiers of Antipas. If Romans, they were coming for Marcus. They would comb the area of Migdal Eder and Beth-lehem. If he was found here against orders, he would not be the lone one arrested. Any who helped him would be guilty of *maeistas* and executed. Zadok. The boys. Perhaps the entire company of shepherds, along with their wives and children, would be in peril.

Zadok stood in the garden as Marcus and Avel arrived home. He gazed toward the north, where a flock of buzzards wheeled above a distant mountain slope. Ha-or Tov sat on the low rock wall behind him.

Emet stood watch on a hill above the lambing caves. The boy waved broadly, indicating that the riders had turned on the road that led into Migdal Eder.

"The vultures are gathering." Zadok gestured toward the circling birds. "Look there. So many. It means they've finished with the crucified bodies in Yerushalayim. They're back over our hills now."

"Riders coming, Avel says." Marcus frowned. "How many, Ha-or Tov?"

"Roman cavalry. I wasn't sure at first. I stayed long enough to count twenty."

"A troop. Heading to Beth-lehem. I must leave. Won't let my presence put you at risk."

The old man appeared unperturbed at the approaching danger, yet held a packed haversack and a waterskin out to Marcus. "I thought you'd want to have a look for me. Up there. Avel and Red Dog will go with you."

"They're coming to arrest me. I can't let a boy and a dog slow me down."

"Avel and Red Dog. Yes. Up there. See the vultures? Two days' journey at least. We've lost a fine big ram in the last fortnight. He took eight ewes with him too. Sometimes they'll get it in their heads to go wild. Start their own tribe. Like Father Avraham, you might say. I fear the old boy may have hurt himself up there. Can't think what else would be drawing so many carrion fowl."

"I'll go alone."

"Take Avel and the dog. One man alone may be spotted and pursued. A man with a boy and a dog? What fool on the run would take a boy and a dog as company? Innocent enough. And you'll need help if that's the ram and the ewes. To bring them back."

"I won't be back, Zadok."

The old man smiled and touched his eyepatch, as if he saw the future played out before his blind eye. "Find my ram. I'm fond of the old fellow and he's stolen my ewes."

It seemed Marcus had no choice. Hide in plain sight. The strategy just might work.

DYING.

Regret mixed with relief.

Manaen would not have recognized himself anymore. Lips swollen and cracked. Ears grotesque lumps of gristle. Tongue useless, wooden and hard from dehydration. Nose leathery, burned by the sun, no longer carrying scents of dust, carrion, sweat, or sage.

All senses but one had deserted him.

Only his hearing functioned.

Vultures quarreled over morsels of ram carcass. How soon would they fight one another for his remains?

Sheep moved about somewhere below him, much farther away. Their sounds tantalized, then tormented him. Sheep meant shepherds—rescue, water, safety.

Gripped by dread in the lightless prison of his body, he feared making a noise, feared attracting vultures before he was dead. What if they devoured him while a spark of life remained?

But no creature came either to help or harm.

He could not call out. Only groan in agony.

One desire urged him to fight back: *Susanna!* Leave her to Demos? If Manaen loved her, shouldn't he try to resist death?

Part of his mind functioned in a detached, distant way. As an on-looker, not a participant. He saw himself seated in the arena, watching gladiators locked in a death struggle. Spectators called out advice: Move this way or that, try this tactic, fight harder!

Then the vision changed.

Manaen in the arena! Manaen about to be killed!

Vulture-headed demons gnawed at his eyes: Demos, Eglon, Antipas . . . laughing.

Blind Peniel was in the stands, shouting. *"Use what you have, Manaen! The answer is near! Listen! Listen!"*

Listen? To what? What else was there to hear besides vultures and sheep? Even the sighing of the wind had ceased.

And yet there was something else! A thin, ready peep! Like a flute hesitatingly played and heard from a distance.

It came again, nearer than before!

Something scratched in the dirt near his foot. A series of chirps caught his attention. A sparrow! Little bird! Close by!

Think, Manaen! Peniel urged from the stands. *Think!*

Sparrow sounds stopped. Fluttering wings darted away.

Manaen grieved. *Friend! Don't go*, he wanted to shout.

What was that? Sparrow! Friend! Piping again. Farther off. Behind him. Higher up somehow.

What does it mean, Peniel?

The bird returned, departed again. Each time the staccato peeps moved from low and near to away and higher.

A tree! Must be landing on a tree branch!

A tree meant shade! Shelter! Hope!

Was there strength left to make the attempt?

Had he waited too long?

The sparrow came back yet again, urging him to the effort.

Try, Peniel encouraged.

The breeze rose again, sweeping up the canyon, pushing Manaen up the slope. The Presence came with it! Manaen felt it near, urging him to live!

Try, the Presence on the wind exhorted. And this time Manaen did not order it away.

Turning over on his belly, Manaen extended one clawed hand, dug fingers into weeds, and pulled himself forward with a heave of shoulders and hips.

Again. Again. Don't stop to rest. Don't think. Pull and pull once more. Better to die moving toward hope than to yield to despair!

The sparrow! Chirping encouragement! It flitted back and forth, drawing Manaen on!

THE WIND ROSE WITH THE DECLINE of the sun. It swirled over the ridgeline, wrapping Marcus, Avel, and the dog in a veil of dust as they struggled upward.

Marcus chose the most direct route toward the summit, even

though it was a challenge to ascend. He desperately wanted to reach the highest ground in the area in order to see what was happening near Migdal Eder.

They fought their way through a thicket of aromatic juniper brush. Marcus and Avel grasped at branches laden with pink flowers to aid their climb up the ravine.

At last they reached the top. Away to the west the terrain dropped precipitately toward the coast, while the bare limestone outcropping on which they stood afforded a view of the sheepfolds, Beth-lehem, and the whole valley.

There was no doubt the warning had been correct: A troop of legionaries were already watering their horses back at the well Marcus had just been tending.

If he had hesitated, or if the warning had come a minute later, he would have been surrounded by soldiers.

Given Marcus' disguise and the presence of Avel, he might have bluffed his way past Syrian cavalrymen. But not past their leader.

Pulling Avel down in the cleft of a rock, Marcus pointed out the burly figure who waved impatiently at his troopers to hurry with their mounts: Vara. Marcus had no doubt that the Praetorian had heard of the connection between Marcus and Zadok and was even now on his way to interrogate the Chief Shepherd.

When the column of mounted men resumed their progress, it confirmed Marcus' suspicion. At a trot the troop skirted the hills on the trail leading directly toward the Tower of the Flock.

His hand rested on Avel's shoulder as Marcus moved the two of them from boulder to brush heap, mindful that they must not let themselves be silhouetted against the evening sky. Like rabbits evading a sniffing fox, their movements were a combination of scurry and frozen stillness: dashes across open spaces and sudden melting into the clumps of sage.

Even Red Dog appeared to understand the need for caution, slinking around rock cairns rather than leaping over them, and creeping on his belly when the humans did so.

Two hundred scampering paces repositioned Marcus and Avel to a spot directly overlooking Migdal Eder. They arrived as the Roman column rode directly through the last pastures, carelessly scattering sheep and shepherds in their arrogance.

Though too far away to hear the words, Marcus could imagine the exchange from Vara's peremptory gestures. *I demand to see the Chief Shepherd*, his motions said. *Immediately.*

A pair of shepherds, anxious to avoid trouble with a man who could order them crucified on a whim, rushed into the tower.

A long time passed.

Vara clearly chafed at the delay, and his mount shared his master's impatience, dancing nervously at the sheep smell and pawing at the ground.

The sun's fiery ball dipped lower and lower.

More angry motions by Vara; more shepherds hurrying to comply.

Zadok knew he would be watching, Marcus thought. The old shepherd was purposely delaying to give them time to escape.

At last Zadok's tall, imposing figure emerged, backlit by the gleam of the light within the ground floor of the tower. Then the sun disappeared behind the western hills, and the scene in the valley below was lost in shadow.

DISMOUNTING INTO THE GROWING DARKNESS, Vara curtly ordered his soldiers to kill any shepherds who offered resistance. Vara followed Zadok into the stone chamber of Migdal Eder. Emet and Ha-or Tov were commanded to remain in the room.

"You," Vara said with a sneering tone. "So you're Chief Shepherd of Israel's flocks. You're the man I nearly cut in two on the Temple Mount. And it was Centurion Marcus Longinus who saved you. So where is he?"

Zadok shrugged. "Have y' misplaced him then? As I recall he was as near to your throat as the point of *his* sword."

With two quick strides Vara crossed the room and backhanded the old man hard on the cheek. Ha-or Tov leapt forward, only to be shoved back hard by Zadok. "Don't move," he warned the boys. "Don't speak."

"Don't play word games with me," Vara warned ominously. "I could have you up on charges of resisting arrest for opposing me at the Temple. *Maiestas* is punishable by death."

"Fine choice," Zadok noted. "Death there or death now for escaping you before. Roman reasoning defies reason." Another blow—this time a clenched fist that sent Zadok to his knees. He rose, slowly, blood streaking his face from a cut on his cheekbone. "Lord high-and-mighty-priest Caiaphas may cooperate with Rome about many things, but abusing the Chief Shepherd of Israel will surely bring a protest from the Sanhedrin to Governor Pilate."

"What's that to me?"

Drawing himself fully upright and staring into Vara's murderous eyes, Zadok intoned, "Do y' take me for some peasant sheepherder you can bully and threaten?"

Another swipe of the fist. This time Zadok ducked his head into his shoulder and took the blow on his skull. It staggered him, but it was Vara who cradled his fingers as if he had injured himself.

"I've got a warrant that covers whatever I choose to do to you. Hiding a traitor and a deserter is also punishable by death," Vara menaced. "Where is he?"

"I hate Romans," Zadok said unequivocally. "What we do here is sacred to the Almighty. I don't allow any but true brothers here. Would I jeopardize our duty to protect a Roman centurion? What's one Roman to me, more or less? Perhaps you and he will meet and kill each other. Two less Romans in my world. A pleasure."

Vara lashed out with fist and riding crop. He pummeled Zadok unmercifully. "Where is Centurion Marcus Longinus?" He followed each clout with a renewed demand for Marcus' whereabouts. "Where? Where has he gone? Did he tell you where he was going?"

Zadok made no reply. A grunt of pain escaped him.

In a corner of the room Ha-or Tov clung to Emet. The younger boy buried his face, not daring to look, whimpering with each blow.

Vara wore himself out pummeling the shepherd.

Beaten to the floor, the old man rose to one knee. Fighting to breathe, Zadok spoke. "You think . . . I wouldn't . . . tell . . . you . . . Roman . . . in a minute . . . if I knew?"

"It isn't over, old man!" One final blow. Vara kicked Zadok in the stomach, then stormed out of the chamber.

To his guard sergeant he said contemptuously, "Old fool doesn't know anything, but I've taught his pride a lesson. Move out. We ride to Herodium."

As soon as the troopers cantered away, Ha-or Tov cried for help.

Emet cradled Zadok's bloody head in his lap. The Chief Shepherd's good eye was swollen shut. Through split and bleeding lips he said to the boy, "Y' mustn't worry . . . about me, boy."

Then he passed out.

36

It was midnight. The temperature in the Judean hill country dropped like a stone. Marcus rose from his fleece pad and used the sheepskin as extra covering for Avel, then returned to fitful slumber.

Dreams of Miryam were interwoven with nightmares of Pilate, Herod Antipas, the high priest, Praetorian Vara, and Yeshua of Nazareth!

Vara. Gladius raised, about to strike! Yeshua pursued, arrested, charged with maiestas. Then stripped, flogged, and stretched out on the wooden cross beam for execution! Miryam calling to Marcus across a vast gulf! Begging him to stop something that was inevitable! The short sword in Vara's hand now a hammer poised to drive the spike into the flesh of Yeshua.

Marcus tried to speak! "Innocent! He's innocent!" Words froze in his throat.

Hand on the hilt of his sword, Marcus struggled to draw it from its sheath. He could not move! The hammer arced downward and drove the spike home! Vara shouted in triumph. "An end! The end of it!"

Miryam turned her eyes to gaze at Marcus in reproach. "Help him! Help him, Marcus!"

But Marcus could not move. Could not speak! "Innocent! Innocent!"

First light. Predawn. Marcus willed himself to awaken from the agonizing vision. He opened his eyes and tried to sort dreams from reality.

The gray-green slopes of grass and sage were brushed with silver frost. Marcus lay wrapped in his shepherd's cloak. Knees were drawn up to his chest as he tried to cover his large frame with an inadequate length of cloth.

The centurion ached with the cold. He lay perfectly still, listening, sensing the danger he had seen in his vision. But was this ominous foreboding real?

Red Dog raised no alarm. Marcus doubted that intruders were around.

He heard the sounds of even breathing: Avel.

And something more: a soft chirping.

Rising slowly to one elbow, Marcus peered across at the boy's bedroll. Avel remained snuggled comfortably under fleece and cloak and the added warmth of Red Dog lying close alongside.

The dog turned his head to acknowledge Marcus, then immediately went back to watching something else. In the uncertain light of early morning, movement flickered in the space between boy and dog.

There, perched on Avel's chest, was a brown sparrow. The tiny creature fluttered its wings, not so much to create a disturbance but apparently just to order its feathers. It did not seem alarmed by the watchful gaze of Red Dog, nor did the canine give any sign of wanting to attack or drive off the avian intruder.

Marcus gazed at this phenomenon for a time. Then he sat up slowly.

Startled, the sparrow flapped its wings again, then took flight. In the instant of the bird's departure Avel's eyes snapped open. A dreamy smile spread across the boy's face. The sparrow did not retreat far, merely darting to a nearby thornbush.

"I was dreaming," said the boy. "Was I? A dream? I was a Sparrow again. A link boy in the night. Carrying torches in Yerushalayim. Light through the streets of Yerushalayim. For Yeshua of Nazareth this time. An old friend. And a sparrow flew before me, showing me the way. Happy. I am happy."

"Well then." Marcus indicated the sparrow perched just feet from Avel.

Avel whispered, "Yes. Well then, a familiar face. Good morning, Yediyd. Small friend."

The sparrow studied the boy and preened on the stem.

Unrolling himself from his covers, Avel also sat up. "A fine dream," he said to Marcus. "Can we have a fire this morning?"

"Better not," Marcus warned. "Don't want to attract attention."

"No matter." Avel reached into his haversack and withdrew a flat cake of unleavened bread. Splitting the matzoh carefully in two, Avel tossed one half to Red Dog, then took a bite for himself. Breaking off another corner, he crumbled it in his fist, then extended his hand, palm upward.

Without hesitation the sparrow returned, perching on Avel's outstretched fingers and politely pecking at the crumbs.

Marcus wondered, unspeaking, at this unusual occurrence. This was an odd place, this hillside. A place of haunting visions. He would be glad to push on.

The eastern mountains were momentarily etched with gold just before the sun leapt into view.

The centurion made a cold breakfast of leftover matzoh, washing it down with cider from an earthen jug. He studied the peak up ahead. With the dawn he again saw a flight of vultures, relentlessly wheeling. "Doesn't look promising," Marcus observed, pointing out the carrion birds to Avel. "Still, that's our destination."

The sparrow, which had left Avel for the thorn limb again while the boy rolled up his bedding, flicked its tail up and down as if also restless to depart.

Marcus, Avel, and Red Dog left the camp as the sun topped the rise. The sparrow went before them, dodging from bush to bush, never more than a dozen yards in advance as they ascended the mountain.

IT WAS AVEL WHO NOW TOOK THE LEAD on their journey. He seemed excited to be on the trail.

Avel darted up the steep ascent as if a spacious path unrolled in front of him. The apprentice shepherd paid no attention to bramble thickets or yawning crevices. He hurtled onward in surefooted confidence.

Always, always, the sparrow flitted ahead of the boy, alighting first on an oak, then on a boulder, then across a gorge to await the struggling humans.

Marcus thought the little bird had vanished after that. But Avel spotted it again leaping from spindle to spindle on a clump of seven-branched sage, like a tiny brown flame flickering on a menorah's lamps.

The sparrow gave the impression that it was leading them . . . some sort of illusion, Marcus was certain. Apparently the bird had a degree of curiosity out of proportion with its species, as if almost eager to see where the humans were going.

Avel adjusted his route up the slope to fit the course of the sparrow.

Why would he do such a senseless thing? Marcus wondered. In any case, he reflected, it did not seem to matter. Their goal was in sight in the form of the orbiting vultures. As long as their path continued upward, they could scarcely make a mistake.

Pausing for breath, Marcus studied the carrion birds. At least two of them were always aloft, riding the air currents in lazy circuits of the cloudless sky. These were the sentinels. Like the regular rotation of a Roman guard detail, their black-uniformed replacements rose into the sunlight on the beating of powerful wings, while the off-duty contingent spiraled back to earth.

Eagerly back to earth, Marcus noted.

Marcus had seen battlefields two days after the bloodletting stopped, once in Germany and again later in Syria. Fat-bodied, evil-visaged birds, gorged almost to immobility on the unburied dead, rending and tearing, haunted Marcus' dreams for weeks.

Hours passed. The sun beat down fiercely. *Miserable high desert,* Marcus thought, *fit for growing thorns. Making men crazy. Getting men lost.*

The end was in sight. Marcus and Avel drew near to the vultures . . . and whatever lay underneath them. Brush rustled around the next bend. Calling to Avel to wait, Marcus whistled to draw Red Dog to him. He readied his shepherd's staff. It could be a lion, a pack of jackals, or worse, a gang of bar Abba's cutthroats.

Where was Avel going?

Instead of returning to Marcus' side, the boy forged ahead, calling out, "There he goes. There goes our friend."

Rushing forward, Marcus brandished his staff, wishing it were a javelin or at least his short sword. He found Avel beside a pair of ewes. A spring bubbled out of the rock, feeding a shallow pool and an expanse of grass.

Red Dog bounded into the thicket brush that ringed the pasture.

Darting in and out, he drove another half-dozen ewes back to the water and then, circling, held them there.

Eight in all. Not one missing.

Then what was the explanation for the vultures? Finding the female sheep was good news to carry to Zadok, but something must have happened to the ram.

Leaving Red Dog to keep the little flock intact, Marcus and Avel climbed the knoll that stood at the head of the draw.

It was as Marcus feared. There, already torn to shreds by vultures, were the remains of the ram. A trio of buzzards fought a three-way tug-of-war over a scrap of fleece. Two more perched on the shoulder of the carcass. They raised their wings and inflated their chests at Marcus' approach, as if to assert their right to the remains.

"We should at least try to salvage some of the pelt," Marcus said. Swinging his staff as he walked, he scattered the vultures. Four of them hopped a few feet out of the way. Others took flight, but only as far as a nearby acacia tree.

Kneeling beside the carcass, Marcus studied it for a time, then called Avel to him. "This is strange," he suggested. "See how straight and clean this slash on the hide? This wasn't done by a wild animal, which would have pulled the body, to jagged pieces. But if by a man with a knife, then why leave it behind? The horns, the fleece." He surveyed the ground, examining the vulture-pecked bones. "All four quarters. Somebody killed it, cut it open, and then left it here. Why?" Scrutinizing the ground, he added, "And what can this mean?" Protruding from under the ram's corpse, held in the grip of a jagged rock, was a bit of cloth as big as a man's hand.

"Not up to us to solve the mystery. Zadok will be glad we've returned with the ewes," Marcus concluded, standing and wiping his hands down the length of his tunic. "Let's get some water at the pool, then head back."

VOICES, DISCUSSING A DISMEMBERED CARCASS. The ram's corpse or his? Manaen listened but could not decide if they were real or imagined. Tantalizing illusion or truth?

Try to call out. Croak, a Voice urged him.

Here I am! Look here!

Was that his voice? Sparrow's chirp was louder. Had he made any sound at all? Had he killed himself? What irony: Fear of dying as a sun-baked husk drove him away from the hillside. Drove him away from rescue?

No matter.

Rest. Shade. Drifting on a cooling breeze. Manaen's back was against the rough acacia bark. Like leaning against the mast on the deck of a ship at sea, the earth rolled with each breath, each heartbeat.

A sense of accomplishment. Manaen would never again say anything was too difficult.

Grim humor, that.

Manaen would never again say anything at all.

The Sadducees taught there was no bodily resurrection. *Hope they are wrong,* Manaen thought. It was his new sense of persistence. He would have liked another chance at life.

If a blind, half-starved, all-burned man can drag himself uphill to a tree, what other things are possible?

If he just had water.

Sparrow chirped a song of congratulations overhead. *Must remember to thank you. Give you a lifetime of bread crumbs, bird . . . if I had bread crumbs . . . if I had a lifetime. Thank you, anyway.*

He saw Peniel, standing, applauding. *Well done, Manaen. But don't give up now.*

Why not? What's left?

The Lord is my shepherd . . . though I walk through the valley of the shadow of death. . . .

Voices—not the bird, not Peniel, not the Presence. Moving away, growing fainter.

Good-bye then, Susanna.

Hope the Sadducees are wrong.

RED DOG GATHERED THE SHEEP without any command from Avel except for a snap of the fingers. The dog formed the flock into a compact clump and turned them toward home.

One old ewe, sorry to leave the grazing, resisted briefly. But Red

Dog went eye-to-eye with her, and her defiance collapsed. When she started down the canyon, so did the rest.

Marcus was troubled by the unexplained mystery of the ram's carcass. Who had killed the animal and why? To be on a hill in the middle of nowhere had every sign of a religious ceremony. But if the ram was a sacrifice, where was the altar? Had something interrupted the rite? Marcus would describe it to Zadok. Maybe the old shepherd could explain.

Avel praised Red Dog as a prince among sheepdogs. Marcus noted the swagger in the boy's step at fulfilling Zadok's orders. Avel took the lead again, obviously keen to return to Migdal Eder and make his report.

Then the boy stopped with a puzzled expression. Marcus watched him cock his head to one side and listen intently. Perhaps the boy's senses had picked up a danger signal Marcus had missed. Red Dog halted also, holding the sheep in check. But the dog gave no signal of unease.

"What is it?" Marcus asked.

"Where's my little friend?" Avel said, scanning the path ahead and behind.

Marcus was momentarily baffled. Had the heat addled the boy's wits? Then he recalled what Avel called the sparrow.

"Decided he'd had enough of his midday scorching," Marcus observed. "Went to look for shade."

Rather than accepting the explanation and moving on, Marcus' comment made Avel redouble his efforts.

Peering intently back up toward the acacia tree, Avel shaded his eyes against the glare, then announced, "He's there."

Marcus likewise examined the tree. Yes, there was a tiny lump that stood out against the sky at the extreme end of one long, skinny limb. The twig bobbed up and down, as if beckoning.

"Smarter than us," Marcus commented. "Resting in the heat of the day."

"No," Avel surprisingly contradicted. "It means something. We have to go back."

"I don't think . . . ," Marcus began, but the boy was already resolutely trudging up the dusty slope again.

No need to give Red Dog any instructions.

Irritated by the detour, Marcus followed Avel toward the lone tree. "Let's go, Avel. We're wasting time." Who knew how long the thorny sentinel had guarded this place, presiding over a kingdom no one wanted. If the sparrow, dancing on a thin perch, wanted company, he had better look for more hospitable surroundings. No living creature . . . the tree moved. While Marcus stared, part of the black trunk leaned sideways.

"Avel!" Marcus ordered sharply. "Get back!"

It was a man. Burnt by the sun. Face swollen, lips split. Dressed in rags. Eyes bandaged. More dead than alive.

But alive.

"Run, Avel! Bring the water jug! Hurry!"

FLOATING. STILL IN DARKNESS. Voice, one older, gruff: "No, Marcus, it's nothing. What's a broken nose to a face like mine or a busted rib? But this fellow! More than half dead, I'd say."

"Water!" Manaen moaned feebly. A jug of water pressed to his lips, and he swallowed greedily.

The one called Marcus, foreign-sounding, replied, "Look here, Zadok. The wounds to his eyes are recent. The look of a professional job. A skilled butcher with a practiced hand burned out his eyes."

Eglon! Manaen wanted to shout. *Demos! Antipas!* And then, *Susanna!* But no words came, only inarticulate mumbling.

The old man, Zadok, came close, bending over Manaen. "He's a Jew. Circumcised. Hands too soft for a commoner. Even so, could he be a Zealot? Or someone caught spying on them, then tortured? abandoned?"

Marcus answered, "On the way down the mountain he called out for Susanna. Does the name mean anything to you? No?"

Someone bent close to Manaen's cheek. He could feel breath. "Who did this to you?" Marcus asked.

"Demos," Manaen murmured, then uttered a string of incoherent syllables. Around the thought of his brother, Manaen wove imprecations, vows of revenge, a sense of deepest loathing.

"Demos?" Marcus repeated. Then to Zadok, "He cursed someone named Demos. Shouted about a wolf."

"And earlier he called the word *Peniel*," Zadok rumbled. "Peniel. The name Jacob gave to the place where he said he saw God face-to-face and lived."

"Maybe that's what he means," Marcus speculated. "Perhaps he saw God."

"This isn't the doing of the Almighty," Zadok told Marcus, then asked the wounded man, "What's your name?"

Manaen remembered the threat to Susanna if he told the details of what had happened to him. He would not answer.

Zadok smoothed soothing oil on Manaen's skin. "Have you got a name, friend?" To Marcus the old one said, "He's blistered from the sun. Sun poisoning. Accounts for the swelling. Saw such a thing when young Lev lost his way in the desert four years ago. Burned bad. But he'll recover right well from it."

Again the water jug was brought to Manaen's blistered lips. "Easy," Marcus coaxed. "That's right. Drink up."

Manaen drank again. Each swallow coursed down through him, cold tingling that radiated from his throat to his stomach and outward to all his limbs.

"Where . . . where am I?" Manaen queried. "What day is this?"

"Highborn," Zadok repeated, commenting on Manaen's accent. "What's your name, young fellow?"

Manaen shook his head in refusal. "Who . . . are you?"

"Zadok. Chief Shepherd of Israel."

"Who found . . . me?"

"Avel, the apprentice shepherd, and I were looking for strays," Marcus answered. "The boy found you beneath a tree fifty yards from a spring where the ewes gathered."

Manaen moaned again. To think that he had been so close to water! If only he had eyes!

Helpless! Helpless! Die of thirst when he might have drunk from a fresh spring!

Questions followed in rapid succession. "What's your name? Where's your people?" Zadok asked.

"No. No! Don't tell."

There was a long pause before Marcus said gently, "Who did this to you?"

"Can't. Don't. Don't ask more," Manaen pleaded. "Sleep. Must sleep."

The weight of his ordeal pressed down on him.

Through the fog of slumber he heard their voices speculating, questioning, drawing wrong conclusions. The voices of boys drifted in and out of the conversation, questioning, wondering, commenting on Manaen's blindness, on the finely embroidered border of his ragged clothes.

A dog came near, licked his hand, whined, and went away. Manaen sipped the broth spooned down his throat, then drank the sweet cider. At last he slept.

Propped up on a rope mattress, Manaen reclined with his back against a wall. Two weeks had passed.

The air was pungent with the aroma of mingled spices: lavender and sage, mint and rue. Occasionally the breeze carried the rank scent of sheep pens through the open window, proof old Zadok was who he claimed to be.

Manaen slowly regained his blunted senses: smell and taste, at least.

Low voices murmured a short distance away; in an adjacent room perhaps? One of the speakers was Zadok. Others were the voices of children.

Footsteps approached his bedside. "Quiet," Zadok cautioned in a husky whisper.

"It's all right," Manaen returned. "I'm awake."

The aroma of lentil stew eddied about Manaen's face, and he knew it was early evening. "I'll feed you," piped a childish treble. "Your hands, see. The bandages. Can't hold a spoon, can you?"

"Thanks," Manaen replied. "Are you Avel? Did you find me?"

"No, I'm Ha-or Tov."

Good Light: what Manaen longed for more than anything else in the world and the one thing he would never again have.

A wooden spoon clunked against a bowl and then pressed to Manaen's lips. He slurped and swallowed. "Good."

"What's your name?" Ha-or Tov inquired politely after five more spoonfuls had gone the way of the first.

"Doesn't matter," Manaen answered.

"You have family? Maybe worried about you? Zadok would send a message."

"No . . . no, no one."

The boy fed him in silence for a time. "I was blind once."

Was? Someone named Good Light had been blind and now could see? A temporary illness maybe.

"Born blind," Ha-or Tov continued. "Wasn't so bad until my mother died. After that I was on my own. Since I never had eyes, I didn't know what I was missing."

"I wasn't born blind," Manaen said bitterly. "I miss everything."

"I'll bet. I wouldn't want to go back."

"What lies are you feeding me, boy?"

"Not lies. Stew. It's all true."

"Born blind? And now you're not?"

"You haven't heard of Yeshua?"

"Everyone's heard of him. Yochanan the Baptizer raised from the dead is the latest rumor. Among other things. What's he got to do with it?"

"Yeshua gave me eyes to see the stars."

"Gave you eyes to see the stars, did he?" Manaen replied caustically. "If that's true, boy, then my name is Orion. Legend is, I fell in love with the Lady Merope, daughter of the king of Chios. The king had me blinded to keep me from his daughter. Or so the story goes. If the facts hold true, my vision will be restored by the rays of the rising sun . . . but I doubt it. I'll never see the stars again. Or the sun."

"Or her?"

"Not the woman I love. No."

"So Orion. It's a good name. Zadok and Marcus will be glad you remembered."

"Could I forget?"

"What about your family?"

"My father is Poseidon. He's in the fishing and shipping business."

"I have Avel and Emet and Zadok for family. Since Yeshua, everything's changed, you see?"

No! Manaen wanted to scream. *I don't see, and I don't believe you, either.* But he merely said, "Good for you, boy. One day your tale will be recorded in the constellations and hung in the stars like Orion for all to see."

"I have a star named for me. I saw it. First thing. Yeshua showed me. Ha-or Tov. Good Light. That's me."

Manaen folded his hands in surrender. "Well then. A good tale. You have a fine future as a wandering troubadour. People will pay to hear stories like these. But for me, I need to sleep. And to think things through. Go away, boy. I've got to think what I should do next."

"ORION, EH?" ZADOK OBSERVED THE next evening. "A noble constellation." Gentle sarcasm infused his tone.

Manaen was finally strong enough to sit at the supper table. "I must go to Yerushalayim," he said abruptly, turning his face to Zadok's voice.

The old man mused. "Orion. Orion? Why a Greek legend? Why not Samson? A good Jewish hero. Blinded by his enemies. Pulled the heathen temple down."

"I've got similar hopes," Manaen interrupted. "I must go to Yerushalayim. Straightaway."

"So! Information at last. Like pulling teeth. You're from Yerushalayim, are you, Orion?" Zadok queried.

"Near enough."

"And your dear father, Poseidon? He's missing your help running the fishing and shipping business?"

"I've got business of my own to attend to."

"Fry a few fish of your own, eh?" Then, without the hint of sarcasm, Zadok added, "I don't know who done this to y'. But they may still be about the city."

"I'm counting on it."

"Vengeance, is it?"

"Justice. Retribution. Call it what you like. Samson had it in the end. I'll have some of it."

"Samson died in the story."

"Died content, no doubt."

"Hard to spot a villain without eyes to see him."

"I'll know his voice."

"And a weapon? Hard to kill a villain without a sword."

Manaen held up his hands. "These'll serve me well."

Zadok cleared his throat. "Against the law of Mosheh to strangle yer sacrifice. Not to mention the commandment about murder."

"Mosheh will understand. An eye for an eye."

Zadok put a hand to his patch. "I don't read it as a life for an eye."

"They took my life when they took my eyes."

"*They*, is it? More than one. They'll stand in line and wait their turn to be executed, will they? Yer going to end up nailed to a cross, young fellow."

"I'm not afraid."

"And where will y' slay these villains?"

"Wherever I find them."

"Would y' not go north first? To the Galil? Find Yeshua. Seek a better way?"

"There's nothing a rabbi can give me that'll take the place of what I've lost."

"Unless he finds what's lost in your life and gives it to you again."

"The legend of Orion, eh? Vision restored by the rays of the rising sun. Legend is legend. I know the difference between reality and legends."

"That which was legend of old has become flesh. He lives among us. Real."

Manaen scoffed. "Not another Messiah! Always the Messiah! The false hope of our people! The world will be better. He'll be our king. Give us freedom! Restore the kingdom of David. I've heard it all from the time I was a boy. It's a bedtime story to help us Jews sleep better at night when the armies of Egypt, Greece, and Rome are marching to destroy us!"

Zadok said kindly, "Yeshua's more than that."

"He'll give me my sight again?"

"A new way of seeing, yes. Light. Peace. Joy."

"Those things were never mine."

"Then you were blind before you lost your eyes."

"That may be. But what's that to you? You can see. What can you know about injustice? What have you lost that compares?"

Avel sat forward and declared furiously, "The old butcher king Herod murdered Zadok's boys and all the baby boys in Beth-lehem! Herod was trying to kill the baby Messiah! Just like Pharaoh did to the babies in Mosheh's day! And Zadok lost one eye fighting to save his sons! To keep Messiah safe! You don't know anything about anything!"

Silence. At last Manaen remarked, "Zadok still has one eye to see the face of his enemy. To cut him down. As for me? I must go to Yerushalayim."

"And there is no persuading y' otherwise?" Zadok asked.

"Never."

"Anything else?"

"Yes!" Manaen replied forcefully. But he did not admit what that something was. Now that he had recovered his strength he found that his hunger and thirst were for information. He could not wait any longer to learn what he could about Susanna.

"And do y' have somewhere to stay?" Zadok pressed.

Manaen had given that question much thought already. Whatever stories were circulating about his fate, and about Susanna's, and about Demos . . . every bit of gossip passed up and down the Temple steps with the daily crowds. Peniel no doubt heard it all and remembered it all.

If Manaen joined Peniel there, he'd be just one more beggar hoping for charity. If and when Demos passed by, Manaen would reach out and . . .

"I have a friend, a brother beggar," Manaen said. He stopped suddenly, seized by the thought that his future might truly be as another blind alms-seeker. He shook his head and resumed. "His name is Peniel, and he keeps to the Temple steps."

"Ah!" Zadok tapped his forehead. "It begins to make sense. You called out Peniel when you were delirious. I thought it was a place. A brother beggar, is he?"

"I know Peniel," Avel asserted from the opposite end of the table. "Sure. Blind. The potter's son?"

"That's him," Manaen thumped his fist on the table.

The boy elaborated. "Peniel sits outside Nicanor Gate. I spoke to him often when I was a Sparrow."

"And how do y' propose to manage this journey?" Zadok's voice held some consternation.

Marcus spoke up for the first time, "I can go with him as far as Bethany."

"I can help," Avel asserted. "I know all the back ways around Yerushalayim. I can take him to Peniel. And then carry the message for Marcus."

Zadok interjected, "It's almost Pentecost. So we're all bound for Yerushalayim."

"All right, then," Marcus said gruffly. "It's settled. Orion—or whatever you call yourself—you'll have my protection as far as Bethany. Then Avel will guide you the rest of the way. He'll take you to this Peniel fellow. After that you're on your own. Don't come back here and put Zadok in danger after you've done what you go to do. Nor mention how he took you in and saved your life. Once you enter Jerusalem, you're on your own."

38

F ive days later Zadok, Marcus, Manaen, and the boys undertook the journey to Bethany. It was late when they arrived. Marcus glanced at the stars. The constellation of Aryeh, the Lion, was just setting in the west. By this he judged that it was shortly after midnight.

The villa of Miryam, El'azar, and Marta was dark and still. A single watch light was set high in the wall. It burned brightly, as if a beacon for travelers. Was someone expected to arrive tonight?

Zadok knocked at the gate. Mere seconds passed before the latch clicked and Miryam, wrapped in a shawl, threw open the door.

She scanned the faces of the weary band and cried, "Marcus! Oh, he said you'd come tonight! He told us you'd come! Master Zadok! And your boys! And, Yeshua said, Manaen bar Talmai!" She winced as light and shadow played on the face of the blind man.

"How do you know my name?" the blind man asked, alarmed. "I've told no one!"

"He—Yeshua—told the servant Naomi before he left. He said you'd come tonight with the shepherd, the lambs, and the soldier."

Marcus stared at Manaen in disbelief. Marcus had met Manaen bar Talmai in the court of Antipas. He was a friend of Felix. They had often gone to the gambling room at the Scorpio baths in Jerusalem. He had been at the banquet when Yochanan was murdered. Could this ragged creature be the same man? Brother of Demos?

Manaen did not reply.

Miryam cried joyfully, "Come in! Come in! He said you'd be hungry too. I've got cheese and bread for you." Then, "Zadok, please, my brother El'azar asked that I show you up to his office when you come. I'll bring your supper to you there if you like. You're all welcome." She smiled into Marcus' eyes. "Welcome." His hand brushed hers as they walked toward the light.

Marcus did not need to ask Miryam how Yeshua knew they would come tonight. "He's gone away then?"

"He'll be in Yerushalayim for Pentecost. Now help yourselves."

She ushered the old shepherd up a flight of stairs.

Torches blazed in the courtyard as they washed. A feast was laid out on a long table.

Manaen bar Talmai was sullen as Avel put a heaping plate into his hands. Then the trio of boys was taken by a servant to their guest room.

Manaen sank down on a couch but did not eat.

Marcus sat across from him. "So," Marcus began.

"Yes." Manaen breathed slowly. "How did anyone know I was alive?"

"Your brother's handiwork, this? Over the girl?"

"It would be easier if I could say this was done because of a gambling debt. But I can't. Demos. After my eyes were burned out, he paid a man to kill me. He didn't kill me after all. You found me. What's to tell?"

It was, Marcus thought, much like the noble families of Rome. Brothers killed brothers, wives poisoned husbands—and all for money, position, and power. Such things were commonplace in Rome.

"What will you do?" Marcus asked.

"Your rabbi isn't here. No magic incantation then to give me back my eyes so I can see my brother as I kill him."

"We'll take you to Yeshua. Nothing is impossible for him."

"Will he give me a sword?"

"No. That he won't do."

"Then he's no use to me."

"Your eyes, Manaen. Light. Worth more than a sword. Worth more than revenge."

"I'll take the dark over light and embrace it too. As long as Demos dies by my hand."

"Kill your brother and it will mean your death as well as his."

"I'll take death over life! *Welcome* death. As long as Demos dies by my hand."

How savagely the bitterness of betrayal had cut into Manaen's heart, Marcus realized.

Zadok and El'azar joined them.

"Manaen bar Talmai," Zadok said. "You're not Orion. Your story is out then."

"Yes," Manaen concurred. "And I know what I have to do."

Zadok touched the scar on his own cheek. "Listen to me, boy, for I know what you feel! Anger is the poison we drink ourselves and then expect the other person to die."

"I'll show him more than anger. More than poison. I was a better man than he when I had two eyes. Maybe we'll be equally matched. But I'll have his soul before it's over."

Zadok said, "God will have his soul. And God will have yours, boy. Are you ready for that?"

Manaen countered, "Is anyone ever ready?"

"Yes. We must all be." Zadok frowned. "Look to it, then. You wouldn't be a man if you didn't do what you could to save Susanna."

"Save her?" Manaen's knuckles became white. "Save her from what?"

"Look, there's Naomi, the servant girl," El'azar interjected as Miryam appeared at the top of the stairs with a woman at her side.

Miryam said gently, "See? Really. He's there, Naomi. Yes. As Yeshua said. Manaen bar Talmai is alive."

"Lord Manaen!" The servant gave a little shriek. Running down the stairs, she fell sobbing at his feet. "Lord Manaen! The Lady Susanna! They've taken her back to Jerusalem! There's a rumor she's to marry your brother after Pentecost! She thinks you're dead. Carried your heart around in a jug, she did. Wolf chucked it away. Lord Manaen! What shall we do? What?" The story of their escape with Peniel and the capture spilled out of her. Manaen asked question after question.

At last satisfied, Manaen said to Marcus. "You see? Not my heart. The heart of a ram. Put a sword in my hand, Marcus Longinus, and I'll die like a man for the sake of her honor!"

Marcus stood. "Do what you must."

"I've got to get to Yerushalayim." Manaen said grimly.

"I'll send word by Avel to Tribune Felix tomorrow that I'm back," Marcus replied. "If I can, I'll meet with Felix. Tell him what's happened to you and Susanna. He can help."

Manaen glowered. "This is my score to settle alone. If I fail? If I die and Demos lives, then I ask you to tell Felix what became of me. Ask him to do what he can. For now I've got a plan. I took a vow. I'll see it through to the end!"

"So be it," Zadok pronounced. "Avel can guide you to Yerushalayim and Peniel tomorrow."

THREE DAYS UNTIL PENTECOST.

Three days before Susanna was bound to Demos.

Three days for Manaen to find his brother and kill him.

Manaen and Avel passed beneath the broad arch of the Eastern Gate and entered the Temple compound. From this gate the rising sun topped the Mount of Olives and blazed directly into the sanctuary twice a year.

Manaen remembered the flash of light that reflected on the hammered gold leaf of the building. Extraordinary. Like a streak of lightning against the sky. An effect meant to be a reminder of the glory of God's presence. *"Blinding,"* Manaen had commented to Susanna at the time.

He had not known what the word meant until now. Sightless, he relied on memory alone. The glory of that sunrise was what he pictured as they shuffled across the stones.

His hand rested on Avel's shoulder. "How will we find Peniel in all this?"

Avel replied, "He's always in the same place. Always. Nicanor Gate."

And so they walked across the familiar courts. Manaen heard the bawling of livestock, the calling of the hawkers in their booths. The clamor of buying and selling drowned out the singing of psalms. Manaen wished he had paid more attention to details. Sounds and smells revived images in his mind. But they were unclear images—partial, indistinct. He was already forgetting the faces of his enemies. He could not get his brain to draw them clearly.

Even Demos.

Manaen feared he had forgotten the sound of his brother's voice. And his sense of hearing would have to be his eyes now.

What if he could not separate his brother's voice from the babble of Jerusalem's commerce?

Three days to find Demos and kill him.

Avel led Manaen up a flight of steps.

"Yes. There's Peniel! That's him! There at Nicanor Gate, like I said. I think he hears me. He's turning his head toward us."

A joyful welcome. "Hey! Shalom, Avel! Herding sheep for sacrifice again?"

"In a way," Manaen replied. "Depends on how you define sheep."

Peniel drew his breath in sharply. "You!" He lowered his voice and reached out, touching Manaen's foot. "You! But they said . . . I heard you were . . . "

"Like a lamb to the slaughter?" Manaen finished the query. "Not yet."

"Well," Peniel replied in wonder. "Well. God be praised."

Avel helped Manaen sit beside Peniel. Manaen explained, "We heard from . . . a friend . . . what happened on the road to Beth-Anyah. How you brought my friends out. And then . . ."

"I failed. But I haven't stopped praying for her." Peniel's words were thick with regret. "I was no help."

Manaen said, "The race isn't over yet."

"I brought him to you. Keep your voices down," Avel hissed. "Your enemies are everywhere. Everywhere." Then, fear in his tone, he said to Peniel, "I've got to go. Shalom, my friend. Shalom tov!"

Avel sprinted off to deliver his message.

Peniel clasped Manaen's hand and whispered, "So you're back from the dead?"

"Unfinished business. It seems I need a blind guide."

Avel leaned against the base of a pillar. He was far enough from the entrance to Antonia Fortress that he would not be noticed but near enough that he could spot the Tribune Dio Felix if he emerged.

The afternoon sun beat on his face. Pulling the hood over his head gave him protection not only from the heat but from being recognized.

Praetorian Vara walked within yards of him. This was the devil Marcus had warned him about! Avel recognized him in an instant. The officer carried his helmet under his arm. His black tunic was sweat-stained. A short sword hung from a blue sheath. The swagger stick he carried as a mark of authority was nicked and dented from bashing skulls.

Avel crouched lower.

Hours passed. He nodded off and jerked himself awake. He blinked unhappily at the changing of the guards stationed on either side of the portal. Had he missed Felix?

Licking his lips, he eyed the fountain in front of the fortress. The thought of Vara just inside held him back.

He had made a promise not to return to Bethany until he had delivered Marcus' message to the tribune.

Hold long would it be?

As long as it took.

Hungry. Thirsty. Avel did not dare budge.

SHADOWS LENGTHENED ACROSS THE WIDE PLAZA of the Antonia. Avel's tongue felt thick and swollen from thirst. His belly rumbled. Eleven hours had passed since his last meal.

Where was Tribune Felix?

Avel caught sight of movement within the entry of the fort. Flashes of red and glimmers of white were framed in the doorway.

The guards stirred and stood more erect, as if anticipating that someone of importance would pass between them.

Avel squinted, attempting to see the uniforms of the men who conversed in the foyer.

No luck.

Long minutes passed. The red tunic withdrew. The white remained within view.

And then Vara strode from the building. A scowl on his brooding face, he tapped his swagger stick against his leg and scanned the courtyard, as if looking for someone.

A junior officer scurried after him.

Avel ducked his head and withdrew into the shadow of the pillar.

"Bring my horse!" Vara commanded.

The assistant sprinted toward the stable gates and returned minutes later with the gray warhorse that had trampled Avel's friend Hayyim several months before.

Vara slapped the junior officer out of the way and mounted his prancing steed. Sparks ignited against the paving stones as the Praetorian galloped out of the compound.

At least that much of the threat was gone.

Avel stood slowly and stretched. His back ached. He contemplated who else might be within the brooding towers. Should he go to the guards? inquire after the tribune? After all, if Marcus was sending a message to Felix, perhaps he wasn't so bad.

Avel hung back, bit his lower lip, and then took a step forward. The guards turned toward him in unison. And why not? Surely they had seen him crouching there all day, waiting.

And then! A miracle of white tunic trimmed in red! Gold fringe along the hem! A silver breastplate secured with a white-and-gold strip of cloth.

The uniform of a tribune! And the man was smiling! He glanced up at the hues of twilight and remarked what a beautiful evening it had turned out to be! He might have been a country gentleman talking to his servants instead of a deadly instrument of Imperial Rome.

Avel resisted the immediate urge to shout out the tribune's name. He walked forward cautiously as Felix chatted cordially with the sentries.

Avel paused. Waited, gazing hopefully at the officer.

"You there! Boy!" a guard barked.

Avel pointed to himself in question.

"Yes! You!" The guard stepped toward him threateningly.

Avel resisted the instinct to run. There was Felix, after all. His goal. The whole reason he was half-starved and parched.

Avel croaked, "Tribune Felix."

The sentries exchanged looks of amazement. What was a Jewish urchin doing addressing the second-highest-ranking Roman officer by name?

"What do you want, boy? You know who you're talking to?" It was good bluster on the part of the sentry, but Felix put a restraining hand on the fellow's arm.

Felix smiled quizzically. "I'm Tribune Felix."

"I'm sent . . . with a message . . . from . . . from . . . a lady," Avel stammered. "Lady . . . Alexandria."

Winks and nudges from the soldiers followed.

Felix shrugged as if to ask what else it could be, then growled, "Back to your posts. I'll handle this. Ah, yes. That lady!" Felix had caught on instantly. Sheepishly, as if caught in some indiscretion, he left the porch and came to Avel. Putting his arm around his shoulder, Felix walked out of earshot of the guards. "Clever lad."

"He's back. He said you'd know what it meant." Avel repeated Marcus' message. "They tried to kill him in Ashkelon."

"I know. Tell him Vara has a warrant. Tell him there are rumors from Rome. I must meet with him."

"I'll tell him."

"On your Shabbat day. At the baths. He'll know. Midday tomorrow." Felix took a coin from his purse. "Here."

"No, sir. I came for him."

"We must make it look like you're a messenger from the Lady. Take it and go. Tell him to keep out of sight until then."

THE COVERED MARKET WAS A PLACE Manaen had strolled through a thousand times, and yet the confusion of noise frightened him now. He could hear the conversation of burly legionaries and Herodians all around. These were men whom, undoubtedly, Manaen had met in the halls of power. Yet they appeared not to notice him.

"There is an advantage to being blind," Peniel explained. "No one really sees you. They see your stick and move out of the way."

Peniel was at home here. His stick probed the empty space and shoppers made way for him.

So the blind beggar brought Manaen supper: fresh bread, cheese, apples, and wine. He led Manaen to the shelter beneath the viaduct, where they ate together.

Over the meal Manaen told Peniel everything that had happened since the night they had been held captive together in the pottery shop.

Peniel told Manaen how he had heard Susanna and Naomi in the thunderstorm. How Susanna had carried what she thought was Manaen's heart in the jar and tried so hard to get away.

"And I failed her." Peniel ended the saga. "I've heard rumors she's to be married after Pentecost. Not of her own free will."

"Not if I can stop it," Manaen said.

"But how?"

"If there's no bridegroom."

"You'll kill your brother?"

"What's he done to me but take my life?"

"You know what they'll do to you? Demos is an important man."

"And what will Demos do to Susanna if I don't make an end to this?"

"I'm sorry for you. You're a dead man."

"I was dead when they took my eyes."

"I've been alive without eyes. My whole life I've been alive. It's not everything. Seeing. You get used to it."

"On Shabbat I'll see the end of Demos. That's what I'm living for."

"Killing him is what you live for?"

"It's all I've thought about."

"Then I'm talking to a dead man," Peniel said sadly.

"Is it right I do nothing? Leave Susanna to suffer?"

"No . . . no. It's just that I'm sorry I couldn't have got her away safely, that's all. Then this conversation wouldn't be happening. But since I couldn't and she's there and you're here, what can I do?"

"Will you help a dead man?"

"Sure. Yes. Tell me what you want from me."

39

F irst light of Shabbat morning. The day before the Feast of Pentecost.

The military presence was out in force along the highways into Jerusalem and within the city. Marcus pulled up the hood of his cloak, lowered his head, and fixed his gaze to the dusty highway as the little band of travelers joined the throngs moving through the gates into Jerusalem. His short sword was concealed beneath his coat. He hoped he would not be spotted among the thousands. The languages and accents of every nation in the Empire were heard.

Yes, Marcus thought, he could hide in plain sight until he met with Felix.

A river of humanity had already flowed up the mountain passes toward the shimmering white marble and gold-topped pinnacles atop Mount Moriah. The city was packed. The aroma of spices and flowers scented the air.

Peniel clutched Avel's hand. Manaen shuffled between Emet and Ha-or Tov.

Zadok and Marcus walked behind them. The old shepherd taught the meaning of Pentecost to the young members of the group. Marcus listened intently to the details of yet another Jewish feast.

Was there anything inherent in this Holy Day that would stir the crowds to riot? Marcus wondered. And this time would Yeshua be at the heart of another controversy drummed up by the Herodian faction or the Sanhedrin?

Zadok explained, "Shavuot, the Feast of Weeks, called by some 'Pentecost,' occurs on the sixth day of Sivan. We celebrate the giving of Torah, God's Word, his wedding gift to Israel. Torah spells out the covenant, which is like a marriage between the Lord and Israel. Messiah is the bridegroom. Israel is the bride. The nation of Israel was betrothed when the Lord led us out of slavery from Egypt and then the covenant was sealed with the giving of the law on Mount Sinai. Every Jew who has ever lived and ever will live, it is said, was there at Sinai when the Voice of the Bridegroom called to his bride, Israel."

Shavuot marked the anniversaries of a score of significant events, it seemed. Mosheh was drawn from the water of the river on Shavuot, and so the ritual washing was practiced in the morning before the Torah was revealed.

King David was born and died on Shavuot.

The Messiah, as Israel's Bridegroom, would descend on Shavuot to claim His bride.

The book of Ruth was read on Shavuot, remembering the Moabite woman married to Boaz, her kinsman-redeemer. She, a Gentile, embraced the Israelite covenant with these words: *"Your people will be my people and your God my God!"*[69]

"And so," Zadok instructed, "the giving of Torah is what God does for us on Shavuot. When we embrace it we become his beloved. Our job is to open our hearts and receive it."

Was it possible for someone like himself, Marcus wondered, to receive what God had to offer mankind? How he longed to open his heart and invite The Word, The Light, to flood his soul!

He said nothing as they passed a troop of legionaries from Syria beside a cistern. Recognizing the men, he touched Zadok's arm and whispered, "For your own sake I'll leave you now, my friend. Farewell. Good luck."

"God go with you," Zadok said as Marcus split off from the group and turned onto the Street of Stairs, which led to the Upper City.

AVEL LED THE TWO BLIND MEN to the Scorpio Bathhouse near the Hippo-drome as Manaen had instructed. They stood arguing beneath the sign of the Scorpion as hadhundreds of pilgrims on their way to the Temple surged past them.

"Don't do this, Manaen," Peniel urged. "Maybe he will come today. Tomorrow's Shavuot! Pentecost! The day the Torah was given on Sinai. Tonight the heavens open and the Voice speaks like it spoke on Sinai! Listen, Manaen! You can't murder a man on such a holy day! You'll miss hearing God's voice if you die."

"I'll hear it sooner if I'm dead."

"No! Don't! Please, come with us! Tomorrow's the birthday of King David. The anniversary of the day David died. Messiah is the son of David, right? Tomorrow is the day the righteous Bridegroom, our Messiah, is supposed to come and call the nation of Israel to be his bride! Shavuot! Pentecost! Have you forgot it all? The Messiah wouldn't miss Pentecost! If he's coming at all to save Israel, he'll be here in Yerushalayim for his own wedding, eh? Maybe he's here now. At the Temple! Teaching! If you stay here . . . if you . . . oh! Don't do it, Manaen! You'll miss him. Come with us, please!"

"Him? Messiah? He'll never come, Peniel," Manaen replied bit-terly. "You're a fool for thinking anyone can save us but ourselves."

"Come away with us and live!"

"What's the point? I'd rather finish what my brother began. And make an end of myself as well. I've lost . . . everything that means any-thing to me."

"Don't do this," Peniel protested. "Even if you find your brother here today—"

"It's Shabbat. Demos will come to the baths as he always does. He'll be here. He never misses a dice game."

"And if your brother comes and you kill him? Then they'll kill you."

"I'll die satisfied."

"You'll die. That's all. And where's the satisfaction in that?"

"It's worth it, isn't it? After what he's done to me?" Manaen chal-lenged.

"Give it a day. Come with me and Avel to the Temple. Just to see.

To listen. If Yeshua of Nazareth comes . . . who knows? Maybe he'll heal us too."

"All lies," Manaen disagreed. "Guaranteed to make us suffer quietly. To keep us meek while men like Demos and Herod Antipas and the rest grind us to dust. No! I made a vow! I'll do what I came to Yerushalayim to do. You said it yourself. You and I survived sword and fire for some reason. If there is a God, I'm sure he won't mind if I step on a cockroach. I'm going to rid the world of Demos."

"Listen! Listen!" Peniel insisted. "No. Manaen. Please. Messiah *will* come, Manaen. If not today, then tomorrow. If not tomorrow, then—"

"Never!" Manaen spat. "Haven't we spent a lifetime waiting? Hoping? Looking for justice that never comes?"

"Come with me and Avel to the Temple," Peniel urged. "Just for today. We'll see, eh? So many thousands. Tens of thousands. Maybe he'll be there. This time, maybe."

"No more, Peniel! And you, Avel! Do what I say! Take me to the place I told you! *Now!* I've got something to do." Manaen growled a warning. "My brother, Demos, is a creature of habit. He'll come to the bath today. Just as he always does. I'll be here waiting when he comes."

"Then . . . " Peniel let go of Manaen's arm. "Shalom and farewell, my friend. We won't meet again."

"Remember me kindly, Peniel. Pray for my soul after I'm dead if you've a mind to. But I'm determined to do this! I hope . . . I do hope . . . for your sake that your Messiah comes. Farewell then."

Today was the day.

Manaen could feel it. After sending Peniel and Avel away, he exulted with the certainty of his plan. Demos always came to the Scorpio Bathhouse on the Sabbath day.

Nor was this any ordinary Sabbath. This was the seventh Sabbath of the Omer, the last Sabbath before Pentecost. It was the last pilgrim feast of the year until the Feast of Tabernacles in the fall.

Pentecost marked the midpoint of the dry season, but more importantly, it signaled the arrival of hot weather in Judea.

After Pentecost the court of Herod Antipas would pack up and move back to Galilee. Demos would go with them.

Today was the day; it had to be. Manaen could imagine his hands around Demos' throat. It was not possible to be this close to his revenge and then have it snatched away.

Demos must come to the baths today! Even though Demos was no early riser and could not be expected before noon, Manaen was taking no chances.

Despite the fact that beggars were not permitted to sit on the semi-circular porch below the columned entry, Manaen still had the perfect location. There was an alleyway immediately beside Scorpio's north wall. The lane was used to deliver firewood for the furnaces for the heated pools, floors, and walls.

But since it was the Sabbath, there would be no deliveries today and the dead-end lane led nowhere else.

Manaen would not attract any attention squatting there, not amid the ebb and flow of pilgrims.

Nor was Manaen any longer worried about locating his brother when he got close. Hour upon agonizing hour Manaen had schooled himself in his brother's voice. Every laugh, every inflection, each turn of phrase or scrap of Hebrew-accented Greek Manaen had turned over in his mind.

Oh no, there was no danger of a mistake! Let Manaen hear but one syllable from Demos' lips, and his brother's fate would be sealed.

SHABBAT! THE FINAL DAY OF THE OFFERING of the firstfruits of harvest before the Lord.

The Feast of Weeks, Pentecost, would arrive at sunset. Today was the forty-ninth day of the heart's preparation to hear God's Voice and receive His Word.

Tonight all of Israel would stay awake and study Torah and listen for the Voice of the Lord!

This was the day on which Peniel rested from the work of begging. He would not cry out for alms today. Like every true son of Abraham, Peniel always sat among the people in the courts of the Temple and listened to the teachings of the rabbis on Shabbat.

Zadok and his boys were waiting near the causeway as Peniel approached.

"Peniel," the old shepherd called, "Yeshua's here! He's already on the steps of the treasury!"

This was good news! Shabbat was not a day Peniel could ask for healing from the Rabbi, but he would learn something, at least.

Avel pulled him along as they threaded through the throng. "Look," Avel cried. "There he is! I see big Shim'on! Ya'acov and Yochanan with him."

"And half the Herodians and Sadducees in Yerushalayim!" Zadok said, concern in his tone. "See there? The Pharisees. More opposition here today than common folk. Look, boys! Temple Guard behind the Sadducees. Look there. Not a pleasant expression on the face of even one."

"Yeshua won't heal on Shabbat," Ha-or Tov remarked. "Or make bread. No work. See? So there aren't so many people coming to hear him today."

"The Temple Guard are writing down names," Avel explained. "Moving along the back of the crowd. Taking down names. People are scared. Going away."

"It's the decree," Zadok agreed. "People are afraid to be seen with him here."

Avel added confidently, "Only about five hundred. They'll all come back tomorrow when it's not Shabbat and Yeshua can work. When they can get something from him they'll be here all right. When he can do works and wonders."

"Then we're in luck," Emet said cheerfully. "We can sit close. See? Go that way."

Avel ducked beneath the portico. "Sure. Close enough to hear him good."

It didn't matter to Peniel that others were being intimidated into staying away. Finally Peniel would hear the teaching of the Rabbi! How Peniel loved Shabbat! Loved to pretend he was as good as any man in Israel on this day of rest! To ask for nothing, beg for nothing! To simply sit, hear the Word of the Lord, and worship! And today! To be in the company of these good friends!

Yeshua's voice boomed out from beneath the portico: "The kingdom of heaven is like a king who prepared a wedding banquet for his son. . . ."

This was an appropriate lesson, Peniel thought, since tomorrow was Shavuot, Pentecost, the day on which it was believed that Messiah would someday descend in fulfillment of Daniel's seventy weeks of years, as a Bridegroom to call out Israel as His bride. Until then each Pentecost was the day the marriage covenant embodied by the commandments between the Lord and Israel at Sinai was remembered.

Yeshua taught the lesson of that future day: "And so the king sent his servants to those who had been invited to the banquet to tell them to come. But they refused to come. Then he sent some more servants and said, 'Tell those who have been invited that I have prepared my dinner: my oxen and fattened cattle have been butchered. Everything is ready. Come to the wedding banquet.'"

Yeshua continued, "But they paid no attention and went off—one to his field, another to his business. The rest seized his servants, mistreated them, and killed them."

"Now he's done it!" Avel whispered. "Look at the Herodians. They know he's talking about how they killed the Baptizer."

Yeshua's lesson became more harsh. "The king was enraged. He sent his army and destroyed those murderers and burned their city."

Yeshua's voice penetrated every corner of the Temple compound and echoed back like a thousand voices from the great halls.

Avel leaned close to Peniel. "You think he means Yerushalayim? There's murder now in the eyes of Herod's men. They're whispering to the Sadducees. Yeshua's *talmidim* are in a circle around him. Protecting him."

But Yeshua was not deterred. "Then the king said to his servants, 'The wedding banquet is ready. But those I invited did not deserve to come. Go to the street corners. Invite to the banquet anyone you find.' So the servants went out into the streets and gathered all the people they could find, both good and bad, and the wedding hall was filled with guests. But then the king came in to see the guests. He noticed a man there who was not wearing wedding clothes. 'Friend,' he asked, 'how did you get in without wedding clothes?' The man was speechless."

Avel interjected, "Hey, Peniel! Yeshua's smiling. He's looking right at Alexander, the brother-in-law of Caiaphas. Alexander owns the concession on ceremonial clothing. Charges the common folk triple what he should for really shoddy stuff. He's not happy to be singled out."

Yeshua's story took an ominous turn. "Then the king told his attendants, 'Tie him up hand and foot! Throw him outside, into the darkness, where there will be weeping and gnashing of teeth!'"[70]

Yeshua used the exact words pronounced when an Israelite was excommunicated! *Throw him outside, into the darkness, where there will be weeping and gnashing of teeth!* The phrase used to cast out any Jew who proclaimed Yeshua as Messiah was being turned back on those who had issued the decree! To be cast out of the synagogue meant loss of friends, of family, of community. No one could give such a person comfort or feed him a crumb of bread. He was cut off from Israel forever.

Was Yeshua telling the political and religious leaders of Israel that they would be cast out by God because they had not accepted God's invitation to come to the celebration of His Son?

Now here was courage! Not what Peniel expected from the Rabbi from Nazareth! Not platitudes or rehashing old ideas. Yeshua was driving home the point that the King of the universe was indeed preparing a wedding feast for His Son, and the guest list at the banquet would not turn out the way anyone expected!

Peniel thought of Manaen, ready to kill his brother and die for the sake of revenge! He must bring Manaen here instead, to hear this truthful man who faced the religious rulers and the agents of Herod Antipas so fearlessly!

"Avel! Will you come with me? Back to fetch Manaen at the bathhouse! Avel! He's got to hear this! Got to hear Yeshua. Please come with me!"

40

arcus walked toward his meeting with Felix by a roundabout route, south past the Pool of Siloam before turning westward and entering the more modern Gentile Quarter of Jerusalem. He purposely dawdled on the way, peering into shopwindows and pretending to be interested in the stalls of sidewalk vendors.

It would not do for a poor Jewish shepherd to be noticed hanging about in front of the Scorpio Bathhouse. Upscale in its clientele for both bathing and gambling, the Scorpio catered to the affluent, like Tribune Felix and members of Herod Antipas' court.

Religious Jews abhorred the nakedness found in Roman bathing facilities, so they never entered, nor would someone who smelled of sheep dung be readily accepted.

Why had Felix insisted Marcus come in person, no matter how urgent the message? Marcus was putting his head in the lion's mouth to walk about in broad daylight where so many Roman officials chose to relax.

It was almost in the shadow of Pilate's palace.

But Felix's reply to his last communication had been adamant.

Marcus wondered if he was going to be arrested. What if Felix had been pressured to either betray Marcus or lose his own position?

Marcus shook off the thought; it was unworthy to think of Felix doing such a thing.

But Felix's reason for the unnecessary danger better be a good one.

THE DAY STRETCHED ON, INTERMINABLY SO. The sun transferred from Manaen's cheek to the top of his head. And still his brother did not come.

The tempo of life in Jerusalem increased. The volume of the hub-bub swelled as excited travelers spoke of seeing the great Temple.

A parcel of Babylonian Jews inquired the way to their synagogue. Manaen hurled abuse, huddled lower, and muttered imprecations on their heads.

The pilgrims hurried away, exclaiming that he was a crazy man or demon-possessed.

Let them think whatever they wanted so long as they left quickly! Manaen could not bear the thought that Demos would slip by him unawares while strangers babbled!

Drops of sweat beaded on Manaen's forehead and ran into his useless eyes. He wiped them furiously. It was not the heat of the day that caused him to perspire. With every passing moment the tension mounted.

Manaen had not fully realized how jammed the streets would be with jabbering tongues! When he was sighted, he never paid any attention to noise, but now . . .

Now that he relied on his ears, the stress was almost unbearable. Every intonation coming into range was analyzed, studied, discarded. Male from female, foreign from native, very young from very old, Manaen had set an enormous task for himself, parsing the speech of thousands of passersby, seeking to identify Demos. Listening for the one voice that he longed to forever silence, to fulfill the one remaining purpose he saw in his life.

THE SUN STOOD ALMOST EXACTLY OVERHEAD. The appointed time had arrived. Approaching the baths from the south, Marcus did not see any sign of Felix. What to do? He judged the street to be crowded enough that there was no immediate danger.

Marcus halted across the road from the Scorpio beside a fruit vendor's cart. Three other purchasers examined the produce, and Marcus attached himself to them.

"What about you, sir?" the fruit seller asked. "Nice crop of early figs. Care to buy some?"

"No, thank you," Marcus replied in Aramaic.

"You're not from Judea or Galilee," the friendly vendor observed. "I'm good at accents. Let me guess: Cyrene?"

"No," Marcus responded. Scanning the crowded lane for Felix, he absently added, "Alexandria."

The three other customers turned round. The tallest said pleasantly, "So are we." Running his eye over Marcus' disreputable attire, he inquired, "What quarter?"

"Delta," Marcus said, naming the Jewish district where he had met Rabbi Onias.

Where was Felix?

The affable tone vanished to be replaced by a suspicious "Oh?"

Marcus thought rapidly through several responses. Each was inadequate and likely to increase the misgivings. So he merely nodded and said nothing.

A particularly thick swarm of pilgrims squeezed past the cart, jostling the Alexandrian Jews so that one of them bumped Marcus' side. The outline of his sword was unmistakable.

"Sicarius," the man muttered to his companions. "Assassin."

The three moved hastily away.

A pair of patrolling legionaries entered the street from the Hippodrome.

If the Alexandrian Jews chose to denounce him, would Marcus be able to escape in the throng?

Marcus knew better than to run. He forced himself to saunter in a direction opposite to the legionaries.

DISTANT RAUCOUS LAUGHTER CAUGHT Manaen's attention. A pair of mature men, speaking Greek, approached from the north . . . from the direction of Antipas' palace.

Manaen swiveled his head from side to side, focusing every bit of his concentration on the scrutiny of tones. One voice, deeper than the other, was not his brother's medium range.

But the second could be.

Manaen inched closer to the corner.

Involuntarily his fingers clenched and unclenched.

Ribald comments about passing women were linked to preemptory commands to get out of the way, move aside.

One of the two men sounded Roman!

It did not matter. Let Manaen get within range of Demos and nothing would stop him. A gladius thrust into his own belly to the hilt would not prevent him from squeezing the breath out of his brother before he died.

Manaen leaned forward to hear even better.

FELIX EMERGED FROM THE SCORPIO, spotted Marcus, and crossed the street toward him.

"Are you trying to get me killed?" Marcus demanded. "What's so—"

"Calm yourself, my friend," Felix urged, smiling. "The news is all good as far as you and I are concerned. Praetorian Vara may not find it suits his taste, but—"

As if mentioning Vara's name had summoned a demon, the bulky form of the Praetorian officer appeared in the crowd less than a block away. Beside him Marcus recognized Demos bar Talmai, Manaen's brother.

"Felix!" Marcus hissed, nodding toward Vara.

A DIFFERENT, FAMILIAR VOICE CAUGHT Manaen entirely off guard.

"There he is! I see him, Peniel! He's right there!"

Avel and Peniel, returned from the Temple!

Not now! Not now!

"We found him!" Peniel called. "The great Teacher is there, in the Temple treasury, right now! You must come with us to meet him!"

"Get away!" Manaen said savagely. "Leave me alone! Go now!"

"He heals people," Peniel said. "Isn't that true, Avel?"

"Me," Avel said. "He healed me. But listen: He healed my friend, Ha-or Tov, who was blind!"

"Did you hear that?" Peniel queried. "He heals the blind! Maybe he'll heal us. Hurry before he leaves!" Peniel plucked at Manaen's sleeve.

"Get away from me!" Manaen shouted again, yanking his arm free. Where was his target now? Was it Demos? How close was he?

"Come with us," Peniel repeated.

Manaen shoved Peniel to the ground. "Go away!"

"Manaen!" Peniel called out in shocked disbelief.

Manaen's name hung in the air like a thunderclap.

THE INSTANT AFTER PENIEL SHOUTED Manaen's name it was repeated, echoing from the opposite side of the street as though in a canyon.

Demos screamed out the recognition of his brother. Drawing a dagger from the folds of his robe, he rushed at Manaen.

Turning toward Demos' voice, Manaen faced the clattering footsteps.

"Look out!" Avel yelled. "He's got a knife!"

Frightened pilgrims scattered from Demos' path. He cursed and dodged around them, waving the blade overhead like a madman. A cluster of travelers fled toward the alleyway, saw too late it was a dead end, boiled back out, clogging the street in a mass of milling confusion.

Marcus, trying to intercept Demos, was stymied by the crowd.

Demos' wild face and flashing knife opened a space in front of him that ended at Manaen. He charged forward.

Avel yelled again.

In the fraction of a second before the two brothers collided, Peniel threw himself in front of Manaen. Demos sprawled headlong across Peniel's back, stabbing the dagger into the paving stones.

Manaen lunged for Demos' neck, missed his hold, then closed both fists around Demos' knife hand.

The two rolled over on the cobbles, Manaen holding the tip of the dagger away from his own throat as Demos tried to wrench it free.

Avel dragged Peniel out of the way, propping him against the wall.

Fiercely the shepherd boy clutched a cobblestone, striking at plunging pilgrims to keep them from trampling Peniel.

"Vara!" Demos yelled. "Help me!"

"Get out of my way!" Vara bellowed. "Before I call the guards!"

The crowd knew what that meant! They scattered, shrieking, fearful of a new massacre. The Praetorian in his uniform was a greater threat than Marcus. The mob pushed past Marcus, carrying him backward.

Vara was closer, was already lifting his sword to strike at Manaen.

Avel drew back his arm, let the cobblestone fly. It struck Vara on the cheekbone, splitting the skin.

With a roar Vara changed direction, swiping his blade at Avel. The boy ducked, and the gladius clanged against the stone wall, rebounding from the force of Vara's blow.

"No! Marcus!" Felix shouted.

But Marcus had reached Vara.

Warned by Felix's cry, Vara turned, deflected Marcus' sword with his own, then drove the hilt into Marcus' chest.

Marcus staggered back.

Vara rushed forward, his gladius upraised, swinging the blade down at the top of Marcus' head.

Marcus barely had time to get both hands on the grip of his weapon, flicking its tip back toward his opponent. He ducked as he stepped toward Vara, getting inside Vara's descending blow.

The force of Vara's charge carried him onward.

The tip of Marcus' gladius hit Vara at the base of his throat, just above his breastplate and below the chin strap of his helmet.

Vara's sword fell from his fingers as he clutched at his neck. His bellow of rage turned into a gurgle and he fell sideways, his weight wrenching Marcus' sword free from his hands.

Behind Marcus, Demos shrieked. Manaen's superior strength turned the dagger. Kicking and madly beating the sides of Manaen's head with his elbows, Demos managed to get free, jumped up to run.

Manaen plunged forward, grabbing his brother about the ankles.

With a cry Demos kicked at Manaen's chin, breaking the hold. But then Demos fell, impaling himself on his own knife. He struggled to his knees, feebly plucking at the dagger protruding from his belly. His mouth worked silently, and then he slumped facedown on the street.

Legionaries hustled up from three directions. At lance point they surrounded Marcus, who raised his hands and stepped back against the wall beside Peniel and Avel.

"Secure this area!" Felix bellowed. "Clear the street and give me a space here."

"But the prisoners—" one of the guardsmen protested.

"Do it!" Felix commanded.

The legionaries had no trouble clearing the street, as all the civilians were avidly streaming away as fast as they could.

Felix approached Marcus. "You all right?"

"I . . . yes . . . ," Marcus panted. "I know I'm done for. Just do what you have to do, Felix. I'll keep you out of it."

Felix looked at Marcus, saying nothing. But an odd half smile crossed his lips. "Take care of Manaen," Felix suggested; then he turned to examine both dead men. Rolling Demos over, he noted the dagger, then took Vara's leather pouch from his belt and opened it. He hummed to himself as he studied what he found there.

Marcus knelt beside Manaen. "Have . . . have I killed him?" Manaen asked.

"He's dead," Marcus said. "But he died by his own knife." Then louder, as if for Felix's benefit, Marcus repeated, "By his own knife."

Aside from superficial cuts on his hands, Manaen was uninjured. "Peniel, Avel," he said, "I'm sorry . . . so sorry. I got you into this. I never—"

Whirling around, Felix ordered, "The prisoner will be silent!" Then to Avel he said, "You, boy! Take that blind beggar out of here. At once, do you hear? You're in the way of my investigation!"

Avel hustled Peniel away from the scene, disappearing into the multitudes.

Manaen and Marcus were left with Felix and the corpses of Vara and Demos.

41

They were too late! Too late!

It was over!

Yeshua gone! Driven from the Temple by the men of Caiaphas' faction!

Avel pulled Peniel forward through the Shabbat crowds. Snatches of conversation filled in details of the confrontation that had taken place between Yeshua, the Pharisees, and the Temple Guard.

"Then they said to the rabbi . . ."

"And Yeshua told them . . ."

"Did you hear what he called the brothers of the high priest? To their faces?"

"A lot of nerve he's got."

"A raving lunatic!"

"They've had men killed for less."

"We came all the way to see him. For what? He's crazy!"

"Maybe a bit too harsh, but honest. I'll give him that!"

"Called them liars!"

"Said they weren't sons of Avraham. Sons of the father of lies!"

"Hypocrites he called them."

"Yeshua may be the only man in Yerushalayim who speaks the truth."

"That's no virtue. You've got to get along if you're going to survive. Honesty doesn't pay the grocer."

"He doesn't get along with anyone! There's such a thing as being too honest."

"Did you hear the way he put them in their places!"

"They'll kill him for it!"

"Yochanan the Baptizer died for less!"

"They picked up stones to stone him."

"He's as good as dead."

"A knife between his ribs. That's what's in store for him and anyone who follows him as well."

So. That was it.

The One Peniel had been waiting for, praying to meet, had vanished into the crowds.

Panting, Avel stopped midway up the Temple steps. "You hear this?" Avel asked. "You want to go back there?"

"He's gone," Peniel replied sadly. "And I've missed my chance. He's gone!"

"We'll find out where Yeshua is."

"Where's Zadok?"

"Probably down at the sheep pens. They'll all be talking about it." Avel linked arms with Peniel. "Come on. Zadok'll know what to do."

Peniel resisted. Disappointment overwhelmed him. How could Yeshua be driven out of Yerushalayim by the Temple priests if He was the true Messiah? It wasn't supposed to happen this way, was it?

Peniel replied, "No. No thanks, Avel. I . . . I can't go. Not now."

"Where will you be?"

"Home. I guess." *Anywhere but here,* Peniel thought. He did not want to hear any more about Yeshua being run off by the high priest!

Avel gave Peniel a shake. "Listen! Everything's gone wrong. I can't hang around. See? Peniel, I've got to tell Zadok about Marcus and Manaen! Tell Zadok they're arrested. I've got to go!"

"Take me to the corner where the papyrus shop is. I can find my way from there."

Avel patted him on the back and led him back down the steps. The two parted at the papyrus shop.

PENIEL WAS CERTAIN MANAEN WOULD BE rotting on a Roman cross before morning.

And what about Yeshua? Such rage overflowed from the religious rulers! Might they execute Yeshua too?

Peniel waited until Avel's footsteps receded.

Peniel did not know where to go. Turning around, he followed his nose along the familiar scents of his neighborhood.

Out of habit his feet carried him to his father's house. Listening, he loitered outside the shop. He could not disturb his father in the Shabbat study.

Peniel heard his mother approach from up the street. She called his name harshly: "Peniel! What?"

"I . . . just wanted to . . . you know? To come home, I mean."

"Well, you can take yourself right off again."

"City's so crowded. People bumping. Things happened. A fight."

"It's a Holy Day. What else do you expect?"

"I was scared of riots again. I didn't know where else . . . " He felt as though he would weep. If only he had tears.

"Stupid! The city's full of pilgrims looking for someone to give their money to! The day's only half gone! Get back to your station."

"It's Shabbat. I'm forbidden to ask alms on Shabbat," he defended, not wanting to return to the Temple.

"Beg. That's what it is. Say it. Beg. You just sit on the steps and look pitiful. You don't even have to open your mouth to speak. That shouldn't be so hard. Look at you. Cracked pot."

"Mama. Can't I come home? One night. Just for tonight. Stay in my old *sukkah?* Only tonight. We're supposed to stay awake all night tonight for Shavuot. Read Torah all night till first light."

"Read!?"

He pleaded, desperate. "Tonight heaven will open. For an instant the prayer on our lips is heard by God, and he answers. Mama! Just for tonight, let me come home. Let me pray here. The city's full of strangers. Nothing ever, ever, ever turns out the way I wish it would. I'm . . . lonely, Mama."

"Stop whining. We've converted your hut into a storage shed. I don't want you near it. Go on. You've got enough daylight to collect a bundle. Now go before I call your father. He'll send you on your way and he won't be nice about it."

She turned on her heel and entered the shop, leaving him outside, listening. He heard the sound of children laughing. Mothers calling. Families.

Peniel stretched his arm out and stroked the familiar wall of home as he left. He told himself that this was what Pentecost was all about. Leaving a familiar place behind and wandering about until you heard the Voice of God commanding you to do or not to do something.

Is anything too hard for God?

The commandment part of it would be easy. If the Voice would just tell him what to do! But how did he live without the faith that somehow, something good waited up ahead in life?

What would he have to hold on to if he could not believe the Messiah could descend as the heavenly Bridegroom to reign in Jerusalem as King over all the earth? What, then, remained for Peniel to look forward to?

Is anything too hard for God?

He made his way up the street and sat slumped against the wall near Abraham's gardenia bush. So near the mountain where God had made provision.

Now Caiaphas and Alexander and the rest had driven Yeshua out of the Temple courts.

So could it be true what the religious rulers said? That Yeshua was not the Messiah after all? It had been a good dream. Like a gardenia flower it had filled Peniel's darkness with a sweet fragrance.

And it had wilted as speedily.

No heavenly Bridegroom this year bringing the light of Torah as a gift to the bride. It would have been nice.

Dreams were just dreams. The Ushpizin were nothing. Air and cobwebs. His dreams had been all wrong.

Peniel arranged his cloak like a sort of bowl in case someone walked by and felt moved to drop a coin in. He would not call out. Men were coming. Talking. Talking all at once. Most likely they would not even see Peniel sitting there beside Abraham's gardenia bush.

But they noticed. They paused.

"Look! What I mean is, if you take this man for an example. How do you sort that out?" one of the men asked.

So Peniel was an example used in a discussion. His mother was right. The cracked pot. Do not say a word and people still notice.

"Yes, Rabbi!" It was the voice of Nakdimon ben Gurion. "Always been blind from birth. A good fellow. Good-hearted. So why?"

"Who sinned? This man? Or his parents, that he was born blind?" the other man said.[62]

A shadow fell across Peniel as someone approached and stood over him. Peniel felt the coolness of it, blocking the afternoon sun. A long moment of silence. Inside his head he heard a whisper: *Peniel, Peniel, your name is Peniel!*

Peniel replied out loud, "Here I am."

Then again, not a voice anyone could hear. Just this sigh, a thought running through his brain. *Peniel, Peniel, the Lord knows your name. Is anything too hard for God?*

Who am I that You would speak to me? Peniel thought.

The voice answered, *It isn't who you are. It's who I AM.*

And then the man stooped near Peniel, as if to study him. Peniel felt it. Did the man know that the same questions these men asked had plagued Peniel for his whole lifetime? *Why? Why was I born blind? What punishment has made me this way? Why?*

There was such compassion in the reply! "Neither this man or his parents sinned. But this . . . happened!"

Peniel recognized the voice. *Yeshua! They didn't stone You!*

Before Abraham was, I AM.

Yeshua touched Peniel's forehead, brushing back a lock of his hair. Then Yeshua explained quietly to Peniel, "This happened so that the work of God might be displayed in your life; as long as it is day I must do the work of him who sent me."

Peniel remembered what Mosheh had asked the Lord as he bowed before the burning bush: *Whom shall I say sent me?*

Peniel questioned in his heart, *What work? It's Shabbat. No one works on Shabbat. Who sent You?*

Yeshua answered Peniel and the men with him, "Night is coming when no one can work. While I AM in the world, I AM the Light of the world."

Having said this, Yeshua spit on the ground and made clay with His saliva. Like a potter smoothing away a flaw on a vase, He put the clay on Peniel's eyes. First the right eye and then the left. He brushed his thumb gently, working the clay until the surface was smooth and perfect. *The potter's hand!* How well Peniel knew the meaning of Yeshua's actions!

Chesed! Mercy! Is anything too hard for God?

"Go," Yeshua told him. "Wash in the Pool of Siloam." The name of the pool meant "Sent"!

There was a smile in Yeshua's voice. He was pleased, like an artisan who had crafted a work of art and was admiring his workmanship.

Yes. Yes. Now this will set it right. This is the work I AM sent to accomplish! Chesed! Mercy! That is the work I AM sent for! Light for the soul! I AM sent, and now I AM sending you. . . .

And so the heavens opened to Peniel. The Voice of God spoke to *him!* The Word, fulfillment of Torah, the commandment was given to *him!*

Does He who forms the eye not see? Go! Go now! Wash yourself in the love and mercy of the One sent from heaven for your sake! Nothing is too hard for God! I AM is sending you!

Peniel obeyed, expectant! Excited! His stomach fluttered as he groped his way down the crooked side streets, down and down toward the Pool of Siloam![71]

Sent!

Could it be? Was it possible?

Peniel immediately rushed headlong toward the Pool of Siloam, the place that had been the setting of his deepest sorrow.

The rabbis said that in all of history, no one had ever opened the eyes of a man born blind. Was it possible such a thing could happen for Peniel?

Nothing is too hard for God!

What would it be like to have sight?

Would it be like the pictures Peniel had built up in his mind, adding layers by his touch the way a potter built up a jar of clay? How big was the Mount of Olives that Gershon had etched on his bowl? What did the fragrance of an orange look like? What was the color of a laughing child? a birdsong? the leaves of a tree rustling in the wind?

"Look out! Watch where you're going!" pilgrims shouted in unconscious irony as Peniel caromed off families heading toward the Temple Mount.

If He was a true miracle worker, why did Yeshua have to daub clay on Peniel? Why did Yeshua not just speak and heal him? And even if the clay had some special property, why send him all the way across the city to wash? There had been water close by, in Nakdimon ben Gurion's garden, in fact. Even now there was water nearer. A fountain in the courtyard where the Herodian Way intersected the Valley of the Cheesemakers was merely a short distance off Peniel's route.

And yet, as the questions crowded his mind, Peniel knew the answers for Yeshua's actions and words. All the Scriptures, everything Peniel had heard as he begged on the Temple steps, flooded his mind!

Everything meant something! Every Scripture was a candle flame—light, alive, wavering in the breath of God!

Yeshua had spoken of work He must accomplish while it was still day . . . and those who heard Him knew that today was Shabbat! When all work was forbidden. Peniel had been afraid to ask Yeshua to heal him because he had not wanted to be a breaker of Shabbat. Had not wanted to be refused by Yeshua!

And yet, *Mercy! Nothing is too hard for God.*

By making the clay, Yeshua had shattered the Pharisee's idea of Shabbat rest! The law had become more important to men than Mercy. And so Yeshua had violated the law for the sake of Mercy! By this He had shown that all His work was to pour out Mercy on those in need! There was no time or day or circumstance when it was not right to do it!

Chesed! Mercy! Show God's love and mercy for all whom you may come upon! This was the true meaning of Shabbat rest!

And why had Yeshua not simply spoken the command and healed Peniel? Peniel remembered what was written in Psalm 94, which was read every Shabbat in the synagogue: "Does he . . . the potter . . . who formed the eye, not see?"

By His actions Yeshua was telling everyone that He had been the One who knelt in the garden of creation and formed man from the dust of the earth!

Who was so blind in his heart that he refused to understand and accept what Yeshua was saying by His actions?

Nothing is too hard for God!

Peniel stumbled in his thoughts and over his feet at the same time.

Sent! Tell them I AM sent you.

He hurried onward. Naaman the Leper had been healed of his

loathsome disease when the prophet Elisha sent him to wash in the Jordan.

Naaman had thought to himself, *Aren't the rivers of my home in Damascus as good as any river in Israel?* But he went and washed in the Jordan anyway. And he was cured.

Nothing is too hard for God!

To obey the voice of the Sent One! No matter how foolish the command might seem! To believe the Word and act on it! Obedience was proof of faith!

The downward slope and Peniel's excitement combined to rush him along. In his haste he missed the turn where the steps toward the plaza of Siloam diverted from the main road.

"Help me!" Peniel cried aloud. "Where is it? Where is the Pool of Siloam?" He sensed pilgrims parting and flowing around him as if he were a rock in a stream. "Where is it?" he called again.

Someone took him by the arm, "It's not far," the stranger said. "Just here."

Peniel felt the wall, recognized the edge of steep stairs underfoot. "Thank you!" he called. "Thank you." He hurried downward, tracing his way by his fingertips to the bottom and around the corner.

He was close. Water gurgled as someone filled a jar to carry home. Children splashed in the shallows.

Once more, on the top step of the entry, he hesitated. What if it did not work? Could he bear the disappointment, here at Siloam of all places?

Nothing . . . too hard . . . for . . . God!

Even if he was meant to bear the disappointment, he would believe! Outstretched, fluttering hands nervously reached for and encountered one of the support pillars of the roof.

"Who am I, Lord?" Peniel cried aloud. "Who am I to expect mercy?"

The Voice replied to his heart, *It's who I AM!*

Dropping to his knees, Peniel crawled forward on his belly to the edge of the pool.

Sent! Tell them I AM sent you. While I AM in the world I AM the Light of the world.

And Peniel remembered the last day with Gershon and why they had been at the pool. Each year on the Day of Atonement the water of

Siloam Pool was drawn out in a golden pitcher. It was carried by the priests through the streets of Jerusalem. Poured out before the altar by the high priest, the water of Siloam was a sign of the outpouring of God's Spirit, of His love and mercy for His people.

Why was Peniel sent to wash in Siloam? Yeshua was saying plainly that the water of God's mercy was an abundant reservoir, not some tiny golden pitcher that needed a parade and a priest to have meaning!

God's Mercy was free for all who came!

It's who I AM!

Peniel hesitated, then sang this prayer: "Blessed are you, O Lord, God of all the universe, who has let me live to see this day!"

Peniel splashed water on his face, once with each hand . . . then plunged his whole face into the pool. He scrubbed at the dried clay, peeling it from his eyelids, then sat quickly upright. With both hands cupped over his face, he scooped out the remaining water, flinging his hands wide.

He opened his eyes . . . and . . . and . . . and . . . "Oh! Blessed are . . . you . . . O Lord! Nothing is impossible with . . . you!"

Dancing diamonds of light refracting in the pool dazzled him. Gershon's description swirled around him. White columns around the terrace reflected in the cool blue water. Water! So much! The blue of the sky overhead was lustrous, framed by dark red roof tiles.

Across the reservoir, a mother and child stopped to stare at him.

He saw! Saw them! Looking at him! Faces! He saw faces!

Peniel started back, dropped his gaze, and saw his own face reflected in the surface of the pool. Wondering, he reached toward the image. It rippled away from his touch.

Then Peniel watched himself touch his nose, his mouth, his eyes. He yanked his hands away from his eyes, from the momentary darkness of obscured sight. All the images and color of the world flooded back instantly.

Peniel laughed, a laugh that bubbled in his chest at first, then erupted from his lips.

"I can see!" he shouted. "I can see!"

He had to find Yeshua, to thank Him for His mercy!

Peniel surged back out of the plaza and up the stairs, exulting in each step as the slightest change of position showed him additional wonders.

Colors, shapes, people, and their clothing were marvelous in their variety! And the shops, displaying mounds of orange and purple and green.

It was the first day of creation, when God said, *"Let there be light,"* *and there was light.* And it was good.[72]

42

To say that Marcus was confused was to completely understate his befuddlement.

Since the deaths of Vara and Demos, Marcus expected no less consequence than to find himself in a dungeon, if not summarily executed.

Instead it was late afternoon, and he and Manaen were in the officers' quarters in the Antonia. They had been given food, wine, water for bathing, fresh clothing. Marcus even had the proper centurion's uniform, and he had shaved for the first time in months.

There were guards outside the door and no one was permitted in or out, but Felix said it was a precaution for their protection . . . whatever that meant.

"These men," Felix said about the sentries, "are personally loyal to me. Stay here and trust me. This won't take long. When I need you to join me, I'll send a special password so there'll be no mistake."

That had been several hours ago.

Perhaps Felix had misjudged Pilate's anger. The killing of Sejanus' protégé by Marcus would no more go unpunished than the killing of Antipas' ward by Manaen.

It would not matter that Manaen had acted in self-defense.

Roman citizens could not, by law, be crucified. Of course, if Marcus was first convicted of treason and *maiestas*, he would be stripped of his citizenship and then nailed to a tree.

As for Manaen, blind or not, his fate was sealed: The crunch of spikes into flesh and bone was what his future held.

PENIEL LAUGHED ON THE WAY UP the Herodian Way and into the bright sunlight of late afternoon.

People thought him mad until they looked into his shining eyes and brilliant smile. "Shalom!" he greeted one and all. "Good Shabbat!" He took foreigners by the hand, welcomed them to Jerusalem, wished them the best Pentecost of their lives.

His smile faltered only momentarily when he retraced his steps to Abraham's Bush and found the lane deserted. Yeshua had moved on. How would Peniel find the Rabbi to thank Him? He did not even know what Yeshua looked like.

What a discovery! Someone's appearance had never been significant to Peniel before. Now he rejoiced in every variation of human features, every nuance of form and shape.

Peniel's joy was too complete, his heart too full of rejoicing to be downcast. He would find Yeshua, he was certain of that. He had committed the Teacher's voice to indelible memory; the exact sound of Yeshua's words would remain with him forever!

After today his life's message would forever be: Is anything too hard for God?

Besides, the gardenia bush had chosen today to erupt in blossoms. Snowy white bundles of delicate waxy fragrance! Aroma and touch and vision all at once; it was overwhelming.

He would go home, he decided. Tell his mother and father of his good fortune . . . and see their faces for the first time!

As he drew nearer to the workshop Peniel grew conscious of people pointing at him and staring.

Suddenly it dawned on him: Though he could not recognize any of them, some of the neighbors could identify him!

"It looks like him," Peniel heard a man say. It was the fruit seller a block away from Peniel's home.

"But it's not him," argued the wheelwright in his bass voice. "It only looks like him."

"It *is* me," Peniel announced joyfully to both astonished onlookers.

"No," the wheelwright argued. "Peniel ben Yahtzar was a blind beggar who sat at Nicanor Gate. You can see."

"I am Peniel," Peniel insisted. "It's me."

A familiar voice called to him from behind. "Peniel? Are you all right?"

It was the shoemaker's wife.

Peniel spun round, faced her. She was beautiful! As beautiful as her voice, as beautiful as her heart! Dark brown hair framed an oval face and a tiny nose. "Peniel?" she repeated.

"You're back," Peniel exclaimed. "I'm so glad. I wanted you to know: I can see. Yeshua put clay on my eyes, I washed, and now I can see!"

THE WHEELWRIGHT GRABBED PENIEL by the arm. "Come on. We've got to see the rabbi."

"Agreed," chimed in the fruit vendor. "He'll know what to do."

Peniel wondered what there was to *do*. He had been blind; now he could see. What was there to do except shout it across Jerusalem?

After years of being led places, Peniel did not try to pull away from the hands that tugged him in a direction opposite from his home.

"I'll tell your parents!" the shoemaker's wife called after him. "I'll tell them!"

The rabbi mentioned by the wheelwright was an elderly Pharisee who spent his days studying regulations, rules, and their commentaries in a working-class synagogue near the Sheep Gate. It was not necessary for Peniel to tell anyone else about his miracle; the wheelwright and the produce merchant shouted it to everyone they passed. "Look; see! This is Peniel, the blind man. You know, Peniel, the cracked pot! Come on, we're taking him to Rabbi Japeth."

By the time Peniel reached the synagogue, an entire crowd from his district followed after.

The wheelwright, towing Peniel behind, burst into the study room. "Rabbi," the craftsman shouted. "A miracle! Look, the marred pot is fixed. Peniel can see!"

The elder scholar raised his gaze from his scroll and fixed rheumy eyes on Peniel. "No, no," he said. "I know Peniel. My brother named him. Peniel begs at Nicanor Gate. This only looks like him."

"Rabbi!" the wheelwright insisted. "This *is* him. He was born blind, but he was healed today!"

"Healed," the rabbi repeated. Peniel saw his mouth working, as if tasting the word and finding it unfamiliar. "Healed today, you say?"

"Today. Just happened," the fruit vendor asserted, wanting to get his share of the glory. "Brought him straight to you."

"Healed on Shabbat?"

Wheelwright and merchant exchanged looks. "Yes, Rabbi. Today. Like we said."

"I know just what to do," Rabbi Japeth said.

Peniel was relieved, and then overjoyed. He remembered what was supposed to happen next and now it would. Now he would be taken to the Temple and presented to the priests, to certify his healing. Then, healed, whole, and able to take his place among men of Israel at last, Peniel would make a Thank-offering to the Almighty.

"Right," Rabbi Japeth said. "There's a meeting of my sect in the Chamber of Hewn Stone. We'll take him there. The Pharisee leaders must hear of this at once. We'll soon get to the bottom of it. Healing on Shabbat!"

By the time peniel reached the Temple Mount and the entry to the Chamber of Hewn Stone, the news of his healing had already reached the Pharisees assembled there. Several of them stared at Peniel suspiciously, as if convinced he was a fraud.

"Impossible!" one of them announced without asking Peniel any questions. "There's never been such a thing since the world began."

"On Shabbat," another announced. "Who did this?"

"Doesn't matter," a third asserted. "It's fake!"

Faces, gestures, shaking fingers, waving fists, sweeps of tunics and robes—all swirled around Peniel. It was overwhelming.

Shutting his eyes against the overload imposed on his new sense of sight, Peniel waited for the tumult to recede. The din of competing voices and arguments threatened to swamp his hearing as well.

"Who claims this man was blind?"

"That's right. What proof do we have?"

"I do," Rabbi Japeth responded. "And I have two other witnesses with me . . . more than that."

"But how? Where?"

"Today, you say?"

The racket churned around Peniel as if he were not present, as if he certainly were not important.

Then a hand was laid on his arm—not harshly but in reassurance. And a quiet, friendly voice close to his ear asked, "Peniel? Open your eyes."

Peniel did so and found himself looking into the broad, smiling face that accompanied the expansive, cheerful demeanor he expected with the well-known tones. It was Nakdimon ben Gurion, and he was built like an ox!

As if the two men were alone, instead of surrounded by a hundred others, Nakdimon inquired, "How were your eyes opened?"

"The man they call Yeshua—"

"What's he say? Who?"

"Be quiet," Nakdimon directed sharply, "if you want to hear his reply." When order and decorum were restored, Nakdimon encouraged, "Go ahead, Peniel. Begin again. How'd it happen?"

"The man they call Yeshua—"

"Stop him at once," Caiaphas said, arriving with his brother-in-law and an entourage of Temple officials. "It's not permitted to speak well of that charlatan."

"It's not permitted to call him *Messiah*," Nakdimon corrected. "You weren't invited to our meeting, Lord Caiaphas," he added. "If you want to hear this testimony, you'll keep still. Go on, Peniel."

"The man they call Yeshua made clay and put it on my eyes. He told me to go to Siloam and wash. So I went and washed; then I could see."

"Where is this man?" Alexander demanded. "Why isn't he here to take credit for his so-called miracle?"

"I don't know where he is," Peniel replied. "I was blind when he touched my eyes. Since I can see, I've been looking for him but haven't found him."

Several of the Pharisees muttered amongst themselves about healing on Shabbat. One of them burst out, "This man is not from God, for he does not keep Shabbat!"

Nakdimon retorted, "How can a sinner do such miraculous signs?"

His assertion was seconded by a young Pharisee named Joseph of Arimathea. "He's right! What evil man possesses such wonder-working power?"

Peniel was baffled by the tumult. He had been blind; now he could see. What was this argument really about?

"Preposterous!" Caiaphas returned. "We know this . . . this man from Galilee . . . is a lawbreaker. He speaks against the proper authorities *and* he's guilty of incitement."

Nakdimon stretched his stout, strong arm protectively across Peniel's shoulders. "You're making unproven statements, Lord Caiaphas. Besides, the reality of what Yeshua does . . . of who he is . . . is here before your eyes!"

Alexander shook his index finger in Peniel's face. "What have you to say about him? It's your eyes he opened."

Peniel thought swiftly. What statement could he make that could not be challenged? What could he say that would not bring danger and retribution on Yeshua's head? Those who could do miracles were sent from God. Yeshua had sent Peniel to wash at Siloam, just like Elisha sent Naaman to wash in Jordan. Elisha was a prophet, doing the work of God. Yeshua spoke of doing the work He'd been given to do. "He's a prophet," Peniel said.

That simple observation was like putting a torch in a barrel of tar. It was a good thing the meeting hall was of hewn stone and not wood, because it most certainly would have burst into flame!

"*Ridiculous!*"

"*Shabbat breaker!*"

"*Possessed by a demon!*"

When the babble once again settled, one of the Pharisees proposed, "Perhaps this is a storm in a wine jug! How do we know this man was born blind? Other blind men have been cured, yes? How do we know the truth about this man?"

Nakdimon's attempt to assert his personal knowledge was overridden, as was a statement by Rabbi Japeth that he had known Peniel since birth.

"*True! How do we know? Are his parents living?*"

"*Send for his parents!*"

"*Let his parents be brought!*"

Those in the hall split into different camps while they awaited the arrival of Peniel's mother and father.

One group asserted it was all a fraud.

Another set of Pharisees noted that healing on Shabbat was not permitted, so Yeshua had done wrong, no matter what.

Joseph of Arimathea urged caution: "Wait until we hear the witnesses speak."

Through it all Nakdimon waited beside Peniel. He smiled into Peniel's eyes, nodding his reassurance that everything would be all right.

Peniel was not so certain about that. In this dispute, few seemed to care that he could *see!* Evidence of a genuine miracle was in front of their faces, but the significance of that fact mattered very little!

At last Peniel's mother and father were hustled into the room.

His mother and father! Peniel looked on the parents he had never before glimpsed, and his heart went out.

Mama! Papa! I'm not the marred pot anymore!

Peniel took a step toward them, but Temple guards surged between them.

Then Peniel gazed into his mother's eyes. She saw him *see* her! Befuddlement and anxiety landed atop a heap of frown lines on her pinched face. Frizzy gray hair framed unhappiness and worry.

Short, fat, bald, and out of breath, Peniel's father appeared uncomfortably nervous. His eyes once met Peniel's, then darted instantly away.

The eyes of Peniel's mother were more hostile: *What have you done to us now? What new trouble have you caused us?*

Caiaphas demanded, "Is this your son? Is this the same one you say was born blind? How is it that now he can see?"

The hall grew still.

"We know he's our son," Peniel's father began haltingly.

"We know he was born blind," his mother added. "We're members in good standing of our synagogue. We always tithe! Always! We keep Shabbat! As for him: I gave him birth; I nursed him. He's always been blind; he's always been trouble and grief to us. He's—"

Caiaphas motioned, and Peniel's mother halted midsentence. "How is it that now he can see?" he repeated.

Peniel saw his father swallow hard and take a deep breath. "How he can now see, or who opened his eyes, we don't know."

A flash of inspiration appeared to come to Peniel's mother. "Ask *him*," she declared, pointing at her son. "Ask him. He's of age. Let him speak for himself."

Peniel's heart was crushed. His mother and father would not speak up for him, would not defend him, would not side with him, would not even share in his miracle.

Instead they gratefully escaped from the Chamber of Hewn Stone without a backward glance.

Peniel's shoulders sagged and Nakdimon noticed. "Don't blame them too much," he said kindly. "They're afraid. You know the decree: Speak approvingly of Yeshua and be put out of the synagogue."

Alexander harrumphed and dismissed the testimony of Peniel's parents with a wave of his hand. "Useless," he said. "All right, so he was born blind. But we don't have an answer to *how* he was healed."

Nakdimon thumped Peniel on the back. "He can speak for himself."

Solemnly, to impress Peniel with the gravity of the inquiry, Caiaphas intoned, "Give glory to God . . . that is to say, tell us the absolute truth. We know this . . . man . . . the one you claim healed you. We know he's a sinner."

Wrath and indignation rose from Peniel's very toes. In tones that rung into the rafters of the hall he stated, "Whether he's a sinner or not, I don't know. One thing I *do* know: I was blind and now I see!"

Raucous clamor again.

"*How?*"

"*What did he do?*"

"*How did he open your eyes?*"

"*Was it sorcery?*"

"*Did he conjure?*"

"*What blasphemy did he utter?*"

"Listen!" Peniel bellowed in exasperation, surprising even himself with the force of his shout. "I told you already and you didn't listen! Why do you want to hear it again? Do you want to become his disciples too?"

The seated audience members jumped to their feet. The standing members shook their fists. All of them talked at once.

"You sinner! You blasphemer! You bastard child!"

"You're this fellow's disciple," one accused Peniel. "We are disciples of Mosheh!"

"Exactly right!" Caiaphas chimed in. "We're Mosheh's disciples. We know that God spoke to Mosheh, but as for this fellow, we don't even know where he comes from!"

His anger under control, but his purpose fixed and his courage at the highest level, Peniel replied in distinct syllables that all could understand: "Now that *is* remarkable! You don't know where he comes from, yet he opened my eyes. We know that God doesn't listen to sinners. He listens to the godly man who does his will. All of you—" Peniel's gaze swept the room, alighted on each face, held each hostile look firmly in the grip of his miraculous eyes—"all of you passed me outside Nicanor Gate. Did any of you ever heal me? Did any of you ever try? Of course not! You didn't even look at me! But I am Peniel ben Yahtzar, the potter's son. Nobody has ever heard of opening the eyes of a man born blind. But if this man . . . this Yeshua of Nazareth . . . wasn't from God, he could do nothing!"

The simmering pot of hostility boiled over.

"You were steeped in sin at birth!"

"You're altogether born in sin!"

"How dare you lecture us?"

Temple guards seized Peniel. Alexander spat in his face. As he was dragged toward the entry portico, Peniel heard Caiaphas utter the words of excommunication: "You are all witnesses! He has broken the edict. *Let him be cast into outer darkness, where there will be weeping and gnashing of teeth!*"

Peniel was thrown out of the chamber, out of the hearing, out of the synagogue, and into the early evening.

THAT SAME EVENING PONTIUS PILATE entered the audience chamber of his palace. When Marcus and Manaen were led into the room, the governor was seated in his *curule* chair, the judgment seat from which official pronouncements—and capital punishments—were handed down.

Lifting his chin, Marcus said to Manaen, "Courage. The governor is waiting for us."

Manaen shrugged as if it were of no consequence. "It doesn't matter what happens to me now. Susanna is safe."

Seated in a second chair of state, but lower than Pilate's and off to one side, was Herod Antipas. Since Manaen was one of Antipas' subjects, Marcus guessed Pilate was showing a courtesy to the tetrarch, though it made no difference to the outcome.

The one jarring note in the appearance of this tribunal was Felix. Resplendent in his dress uniform, the tribune stood in front of Pilate's chair . . . faintly smiling.

As Marcus approached and saluted, Felix gave a slight nod, but no clue as to what it all meant.

"My Lord Antipas," Pilate said, "I have this day received important news from Rome. Since it concerns not only Imperial rule but also the matter before us, I will share it before we begin: The Praetorian Prefect Sejanus . . . "

Marcus' heart sank. So Sejanus had succeeded in his coup, making him master of Rome and the world.

"Prefect Sejanus," Pilate continued, "has been found guilty of treason and *maiestas* and has been executed."

Wildest hope soared through Marcus. Sejanus dead!

"Not only was he guilty of treason," Pilate added, "but his highest deputies are also suspected of complicity. The ranks of the Praetorian Guard are being purged even now. Thank the gods the emperor is safe."

Antipas looked piously upward and raised a hand toward heaven.

"We have not been free from the pernicious influence of Sejanus even here," Pilate noted. "The excesses of the Praetorian officer Vara, which because of his unnecessary savagery led to the Passover killings, are well known. And Vara, I am told, is also responsible for the brutal blinding of your ward, Manaen bar Talmai. Ah! A chair for bar Talmai."

Marcus struggled to understand this. That Pilate would try to distance himself from Sejanus and the Praetorians was easily recognized, but what did it have to do with Manaen?

At a gesture from Pilate, Felix picked up the story. "Apparently, Lord Antipas, Vara conceived a hatred for both bar Talmai brothers: a hatred increased by a dispute over a gambling debt. I'm sorry to inform you that as a result of that bitterness, Vara killed Demos bar Talmai today."

A flame of comprehension flickered in Marcus' mind, and he

guessed what Felix would say next. "Centurion Marcus Longinus was nearby and intercepted the rampaging Vara . . . unfortunately too late to save Demos, but in time to save Manaen. Armed as he was with the governor's own writ of special powers—" Felix brandished the parchment he had plucked from Vara's body—"it says here in the name of Pilate, that what is done is done for the good of the Empire. Marcus, having this warrant in his possession, did not hesitate to confront Praetorian Vara and then defeat him. Vara is dead."

"Well done." Herod Antipas applauded. "So the centurion saved you the trouble of arresting and trying the traitor Vara."

That was it exactly. Marcus had unintentionally done Pilate a huge favor. By killing Vara, Marcus had freed the governor from any embarrassing revelations that might connect him to Sejanus. The writ of special power was found by Felix in Vara's pouch; another thing Pilate would not want known, if he was trying to blame a dead man for the riots in Jerusalem. Best for all to pretend that Marcus had been the one given this document.

Pilate stretched out his hand to take the decree from Felix. He scanned it and smiled. "Yes. Yes. My seal. Well done, Centurion Marcus Longinus. I congratulate you for putting an end to Vara on my behalf."

Marcus saluted and bowed curtly in acceptance of the accolade. Pilate placed the document against the flame of his lamp and let it drop to the floor and burn. Then, with a snap of his fingers, he called his scribe to him. "Bring out the Lady Susanna," he commanded.

Manaen breathed, "Susanna?"

She was brought into the room. Her astonished gaze fell on Manaen. "Manaen?" she cried. "Manaen! Alive!" She ran to embrace him. They melted into one another's arms, and Marcus was uncertain if they heard the next words of Pilate.

"One more piece of news from Rome concerns you, Lord Antipas," Pilate said. "It seems that by Imperial decree—from the emperor himself—that the Lady Susanna bat Maccabee is confirmed in her inheritance . . . and specifically freed to marry whomsoever she chooses."

Tonight every synagogue in Jerusalem would be packed with men reading through the Torah and Psalms, urging one another to stay awake, to listen for the instant when the Voice of God descended from heaven.

And then there was Peniel. Cast out. Thrown out. Cursed. Cut off.

But Peniel laughed as he walked through the deserted streets. He decided this brand of outer darkness was not as bad. It was much brighter than inner darkness anyway.

He found his way back to the beginning. Where else? Abraham's gardenia bush was frosted over with white flowers. Yeshua of Nazareth was not there. He had moved on quietly, no doubt touching others, healing wounded bodies and hearts. Peniel was not surprised.

The sun was setting. The sky looked like the smell of cinnamon. Baking apples? Red? Is that what Gershon had called it? Cinnamon banners.

Shabbat was ending, the last Shabbat of counting the Omer. Seven times seven weeks, forty-nine days since the Passover massacre that began Peniel's odyssey.

Nothing is too hard for God!

Tomorrow was Pentecost. Feast of Weeks. The cycle that began with *Chesed*, Mercy, was complete. Maybe Messiah would descend tonight or tomorrow to call His bride from the world.

If He did, Peniel would be here. In Jerusalem. Where it all began. He began to sing the ancient hymn:

O come, O come, thou Lord of Might
Who to thy tribes, on Sinai's height,
In ancient times didst give the law
In cloud and majesty and awe.

O come, thou Dayspring from on high
And cheer us by thy drawing nigh;
Disperse the gloomy clouds of night,
And death's dark shadows put to flight.

Fascinated, Peniel watched lights wink on all across Jerusalem. In simple homes and mansions, atop towers and the great Temple people trimmed their wicks and lit their lamps. Waiting, waiting for heaven to open and hear their prayers! Waiting for the voice of Messiah to call their names! Waiting for The Light of the World to descend from heaven and dwell among men! The true Light! Glorious, wonderful, darkness-dispelling!

Peniel inhaled the fragrance of the flowers. He gazed up at the myriad of stars and knew: The Light had come.

DREAMING AGAIN. It was early morning, Pentecost. Peniel was the one man in Jerusalem who could not stay awake for the Voice.

Peniel. Peniel.

The breath whispering his name was as fragrant as gardenia blossoms. Warm as lamplight. Near as the touch of the breeze on his face.

"*U-lu Ush-pi-zin* . . . enter, exalted guest. I've been waiting for you."

Yes, I know.

"And what is your name, please?"

I have many names: Metatron. The Angel of the Face. The Angel of the

Lord. *The Anointed One. Messiah. The Servant of the Lord. Prince of Peace. Wonderful. Immanu'el—"God-with-us." Son of God. Son of Man.*

"What should I call you?"

Before Avraham was, I AM.

In his dream Peniel bowed his face to the ground, pressing his fore-head to the red clay from which his eyes were made. "Who am I, that you come to me?"

A hand on his shoulder touched him gently, then cupped his chin, urging him to rise up.

It's not who you are; it's who I AM. I know how you are formed; I remember that you are clay. Look around you. Behold the glory of creation.

Lifting his eyes to the night sky, Peniel gasped. "There are lights in the heavens," he said breathlessly. "Points of fire and ice . . . broad brush strokes that gleam like the sun on the Pool of Siloam . . . spiraling curls and luminous jets of fire."

Yes. Echoes of My first words at creation: Let there be Light.

"Echoes," Peniel repeated. "Yes. I see! I see the Hymn of Creation! With my eyes my soul hears the Moment of Beginnings." He paused, then said, "Lord, I can't ask you for a story. It wouldn't be right. You aren't just one among the Ushpizin."

No, but each of their stories provides clues about Me. I am on a journey from My Father's house, as Avraham was sent from his father's house. And I have come to show the Mercy of the Father to the world, as mercy was shown to Avraham. And I will lay down My life obediently, as Yitz'chak did. And as Yitz'chak, Ya'acov, and Mosheh all did, I have come a long way, seeking My bride.

Moon and stars spun overhead. Peniel listened to the Hymn of Creation. And in the reverberating sagas of the Ushpizin he recognized the truth that everything means something. No tale of the fathers exists except to point the way to the coming of the Bridegroom, as every candle flame hints at sunrise but cannot prepare the eye for the sun.

"Nothing is too hard for God," Peniel murmured.

You are a living testimony to that truth. This happened so that the work of God might be displayed in your life.

The dream receded in Peniel's mind. The Voice swirled away. The leaves of Abraham's gardenia bush stirred with the breeze.

Peniel called out, "But I still don't know what to call you, Lord. Please! And tell me! When will you call us out as your bride?"

Peniel! Everything written in the Word means something! Peniel! When all is accomplished that is written in the book, then look up, Peniel! I AM . . . coming soon. . . . Look up, Peniel! Peniel! Look up!

He said no more. And then it was . . .

First light.

A cock crowed, announcing the approach of morning. Peniel's first morning.

He opened his eyes. Awake. And there was light. Color. The world swirled around him like the aroma of the flower seller's cart. The stones of Jerusalem glowed golden. The sky was a soft blanket over his head.

A man stood above him. The rising sun was at the man's back, framing Him in light. Dark eyes. Peniel noticed His eyes first, before anything else. Eyes smiling into him. Seeing everything. Everything.

The light shone brighter around Peniel.

The man said, "Peniel. It's a good name for you, don't you think?"

"You," Peniel said softly, knowing, recognizing the voice. "You came back."

"Yes. To where it all began."

"I wanted to thank you."

"Peniel. I've been looking for you. It's First Light, you see."

"Yes. I was blind. But now—" Peniel swept his hand toward the sky! The eastern horizon glowed orange, backlighting the Temple Mount.

"Tell me, Peniel," Yeshua asked. "Do you believe in the Son of Man?"

Blinking in the morning light, Peniel could only stammer, "Who . . . is he . . . sir? Tell me! Tell me so I may believe in him!"

Yeshua smiled. "Peniel, my friend, you have now *seen* his face. In fact, I AM the one speaking with you."

Peniel shouted with joy. With both arms he embraced Yeshua around the knees. "My Lord," he cried, "I believe! Oh! I do! I believe! And like our father Ya'acov, who wrestled you beside the river! I will not . . . *will not* . . . let you go, Lord! Until you bless me!"

So Peniel, seeing Him face-to-face on Pentecost morning, worshipped Him as Ya'acov had done at dawn beside the river.

Yeshua laughed, sharing Peniel's joy. Stooped beside him, the Lord touched Peniel's head, his face, his chin. Clasping him by the shoulders, Yeshua raised Peniel to his feet, then gazed into his eyes. "For judgment I have come into this world, so that the blind will see . . . and those who think they see will become blind. Come on then, friend. Follow me, Peniel. This is the first light of a new day, and life will never be the same."

Epilogue

SILENCE.

The library beneath the Temple Mount was perfumed with the fragrance of gardenias. The soft touch of a breeze ruffled Shimon's hair, as if someone unseen had walked past and touched him.

Shimon closed the scroll and wiped his eyes with the back of his hand. He glanced up, meeting the knowing gaze of his father.

Alfie put a hand over his heart. "Peniel. His name . . . the meaning of it? In here! He saw God's face . . . in here, first."

Moshe nodded once. "Before the Potter gave him eyes to see the sunrise, he understood light."

"First light," Shimon whispered. "I understand now, Papa."

Moshe pulled Shimon into his arms as if he were a small boy in need of comfort. He stroked Shimon's hair and kissed him on his head. "My boy. First light! Yes. First is only the *beginning!* And I promise you, my son! My son! This is only the beginning of the light that will flood your heart!"

Shimon clung to his father as the two gazed at the triangle of summer stars shining brightly above them. "I was blind, Papa. I was . . . but *now* I see!"

Blessed are the pure in heart,

for they will see God's face!

MATTHEW 5:8

Authors' Note

The following sources have been helpful in our research for this book:

- *The Complete Jewish Bible.* Translated by David H. Stern. Baltimore, MD: Jewish New Testament Publications, Inc., 1998.

- iLumina, a digitally animated Bible and encyclopedia suite. Wheaton, IL: Tyndale House Publishers, 2002.

- *The International Standard Bible Encyclopaedia.* George Bromiley, ed. 5 vols., Grand Rapids: Eerdmans 1979.

- *O Jerusalem!* Larry Collins and Dominique Lapierre. New York: Simon and Schuster, 1972.

- *The Life and Times of Jesus the Messiah.* Alfred Edersheim. Peabody, MA: Hendrickson Publishers, Inc., 1995.

Scripture References

[1] Ps. 84:10
[2] Deut. 6:4
[3] Gen. 1:1
[4] Isa. 53:7
[5] Isa. 53:4-5
[6] Isa. 53:7
[7] Matt. 16:25
[8] John 3:16
[9] Matt. 13:17
[10] Isa. 53:5
[11] Ps. 121:8
[12] Eccles. 3:1-8
[13] Rom. 3:23
[14] Luke 13:1-5
[15] Rom. 6:23
[16] Isa. 64:6
[17] Luke 13:6-9
[18] Luke 12:54-56
[19] Luke 12:13ff
[20] Luke 12:16-21
[21] Luke 10:38-42.
[22] Luke 12:3
[23] Luke 12:4-7
[24] Gen. 12:1-3
[25] Luke 12:8-12
[26] Gen. 18:1-15
[27] Isa. 32:1-2
[28] Luke 13:18-19
[29] Matt. 13:24-30
[30] Matt. 13:3-9

[31] Matt. 11:13
[32] Luke 13:10-13
[33] Luke 13:15-16
[34] Ps. 67:1-7
[35] Hos. 11:1
[36] Judg. 16
[37] Ps. 94:1-3
[38] Ps. 94:4-5a
[39] Ps. 94:6-7
[40] Ps. 94:8b-9
[41] Ps. 84:10
[42] Jer. 29:11
[43] Gen. 22:1-3
[44] Gen. 22:5
[45] Gen. 22:6-7
[46] John 3:16
[47] Amos 3:7
[48] Mic. 5:2
[49] Jer. 31:15; Matt. 2:18
[50] Hos. 11:1; Matt. 2:15
[51] Ps. 91:1-8
[52] Ps. 94:9
[53] Ps. 91:11-12
[54] Ps. 3:1-8
[55] Isa. 9:1-2
[56] Gen. 1:3
[57] Ps. 35:4-9
[58] Gen. 32–33
[59] Jer. 31:16
[60] Jer. 31:34

[61] Matt. 1:17
[62] Luke 2:29-30
[63] Luke 2:1-15
[64] Matt. 2
[65] Exod. 3:4-10
[66] Ps. 91:1-2
[67] Ps. 91:3-4
[68] Ps. 23
[69] Ruth 1:16
[70] Matt. 22:1-13
[71] John 9:1-7
[72] Gen. 1:3-4

BODIE AND BROCK THOENE

The Zion Legacy Series

Shiloh Autumn

The Twilight of Courage

The Zion Covenant Series

The Zion Chronicles Series

The Shiloh Legacy Series

The Saga of the Sierras

The Galway Chronicles

The Wayward Winds Series

Writer-to-Writer

the middLe east

FIRST CENTURY A.D.

SAMARIA

Jordan River

Mediterranean Sea

PEREA

Jericho •

Jerusalem • + Mount of Olives

← to Alexandria

Ashkelon • Bethlehem • • Bethany

• Herodium

JUDEA

Dead Sea

IDUMEA

EGYPT

N

Red Sea